This Game

Has

No Loyalty

L. J. Miller

This is a work of fiction. Any references or similarities to actual events, real people, living, or dead, or to real locals are intended to give the novel a sense of reality. Any similarity in other names, characters, places, and incidents is entirely coincidental.

Pilot Publishing Group
9122 Mackerel Drive
Texas City, Texas 77591
www.pilotpublishinggroup.com

ISBN 13: 9780976102540
ISBN 10: 0-9761025-4-4

First Printing February 2008
Printed in United States of America

Cover Artist: Marion Designs

Acknowledgements

The road traveled to become successful is a very difficult one to follow. Your success is measured on the basis of what goals you have accomplished as an individual. I have traveled a tough road as many before me have traveled to accomplish this goal to have a published book. On my journey I have had people in my life that have inspired me, supported my quest, and educated me further about life. These people, along with many others are whom I want to personally thank for having a positive impact on my life directly and/or indirectly.

Mother – Your faith in the Almighty and your endless prayers for me is what spiritually kept me grounded through my years. Thank you mother for trying to raise 4 children to be positive and successful with the little resources you had when we came to this country some 30 years ago. You wanted to give us a better life and provided, to the best of your ability, for your family through hard work and perseverance. I thank you.

Father (my namesake) – Thank you for the talks, although infrequent, they help mold me mentally.

Dina (Sis) – Wow…you have always been my best friend (I think we were supposed to be twins). Throughout our years we've remained close-ly knit. Thank you for your support and confidence in my abilities. Thank you sis for being there for me in my darkest hours and providing the tough love that only you are able to give to me. You are my rock and I love you for that.

Cirilo (my other big bruh) – I took a lot from you when we were young-er, you fueled my thirst for education and reading. It is you that made me an organized and structured person. I thank you for that.

Nathan (my youngest older brother) – You are hands down the most sup-portive person in my life. With every idea I've approached you with, you've never denied me, put me down or told me it was far-fetched and not feasible. I may be slightly older than you but you have taught me so much through your wisdom.
I appreciate all you've done for me and for being there to hold me down when I was experiencing hardship. I will never be able to repay you for that. Thank you babe bruh, I love you.

Sha-Juan, Shaaid, Shadiya, and Shamel (the four Sha's) – Shajuan, my baby girl, you were one of daddy's first inspiration to change his life, your birth is responsible for making me the man I am today. Shaaid, my lil' man, I see myself in you when I was your age. You are my manchild and you helped me realize a man has to be present to raise his son, I will not fail you son. Shadiya and Shamel, my girl and last boy, daddy loves you guys and your presence and purpose are defined through me. I love you all, my four Sha's.

Cuwan, Chanae, Mark (my other three) – Cuwan, I'm hoping you learned from your mistakes. Remember, you make the choices in your life. I hope this book will incite some of the realities of the environment in which we grew up. You have the ability to change and control your destiny, be strong and be a leader. Chanae, you have grown up to be a beautiful young lady, continue to stay focused on your dreams, I think you are a great dancer lil ma. Mark, your love for art is what makes you special. Don't forget that education is key. I love you all.

Millette – I know I was not the easiest person to get along with. When I started this project, you were the first to know and you read my chapters and pushed me. You told me I was my own worst critic and continued to support me in every way possible. I thank you for all you've contributed to this project.

Donnell (D-Boy) – We've been homies for an eternity. You've been by my side throughout my adult life. Throughout our years, we've expe-rienced a lot together and grew to be responsible men to our families. You are my brother from another mother and I thank you for being a true homie and holding me down when I had no one else.

Peaches (Sara) – We've both made a beautiful daughter together which was my one of my strongest inspirations to change. You have remained my best friend throughout the years and I cherish our relationship. You have always been the shoulder I could lean on and be myself without worrying if I looked weak. I thank you so much for being real throughout our friendship.

Norris, Monica, Tuwoski, thanks for reading my manuscript and giving me honest feedback, you are one of my first supporters. Adrian (A.D.) you are my homie for life, we've been through so much together and I cherish our friendship, thanks for being a true friend. My Little Washing-ton family (L dub), Eva Keys, Peaches, Ziggy, Rat (Mouse), Stacy Keech, Faye Keech, Sleepy, Stick Man, Omar (Scarnitti), Bunky, Beanie (Bink), Big A, Johnnie Lonnie, Cool

Whip, Mikki, Ant, Al Green, Shawn, Bolo, Sammy, Eric T., Fruit, Pat W., Tasha, Aimee P., Lil D, Alton R., Flava Man, Niyoko, Kelly, and the rest of the L dub crew y'all know who you are, if I missed anyone, my apologies. You all made me feel like I was born and raised in L.W. I love you all for that and I'm glad throughout the years we maintained our friendship.

To my homies from 'round the way – Ramel, Ra Dollar, Detail, Cleve, Bazz, DuSha, Big Moe, Billy Bang, Big L, B.Z., Sheeny boy, Shrimpo, Crazy Ty, Sunshine, Uncle D, Jamel, my homie Divine, 1100 (keep pim-pin'), Mizzo, and the rest of my homies (you know who you are), this is about us for us, ya heard!

Lady Scorpio (Brooklyn) – Special thanks to you for being one of my first supporter on line and now a true big sis, thanks from my heart and soul.

Tameeka – Thank you for your support. You have really been a very im-portant person in my life, thank you so much.

My myspace homies, C2C, all my readers and supporters, thanks for the love and support you've shown me by reading my excerpts and com-menting honestly. Without you guys, this would not be possible; I thank you all from the heart.

G.C. Miller (older bruh) – I held you last because the last shall come first. You are my role model. Although many may not understand you and see you as complex (I once did), I thank you for your overall support and teachings of life to me. I hold you dear and I'm glad you've em-braced me and cared enough to assist me in getting ahead and being suc-cessful. You can easily take up a whole page so I'm going to cut it short and tell you that I love you and thank you for being there for me.

Dedication

This book is dedicated to Eric Jerome Keech, (my best friend) who left us way too early in this lifetime. You have inspired me to write in hopes of reaching the misguided and misinformed youth in words, their words and our words, which they can relate to and gain a true understanding of what really happens behind the scenes on the mean streets of any hood. You've left a lasting imprint on the souls and minds of those who knew and loved you. You will continue to live on through your son, Jahiem and daughter Erica. I love you Black and you are never forgotten, you are a true soldier in our war of survival. I also dedicate this book to all the fallen soldiers that left this world early because of the game, there are too many to name but I will name a few…Tyran, Kirk, Eugene, JoJo, and many more. God Bless you all.

Baptiste Housing Projects, Brooklyn 1988-89

Lakim and Kendu were sitting on the benches in the back of Lakim's building smoking a blunt and drinking on a 40 oz. of Old Gold. It was almost midnight and in the back where they were at, it was packed with people talking and getting high off the drug of their choice while music was blaring out of the window of a tenant on the first floor of the building.

"Yo nigga, pass the blunt. You sucking on that shit like a Hoover!" Lakim said to Kendu.

"Chill man, you just passed it to me." Kendu replied sucking as much smoke into his lungs as possible.

"Shit nigga, you already steamed it down to a roach." Lakim said as the now small blunt was finally passed to him.

As Lakim sucked down the last of the weed, Kendu switched his attention to the girls that were dancing and shaking their ass near the back exit of the building.

"Damn them shorties over there is holdin'" Kendu said to Lakim.

Lakim brushed some ashes off his pants and looked at the girls his friend was referring to.

"Damn! What they putting in the water making them girls fill out like that? Them bitches is thick as fuck. I'm gon'get at one of them fo' the night over with while you sittin' here just watching them."

Kendu got up from the bench and was about to make his way to where the girls were when he heard someone call his name. He turned to the voice and noticed one of his old friends from school approaching.

"What's up KB?" Kendu greeted him by slapping him five.

"Ain't too much, just chillin'." KB replied.

Lakim gestured to KB with a nod of his head.

"I ain't seen you in a minute, where you been bruh?" Kendu asked KB.

"You know my M.O. kid, still stickin' up spots and these fake ass drug dealing niggas." KB said boldly.

"I hear that." KB replied.

"I hear that fly shit too but ain't no fake ass drug dealer over here." Lakim said taking offense to KB's comment.

1

"Nah kid, I ain't talkin' 'bout you, you fam." KB replied.

"Oh, I thought you was trying to play me." Lakim said.

"So y'all niggas getting money out here now huh?" KB asked.

"Look, kid," Lakim said to KB, showing off a wad of bills, "I made this today and I just came out at seven!"

"Damn, what the fuck you do, man, rob an armored truck?" KB asked, acting clueless.

"Nah, kid, knocking off these jacks. Matter of fact, I gotta go beep my man so I can re-up."

"Who you slinging for?" KB asked.

"My man Junior from the Fort," Lakim replied, counting his money again. "Damn, I didn't know that I made this much dough already," he said, not really addressing KB.

"Damn, he getting money like that way over here, kid?" KB asked.

"Yeah, he bubblin' too. Yo, I gotta go beep this nigga right now. I need some more work. I can't afford to run out now," Lakim said as he walked toward the corner to use a payphone.

KB became interested in this guy Lakim was talking about because he sounded like someone his colleague would be interested in, so he decided to get some more information about Junior while La was gone.

"Yo, 'Du, who this nigga La talking 'bout? You know him too?" KB asked Kendu.

"Yeah, I fuck wit' him sometimes. I made like fifteen hundred today gettin' rid of that shit," he said proudly, knowing he was lying.

"Word, kid, it's money out here like that?"

"Yeah, nigga, the heads don't never stop chasin' this shit, plus duke shit is the bomb, a scud missile."

"I didn't know you was a worker bee," KB teased, hoping to get him worked up. "I thought you was holding your own self down, nigga. What happened?"

"I'm gettin money, that's what happened, nigga. Can't you tell?" he asked as he pulled out a mountain of bills from his pocket.

"Aight, nigga, I see you getting paid. Where he from again?" KB asked.

"He from Fort Green projects but he be staying with his girl, Shondra, you know the dark-skinned bitch with the fat ass?" KB started giving out the information KB was looking for.

2

"Yeah, I know her. Her brother is Ru-Ru, right?"

"Uh-huh. I think he been dealing with her for a coupla years now." Kendu said.

"He live in the crib with her?"

"I think he might 'cause he be out here hustling every day, all day."

"You cool with that nigga?" KB asked.

"He aight but he not my man like that." Kendu answered.

"Him and your man La tight?"

"Not like that, La's my main man, he just work for the nigga."

"I'm saying, would you set the nigga up?" KB asked hoping he would.

"What I'm gonna get for doing it?" Kendu became interested.

"You get a percentage of what we get from that nigga." KB lied.

"And how much is that?" Kendu asked.

"You tell me. Where do the nigga keep his stash, in his girl's house?" KB asked.

"I don't know all that but I know he be having money on him when La go to him to re-up. Matter of fact tomorrow's the first and that's when he be having mad money on him because he go pick up from everybody that owe him money. He'll be out tomorrow early because he be holding they welfare cards and shit so he don't have to worry about them not paying him." Kendu told KB.

"You know the ones that owe him?" KB continued with his questions.

"Shit. Everybody that smoke out this muhfucka owe him." Kendu replied.

"But do you know all the ones he pick up from?" KB elaborated.

"I don't know all of them but I know a couple. He definitely gonna pick up from this closet smoking bitch name Lizzette that live on the other side, he always give her credit. I think he hittin' it on the low." Kendu answered.

"Aight, I'm gonna let my man know what's up with him and we gonna watch that nigga's move early in the morning and when he pick up we'll get him."

"Just make sure I get my cut and don't try and beat me outta my share." Kendu said.

"Don't worry son, I got you." KB replied.

"I hope you bring heat with you 'cause that nigga got mad guns." Kendu warned.

KB pulled out a black .38 revolver and showed it to Kendu.

"I stay strapped with a biscuit nigga!" KB said feeling a surge of power.

KB pointed the pistol in the air and let off some shots, everyone, including Kendu, scattered for safety. KB smirked then walked away towards home, he had to call Stump and tell him about Junior.

Chapter 1
It s all over. I got you.

Junior was ready to go in the house after serving his last customer, but before he made it to the entrance of his girl's building, he heard gunshots coming from across the street. Everyone standing in front of the building with him ran in different directions, Junior ran into his girlfriend's building, then peeked out the door to see if he could get a glimpse of the shooter. He didn't see anyone, so he figured whoever was shooting must have been testing out their new toy, something that was common in the hood. A few minutes later a police cruiser drove slowly by the building. The police usually never got to the trouble that fast, so they may have already been in the area patrolling when they heard the gunshots. They never got out of their vehicle to investigate. They just circled the block and shined a bright light at the building across the street. Once Junior knew the police were gone, he went into the house to get his gun from his girlfriend's room. She was fast asleep, or seemed to be, and didn't stir when he came in, nor when he went into the closet. He took out a duffel bag full of automatic guns and revolvers. He chose a black .357 revolver with a rubber handle and stuffed it into the pocket of his Fila sweatpants. Then he went back out as silently as he came in. He opened the backdoor of the building and stood by the benches near a black gate. He pointed the gun in the air away from the windows in the projects and let off three thunderous booms from the snub-nosed revolver. The fire from the barrel lit up the cool summer night. After the echoes from the blast of the powerful handgun subsided, he looked around, hoping someone recognized him, because he wanted them to know his gun had a bigger bang. Satisfied that he had sent his own message, he went back into the house and got into bed with his girl.

Junior woke up to the familiar smell of bacon and eggs. The scent traveled from the kitchen to the room in the back where he slept. He turned over, stretched then sat up in the bed and reached for the Newport that was half smoked in the ashtray. He lit the tip of the cigarette, took a long pull, and blew out the smoke as he got out of bed. He knew Shondra would be coming in soon with his breakfast, so he went to the bathroom to wash

5

his face and brush his teeth. When he got back in the room he slipped on the Fila sweatpants he had on the night before and headed to the kitchen.

Shondra was standing over the stove in a tattered, floral print housecoat with a tear in the side that revealed her brown skin. Her body was tight. She had firm breasts with perky nipples that showed through any light clothing she wore, and a small waist accentuated her nice, round hips and bubble ass. He loved her. She was his queen, best friend, and confidante. She was his Bonnie and he, her Clyde. He grabbed her gently from behind and wrapped his arms around her waist, letting his hand rest in the comfort spot of her crotch. She squirmed slightly and threw her head back to his shoulders, revealing her discolored wino lips. He gently kissed her on the temple as he grabbed one of her breasts. He felt a rise as he caressed her. She quickly turned around and put her tongue in his mouth, moving her snatch around until she felt his hardness. He grabbed her ass with both hands and drew her to him hard, moving in a circular motion as he enjoyed their good-morning kiss. She moaned as their bodies moved as one. He stiffened more, alerting him it was time to take things a step further. He pulled the snaps of her housecoat and revealed the two beautiful stacks that jumped out at him in eagerness to be held. He moved her over to the sink and put his mouth on her breast, sucking her nipple gently. Suddenly the smoke alarm went off and they both stopped abruptly. His breakfast was burning.

"See, boo, you made me burn your bacon," she said, her breathing slowing back down to a normal pace.

"Fuck that bacon. That's not what I was trying to heat up," he said as he patted her on her ass.

"Well at least all the bacon didn't burn. You want me to make you some more, or is this enough?" she asked, showing him the portion of bacon that wasn't burned in the pan.

"It don't matter, Mooka," he said, walking back to the bedroom.

Shondra's room was steel gray. He had painted it that color, but couldn't remember why. Now as he looked around, he realized it was a depressing color. He had also put down a gray carpet with black specks because he wanted the room he stayed in to be comfortable and different from the rest of the rooms in the apartment.

"Here, boo," Shondra said, placing the plate of food on the edge of the bed.

6

Junior picked up the remote and turned the television on to *Jerry Springer*. He loved watching this talk show because Jerry always had some crazy people on there. Junior ate his breakfast while Shondra and he watched Jerry together. The caption on the bottom of the television screen read, "Revealing Secrets: My Girl is a Man." Shondra lay down, her head resting on his lap.

"What happened last night, boo? I heard gunshots."

"Them stupid ass niggas trying to let me know they got guns," he said as if he wasn't troubled at all.

"You gotta be careful. You know they don't really like you around here."

"Like I give a fuck. Ain't no nigga gonna stop me from getting this money unless he willing to lay down."

"I just want you to be careful, that's all, boo."

"Get up, Mooka. I got to get dressed. It's the first of the month," he said, placing his finished plate on the bed.

Junior already knew that most of the niggas around her way didn't like him and it wasn't just because he was hustling it also had something to do with him being with Shondra. He sat on the edge of the bed and thought back to how he met Shondra four years ago in the summer of '89.

Junior met Shondra one summer while hanging in her projects. He knew a couple of the guys from around there through his homeboy, Larry, who also lived in those projects. Since Junior lived way downtown Brooklyn, he always wanted to find a girl around there so he could have somewhere to lay up when he didn't feel like taking the long ride home on the train.

Puerto Ricans predominantly inhabited Baptiste Plaza Projects and Junior always thought he would end up with a Boriqua mami until he noticed a girl he never saw before buying an ice cream cone at the Mister Softee ice cream truck. She was a sista. He rarely saw black girls in those projects, and the ones he did see usually acted like they were Spanish. The first thing he noticed was that she had a fat ass. He asked Larry about her and Larry told him she was a firecracker, a little on the wild side, and that he went to public school with her brother, Rudolph, back in the day. Junior walked over to the ice cream truck and tried to kick it to her.

"What's up, miss? Can I talk to you for a minute?" he asked her as she turned around and looked into his eyes.

"Excuse me?"

"I mean, are you in a rush or something? You got a minute to talk so I can get to know you?"

7

"Not really. My man is waiting for me. And who are you anyway?" She began walking back toward her building on the corner.

"I don't mean no disrespect, ma, but I just noticed you, and I wanted to get to know you. I'm Big L's man."

She stopped, turned around, and looked at him.

"OK, mister, here's your minute."

That response caught him off guard, but he recovered quickly.

"I don't know you, and I know you don't know me, but I think we should get to know each other better. I want to know everything about you that you would be willing to reveal, and the things you conceal I will learn about later as we get to the next level of understanding one another. All I need is a chance, and if you're not willing to take a chance, give me the chance to develop a friendship with you that is like no other friendship you've had with any nigga. So, can we get to know each other, luv?" He spit sixteen bars like he was in a studio. She smiled a wide grin and shuffled on down the street without saying a word.

"Hold up!" he yelled, running behind her. "Why you slidin' off like that, ma?"

"My man is in front of the building."

Junior caught a glimpse of the guy standing in front of the building. He was a light-skinned guy with a dark seazer haircut, and was sort of on the heavy side. Junior followed her to the front of her building and watched them go inside together. She had a nice shape, but her grill wasn't all that attractive. It was the roundness of her ass that made him want to pursue her.

Junior made it his business to go past Shondra's building the next day. He kept passing by there all day hoping he would see her. He went to the store on Siegel Street and on his way back he saw her walking with a little girl toward the Chinese restaurant. He decided to follow her, then act like he just happened to bump into her, but it didn't work because she spotted him before he could get to her.

"Are you following me?" she asked as he came up on her.

"Yeah, you busted me," he said, smiling. "I just wanted the rest of my minute."

"Well, my man didn't appreciate you following me last night."

"Like I said yesterday, I ain't tryin' to be disrespectful, but fuck that nigga. If he didn't like it, he shoulda said something to me."

"Look, I don't want no problems with him, so you need to keep it movin'," she said as she grabbed the little girl's hand to cross the street.

"Look, ma, I ain't trying to get you fucked up. I just want to get to know you. Is something wrong with that?"

"Yeah, the problem is that I already have a man."

"And how long have you had that problem?"

8

"You ain't funny, nigga," she said, smiling. "Seriously, he's real jealous and I don't want no problems. That's all."

"Look, let me worry about that problem. I can handle myself. Can you?"

"I ain't worried about me. I'm worried about you."

"Look, ma, if you trying to get out of your fucked up relationship by getting me to beat that nigga's ass, just let me know so we can cut this shit short."

She laughed real hard at his comment, then stopped in front of the restaurant and looked him in his brown eyes.

"Get a pen and give me your beeper number. I'll beep you when he leaves later on tonight, aight?"

Junior went into the restaurant for a pen, then gave her his number and walked away. He knew he had her. She couldn't resist his chinky, bedroom eyes.

Later that same night Junior was standing in front of a bodega on Graham Avenue talking with some guys when Shondra paged him. There was a payphone on the corner so he was able to return her call quickly.

"Hello."

"Hello?" a woman's voice replied.

"Umm, can I speak to Shondra?"

"She not here. Who is this?"

"Can you tell her that Junior called?"

"I sure will. Where you at right now?"

"I'm on the corner of Humboldt. Why?"

"This is me, crazy. Didn't I just beep you? How you didn't know it was me? You forgot the sound of my voice already?"

"I shoulda known it was you by that sweet voice. I just needed to make sure it was you and not your moms or somebody."

"You crazy, boy. What you doin' right now?"

"I'm out here chillin' on the Ave. Why, what's up?"

"Come to the back of my building so we can talk, if you ain't too busy."

"I'll be there in twenty seconds."

He walked to the back of her building and waited by the benches for her to come outside. When she came out of the building she walked over to him and sat on the benches. She looked up at him, smiled, and grabbed his hand.

"I've been thinking about you since you gave me your beeper number. I couldn't get you out of my mind. I don't know what to expect, but I like how you came at me."

9

a! That's deep, ma. I didn't know you was feelin' me like ...you told me you got a man and shit, I thought you and him was ...e that. I didn't know I had a chance."

"You know everything ain't what it seems. I do have a man, but he been actin' up lately, doing foul shit so we 'bout on our way to a break up. I always said if I found a nice nigga, I might hafta speed up the process. So now that we're here, what's up, daddy?"

"I ain't tryin' to step on a nigga's toes, but if his shit ain't right, then he gonna hafta get lost. I'm saying, baby, what you want to do?" he asked, dragging her up from the bench and pulling her close to him.

"I'm down for whateva." She replied.

"Let's get outta here, then," he said, leading her through the building.

"Hold up, daddy. Let me go get my bag," she said to him as she went to her door.

While Junior was waiting in the hallway for her to come out, he saw her man come into the building. Her man walked right past Junior and into her apartment. Junior didn't know what to do. He didn't know if he should stay or leave, but then he decided to stay in case something jumped off. He walked out of the building and sat down on the benches to wait for her. Shondra lived on the first floor and her living room window faced the back of the building, so that's how he was able to hear her arguing with her man. He went up to the gate and peeked in the window, watching as Shondra's man stood there shaking her and slapping her in the face. He saw Shondra run out the door and into the hallway, screaming as he followed behind her. Then Junior did something he had no business doing. He went back into the building. He didn't know what he was going to do, but he knew he didn't want to see her get her ass beat by that nigga.

"Get the fuck off of me, motherfucker!" Junior could hear Shondra screaming.

"Get outa here, bitch!"

When Junior opened the door he could see her man choking her by the exit. Junior wanted to do something, but he didn't want to seem as if he was coming to her rescue, so he walked into the lobby as if he were cutting through the building. Her man didn't stop choking her and she looked like she was about to pass out, so Junior asked him what was wrong.

"Yo, man, she 'bout to pass out."

Her man turned around, not taking his hand from around her throat.

"Yo, mind your fuckin' business, aight?" her man replied.

Junior looked at Shondra and her eyes were pleading with him to help her.

10

"I'm saying, duke, she a girl. You gotta take it easy or you gonna really hurt her!"

"Didn't I tell you to mind your fuckin' business, nigga?"

"I'm just looking out for you, nigga, so you don't catch a murda charge, but if you don't want to listen, then fuck you!"

The guy then let go of Shondra and put all his concentration on Junior.

"Yo, son, who the fuck you supposed to be, Captain Save a Ho?" He was walking toward Junior.

Junior timed him perfectly and caught him with a hard right hook to his temple. He was unprepared for the blow and fell backward onto the stairs behind him. Shondra was on the floor catching her breath and holding her neck. Junior ran over to where he stumbled and commenced to hit him with lefts and rights as Shondra's man tried to cover up the blows. Junior stopped when Shondra got to her feet and started to stomp him.

"You fat bastard! You think you gonna keep beatin' on me like that?" Shondra screamed.

Her man groaned at every foot that caught him in a tender spot, then she stopped and ran into her house. Junior backed up and waited for him to get up, not knowing if he was going to charge after him or go after Shondra. As Junior waited to see what his next move would be, Shondra returned with two big steak knives in both hands and lunged at her man as he was getting to his feet. Junior tried to get to her before she plunged the knives into him, but he moved too slowly. She slashed her man on his back with one knife and the other one found itself buried in his thigh. He let out a loud yell as Junior grabbed her and pulled her away from her victim. She fought with him furiously, but he held her tightly as her man hobbled to the entrance of the building, hoping to get away before she carved him up like a Thanksgiving turkey. Shondra buried her head into Junior's chest as she wailed and he held her tenderly.

"All right, baby, it's all over. I got you," he said, comforting her and rocking her back and forth in his arms.

That incident consummated Junior and Shondra's union, and because of what happened, some of her ex's homeboys held animosity toward Junior. He started to hustle in front of her building, and this made them dislike him even more, not because he was selling, but because he was one of the first guys selling in their hood. None of them said anything to him directly because of his street credibility, but they would do things, subliminal things, to let him know they didn't like him. When he would go in at night, they would rob the crack heads that came looking for him. The crack heads would tell him they were robbed or someone sold them soap. Junior would tell them that if he wasn't out there to make sure they didn't cop from anyone around there.

This way he got all the money that came through that building. What they tried to do didn't bother Junior. He wasn't going to let them or anything they tried to do stop him from getting his money.

Shondra came back into the bedroom with a glass of Pepsi and interrupted Junior's daydreaming. He grabbed the glass out of her hands and took a deep swallow as he stood up. He was 5'4" but was built like he worked out. He had broad shoulders, a wide and firm chest with muscular arms attached. His complexion was a tint lighter than caramel and his teeth were pearl white. His chinky eyes were complimented with long curly eyelashes that made him look sexy whenever he blinked slowly. Shondra lusted at her beautiful specimen of a man then suddenly disrobed and pushed him down flat on the bed with his feet still on the ground. She straddled him and positioned herself so she could feel him stiffen. He grabbed her hips, brought her down to him, and kissed her softly. They moved as one for a moment, and then she pulled his sweats down to his thighs, grabbed his pole, and stroked it. He moaned a little, enjoying the sensations she sent through his body.

Junior felt a snowy feeling coming over him and quickly repositioned himself so he wouldn't explode prematurely. The way she handled his body would make any nigga blast off unexpectedly. She was just that good. He grabbed her hands, stretched them above her head, and kissed her neck, licking around her mountains and working his way to her valley. She squirmed with each lick, and the movement of her body enticed him more. He moved his hands down to her waist and caressed her ass, then moved them to her thighs and opened her legs slightly so he could view her hairy cavern. He licked her clit and rotated the tip of his tongue around her opening, listening for the grunts and moans she released from every good feeling. He proceeded to suck on her clit and moved his tongue rapidly like a hissing snake. He gripped her legs firmly and locked onto her like vice grips. She moaned out in pleasure as she creamed on his chin. He flipped her over on her stomach and slid his pole inside her pulsating hole. She let out a howl, then relaxed. He went in and out slowly, feeling her wetness, the friction sending waves of satisfaction through his body. As the sensation increased, he moved more rapidly until he fell limp inside her.

Junior rolled over on his back for a minute to catch his breath. She held him close and put her head on his chest as they both lay naked in ecstasy.

"Damn, boo, you make me feel soooo good," she whispered in his ear.

"I love making you feel good," he replied, his breathing coming back to normal.

"Go in the safe and give your moms five hundred dollars for the rent," he told her as he got up and went to the bathroom.

"Can I have some money so I can buy me some sneakers?" she asked as she went into the safe. She rarely asked for money, and that's how Junior knew she truly loved him solely because of his character. Most broads wanted niggas that had bank, but she was different. Although she didn't have shit, she wasn't a gold-digging whore.

"Take what you need," he replied. "But make sure you lock the closet when you're done."

Junior had an everyday routine when he came out of the building. He always checked the back and front of the building for anything or anyone that looked suspicious before starting his day. A lot of the niggas in the hood respected or feared him, but he had to be real careful of the snakes that did you dirty behind your back. That's why he was always on the lookout for the stick-up kids and the police. He didn't want to get caught slipping. It wasn't easy being in the game, and he was only three years into it, so he wasn't a vet yet. He was still trying to perfect his craft by taking things slowly and getting advice from his cousin Craig who was a "boss" in his hood. One of the most important things for him was to try and be observant of everyone and everything around him, he couldn't trust shit.

Nothing seemed out of the ordinary on this day, so he walked to the back of the building. As he approached the opened backdoor, he saw Sugar coming through the lane. When she saw him she put up one finger to let him know how much she wanted to cop. He nodded at her and looked around to make sure there were no police around or on the roof looking down. He went back into the lobby so he could make the transaction on the inside.

"What up, Suge? I got it good for you, baby."

"Let me get one, my sweet prince."

He held his hand out for the money and she stuffed her grubby hands into her pocket and produced some folded bills. She passed him the wrinkled up money and he counted it out to make sure it was the exact amount.

"Didn't I tell you stop bringing me this wrinkled-up money?" He hated wrinkled money because it took too much time to unfold and count, and at any moment you could get caught if Jake (the police) came into the building. "Wait right here," he told her as he went to the mailbox to get his stash. "Here, baby," he said when he returned. "And the weight is nice, so don't stand there staring at it like you gonna get another one."

She took the product in her dirty hands and looked at it, plucking the bottom of the bottle with her finger like so many veteran crack heads to see if the little rocks inside settled down.

"Come on, baby, you can do me better than that."

"Look, Suge, I'm just coming out. Don't give me no drama this early."

"That's right, baby, I'm just coming out too, and I want my first hit to be a major," she said, her smile revealing her missing teeth. Sugar's beauty was destroyed by her addiction to the little, hard rocks. She was once a beautiful Puerto Rican about a year before her druggie boyfriend turned her onto the drug. He introduced her to the drug for his own selfish reasons. He was unable to support his own habit, so he figured he would turn her out and once she became addicted to the drug, he would use her to sell her body or provide oral services for money to get high. That lasted for about three months until she realized she was the only one making money to support their habit, so Sugar got rid of him. When she first got hooked on the drug, every nigga that ever wanted her sexually paid for her services. She was the most desirable crack head at that time and was rewarded for her amazing skills. As time passed her beauty and physical attributes faded from the excessive use of the drug, and she was unable to support her habit by performing sexual favors around the way. She was reduced to going on the "ho stroll." This was a designated block for women that were strung out on drugs. Sugar would turn tricks with Mexican immigrants and other strung-out druggies, and because of the volume of partners she had, she was believed to have contracted the "monster."

"Aight, fuck it, Sugar. Give it back and I'll see you later on," he told her, digging in his pocket to get out the money she had given him.

"Please, baby, just let me get a better one and I'm gone."

"I'm not fucking wit' you, Sugar. I got something to handle and you holding me up. Take it or leave it."

"OK, baby, but you owe me," she said as she headed for the front entrance. "Be careful. You know they hot out today. It's the first."

Sugar was referring to the narcs. They would be out in force trying to make busts because they knew the first and the fifteenth of every month was the day welfare checks came out, and most drug users would be out trying to score.

"I know, baby. Thanks for letting me know."

Junior was on his way to the other side of the projects to pick up money that was owed to him. He was going to Lizzette's house. She lived on the fourth floor in his homeboy's building. She was a closet smoker who wasn't strung out on the shit yet, but it would just be a matter of time before she looked like Sugar or worse. He walked up the steps to the third floor, walked to the end of the corridor, and knocked on the door three times. She came to the door and he could hear her opening the locks. She opened the door wide, her way of inviting him in without actually saying so. He walked in and looked around before coming all the way inside. He wanted to make sure she was alone.

"What's up, papi?" she asked with her strong Spanish accent.

"You," he replied quickly, looking at her stunning figure.

"Give me a second to get dressed. I was making some breakfast," she said, walking back into the kitchen. "You not in a big rush, are you?"

"Nah, not really."

She was wearing some thin, yellow shorts that showed the roundness of her ass, and she couldn't have been wearing any panties as short as the shorts were. Her white T-shirt was dingy, but he only noticed her nipples poking out of the thin fabric. Her skin was pretty. She had a butterscotch complexion and not one mark or blemish on her body. She was damn near perfect. Although he loved Shondra, the man in him had always wanted to hit it but she never showed any interest in him like that, and he didn't want to use drugs to try to persuade her, because he didn't want her to think he was a trick.

"I'm sorry, papito. Ju want sonthin' to drink?"

"Yeah, something cold if you got it."

"I have only Kool-Aid, sherry flavor."

"That's good, thanks."

15

She passed him the drink, but the red fluid in the cup looked like an oil spill, which killed his thirst, so he put the cup down on her center table.

"Look, papi, I'm gonna take a quick shower before we go to the check cashing place, OK?" she asked, walking past him toward her bathroom.

"Sure, hun, but don't take too long in there," he said, watching her ass jiggle as she went into the bathroom.

Once Lizzette was out of sight, Junior took the cup of Kool-Aid and emptied it out in her sink, washed the cup, and then deposited it in her dish tray. Her apartment was very tidy but her furniture was battered and old. The couch was a dingy beige with stains on the pillows. The tiles on the floor were clean but also had visible stains on them. About fifteen minutes had passed when he heard the bathroom door opening. He purposely sat facing the bathroom, hoping she would come out revealing her naked body. She emerged from the bathroom with a small towel wrapped around her upper body, and he watched her go into her room.

"Hey, Liz, can I use your restroom, ma?"

"Sure, papi, go ahead."

He had never been past her bathroom before, but he had hopes of getting past it one day soon. He really did have to urinate, though, so he went into the bathroom and relieved himself, but left the door open, hoping she might come in. The bathroom was pink and very clean. It smelled like apples and cinnamon and the aroma just made him want Lizzette more. He walked out of the bathroom slowly, hoping to get a glimpse of her putting on her clothes in her bedroom. Suddenly she came out in her bra and panties.

"Oops! I thought you were out the bano already."

"I'm sorry," he replied, his eyes fixed on her goddess-like shape.

She gave him an alluring look like she wanted him, so he went for it. He moved to her slowly, his eyes fixed on hers to make sure he was reading her right. She moved toward him and he grabbed her shoulders, gently pushing her up against the hallway wall. He could hear her breathing getting heavy and he gently kissed her as he let his hands explore the regions of her body. His heart was racing, but he kept his composure. He couldn't lose control, not when he finally had her. She smelled sweet and she was soft to the touch. Her hole was wet, so he played in her with his middle finger while she moved with his motions and moaned while they kissed. He slid down on the cold tile floor and laid down. She followed his every lead, and he kept the pressure on by continuing to kiss her passionately. As he began to pull down his sweats, she whispered in his ear.

"Ju have a rubber, papi?" she asked.

He didn't have a rubber band, much less a rubber, so he didn't know how to reply to the question.

"You clean, right, mami?"

"Yeah, papi, but that's not it. I need to protect myself, and ju do too. I don't want any bambinos."

"Ahhh, come on, Liz. I'll pull it out before I nut."

"No, papi. If you don't have nothing, we can't do nothing. I want to, but I need to make sure we do it the right way."

"Aight, mami, let's finish this another time," he said reluctantly.

"Mmmmm, damn, you big, papito. I wanted you inside me," she moaned as she got up and went into the bathroom.

He walked back to the living room and tried to pull himself together. She came out of the bathroom and disappeared into her room. He got his senses together and walked to the front door as she came out of her bedroom. She was fully dressed and was looking edible. She had on black riding pants that showed the curves of her body and made her hips stick out like gun holsters. She had on a long, white T-shirt that covered the front of her, slightly revealing the V-shape of her vagina in the tight, black pants.

"How I look, papi?"

"Like a Puerto Rican queen, baby," he replied, turning the knob on the door. "Now let's get to the check-cashing place before it gets crowded."

L. J. Miller

Chapter 2
I'm the landlord of the hood.

"Where the fuck is this dude at?" the six foot tall, stocky guy asked. He was talking to KB, a short guy who was on the chubby side, but not really overweight. "I'm getting tired of waiting, KB."

KB was the flunky or TIT (Thug In Training) for Stump, the six-foot tall, thug lord of his hood. Stump was a career criminal with armed robberies, grand theft auto, grand larceny, and attempted murder on his long list of crimes. He was just coming home from doing four years on a three- to six-year sentence. He lived in Bushwick projects, one block away from Baptiste Plaza Projects. He was well known and feared for his crimes in the neighborhood. He had more enemies than friends, and the enemies that lived in the neighborhood preferred to stay away from the places he frequented to avoid a disastrous confrontation.

Stump had been shot over five times about five years ago. Half the hood was glad when they heard he had been shot, and many wished him dead. His enemies breathed a lot easier and hoped for his demise. The few friends he had were devastated, some saying they expected nothing less because of the kind of life he was leading. But Stump survived the attack, and that made him look invincible and unstoppable, which increased people's fear of him. A lot of people began to think that if Stump could get shot over five times in the upper body, live, and then come right back to the hood and wreak havoc, he had to be indestructible. He stayed in the hospital only six days after being shot, and when he came home he seemed to be more ruthless and dangerous than before. Stump was a real thug—a true thug to the death.

KB wasn't anything like Stump. He wasn't built for a life of crime but he wanted to portray that image to the people that knew him. When he was younger he wasn't much of a threat and always looked up to the "bad boys" and liked the attention they received from other people. He also lacked confidence when it came to girls and never really had a girlfriend. He saw hanging with Stump as his way of building his confidence, gaining respect, and getting girls. He was looking to earn some recognition in the hood, but he never expected to get in as deep as he did.

19

"Go 'round the corner and see if you see that nigga, K," Stump told KB.

"Aight."

He went around the corner, but then he decided to go to the store instead. He never noticed Junior and Lizzette coming out of her building.

"Hey, papi, I want to see you later on tonight, and not just for business," she said to Junior seductively.

"No problem. I want to finish what we started up there with no interruptions. Feel me, ma?"

As they got closer to the corner Junior started ruffling through his pockets looking for her welfare card.

"Shit, I think I left your card home," he said, a little frustrated. "I have to go get it. You just go ahead to the check-cashing place and get on line. I should be there before you get to the window."

"OK, papi. It's probably crowded by now anyway."

Junior kept walking straight toward his crib as Lizzette turned the corner and began walking toward the check-cashing place. KB emerged from the store just as Lizzette turned the corner. He caught a glimpse of her beautiful shape, so he walked behind her quickly to get a full-body view. He figured she was going to the check-cashing place. When he recognized who she was, he hurried to Stump to let him know.

"That's the bitch he be seeing on the side," KB told Stump, pointing at Lizzette.

"That's the bitch, huh?" Stump asked, looking at her cross the street. "She don't look like no fiend to me. You sure she smoke?"

"Yeah, man, she get high, and I saw him go in there earlier."

"Well, where the fuck he at then?"

"I didn't see him. He musta left or something. I don't know."

***

Shondra was in the shower when Junior got to the crib. He went into the bedroom and looked on the bed and floor for the missing welfare card. He couldn't find it so he unlocked the closet to see if he had dropped it in there by mistake. It wasn't in the closet either, and he became worried because he needed it to get his money.

"Ay, Mooka, did you see a welfare card anywhere in the room?" he yelled to Shondra, who was still in the shower.

"Huh?" she screamed from the bathroom. He walked over to the bathroom and opened the door. The steam billowed out like a back draft. The thick, white smoke stifled him as he asked Shondra again if she had seen the card.

"Oh yeah, boo. I put it in your black Fila jacket hanging in the closet."

He could hear the shower water beating off her body and he saw her silhouette through the thin shower curtains. He was getting excited, but refrained from his impulses because he was in a rush. He would come back and tear dat ass up later. As he checked the pocket of the jacket, he looked up on the shelf at the pistol he shot off the night before, along with two nine-millimeter, automatic Glocks, and a .38 he had taken out and forgotten to put back in his duffel bag. He had all those guns in the house in case he ever had beef in the streets, but so far he never had a reason to use them, and he hoped he never would. But after what happened last night, he had a strange feeling that was all going to change. All of a sudden he had a strong urge to take one of the guns with him.

Junior found the card and put it in his pocket, then stood in front of the closet contemplating on taking one of the guns. His reasoning for not taking a gun was because he had on sweats, which provided no support for the gun in his waistband, not to mention it was risky to be strapped on the first of the month, when the cops were out in full force, waiting to catch someone using their welfare money to cop some drugs or catch a dealer making a transaction. His reasoning on why he should take it was because since it was mother's day, the day welfare recipients received their budget, there would be more thieves out in flocks looking for a quick stick. He was having a hard time trying to decide because his reasoning on both sides was valid. He thought of something he was told by his cousin Craig, *"It's best to have a gun and not need it, than to need one and not have it."* Junior took the gun.

Shondra came into the room smelling like Dove soap with her towel covering only a portion of her voluptuous body, showing off how her breast and hips shaped the terry cloth fabric. Junior looked up at her and lusted, but he couldn't act on his impulses because he had more important things to take care of at the moment.

***

21

The check-cashing place was packed with customers trying to cash their welfare check, social security check, or employment check. The women picking up welfare checks had on their house clothes, some in house slippers with headscarves tied up on their heads. The younger females were there with their infant children or toddlers dressed in the newest fashions. The ones picking up their Social Security checks were older or disabled, and the working part of the crowd was dressed in company uniforms or in slacks and shoes. Junior walked over to Lizzette, who was talking in Spanish with another woman, and placed the welfare card in her hand as she turned around and smiled at him lovingly.

"I'm going to stand outside and wait for you," he whispered in her ear.

She nodded her head with understanding and continued her conversation with the Spanish woman. He walked out of the crowded check-cashing place and stood by a pay phone on the corner just as his beeper went off.

Stump and KB were still standing on the corner hoping to run into Junior.

"You know what?" Stump asked KB. "You would think he knew I was waiting for his ass today. Shit, I just want to talk to the brotha 'bout some things I been hearing about him in the hood."

"Things like what, dawg?" KB asked, engaging in the light banter Stump was starting.

"I heard the nigga been making some cream out here in the hood and ain't paid me no rent yet."

"Is that right? But why would he pay you rent, Stump?"

"'Cause I'm the fucking landlord of the hood, nigga. That's why. That nigga ain't even from around here and he making money out here like he paid dues already. Fuck that! He gotta pay or change locations."

"I feel you," KB said. "They said the nigga make at least five hundred on a bad night."

"That's why he gotta pay to play, he can't come through here and blow up and don't give back to the fuckin' community. I'm not having it!"

Stump only robbed drug dealers but his main focus was on the ones that supplied the product. He would get the street peddlers as a bonus occasionally, since their operation was always done out in the open. He would rob the ones in his neighborhood because they were easy targets, so he thought.

***

Junior checked the number in his beeper and fumbled in his pocket for change to return the call. He dialed the number, then turned around as he spoke to the person on the other line. Because he was so observant, he noticed KB and Stump up the block standing on the corner. He looked at the two as he spoke on the phone, and when he hung up he stood there and watched them. He knew who Stump was from his rep on the streets. Junior was alert because it was highly unusual to see Stump out this early, especially on the first of the month. He also recognized the guy Stump was with. He was the guy Kendu hung out with from time to time. Junior had never seen him with Stump before, and that was also unusual in itself. Junior stood there trying to figure out why KB was with Stump, and what they were up to. He wondered who they were scheming on.

Lizzette came out of the check-cashing place with Junior's money bundled up in one hand, and a receipt in the other. Junior took the money that was owed to him and whispered something in her ear. Then she walked off in one direction, and he in the other.

Lizzette was walking past the bodega when KB noticed her.

"That's the bitch he was with this morning," KB said to Stump.

"I know, nigga," Stump replied. "Ask her if she knows where Junior is when she comes out."

"Aight."

Lizzette was buying some milk, eggs, and bread when KB opened the door and walked into the bodega.

"You want me to help you wit' your bags, miss?"

"No, I'm OK, thank you."

"Oh, aight, ummmmm . . . I wanted to talk to you when I saw you earlier, but I saw you wit' Junior. I didn't want to be disrespectful, so I didn't say anything. Since he not wit' you now, I figured I could talk to you unless he your man. Is he your man?"

"Que?"

"Junior. Is he your boyfriend?"

"Oh, Junior, yes, yes. I know Junior. He very nice guy."

"So is that your man or not? I mean is it OK for me to talk to you?"

23

"No, I . . . ah . . . no . . . don't know," she said in her worst English.

"I'm talking about the guy you was wit' earlier, a lil while ago?"

"Today, yeah, I see him today, but I don't know where he at," she said as if she didn't understand what he was trying to ask her.

"Oh . . . OK . . . sorry to bother you, luv."

KB walked back to Stump and told him what Lizzette had said.

"That bitch was lying through her fucking teeth," KB said, "acting like she don't understand English. I saw that nigga go to her building early this morning and he didn't come out," he said to Stump.

"Ah, shut the fuck up. You don't know if he came out or not, 'cause your dumb ass wasn't looking. He mighta came out," Stump retorted. "Fuck it. I'll get him later on tonight or tomorrow. Now if I catch him later and my pockets is kinda low, then ain't no telling what will go down."

When Junior got back to Shondra's place he went into the bedroom closet and put the money Lizzette had just given him into his safe. There was a reason for the funny feeling he had earlier, and seeing Stump and KB confirmed the negative feelings he was having. They didn't do anything, but it just seemed really odd for them to be out so early in the morning standing on the corner.

Junior pulled out a bomb of work, put it in a plastic bag, and then put it inside the front of his pants. Shondra was sitting on the bed dressed in a Crème European, silk pants with a matching top watching TV. She had on two pairs of doorknocker earrings, and she wore three modest-sized gold chains. One chain was a herringbone Junior bought off a crack head for one hundred dollars, which was appraised at eight hundred dollars. It had a heart pendant outlined in diamond chips hanging from it. The second chain was a Figaro with a crucifix pendant, and the third chain was an eighteen-inch herringbone with a diamond pendant of a Nefertiti head. Shondra wore fine attire because Junior loved for her to look good. It didn't change her attitude in any way. She was the same humble, funny, loving girl he met three years ago.

"I thought you were going shopping?" Junior asked before leaving out again.

"I am. I'm waiting for Gloria to come downstairs, then we goin' downtown."

"Oh, OK. What you gon' cop down there?" he asked, forgetting what she had told him earlier.

"I want the new Carolina blue Air Max. They only got them in Dr. Jay's downtown."

"You know what, pick me up a pair, too, but I want all white ones."

"OK, boo."

"Thanks, Mooka."

Shondra was concerned about Junior. The night before she had heard gunshots and was afraid because she didn't know if he was involved. He didn't allow her to be out late at night while he hustled because he always said niggas could use her to get to him. That night she waited patiently for him to come in, and when she heard the front door close she played like she was asleep. She heard him open the closet and leave again. Soon after he left she heard more gunshots. She was terrified, but remembered he had told her never to get involved in anything when it came to him. If there was something he wanted her to know, he would tell her. Although it was hard to follow his rules, she respected and trusted his word.

Every one of Shondra's old boyfriends were always from different neighborhoods, and the guys in her hood didn't like that. The guys in her hood that liked her couldn't get past the friendship stage with her because she wouldn't talk to anyone in the area romantically. Shondra wasn't the prettiest girl in the world, but what made her attractive and intriguing was the fact that no one in the hood could ever say they hit it, which made her somewhat like wifey material. Shondra was not known for sleeping around and didn't have a bad rep or carry the moniker of being a whore in the hood. She wasn't stuck up, had a beautiful shape, and most importantly she was friendly and demanded respect.

Shondra was known for her temper and how thorough she was when it came to fighting. Most of her fights were violent. She would fight like a beast in the wild, making sure her opponents came out looking other than themselves. She had respect from every girl and many of the women in the PJs and although she was a really nice person, females knew not to fuck with her because of her brutal fighting skills.

Shondra didn't care if the guys around the way didn't like her man, because she was behind everything he did 100 percent. She had his front and his back, and would not let anything happen to him if she was able to prevent it. She was his eyes and ears on the streets and in the hood. She was someone whose word he could trust, and she loved him dearly because he took care of her and loved her unconditionally. He increased her self-esteem by making her feel beautiful. Junior was a good man to her because they did things together she had never experienced with any man before him.

Chapter 3
You tryin to set me up.

Junior ran into Lakim as he came out of Shondra's building.

"What the deal, dun-dun," Lakim asked, slapping Junior five.

"Ain't nothing, kicko. I got you," Junior told him. "Come on, let's go take care of this in the building."

They got on the elevator and Junior pressed the sixth floor. They got out when the doors opened and walked to the stairway door to make the transaction. First, though, Junior walked up some of the stairs leading to the roof to make sure no one was up there getting high. He didn't like to conduct business inside apartments because he felt it was a "get had" spot. If you handled your business in an apartment, it wouldn't be long before somebody peeped it and set you up. He figured if he was in the building he could hear anyone coming up the stairs or coming off the elevator, which would give him time to get away or deal with the situation.

Lakim pulled out a bankroll and counted out forty-two hundred dollars.

"Kendu's in here, too, but he still got a bomb left. I knocked all mine off last night."

Junior counted it and put the roll in his pocket, then pulled out a Ziploc bag full of work and handed it to Lakim. Lakim looked at the bag, then stuffed it inside his jacket.

"Yo, why don't you hit me off with more work?" he asked, not waiting for an answer before continuing. "I be knocking off like five Gs every two days, and you still spoon feeding me, bruh."

"You want me to hit you with a ten-G pack?" Junior asked, tilting his head and looking at Lakim sideways.

"I'm just saying, yo, when I finish my last pack I always got to find you, and I be losing money on the block like that. Like this week I finished my pack last night after you went inside. I couldn't re-up because you don't want nobody knocking on your door after you go in. I lost like five hundred dollars last night and I'm a late hawk. You know my motto, kid. I don't close, I doze. Ya feel me?"

"Why didn't you get some work from 'Du and knock his off then?"

"'Cause that nigga don't be out late like me. He mostly be out in the morning, then he go in when he make like four hundred or something. That's why his pack ain't finished."

"Aight, check this out. Take whatever 'Du didn't finish and knock off the pack I just gave you. That should be about seven Gs worth of work. If I see you Thursday to re-up, then I'll keep you on that, bet?"

"Aight, then, but 'Du gonna be vexed if he don't get no more work."

"Tell 'Du come see me 'bout that. I need to talk to him anyway."

Junior wanted to see Kendu because he had a bad feeling after seeing Stump and KB earlier on the Ave. He knew KB hung out with Kendu, so he was wondering if Kendu said anything to them about him. Because of Stump's rep, Junior knew if Stump heard about him making money in the hood, Stump would be paying him a visit. And Kendu had been acting suspicious lately. He wouldn't be around as much, he was taking an unusually long time to knock off the work, and he was always coming up short. Junior had a strong feeling something shady was about to go down soon. He just wanted to be one step ahead of the bullshit. He was a naturally cautious guy and stayed on point most of the time, so he wanted to make sure he wasn't caught slipping if somebody was scheming on him. Junior had so much to worry about—the cops, the crack heads snitching, stick-up kids, and haters, just to name a few. Shit was really hectic out in the jungle.

Shondra opened the door when she heard Gloria yelling her name in the lobby for her to come out.

"Damn, girl, you deaf. I been calling you for ten minutes."

"Shut up, bitch. That's why they say we so damn ghetto. We don' forgot how to knock on doors like normal muhfuckas," Shondra said, locking the door behind her. "Not to mention how much we fucking curse."

"Come on, ho, let's get moving before them ghetto bitches buy up all the shit in the shoe store."

Shondra was in Bakers Shoes looking at some sandals when a guy with a mouth full of gold teeth came up behind her and rubbed himself on her ass.

"Damn, you soft, mama," he whispered in her ear.

She reacted so swiftly that the blow threw him off guard and he fell back into the display of shoes.

"What the fuck is your problem, muhfucka!" she screamed, looking for the box cutter Junior always made her carry in her Gucci purse.

"What the fuck you hit me for, bitch?" he asked, getting up from the floor.

"You crazy, nigga? You don't know me to be rubbing up against me!"

"I made a mistake, bitch. It's crowded in here!"

Gloria was coming from the front of the store trying to see what the commotion was all about.

"What's wrong, Shondra?"

"That stupid muhfucka over there tried to cop a feel on me like I'm a ho or something. That nigga don't know me like that!"

"Fuck that, bitch. I was just trying to get by her ugly ass!"

The manager got between Shondra and the guy right before she could swing the box cutter.

"Wait, don't do something that you'll regret later," he said, grabbing the hand that held the razor.

"Get the fuck off her!" Gloria screamed as she pushed the manager off of Shondra.

As a crowd gathered in front of the store the guy who had grabbed Shondra slipped out of the mayhem unnoticed.

"Where the fuck he at? I should have sliced off his dick, that faggot ass nigga. That's why I don't like coming down here. Niggas don't know how to act. They think that every girl they see is a ho or something. And what the fuck he doin' in a woman's shoe store anyway?"

"You ain't lying, girl. Fuck it, let's get outta here."

"Damn, I forgot to get Junior his sneakers. Let's go to Tom Dick's around the way and get them," she told Gloria as a cab pulled up.

"I'm wit that."

***

Kendu was sitting on his bed watching TV when he heard a knock on the door.

"Who is it?"

"Me, nigga," La said.

Kendu opened the door to let Lakim in, then headed back to his room. Kendu's room was almost bare, only furnished with a twin mattress and box spring that lay on the floor, and a thirteen-inch, black and white television that sat on a broken wooden dresser. Lakim sat on the edge of the unmade bed, picked up an unlit blunt in Kendu's homemade ashtray, and lit it.

"What up, my nigga?" he asked, taking a pull of the blunt then passing it to Kendu.

"Ain't nothin', man. Just chillin', ya know."

"I just got right. How much work you got left?"

"I still got like a half a bomb left," Kendu said, putting out the blunt.

"Today's the first. You 'posed to get right. Why you ain't out on the block, kid?"

"That money ain't goin' nowhere, man. Them heads want that shit 'round the clock. I ain't stressin' getting' rid of that shit no special time."

"Well give me what you got left and I'll knock it off. Plus Junior wants to see you."

"What the fuck that nigga want with me? He wanna know why I ain't on the block, huh? He be actin' like he really my boss and shit, stressing me on how fast I move a pack. He act like this shit is legal and he gon' dock me my pay for not getting rid of his shit quick enough!"

"It ain't like that, man. The nigga just want to make fast money, and if you making it slow, then you holding up the process. Feel me?"

"You act like you on his love, nigga. Let me find out. What the nigga told you, to come over here and get his work from me 'cause I'm slow? What, he scared to tell me himself?"

"Come on, 'Du, you know how it is when a nigga want they money. They don't want to wait, and they definitely don't want to hear no excuses."

"Fuck it, man, take this shit. I don't need shit from that nigga. He think he the man 'round this muhfucka anyway, and he ain't even from our hood," Kendu said as he got the rest of the work from under the mattress.

Lakim felt that Kendu was overreacting and that there was something else contributing to his anger, more than he was letting on.

"It ain't like that, 'Du. You know how the game goes. Do you and the man got beef or somethin'? I mean the way you sounding off, you make me think the nigga said something or did something foul to you. Did something go down between y'all two?"

"Man, La, you got it twisted real bad. That nigga ain't nobody. All he doin' is making money in our hood and breaking us off a little bit. Shit, we can do this shit on our own and run his ass outta here."

"Yeah, you right and shit, but what did the nigga do to you to make you feel like this? I mean, I'm sure we can get down with him if we wanted to. What I'm trying to ask you is why you feel like this all of a sudden?" La knew what Kendu was saying was right, but he was going about it the wrong way.

"This ain't all of a sudden, nigga. You know the boys ain't feelin' that nigga like that. It's 'cause of Shondra that nobody ain't really moved on his punk ass yet. I'm telling you, La, niggas is ready to move that nigga out the hood, so you gotta keep it real out here, kid, or niggas gonna think you down with him."

"Damn, I know niggas ain't really feelin' him like that, but I didn't know they was talkin' like that. I mean, the nigga mad cool with me and he don't be actin' up out here. He just be chillin', drinkin' his beer, and smoking his weed. Who saying that they want to move on him?"

Kendu lit the blunt again and took a deep breath.

"Everybody saying they ready to move on him, the whole projects, bitches, too."

"Get the fuck outta here, man. You bullshittin'. The whole projects can't be saying that. But check it, 'Du, fuck them other niggas. I'm talking 'bout you. Why you so salty with the nigga? He looked out for us when we ain't really have shit. When you short with the dough, he don't beef. He just tell you to double up on the next pack. The nigga don't stress nobody and he basically keep to himself. You know you my man and I'm down with you, kid, so just tell me what the problem is."

"Why you actin' like that nigga's sponsor? You act like he saved your life or something. La, come on, man, don't change sides. The nigga not worth it. I don't like him 'cause he think he big shit and he ain't. That's what my problem is. Fuck him, La. He ain't no fuckin' body."

Lakim saw Kendu was too upset to reason with him so he got up off the bed, picked up the work, and headed for the door.

"Yo, La, seriously, kid, don't get too tied up with that nigga. You know you one of us and nothing is gonna happen to you when shit goes down. Feel me, my nigga?"

"I hear you, son. I'm not getting caught up."

As he walked to the elevator, Lakim felt a bad vibe. He knew something was about to go down and when it did, it was going to change everything in the hood. Shit was about to get real fucked up out there. Junior was cool as hell and Lakim really liked him, but he didn't know if he should tell him what Kendu was saying. He rode down the elevator and thought about how fucked up it would be if something happened to Junior for nothing, just for hustling in their hood.

Junior was coming from the other side of the projects collecting the rest of his money when his beeper went off. It was Lizzette and he knew what she wanted, so he turned around and started back toward her building. When he got to her floor, he fixed the gun in his waist, then knocked on her door.

"Come in," she said as he turned the knob of the brown, metal door and walked into her apartment.

"What up, ma?"

"You were right, papi," she said, coming from the back of the apartment wearing a see-through shirt with no bra and panties. "The short guy was asking me questions about you."

"What did you tell him?"

"I don't tell him anything. I just listen to what he ask me about you."

"What did he ask you?"

"He ask me if you my boyfriend and if I see you early today, and I tell him I see you but then he ask me if I know where you go, and I tell him no, but he don't look like he believe me."

"Did the other guy say anything to you?"

"No. He just whisper something to the other guy and he stay outside and just look at me. Wha, they no like you or sunthin'?"

"I don't really know because I don't know them like that."

Junior didn't want Lizzette to know what he was really thinking so he avoided answering her questions. One thing was for sure, his suspicions about Stump and KB were right.

"Well, what you got good for me, papi?" she asked, walking to the back of the apartment.

"Whatever you want, luv."

She returned with a small, plastic bag, then sat down on her couch.

"Give me five." She poured the contents in the bag on the oval glass center table.

Junior pulled out six of the skinny, clear, plastic bottles and put them on the table.

"OK, papi." Her eyes got big after seeing the drugs. "I'm gonna get right. I hope you don't mind."

"Nah, go ahead. Knock yourself out," he said, getting up from the couch.

"Where you goin'?" she asked, splitting open a cigar with a rusty razor.

"I gotta jet. I got some shit I need to take care of on the other side. I'll be back later if you need me."

"I thought that you was gonna stay a lil while with me. I hope I'm not turning you off doing this."

"Come on, ma, I ain't no judge. I sell the shit," he said as he changed his mind and went to the bathroom to relieve himself.

When he returned from the bathroom she was crushing the small, white rocks in a dollar bill and then emptying them into the cigar that was now filled with weed. He stood there and watched her roll up the cigar, then put it in her mouth and twirl it around, allowing her saliva to act like glue and seal the edges. She looked up, her head half-tilted, and lit the cigar. Then she drew a deep breath, blew out the smoke, and sat back looking like she had just had an orgasm. Junior stood there and looked at her, wondering how the hell someone so beautiful could be on that shit. It was so powerfully addictive, and it slowly stripped its users of their dignity. It turned them into different beings that would sell their souls to the devil to acquire a false sense of euphoria. She looked at him, took another deep drag, and blew out the smoke. He started to smell a sweet, tangy aroma, signaling him that it was time to go.

"Aight, ma, I'm out. Call me when you need to see me."

"I need to see you now," she said seductively, rubbing her breasts and smiling a crooked smile that formed from the effects of the drug numbing her mouth like Novacaine.

"I'll come back later on. I just gotta take care of some business real quick," he said, closing the door behind him.

Lizzette sighed when he left, she was hoping to turn him out like she did so many other niggas that wanted her for her body.

Lakim was coming out of the building after serving a customer when he saw Junior coming up the block.

"Waddup, kicko?" La asked.

"Nothing. I just left that Puerto Rican broad's crib collecting some of my dough. It's fucked up to see how that shit can fuck up some perfectly good ass. That bitch was getting fucked up with me in there. I don't trust bitches like that, 'specially when they know I can supply they ass with that shit that keeps they pussy wet," Junior said, laughing.

"I got that work from Kendu. He had a buck left," La said, getting down to business.

"Did he give you the rest of my money?"

"Nah. He said that he would give it to you himself later on," Lakim lied.

"You told him what I said?"

"Yeah."

"What he say? Was he mad when you took the rest of the work from him?"

"Yeah, man, he was heated, but I told him he was slowing shit down 'cause he takin' his time to get rid of the work. He tried to tell me why he wasn't finished, but I wasn't really listening to what he was saying. I was trying to get the work so I could come out here and get this money."

"So you all right now?"

"I'm good. I made like six already, so I'm 'bout to go to the crib and chill for a minute, then come back on the block lata on."

"Cool. I'm going to Williamsburg to go pick up the rest of my money. I'll be back in a few. I'll see you on the block when I get back."

Shondra and Gloria were walking up Graham Avenue talking about going to club Red Parrot that night while Kendu was standing on the corner of Siegel Street talking to KB about Junior.

"My man La came to my crib and told me the nigga don't want me to work for him no more because I move his shit too slow. I started not to give him the rest of the work and tell him to tell that nigga come see me if he wanted it, but I figured I'd just keep the dough I already had. He thinks I'm his son or something, sending my man to do shit he scared to do himself. I know that nigga scared of me. I'll fuck his ass up and he know it. He sent my man because he know if he tried to come at me like that he would have problems and he better not come ask me for no money or I'm gonna beat the shit outta him. He be knowing who to go to with that bullshit."

"I feel you, bruh. About how much shit he be moving out here?" KB asked.

"I don't know, eight or nine Gs a week, about," Kendu guessed.

"You and La the only niggas he got slingin' for him?"

"Yeah, I think it's only me and La right now. He sell most of his shit himself, though. He got La working our building, 155, and 215. I work my building in the day and sometimes I go in front of 300 and catch the heads going to Bushwick, but I do it when I felt like having cheddar in my pocket. I ain't out here like my man La, every day and every night. Junior slings in front of Shondra's building during the day, and at night he goes in the back. He be sittin' on the benches late at night, and sometimes some nigga from Tompkins be out there with him."

"He don't be by himself when he be out there slingin'?"

"Sometimes, but late at night that nigga be out there with him. I guess he be holdin' him down or somethin'."

"Who the dude is?"

"I don't know who he really is, but I know he from Tompkins," Kendu told him, trying to remember what La had said about the guy from Tompkins.

"Do the nigga be out there all night wit' him?"

"I don't know. I don't hang with the nigga like that. I just smoke his choke up and drink all his beer, and when it's gone I jet."

Shondra and Gloria walked past Kendu and KB as they were talking. Kendu glared at Shondra as they walked by, and Gloria stared KB down. Gloria thought KB was cute, but Shondra was wondering why Kendu was glaring at her like that.

"Stump ready to move on that nigga, you know," KB told him as the girls passed them.

"I hear you. I don't like that faggot ass nigga no way. When y'all ready to get at him, let me know, 'cause I'm down for whatever."

35

"Ain't that his wisdom that just walked by with that dark-skinned chick?" KB asked.

"Yeah, that's his bitch. I don't like her fronting ass neither. She be actin' like she all dat, and she used to be a bum ass bitch back in the day."

"He must be getting money 'cause they look like they just came from shopping with all dem bags they had, plus she fly as fuck."

"Yeah, yeah, that trickin' ass nigga probably is giving that ho all his money. That's why he stressin' me for his money and shit."

"I'm saying, though, she draped in jewels and the whole nine."

"Fuck that bitch, son. She ain't nobody. She ain't shit either, just like her punk ass man."

When Shondra and Gloria got in her house, Shondra threw the bags on her bed and Gloria turned on the Sony CD/cassette recorder on her dresser.

"Let me call my boo to let him know I'm home."

"You gonna tell him about what happened downtown?"

"Hell, yeah, because he know a lotta people and we was downtown where everybody hangs out and if somebody he knows seen it and tell him instead of me, he gonna be pissed off with me."

"I hear that fly shit. Most niggas don't give a fuck." Gloria was thinking about how most guys treated her.

"You right. Most niggas," Shondra said, smiling and dialing his beeper number.

Gloria started dancing to the music playing on the radio.

"Don't forget to tell him that you want to go to the club tonight too, bitch," she said, shaking her round hips to the rhythm of the music.

"We going. Don't worry, ho."

Shondra pulled out the Nike box with Junior's sneakers in it and put it in the closet on top of his other sneaker boxes. She had also bought him a matching Nike shirt.

"That color is nice," Gloria said.

"I know. I got good taste, bitch."

"What you gonna wear tonight to the club?" Gloria asked. She didn't have as many clothes as Shondra, but every time they went shopping Shondra would pick something up for her because Shondra knew Gloria didn't have money to buy the expensive shit she was able to buy with Junior's money.

"I didn't even think about it yet. I might wear that purple, butter soft, leather dress with the back out, and my Nine West hooker boots."

"I'm only going out to listen to some music and enjoy myself. We should ask Elaine and Cheryl to come too, right?" Gloria asked.

"I was thinking about that, too, so we can make it girls' night out. You know that guy that we passed on Graham Avenue that was talking to that dirty ass Kendu?" Shondra asked Gloria.

"Yeah, I don't like Kendu. You see how he looked at you all funny and shit when we walked by? But the guy he was standing with was kinda cute. I was going to say something to him, but that jealous ass Kendu probably woulda cock blocked."

"I think the dude he was with is from Williamsburg."

"Yeah, I think he is, and I heard them niggas over there are real grimy. I heard they be beefing with niggas from our projects and setting them up and shit."

"I heard that, too. I don't know him, but he be with Kendu a lot. They be in the back smoking choke and drinking."

"Well, I think he's cute, and the next time I see him I'm gonna make it my business to get with him if he's alone," Gloria said, shaking her wide hips.

"Well don't give the pussy up until you know the nigga's name at least, ho."

"You don't worry about who I put this good pussy on, bitch. What I'm worried about is if the nigga is hung like a horse."

Gloria envied Shondra's relationship with Junior. She wished she could find a man that treated her the way Junior treated Shondra. Gloria was a shiny, black girl with an hourglass figure. Her face was perfectly round with full lips, a straight nose, and a good grade of hair, thanks to her Cherokee heritage. When Gloria was younger she was loose and had been dogged out by a lot of the guys from the projects. She was labeled a ho because she was so easy to get with. The truth was that Gloria had low self-esteem and desired the affection and attention she was missing from home. If a guy told her she was pretty or that he really liked her, she would sleep with him in hopes that he would be her man, but once he got the puss, he would only come around when he wanted some ass.

Once the rumor got around that Gloria was an easy lay, every nigga and his man was in her ear trying to hit it, and she loved the attention. She soon became notorious in the projects for her mean ass head game, as well as how freaky she got between the sheets. She was having threesomes and gangbangs with well over five niggas, and was compared to the porn star Vanessa del Rio. Gloria was so far gone with her "celebrity" status that she never realized she was being mentally and physically abused by all her partners. Her reputation was being trashed and she had no idea of the adverse effect it would have on her life.

One day one of the guys she saw regularly had called her and said he wanted to see her. Since she wasn't doing anything that day she decided to go see him. When she got to his house she went to his room where he lit a blunt and they both got high and had sex. When he was done he asked her if his boys could get down too, but she refused, which didn't make him too happy. He rose from the bed and tried to smooth talk her into changing her mind, but her mind was made up, so he walked out of the room and came back with seven dudes. Gloria's heart started racing because the look on their faces said they weren't taking no for an answer. She tried to go out the door, but they blocked it so she couldn't leave. One of them put his finger over his mouth, motioning for her to keep quiet as he fondled her. She couldn't believe what was about to happen. She never thought anything like that could happen to her. She lay down on the bed reluctantly and closed her eyes, letting them all take turns on her, hoping it would be over quickly.

When they were finished with her they left her sprawled out on the bed ravaged like she had been in a car wreck. Gloria was left alone in the room—naked, cold, and numb. She felt worthless and she was contemplating ending her life. She rose to her feet and walked out the door half-dressed. She didn't know where she was going because she was in shock. She walked out of the building and the cold November breeze brought her back to reality as she tried to gather her clothing around her properly.

Shondra was coming from Cooper projects when she noticed Gloria walking in the direction of home. She caught up with her so they could walk home together, although she didn't hang out with Gloria because of her bad reputation. When she saw Gloria and looked in her face, she knew something terrible had happened to her, and that's when their friendship was formed.

Shondra took Gloria under her wing and taught her how to love and respect herself. She made Gloria realize she was searching for something outside of herself that she always had on the inside. Once Shondra was finished with Gloria, Gloria was a totally changed woman with a brighter outlook on life. There were still some guys that would try to break her will, but everyone soon realized that she had changed.

***

Stump got up and sat on the edge of the bed from resting that morning. He was still tired and needed more rest, but he wanted to go back to Baptiste in hopes of finding Junior. He grabbed his handgun from under the pillow and took it with him as he went to the bathroom. Ever since he'd been shot, Stump never went anywhere without being strapped. He had made a promise to himself while recovering in the hospital that he wasn't ever going to get caught without his iron again.

It bothered him to think about the day he was shot, but that experience made him more aware of his surroundings when he was coming and going and had hardened his heart even more than before. He pulled up his shirt, looked at the scar on his shoulder, and felt the long, ugly scars on his back. Those scars proved he was a survivor and a real soldier in the field. He put his gun in his waistband, grabbed his jacket off the chair next to the bed, and headed for the door. He checked to make sure the safety was off his gun before he opened the door, and then he bolted down the stairs to the lobby of the building.

Junior had just reached Williamsburg when he felt his beeper vibrate, so he went into the corner bodega to get change. He bought a pack of Newports and a Heineken, then asked for change for a dollar and went to the pay phone. He dialed Shondra's number and listened to her tell him about her episode when she went downtown. He was only half listening because he was thinking about what Lizzette had told him about KB. After telling Shondra he would be home after he picked up his money, he walked up the street to the building where the guy that owed him money lived. After he picked up his money, he headed back to Shondra's house.

Kendu was in the building across the street from his with Joyce, a booster from Baptiste who was strung out on crack. He was looking at some items of clothing she was trying to sell to him for a hit.

"These shits are hot and dey just came out, so ain't nobody got 'em yet, I took dem scrait outta da box in da stockroom, so these muhfuckas not even on display yet," she said about the Georges Marciano shirts she had in the Macy's bag.

"They aight. How much you want for this black and blue one?" he asked, holding one of the shirts up to his chest to see if it was his size.

"Gimme twenty dollars and two nicks."

"Two nicks and twenty dollars?"

"Yeah, nigga. These not even out yet. You'll be da first nigga wit' it. Shit, I can get thirty dollars easy for one."

"Yeah, but they don't have a price tag on them, so you don't know how much they really cost. They might only be thirty dollars for one and I'd be gettin' beat."

"Nigga, I jus' tole you dat I got dem scrait from da stockroom, so dey ain't gon' have no tags on dem. Come on, nigga, you know Guess cost sixty dollars off top, so stop frontin' and give me da twenty and two nicks."

"Aight, Joyce, but look, I gotta give you the nicks when I come from the crib, and I don't have no money on me right now."

"Nah, nigga, you gotta give me all my shit now," she said, putting the garments back in the bag.

"See, Joyce, see how you tryin' to play me like a crab. I'm not going to beat you outta your shit!"

"Come on, nigga, I wanna blast off and you bullshittin'. I wanna take a major and you talkin' reckless. Fuck it. I'm gonna go see La. He always holdin'. Shit, nigga, you ain't neva got no work when I come to cop from you. What, you smokin' your own shit?"

"Fuck you, you crack head bitch!" he said, throwing the shirt on the floor and stomping on it.

"Ah! Why you gotta do dat dumb shit for, muhfucka?" she asked picking up the shirt and trying to clean it off. "Did I hit a nerve or sumthin'?"

Kendu walked out the building in a huff and headed for his building. Joyce grabbed up her clothing and muttered to herself, "That nigga in the closet!"

Kendu was furious and slammed the door to his bedroom. He opened the closet door and went into the pocket of a jacket that was way in the back. He pulled out a cigar and a small, clear, glassine bag. The small mirror from off his nightstand was placed on the unmade bed as he split the blunt open and emptied the contents of it in a brown, paper bag. He poured some of the stuff in the glassine bag onto the mirror, put a dollar over it, and used a lighter to crush the small rocks into a powder. Then he took the razor and scraped the white powder together in a small mountain, and licked the residue off the dollar bill. The weed in his pocket was poured into the cigar, then he scooped up the white powder with the dirty razor and sprinkled it over the weed in the cigar. He scooped up some more and spread that evenly over the reefer, then used his index finger to pick up the remainder and licked up the residue. Finally he rolled up the cigar, transforming it into a woola blunt. He lit it, inhaling deeply and trying not to let any smoke escape his lungs. He held the smoke in for as long as possible, then exhaled as the cloud filled his dimly lit room. He continued to smoke until the blunt was burning his thumb and index finger.

The combination of the weed and crack gave Kendu an immediate rush, and he began to feel light-headed. He tried to get comfortable on his bed, but for some reason he couldn't find a position that suited him. He kept looking around as if he lost something, and then his mind told him he was bugging out from the drugs. He laughed to himself, then tried to enjoy his high. His mind was flooded with all kinds of thoughts. He was sitting in a room getting high because he didn't want anyone to know he was smoking crack, and another crack head had just called him out. His anger was resurfacing again.

Kendu blamed Junior for getting him addicted to this shit he was smoking. If Junior never gave him the packages to sell, then he would never have met that bad ass Puerto Rican bitch that showed him how to tap the bottles and increase his count. While she showed him, she offered to suck his dick for a hit. The average man would never know she was smoking that shit, because she looked so damn good and kept her body tight. It was a good feeling to get served by a bad bitch like Lizzette. It was mad niggas 'round the way that wanted her. Even the Puerto Rican niggas was sweating her when they saw her walk past them in some skin-tight jeans.

Lizzette was the one who got Kendu addicted. One day he went to her house to serve her and while she got high, Kendu rolled a blunt. She came over to where he was sitting, sucked on his earlobe, and asked if he wanted

41

some head. He thought fucking was next after she sucked him off—at least that's what he was expecting anyway—so he told her yes and wanted to see how much it was going to cost him, but she never said anything. She just took off her stretch pants and oversized T-shirt, and started rubbing her pussy in front of him. Kendu was aroused and started stroking his manhood in preparation for what was to come next, but then she did the okie doke. She told him she wanted to take a hit first because it made her more horny and wet. He fumbled in his pocket and took out one of the tapped capsules he had made from Junior's pack. She took it, then put it in her mouth and sucked it like a lollipop. She was fucking with him.

As he sat there massaging his piece, she asked him if he had anymore weed. When he told her yes, a smile grew across her face because she knew it was time to set her plan in motion. Kendu pulled out the weed and the blunt, and then she asked him to fix it up for her while she crushed the rocks into powder. He did as he was told. Then she took if from him when he was done and prepared it to be smoked. He lit it for her, and as she put it in her mouth, she got on her hands and knees and crawled to him, the blunt dangling from the side of her mouth. Kendu thought the smoke had a sweet smell. He patiently waited for her to reach him. When she got to him she pulled off her panties and stood over his dick, positioning herself right over his pole. He grabbed her by her waist and tried to bring her gently down on his tool. As he did that she put the blunt in his mouth. In that moment of weakness he "ate the forbidden fruit."

It seemed like an hour had passed as Kendu sat in his room, high and blaming his fuck-ups on Junior and anyone else he could think of. He was in denial big time. Kendu heard a knock on the door and sat still, trying to hear if someone was outside his room. After about ten minutes of listening, he decided to see if someone was actually there, but when he opened the door there was no one there, so he closed it back, sensing his own paranoia. He walked over to his broken, full-length mirror and gazed at his reflection. The guy in the mirror had eyes as wide as saucers and white lips that didn't resemble Kendu. The guy in the mirror was tired, confused, and in desperate need of help. Kendu grabbed the mirror and threw it to the floor—seven years of bad luck.

***

Shondra was explaining to Junior what happened downtown in detail and that she and Gloria were planning to go to the Red Parrot that night. Junior really didn't like her going out, but he didn't want to act like he was her father by telling her not to go. She was already dressed and looked good in the leather outfit she had on. Her ass stretched it out and it clung to her thick thighs.

"With that dress on, a nigga might kidnap your ass if you don't give him no play."

"Oh, boo, ain't no nigga out there want me. Plus, this rock on my finger lets them know I'm taken."

"Bullshit. Look what happened today downtown. The nigga wanted to put your lights out because you wouldn't give him no rap."

"Yeah, but I put that shit in check with the quickness. I just don't like the fact that niggas think that they can say and do whatever they want to a female. I be getting tired of that shit."

"Then why you going to a club where there ain't nothing but niggas like that?"

"It's just me, Gloria, Cheryl, and Elaine going. It's girls' night out, and we ain't all hung out together in a long time, baby."

"Yeah, but none of dem bitches got a man, and you do. They purpose is to meet niggas."

"You right, boo, but you don't got shit to worry about, 'cause I love you. I'm not looking for nobody. I'm just going to listen to some music and have some drinks. That's all. I know you trust me, baby. I would never step out on you, ever."

"I'm just saying, them chicks you hang wit' is wild, 'specially Gloria. She a ho."

"Come on now, you don't have to disrespect my homegirl like that. You know I ain't no follower, and I definitely ain't no ho. If anything, I'm the chief and they the Indians."

"I ain't call you no ho. I was just saying . . . ahhhh, fuck it," he said, knowing he wouldn't be able to win this argument.

She walked over to the closet and pulled out the sneakers and shirt she had bought him earlier, hoping it would change his mood.

"Look, I bought you the shirt to match the sneakers. Try it on so I can see how it looks on you."

"That's cool." He grabbed the shirt and looked at it. "Yeah, it'll fit. What time y'all leavin'?"

"'Bout eleven o'clock, and I'll be back 'round two or three."

"Aight, I'm out. Take this. You buy your own drinks," he said, giving her some money.

He gave her a long, sloppy kiss and headed out the door.

"I love you, boo. Thank you, daddy."

There weren't many people out and the night air was thick. Junior went to the store to get a forty-ounce of Ole Gold and sat in his same spot on the benches behind Shondra's building. He cracked open the cold beer, tilted the bottle up to his mouth, and took three long gulps. As he put the top back on the beer he noticed one of his regulars standing by the back door of the building. The customer flashed three fingers as he approached. They went into the vestibule of the building and made the transaction smoothly. Junior returned back to his spot on the bench. He guzzled down some more of his beer and waited for the paper chase to begin.

La was coming out of his building when he saw Kendu coming up the block. La was getting ready to go chill with Junior like he did some nights but when he saw Kendu he changed his mind.

"Yo, La, where you headed?"

"Nowhere but right here, bruh."

"Did you see Joyce?"

"Yeah, she had some fly ass Guess shirts. I copped four of them."

"You know that crack head bitch ain't want to let me go for ten dollars?"

"Word? That's fucked up."

"You just comin' back out since the last time I saw you?"

"Yeah, man, I had to cop some Zs. I been out all last night. I'm 'bout to go get me a beer and some choke from the black gate."

"Aight, let's go," Kendu said and they started walking in the direction of the weed spot.

As they were walking up the Ave someone was calling Kendu's name. When they turned around, KB was standing on the corner with Stump.

"YOOOOO!!!!" he called back to them, then turned to La. "Let me go see what these niggas want. I'll catch up with you in a minute."

Kendu jogged toward them and La watched, figuring his man was up to no good. He turned around and started walking to the spot, thinking of how fucked up shit was about to get in the hood. He now figured Stump was the one Kendu was talking about when he said niggas were ready to move on Junior. He knew Stump was a dangerous and ruthless muhfucka, but he wasn't sure if Junior would be an easy win if he didn't come correct. He copped his smoke and headed back around the way to the projects. When he got to his building he checked the back to see if Kendu was out there. La was feeling uneasy. He was used to seeing KB with Kendu from time to time, but seeing Stump meant danger, especially after how Kendu was acting. Everyone in the hood knew how Stump got down. If he heard a nigga was getting money, he was on them like a fly on shit. Kendu must have told him Junior was getting a lot of money out there, and from what La was taking him every four to five days, they were right. Junior had Baptiste on lock, and now it seemed that Stump wanted a cut of the dough, or just wanted a big payoff. Either way, it was looking grim for the home team.

When La came back from the weed spot Kendu wasn't anywhere to be found, so he decided to go chill on the Ave. He had a bad feeling his childhood homey was about to get into something that he was sure would get him hurt or killed if he didn't think it out properly.

"Damn!" he said out loud, not knowing he was talking to himself. "Why this nigga got to go and fuck wit' them grimy ass niggas? He know them niggas don't give a fuck 'bout him like that. Damn, 'Du!"

He decided right then that if something was going to happen, he would have Junior's back. He was just stuck between a rock and a hard place when it came to him telling Junior what Kendu was saying. Kendu was his childhood homey and Junior was just his boss, his loyalty to Kendu went as far as friendship. He told himself telling Junior about what Kendu was saying wasn't being disloyal. As far as he was concerned, he was keeping it loyal to the *money*. La didn't want to go against the grain, but the reality behind it was that his love of money was truly stronger than his friendship with Kendu. Junior looked out for him when it came to money. What Kendu was plotting to do was impulsive and La knew he wasn't thinking straight, he was just reacting. La believed he had the right idea but was just using the wrong resources. If he was going to do that, he would not use someone that Junior would suspect.

Stump, KB, and Kendu walked over to an adjacent building while they talked.

"Did you see Junior yet?" KB asked Kendu as they all sat on the benches in the back of the building.

"Nah. He should be in the back of 110 by now. Did y'all check over there?"

"Nope. Wasn't that La you was walking wit'?"

"Yeah, we was going to cop some smoke and some brew."

Stump didn't say anything. He just sat quietly and listened to them, periodically feeling for his gun.

"You know we ready to get at that nigga tonight, right? You down wit' us or what?"

"I already told you I'm with it. I'm down for whatever."

"We gotta find out if he out there first. What you need to do is go check to see if he's back there and come back and let us know. Even if he ain't out there when you get there, just wait 'til he comes, then come back and let us know. You got it?" Stump was serious.

"I got you. I'll just go over there with La when he comes from the store. He usually goes back there and smokes wit' him."

"Aight, then, we gonna chill right here in the cut and wait for you to come back. Listen, make sure you come back and let us know something," Stump warned.

"I gotcha, man, trust me. I'll be back so we can get that nigga."

Junior saw a figure coming from the street side of the building and got off the bench to try to figure out who was coming toward him. As the person got closer he realized it was Kendu.

"What up, 'Du?" he asked, slapping him five.

"Ain't nothin'. What up with you?"

"Same ol', same ol'."

"You seen La?" 'Du asked.

"Nah, not since earlier. He said he was coming through later on, though."

"Oh, yeah, he told me you wanted to see me about somethin'."

"Yeah, let me go take care of this custy real quick and then we can talk, aight?" Junior said, walking toward the building to go serve someone that was waiting impatiently for him.

Kendu sat on the bench and looked at Junior with disgust. He hated how he thought he was so cool. This made him want Stump and KB to get him that much more. He figured he would sit with Junior until La came by so he could warn him about what was about to go down, because he didn't want him to get caught up. After serving the customer, Junior came back to the benches, sat down, pulled out a half-smoked blunt, and lit it. He took a couple of drags, then passed it to Kendu.

"I want to talk some business wit you," Junior said.

"I'm listening."

"When I first hit you off with work, I told you that if you wanted to make money you would have to be dedicated to what you do. In the beginning, you was flipping more than La, but then you just slowed down out of the blue. I'm not trying to put a rush on what you do, but what I'm concerned about is what made you slow down so much. To me it seems like you lost interest or somethin', or you makin' too much dough. Is that what happened?"

Kendu couldn't believe he was talking to him like they were really at a board meeting.

"Nah, I just had other shit I been taking care of. That's all," Kendu replied, flicking the blunt in the grass.

"Why you ain't just tell me? I mean, I don't want to know your business. You coulda just told me you had some other shit to do and I coulda worked something out with you until you got ready to get back to makin' some dough."

"I know, but everything is all right now." Kendu was not feeling the conversation. Junior was really taking that boss shit to heart.

"It's just that when I'm done with my package and you still have work left, I have to wait on you to finish so I can go re-up, and that slows down the process. I gotta make sure my count is right with the losses and everything else. I can't go to my connect with less than what I usually cop because he won't give me nothing on consignment, so if I come short, he ain't gonna hit me with what he usually do and I don't like making two and three trips for nothing. You feel me?"

"I hear you. I got the rest of your dough upstairs. I'll give it to you tomorrow unless you need it now."

"Nah, I'm cool right now. So, what's up? If everything is cleared up wit' you, you ready to get back on the block again?"

"Not right now. I'll let you know when I'm ready."

"That's cool. Just let me know when you ready to get started again. You need any money or anything? I mean, if you need some extra dough, I can hit you wit' a lil' sumthin'."

"Nah, man, I'm OK, but good looking out." Kendu was getting furious. He felt like Junior was trying to son him.

"Well, just keep what you got, and when you ready to start up again, then let me know." Junior still wanted to ask him about seeing Stump and KB, but he wanted to wait for the right time.

They sat on the benches talking shit for a little while longer, then Junior's beeper went off. He looked at it and told Kendu to chill for a minute. Kendu rose to his feet and tried to dismiss himself, but Junior was insistent on him staying.

"Just hold up for a minute. I just gotta tell my cousin something real quick."

"Aight, I'ma chill," Kendu said reluctantly.

Junior walked to the street and Kendu watched to see where he was going. He noticed Junior walking toward the corner. He observed Junior talking to someone in a 190E Mercedes Benz with alloy rims.

Junior got into the red car and immediately turned the music down. Craig was pumping En Vogue's "My Love (You're Never Gonna Get It)." Craig was Junior's cousin. He was a dark chocolate brother with a smooth complexion and wavy hair. He was tall, thin, and good-looking, and he lived and hustled in Tompkins projects. Craig usually came through to check on his cousin every night to make sure he was OK, because he knew Junior was fairly new to the game. He didn't want Junior slipping and making rookie mistakes, because in this game, any mistake could prove to be fatal. Craig would put some of his money with Junior to help him get his weight up, and they would take turns going to cop. He didn't really approve of Junior selling, but if he was going to be in the game Craig preferred that he learn it from somebody that would keep his best interests at heart. There was so much shit a nigga had to watch out for that he had to have eyes in the back of his head to see everything that was coming at him. You had to be one step ahead of everyone. You had to think like your worker, like the detective that wanted to bust you, like the nigga that wanted to rob you, like the nigga that was jealous of your status, and most importantly, like the woman you slept with.

"How you did this week?" Junior asked him.

"I did like fifty-seven thousand. What about you?"

"I did like eighteen thousand, give or take a G. You know I gotta pay my workers, so I made a little less."

"Me too, nigga, and you know my team bigger than yours. Anyway, nigga, I got my shit sucked so good today. I mean that broad sucked me so good I thought she had a bachelor's in cocksucking from Big Dick University," Craig said, grabbing his crotch and laughing.

"Yeah, well I got this Spanish mami that got a bangin' ass. I almost laced her, but she wouldn't let me go raw."

"Nigga! Is you crazy? You betta' not fuck none of dem broads raw. You know they can give you some shit you can't get rid of."

"I know, man. I was slippin', but she look good as hell and the ass is soooo fat."

"Yeah, but you can't let that shit cloud your judgment, kid. It's all good when you hittin' it, but three days lata' you gonna wanna kill the bitch 'cause she fried you."

"I can dig it."

"Just think about if you bought something home to bugga."

"It's Mooka, you stupid muhfucka."

"Oh, my bad," Craig said, laughing. "Nah, but for real, you gotta think about that shit. She not gonna wanna hear no sorry and shit, so you better think with the right head from now on."

"You right. I'm 'posed to see the broad tonight before I go in. Shondra went to the club and she ain't comin' in 'til late, so I got a chance to go hit that real fast."

"You love playin' dangerous games, nigga. Why in the world would you fuck with somebody that lives in the same PJs as your girl? That ain't nothin' but problems, kid. You need to go somewhere else with that shit, especially a crack head. You know how they blow the spot up when they want a hit."

"I ain't worried 'bout no bitches. If she try to flip out on me, I'll tell Shondra she lyin' 'cause I won't give her no credit."

"Aight, whatever, nigga. Don't say I didn't warn your ass when Shondra got your nuts in a grinder," Craig said, laughing. "Now come on and let me count out this money for you."

Craig reached in the backseat and pulled out a brown, paper bag full of money.

"I be trying to get these dollar bills changed over so my knot won't be so fat, plus I'm tired of counting all these ones," he said, pulling out the wad of money.

"I know. I be telling the heads that I don't take dollar bills at night. I make them change that shit and I definitely don't take change," Junior said.

"Well, that's all of it. When you going to go re-up again, or is it my turn?"

"You know it's my turn, nigga. You ain't funny. I think we need to up it to at least five kees now. We see Cheech almost three times a month, and I hate goin' up there 'cause it be so fuckin' hot with the po-po and TNT. What you think?"

"I think you're right. I'm tired of going up there my damn self, but who the fuck we gonna trust with all this dough?"

"Nobody." Junior tried to stuff the money in his pants, but it wouldn't fit.

"What you doing with a tool on you, nigga? You got beef?" Craig asked Junior after spotting the gun in his waistband.

"I hope not. I just got a feeling that something shady is 'bout to go down."

Craig looked real disturbed by Junior's statement.

"What you mean you got a feeling? Did something happen out here?"

"Not really. It's just that some cat out here been asking 'bout me, ya know. That Puerto Rican girl told me that this nigga named KB was asking her was I with her. Him and this dude, Stump, was on the corner of Graham when I went to the check cashing place to collect my money from her, and when she was on her way back to her crib he started questioning her and shit," Junior said, fixing the gun in his waist.

"Who are they?"

"I seen KB before hangin' with that nigga 'Du, the kid that work for me. I think he from Williamsburg. He ain't no real threat. But the other nigga he was with is the one to worry about."

"Why? Who the fuck he 'posed to be?"

"I don't know him like that. Today was my first time seeing him around here. They say he one of dem stick up kids that always into some shit. He don' robbed almost every nigga 'round here that get paper. I heard some niggas shot him up but they say that shit only made his ass worse," Junior said, trying not to sound worried.

"You know where he rest at?"

"I heard Bushwick PJs, but I'm not really sure. That nigga 'Du is in the back. I was goin' to ask him since he hangs out wit' the nigga, you know what I mean?"

"I feel you. We need to find out what the fuck is goin' on. Let me talk to that nigga 'Du and find out what's really goin' on," Craig suggested.

"Nah, kid, I got it. I don't want him to think I know somethin' just in case he got some information. Matter of fact, let me go holla at him now before his ass leaves. I kinda think the nigga know somethin', 'cause he been actin' suspect lately. He been slow getting my money to me and I ain't been seein' him around like before. You know you can tell a nigga actin' funny by how they change up what they do. He don't really hang around me like he used to and shit. I been peepin' his flow and he been actin' real shady."

"Well, I'm gonna run up to my man's crib in Bushwick real quick and get me some heat so I can hold you down tonight, aight?" Craig asked as he started up his car.

"Cool."

Junior got out of the car carrying the bag of money because it wouldn't fit in his pocket. He walked to the front of the building so Kendu wouldn't see what he was doing. After he put the money in the closet in his room, he headed to the back of the building to finish quizzing Kendu. As he got to the backdoor he could hear Kendu yelling, and when he opened the door he noticed it was Kendu and La, and they were arguing. He tried to hear what they were saying, but when Kendu saw him he just walked off quickly.

"What up, La? What was all that about?" Junior asked.

"Ahh nothin', man."

"Why 'Du just walk off like that? He looked real vexed," Junior said, keeping his eye on Kendu as he walked away.

"Look, Junior," La started, "I need to tell you something. I think Du is trying to set you up. I'm not real sure, but he been saying some ill shit about you."

"Like what?" Junior asked, his full attention now on La.

"Like when I went to go get the rest of the work from him he just started talking reckless and shit. I asked him did you say something to him for him to be feelin' salty, but he just said 'fuck you' and then started sayin' that niggas 'round here was ready to move on you and shit. . . ."

Junior stood frozen, listening to everything La was telling him about Kendu. His heart was beating fast as hell and he was a little nervous knowing what he was thinking all along was now confirmed. He listened intently, thinking that his life was about to take a drastic change.

"He even told me that I better stop hangin' 'round you before they move on you, or I might get it, too," La finished.

51

Junior was speechless, but he couldn't show La any weakness. He had to stay in control and make sure his response was strong and direct with no indication of fear. He knew what La was doing would eventually jeopardize his rep in the hood, and he really didn't want to involve La because he knew the outcome could be deadly. He had to make sure La stayed confident so he wouldn't think he made a mistake by telling him about the setup.

"This is what that nigga just told you, just now?" Junior didn't realize that he was yelling.

"Yeah, man, he told me the shit is about to go down now and . . ." La trailed off from what he was saying as he began to wonder if he had done the right thing by telling.

"WHAT!" Junior screamed. "That black muhfucka, where the fuck was he going, La?" Junior grabbed his gun from his waist and headed toward the direction Kendu was walking when he left.

"Chill, son. I know you heated, but you gotta think first, man," La said, trying to stop Junior from leaving.

"Yo, get the fuck off me! I looked out for that faggot ass nigga and he tryin' to set me up. That's some real crab shit. That's my word. I'm gonna put a hole in that nigga's wig and leave his ass leaking on the sidewalk. Get out of my way, La!"

"Come on, Junior, he probably want you to go looking for him. He probably hopes you go looking for him so he can ambush you in the building or sumthin'. Just chill, man, and think for a minute."

La was right. Junior was just reacting. He wasn't thinking logically and strategically. He knew Kendu couldn't be the mastermind of this shit. He was just a pawn in this setup. Junior had to think. He had to devise a plan on how he would move, where, and when. He didn't know how much time he had left to think of a plan, but he needed to move soon. He needed to calm down, and he needed to cool out for a minute.

Junior sat down on the benches and looked down at the gun in his hand, then looked up at the roof from instinct to see if any police were up there peeping, and then he blew out a long sigh. He wasn't prepared for what he knew he had to do, and he wanted to leave and say "fuck it," but he was already knee deep in the game, and if he abandoned his spot his rep would be ruined and he would lose what little respect he had in the hood. If he left, niggas would think he was weak and he would have more niggas trying him than a winning slot machine in Atlantic City.

Kendu was furious, he couldn't believe La was defending Junior. La was acting like Junior was more his man than he was. Kendu tried to warn La to leave Junior alone, because Stump and KB were about to get him. La had the nerve to argue with him and tell him he was jealous of Junior and he *was* jealous of Junior. He hated the fact that Junior had so much love in his hood, more love than he had. Look how he had his man turning on him. He hated the fact that Junior was making major paper. He hated the fact that Junior had a girl from around Kendu's way. Shit, there were a thousand reasons why he was jealous of Junior.

When Kendu got to the back of the building, KB and Stump were on the bench talking.

"He out there. I just left him," he said as he walked up on their conversation.

"OK. Who was out there with him?" KB asked.

"My man, La. You know, the one I was walking with earlier. He's out there with him right now. I told him to get ghost because I didn't want him to catch no fever when we go over there."

"You told him what we plannin' to do?" Stump asked, his brows lowering.

"Yeah, that's my man. I had to let him know so he don't get caught up in this shit."

Stump stood and slapped the shit out of Kendu. The blow caught Kendu off guard and knocked him to the ground.

"What the fuck is wrong with you, muhfucka?" Stump boomed. "You put the nigga on to what I'm 'bout to do? Huh?" he asked as he grabbed Kendu and held him by his collar. "You might be tryin' to set me up for all I know. How the fuck you gonna tell somebody what the fuck I'm gonna do? Did you tell the police too, muhfucka?"

Stump smacked Kendu again and Kendu's bottom lip started to bleed as he stumbled backward, unable to defend himself because Stump never let him regain his balance.

"You dumb bitch. What the fuck was you thinkin'? I didn't tell you to go ova there and tell nobody shit. I told you to see if the nigga was out there. Nothing else!"

Stump was very serious about what he was saying. He knew from experience that niggas got caught because of other niggas running off with the mouth before shit even happened.

53

"Suppose he tell that nigga what you told him, huh, muhfucka?" Stump yelled, grabbing at Kendu again, but Kendu got to his feet and wiggled out of Stump's grip.

"Look, man, he not gonna tell that nigga shit," Kendu cried as he backed up out of Stump's reach.

"What! How the fuck you know?" Stump was still trying to get a hold on Kendu.

"'Cause, that's my man. KB, tell him I ain't tryin' to set y'all up, please, man."

The whole time KB was just watching. He wasn't going to agree with anything because he didn't want to catch a backhand from Stump. Those blows looked like they hurt.

Stump finally got a hold on Kendu and punched him hard in his face. Kendu let out a loud yelp and covered his face in anticipation of some more blows to the head. He couldn't fight Stump back, and he just wanted him to stop. He wished he had never told La anything, and now he wished he had never told Stump that he told La some information. He was hoping that La didn't tell Junior anything, because if he did, Kendu knew that would be the end of him. Stump was not the one to play with.

"You better hope that nigga not hip to what's about to go down or you're a dead man," Stump said as he let Kendu drop to the ground.

"You think we should still go ahead and get this nigga?" KB asked cautiously.

"Fuck yeah! And this nigga gonna lead the way!" Stump said, grabbing his gun.

Kendu was getting to his feet, trying to regain his senses.

"I'm not tryin' to set you up, man. I wouldn't do that. That's my word on my momma, man."

"I don't want to hear that shit. Just show me where the nigga at!"

"He's in the back of the building with La."

"I want you to go back ova there and tell him to come in the building. I'm gonna be in the building. Once I see you go through the front, I'll have the drop on him. It should all come as a surprise for his ass, and if it doesn't, that means you or your man told him, and in either case, all y'all gonna be dead men tonight. You hear me, muhfucka?" Stump pointed his gun at Kendu's head. "Don't do nothing other than what I just told you, nigga. I'm gonna be right behind you, so you ain't gonna get far if you try to run."

Kendu didn't know what he had gotten himself into, and he wanted to get out of that shit immediately, because it was a lose-lose situation for him. He was so afraid at that point that he didn't know what to do. He wasn't 100 percent sure La didn't tell Junior, because La had taken Junior's side when Kendu told him what was about to go down. Kendu didn't have a gun on him, so if he just walked up on Junior, there was no telling what his reaction would be. His heart was racing and he didn't see a way out of his dilemma. He was deathly afraid. The tables had turned drastically for him. He knew he had gotten himself into a world of shit, and he was sinking deep and fast.

L. J. Miller

Chapter 4
Why you pullin☐out on me?

Junior and La were standing on the corner—Junior with a gun in his hand, and La with his back against the black gate. They were both on alert for anything or anyone suspicious. Junior was praying nothing happened. He kind of wished what La told him was just bullshit, but it was truly wishful thinking on his part. It seemed like La was going to hold him down, since he didn't have to tell him what Kendu said, and he didn't have to stand there with Junior, knowing something was supposed to go down. It was like La didn't care what the outcome was going to be. Junior was finding it hard to believe a nigga would go against his childhood friend like that, and it raised some questions on La's loyalty, but Junior was just glad La was on his side, this time. Junior's mind was racing a mile a minute. He was trying to figure out what he was going to do. He knew he had to warn Shondra because he definitely didn't want her caught up in anything. He didn't want anyone to use her to get to him, and there was no telling how grimy those guys were.

Junior and La both stood silently on the corner like sentries, looking up and down the block. Junior saw headlights coming from the south corner of the building, so he put his back against the wall and held up his gun. La saw his reaction, and because he didn't have a gun, he moved closer to the entrance of the building in case something jumped off. As the car got closer, Junior realized it was his cousin's car, so he pointed around the corner to let him know to park on the side of the building.

"That's my fam, La. Chill right here for a sec. I'm just gonna let him know what's goin' on, OK?"

"I got you, kid." La said.

Junior handed him his gun.

"Hold on to this. If you see Kendu or any of dem other cats, holla so I'll know, but if you don't have a chance, I don't have to explain to you what to do."

"Right." La replied holding the gun firmly in his hand.

Junior walked around the corner as Craig was getting out of the car dressed in a black fatigue suit with a gun in his hand. "I saw you with the heat in your hand when I was coming up. I was thinking something went down already. Did you see that kid yet?"

57

"Nah. My man La just told me the nigga tryin' to set me up to get robbed. He said the nigga told him the shit 'posed to pop off tonight. He told me this as soon as you pulled off. Can you believe that shit? You know I'm gonna blow that nigga's head off when I see him, right?"

"Hell, yeah, I believe it. What makes you think these niggas got love for you in their hood? You a money machine for the niggas that work for you, kid. These muhfuckas don't give a fuck if you live or die. The only thing they care about is if you still gonna hit them off with work. Smarten up, nigga. This game don't have no love for you, and the hood you in don't have none for you either. The sooner you realize this, the better off you'll be, 'specially when shit like this pop off. Well, where the nigga live at? Let's lay in his building and wait for him to come in or go out."

"No. He just told La, so he might be expecting me to move like that, so I'm trying to think which way to move on him."

"So what we gonna do? Just sit here like ducks waiting on some niggas to pick us off?" Craig asked with frustration.

"What you think we should do, Craig?"

"I think we should go to the nigga's crib, drag him out his house, take him on the roof, and blow the back of his head off. That's what I think we should do!"

"Yeah, I know, but we can't do that right now. I don't know if the nigga expectin' me to react all crazy and shit without thinking and run over to his building and turn it into the OK Corral. I should chill right here like I normally do and see what he gonna do. I mean, I know it's coming, and that means I'm not gonna let him catch me sleeping. I got my man La in the front of the building so he gon' holla if something ain't right, you know what I mean?"

"You trust that nigga? Shit, he could be the one tryin' to set you up, too. You forgettin', this ain't your hood, nigga. This they hood. They gonna stick together. I don't trust none of dem niggas when it comes to beef. I think you already slippin'. Don't let your fear interfere wit' your better judgment, nigga. That shit can have you laying real still in a pine box."

"I hear you Craig, but that nigga ain't like that kid. He got love for me. He in the front lookin' out for them niggas right now." Junior was hoping he was right and that the betrayal stopped at Kendu.

"Whateva, nigga. If you feel that nigga gon' bust his gun with you, then fine by me. Go ahead. I'm gonna watch the nigga real close just in case, though. You know what I'm sayin'?"

"Come with me to the crib real quick so I can get my other toast. I let La hold onto the other one."

"You gave the nigga your gun, too? Is you all right, nigga?"

Kendu could see La standing in front of the building. He was nervous, but he had to go over there. Stump and KB were in the building across the street watching his every move. He didn't have a gun on him, and he didn't know what La's response was going to be when he got closer. He walked slowly, his hands showing so La could see he was unarmed, but as he got closer he noticed a gun in La's hand, so he stopped abruptly.

"What up, La? Why you pullin' out on me?"

"Get lost, 'Du. I'm not tryin' to hear shit right now, dawg."

"Come on, La, you my man. Let me talk to you for a minute, kid."

"I'm tellin' you, 'Du, don't come over here, son. Get gon' before Junior come out here," he warned, noticing the bruises on 'Du's face as he got closer.

"You told him what I told you?"

"Yup. You going 'bout this all wrong man. I ain't wit' it."

"You told him . . . aaaaaahhhh shit, La. You just got me killed."

"Fuck it, son. You played yourself. Just get lost before this nigga come back out here. I'm tellin' you, man."

When Junior and Craig came out the house they went to the back of the building because they heard La talking.

"I think he talking to that nigga, 'Du."

"I'm goin' 'round the other side. You take the side your man is on. When I see him I'm blastin'. Once I let off, just make sure he's not comin' in your direction," Craig said, cocking his gun and then trotting to the other side of the building.

Junior pulled out the big, silver gun and cocked it back, holding it down to his waist. He walked along the other side of the building to where La was. When he reached the corner of the building he peeked around slowly. He could see La with his gun drawn, telling Kendu to leave. Kendu was walking slowly toward La with his hands outstretched and seemed to be pleading with him. Junior watched closely. There was no one out except for a

59

few Puerto Rican kids who noticed La holding a gun and decided to watch and see if some drama unfolded from a safe distance across the street, cowering behind parked cars. Just then Junior heard what sounded like an explosion, and La backed up toward the entrance of the building. Kendu took off like a jet across the street, and Junior realized Craig had let off a shot. Then Junior heard two or three more thunderous booms. Kendu was running across the street, heading in Junior's direction. He saw Craig running behind him, his gun pointed at Kendu's back. Junior jumped into action and let off some shots toward Kendu as he was running and ducking at the same time.

"Don't let that nigga get away!" Craig yelled.

Junior was in pursuit and heard some more loud blasts, but these were from a different gun. His adrenalin was pumping. He glanced in the direction of the noise and saw a tall figure running behind his cousin, letting off a barrage of shots.

"Somebody bustin' at you. Watch out!" Junior screamed to Craig.

Junior turned his gun toward the tall figure and let off some shots. The figure ducked behind a car and Junior made sure Craig was out of danger. Kendu had cut through the back of a building and Junior continued his chase. Craig was right behind him.

"Who the fuck was that bustin' at me?" Craig asked Junior as he caught up to him.

"I don't know. I think it was them cats that was with Kendu," Junior said, breathing heavily.

"Come on, we can't let that nigga get away. I'm gonna kill that muhfucka," Craig said with determination in his voice.

"He went into that building," Junior said, pointing his gun at the backdoor.

"I don't think he got a burner on him, or he would have been bustin' back at me," Craig analyzed.

"Fuck it. Let's get outta here 'fore the police come. We'll catch that nigga on the late show another night!" Junior said.

They ran back toward Craig's car, and as they crossed the street they heard some more shots. Craig turned around and emptied his clip at the tall guy shooting at him. Junior stooped behind a car to get a good look at the guy shooting, then La came out of the building and Junior saw him bustin' in the guy's direction.

"Come on, muhfucka!" La yelled.

"Let's go!" Craig called out to Junior.

Junior rose slowly and let off three more shots, then quickly made it to the other side of the street where Craig was putting another clip in his automatic.

"Come on, man, we gotta get the fuck outta here before the fucking police come!" he said, running toward his car.

"Yo, I can't leave La like that, man. He still bustin' at them niggas!"

"Man, fuck that nigga. We gotta blow," he said, pulling the car keys from his pocket.

"Go start the car, man. I'm gonna go get him. He gotta come with us!" Junior said, going back to where La was.

Junior could hear more gunshots as he ran through the back of the building.

La was hiding behind one of the columns in front of the building, peeking to see if the guy shooting would advance on him. He had no idea how many bullets he had left in the gun, and he didn't want to waste what he had. He was petrified. His heart was beating rapidly and his legs felt weak, but he had to hold on. He was never in a shootout before, and he didn't know what to do next, but he knew he didn't want to get shot, so he held fast.

"Yo, La!" Junior yelled from inside the building. "Come on, man. Let's get the fuck outta here!"

It was as if he heard an angel speaking to him. He fired off the last shots and watched the slide on the barrel of the automatic freeze in an extended position, letting him know the clip was empty. He ran into the building and followed Junior to Craig's car.

Stump was furious. He couldn't believe those niggas had the heart to shoot back at him. When he heard the first shots he knew Kendu had lied. He had underestimated them, and didn't expect them to react the way they did. He told KB to wait in the building while he found out who was shooting. When he got outside he saw Kendu running and somebody chasing after him. He shot at the guy that was chasing Kendu, and then he heard return fire from somebody else. That's when he knew they were prepared to go all out, and he really wasn't ready for a gunfight. He knew he had rushed the decision to move on Junior, but he hadn't wanted to wait any longer. He expected to get the drop on him, but now he knew it was really on. He had to respect Junior because he wasn't a pushover like the other niggas he had robbed.

"Where the fuck is Kendu?" Stump screamed at KB.

"I don't know, man. What the fuck happened out there?"

"Them niggas was expectin' us. They seen Kendu and just started blastin' off!"

"I heard. It sounded like Beirut out that muhfucka. How many niggas was out there?"

"It was a nigga in all black bustin' at Kendu, then another nigga I couldn't see too good. I guess it was the nigga Junior and the kid that was with Kendu. The nigga with Kendu was in front the building and was bustin' at me when I started shootin' at the nigga in all black!"

"That must have been Lakim."

"I don't know his name. All I know is I'm gonna put that nigga Kendu to rest and then I'm gonna flatten all dem other niggas that was bustin' at me. I knew when he said he told that kid what was goin' down that Junior would find out. That's why I wanted to move right away. I shoulda waited and caught that nigga sleepin'."

They could hear police sirens in the distance and knew it was time to get gone. They decided to go stash the guns at KB's friend's house in the next building.

Kendu had run to one of his friend's houses to get a gun, but by the time he headed back downstairs he could hear the screech of walkie-talkies and people talking in the lobby, letting him know the police were obviously on the scene. He returned the gun he had gotten and waited a while before he went back to his building. When he got over there he blended in the crowd that had gathered outside and snuck into the building, running up the stairs to his place. His heart was still racing as he sat on his bed thinking about how his childhood friend had betrayed him. He couldn't believe La had flipped on him. La was his enemy now. Although he had never let off a shot, La held a gun on him, and that was something he never thought would happen between them. Kendu was enraged.

Kendu originally thought Stump was the one shooting at him until he glanced over his shoulder and saw a guy in all black chasing him with a big ass gun. When he realized it wasn't Stump, he tried to get the fuck out of dodge, and while he was running he noticed Junior was shooting at him, too. He never actually saw La shoot, but he might as well have, since he was with the niggas that was busting at him.

As Junior and La ran to Craig's car, Craig yelled at them to hurry. As soon as the pair reached the car, Craig pulled off and made a right tunr toward Bed-Stuy.

"Did you hit anybody?" La asked Junior.

"Nah, but I was trying to take Kendu's head off!" Junior said.

"Who the fuck was the kid bustin' at me?" Craig asked.

"That was Stump," La replied.

"So Kendu *was* trying to set me up. I should have killed that nigga!"

"I was trying," Craig said. "But the other nigga that was shooting threw me off."

"When Du was walking up on me, I heard somebody let off and I ran in the building. I didn't know who was bustin' off. I stood by the mailboxes thinking somebody was coming in. I was gonna blast they ass as soon as they came in the building," La said.

"That was me. I didn't know if the nigga was holdin' heat or not. I was aiming for his melon, but I wasn't close enough," Craig said.

"When that nigga heard the shots, he jetted," Junior said. "I was chasin' the nigga until I saw that nigga Stump bustin' at Craig. I can't front, that nigga had some big shit. It was loud as hell too. I think he had a fifth or a .44."

"Yo, you know you can't go back over there right now, not 'til shit cools down," Craig was telling Junior.

"I know, man, but my girl lives over there and I don't want them niggas trying to do sumthin' to her to try to get to me, and I can't let them stop me from getttin' money over there either," Junior said, visibly upset. "Fuck dem, niggas! I'm just gonna' hafta' be a lil' more careful that's all!"

"You buggin'. It's gonna be hotta' than fish grease ova there. You gotta be easy, man, 'cause if you go over there slippin', you gon' fuck around and get locked up, or you might get your ass flattened."

La was sitting in the back not saying anything because he was wondering what he was going to do now.

Shondra was thinking about how mad Junior was going to be if he was already in the house, because she was coming in later than she had originally planned. She was having such a good time with her girls that she had lost track of time. When the cab pulled up in front of her building there was a crowd out front and police cars on the sidewalk with their lights flashing. Her mouth got dry and her heart rate increased. She immediately thought the worst and wasn't prepared for any bad news.

"Stop the car!" she screamed. "Let me out!"

The cab driver pulled over behind a police car and Shondra snatched the door handle, breaking one of her manicured nails. Gloria paid the fare and followed behind her. Shondra ran up to a girl named Gina who lived in her building.

"What happened out here?"

`"I don't know, girl. I just heard a bunch o' shootin' out here. It was loud as hell, too, because that shit woke up me and my son."

"Did you see who . . . I mean, did anybody get shot?"

"Not that I know of. I just know there was a lot of damn shootin'," Gina said, taking a long pull from her cigarette.

Shondra walked quickly to her building and broke one of her heels as she entered the lobby.

"Shit!" she squealed.

When she got in her apartment, she yelled out for Junior, but didn't get any answer. This worried her more and she rushed into her room for any signs he had been there. Gloria was right behind her to make sure she was all right.

"You have to calm down, girl. I know what you thinkin', but you ain't really sure what happened out there. Just call him and see if he knows what happened out here."

"I gotta call him, Glo. I'm scared," she said, shaking nervously. "I don't know if he's OK."

"I know, girl, but you don't know if he was mixed up in that shit out there."

"I know he was, 'cause he not here. Where the hell is he?" She was crying.

"Give me his beeper number so I can beep him for you," Gloria said, picking up the receiver to the phone.

Shondra lay down on the queen-sized bed she shared with Junior with a worried look on her face. She was trying not to think the worst, but she couldn't help it.

"I shouldn't have gone out. I shoulda stayed home. At least I would know if he was OK or not."

"Look, Shondra, you buggin' out. You can't do that to yourself. Number one, you don't know what happened, and number two, you can't blame yourself if something did happen. You not God."

Chapter 5
Take a picture, sweetie.

It was late in the afternoon when KB came out of his house the next day. His mother had been trying to wake him up earlier to answer the phone calls he was getting, but he was worn out from the night before. He knew it was Stump calling, because he rarely received phone calls at home. It was kind of warm out, so he decided to go back upstairs and change his gear. He had on a long sleeve Polo shirt with a hot ass Polo jacket.

The phone rang again when he walked into his house.

"Hello?"

"KB?" Stump asked.

"Yeah, what's good, man?"

"Where you been? I been callin' you all morning."

"Shit, I was knocked out. What's up?"

"Did you hear anything about last night?"

"Nah, I ain't been out."

"So you ain't hear nothin' about Kendu?"

"Nah. I was gonna go by his crib to see what's up with him later."

"Yeah, 'cause I wanna know what the deal is with that joker. I should have put a hot one in his ass last night. Them niggas was on point."

"I know, and I didn't even have a burner on me to help you out."

"Meet me by the projects in twenty minutes and I'll go with you to see Kendu."

"Aight. I'll be in front of Adbul's."

"Cool. I'll see you in twenty."

KB tucked his burner in his waist and headed for Baptiste.

La was lighting a blunt when Junior came back from the store with a turkey and cheese hero. They were in Tompkins Park waiting for Shondra. Junior had spoken to her when she beeped him last night. He was taking every precaution and told her to bring the money, guns, and drugs he had in her house in case someone started snitching. He also made sure he told her not to tell anyone what little bit he told her about what happened that night, especially her homegirl. Times like these were when he realized she was a real trooper, because she always came through for him when he needed her.

"I don't think nobody gonna say it was us that was shooting out there last night," La was saying to Junior.

"You never know. Them faggot ass niggas might. You know they don't like me like that. They'll be glad for me to get locked up."

"I'm not sweatin' that shit. All I'm thinking about is this money," La said, blowing the white smoke out of his lungs.

"Me too. I'm not gonna lay low too long because I don't want nobody takin' my spot over. Right now I'ma work off my beeper 'til we find out how hot it is ova there."

"I don't really give a fuck. I rest in those PJs. Them niggas not gonna run me out my own hood!"

"I hear you, La, but it wasn't them niggas that was bustin' at us."

"I know, but I been livin' there all my life, and I don't have nowhere else to go. I can't stay ova here forever. I know them dudes probably mad 'cause I fuck with you on the money tip, but I don't give a fuck. I ain't neva had no beef with them cats, so I should be OK going back ova there. I know Kendu did some foul shit, and I know he gotta get his, but his hand called for it."

"Aight, La, I got you, man. Just let me find out if they callin' out my name 'round there first, and either way it goes, you can go back out there and I'ma let you run the spot. I just gotta be sure that I don't send you out there blind and put you in jeopardy. Believe me, son, I'm not gonna let nobody stop the flow of my dough!"

"That's what I'm talking about. Fuck them niggas. This shouldn't stop us from eating. If anything, we should be able to eat lovely now that they know we ain't no pushovers," La said, passing Junior the blunt.

When Shondra saw Junior she ran toward him, arms outstretched and held him tightly.

"Are you OK, baby?"

"I'm good, Mooka. Did you find out anything?"

"Mmmmhmm. Talking ass Terry was telling Gloria that he heard some guys from Bushwick was trying to rob you, and that y'all was shooting out."

"Did he say any names?" Junior asked.

"No. They didn't say any names." She replied.

"What about the police? Did he say the police knew who it was?"

"No. He said they was asking people, but he didn't think nobody said anything."

"Good. No police came to your house, right?"

"No. They was just outside asking people questions. Oh, I'm sorry, La, how are you?" Shondra asked, remembering her manners.

"That's aight. I'm OK too, Shondra."

"What you gonna do now, boo?" she asked, turning her attention back to her man.

"I don't really know yet, but I do know I gotta get that nigga Kendu and the niggas that was bustin' at us. Anybody call they name out or anything?" Junior knew it was Stump. He just wanted to know if the hood knew.

"Not that I know of. They never said Kendu's name either. Was he the one that tried to set you up?"

"Yeah, he the one that sicked them niggas on Junior!" La blurted. Kendu was his man, but La knew he went about what he was trying to do in the wrong way.

"I can't stand his dirty ass," Shondra said. "When we was coming from Graham Ave. he was talking to some guy and he gave me the dirtiest look. I should have known something was up right then."

"Well, fuck him. He gotta take a dirt nap now!" Junior said.

Junior grabbed the bag Shondra was carrying and inspected the contents, and then they all walked off to Tompkins Projects.

KB waited for Stump in front of the bodega on the other side of Baptiste, knowing things had gotten out of hand. After what happened last night he knew he was about to get involved with murder, and he wasn't prepared for that. He also knew that hanging with Stump involved criminal activity, but the most he was expecting was armed robbery. Now he had a dilemma. He had to find his way out before he ended up doing a life bid behind bars, or up in Dante's Funeral Home.

"What up, boy?" Stump asked as he approached KB.

"Ain't shit. You holdin'?"

"Always. Did you see that bitch ass nigga?" Stump asked, tapping both sides of his waist to let KB know he had two guns on him.

"Nah, I think he blew. I doubt he gonna be out here."

"Well, let's go to his crib just to be sure," Stump said, walking in the direction of Kendu's building.

They walked to Kendu's building and knocked on his door. Nobody answered, so they left and sat on the benches in the back of his building. Stump wanted to wait to see if Kendu showed up.

A young kid walked up to KB and asked him for fifty cents. KB went into his pocket and gave him a dollar bill. The kid took the money, thanked him, then walked off. KB called the kid back and asked him if he knew Kendu.

"Yeah, I know him," the kid responded.

"You seen him today?"

"Nope. I don't think anybody's gonna see him no time soon," he replied, looking at Stump.

"Why you say that, lil man?" KB asked.

"'Cause I know," he replied, still looking at Stump.

"How you know?" KB tried to get him to look at him.

"'Cause he's my brother," he replied, looking at Stump as if he was waiting for a reaction.

Stump lit up like a light bulb.

"Do you know where he at?" Stump interjected.

"Yeah, he at my cousin's house."

"And where's that at?" Stump asked, very interested in the little guy now.

"Why you want to know?"

"I need to give him something," Stump said, sensing that the little boy didn't trust him.

"Give it to me, and I'll make sure he gets it," he replied, holding out his hand.

"How 'bout I give you something for yourself and you tell me where your cuz lives at?"

"That's cool, but I'm still not gonna tell y'all," he replied, shifting his eyes from Stump to KB.

"Look, shawty, if you don't tell me where your cousin lives, I'm goin' to make it so you don't see your mama no more!"

"Fuck you, nigga. My mama dead!" he said and ran off.

"Go get that lil muthafucka so I can get the address from him!" Stump yelled.

"Chill, man. He ain't gonna give you the address now, even if we do get him," KB reasoned. "At least we know where Kendu at."

"Yeah, but how long he gonna be there? We need to find out where his cousin lives."

Stump decided to stay around all night. He wanted to be sure Kendu didn't tell his brother to say that to throw off anyone that asked questions regarding Kendu's whereabouts.

Steam seeped from the pots on the stove, and the kettle was whistling, informing Gloria that the water was boiling. She was cooking dinner and making tea for Shondra. She brought the tea out to Shondra and sat down beside her on the couch.

"I can't believe some niggas from Bushwick was trying to rob Junior," Gloria said.

Shondra remembered what Junior told her about not giving up any extra information on what happened that night he had the shootout.

"I'm so scared for Junior now," Shondra said, sipping the hot tea.

"I know, girl, but you know niggas bound to get into some shit sooner or later."

"Yeah, but you never think it'll be your man or someone that close to you."

"Think about it. 'Member when they killed Byron in front of the building? I didn't even know he was selling drugs until the police found all that money and shit on him," Gloria remembered.

"I always wondered how he drove all dem pretty cars, though. He was so cool. His sister Alyssa always stayed to herself too," Shondra added.

"I heard she runnin' his business now," Gloria said. "I don't know how true it is, but you know how the streets be talkin'."

"Well, I don't want anything to happen to my baby, and I hope the niggas that tried to violate stays the fuck from 'round here."

"You want to smoke?" Gloria asked as she pulled a plastic bag full of weed from her Louie purse.

"Yeah, I need something to calm my nerves and shit." Gloria ruffled through her purse and pulled out a blunt.

"Shit, it's broke. I'm going to run to the corner and get another one and something to drink. You want something?"

"No, I'm OK with this tea."

The door slammed and Shondra laid her head back and thought about how her man was getting along without her.

The store on the corner was closed, so Gloria had to go to the twenty-four-hour store on Graham Avenue. As she turned the corner she saw KB walking toward her.

Oh, shit, it's that cute ass nigga, she thought.

She fixed her hair and slowed her walk to a sexy gait, hoping to entice him. KB noticed her and he could see the roundness of her hips in the tight Calvin Klein jeans. When he got close enough, she dropped her purse purposely, turned around, and bent down, giving him a full view of her perfectly round, apple ass.

"Damn, lady, you can hurt somebody wit all dat," he said, bending down next to her.

"'Scuse me?"

"I'm saying, you bending down and exposing all dat ass is dangerous."

"I dropped my purse, sweetie. How else am I supposed to get it?"

They stood up at the same time and he moved closer to her.

"I would have gotten it for you if you gave me a chance," KB said.

"Second times the charm," she said as she dropped her purse again.

KB bent down and picked it up, but didn't give it to her.

"I see you like playin' games, huh?"

"I don't play games, hun. I'm grown."

"Was that some type of trick to see if I would pick it up?" he asked, holding the purse out to her.

"Like I said, hun, tricks are for kids, and I'm grown." She grabbed her purse and continued to walk toward the corner.

She was hoping he would walk her to the store, but she noticed from the small talk that her game was a little more advanced than his. She turned around to see if he was coming

70

behind her, but he was just standing in the same spot watching her.

"Take a picture, sweetie. It'll last longer."

KB was checking out her fine body. He couldn't believe somebody as fine as her would even be interested in someone like him.

"Hold on, chocolate. Where you going?"

Got him, she said in her mind. "I'm going to the store," she said to KB.

"Let me walk with you."

Gloria stopped and waited for him to catch up to her.

"What's your name, lady?"

"Gloria. What's your name?"

"KB. You live around here?"

"Duh, yeah. Why would I be out here this late going to the store?"

"Because, I'm not from around here," KB said.

"Well, where you from?"

"I live in Williamsburg."

"Oh OK. What you doing over here so late?"

"I'm just chillin', on my way to the crib."

Gloria put two dollars in the square, Plexiglas cube.

"Let me get a Philly and a sixteen-ounce Pepsi," Gloria asked the man behind the glass.

"You smoke choke?" KB asked her.

"What are these, trick questions?" she asked. She couldn't believe his game was so lame.

"Why you so uptight, love? I'm just trying to make conversation."

"I'm sorry. I ain't tryin' to be mean. I'm just joking with you."

They started back toward the projects and KB grabbed her hand and stopped her in the middle of the block.

"Look, luv, as you can tell, I'm not really good when it comes to kicking it to a female, so I'm just gonna be forward with you if that's all right."

Gloria looked into his eyes and could tell he was serious.

"Go ahead, hun, say what's on your mind."

"I like the way you look, I like the way you dress, and I like the way you talk. I want to get to know you better. I don't know if you got a man, and I really don't care, but if you feel close to how I'm feelin', I think we should see where this takes us."

71

Gloria was taken aback. That was the realest and most honest line she had ever heard from any of the guys that had ever tried to talk to her before.

"You know something, K, I like the way you look, too, and I like how you're kickin' it to me right now, so I want to see where this goes. And by the way, I don't have a man."

"Good. So what do we do from here?"

"I don't know. Why don't you give me your number and I'll call you tomorrow so we can hook up."

"Sounds good. Ay, you didn't say you like the way I dress. Is there something wrong with my gear?"

"Nah, baby, you dress fine. You dress real fine," Gloria said with a smile on her face as she walked back into her building.

Shondra was lying on the couch nodding off when Gloria walked inside.

"Girl, you ain't gonna believe who I just ran into on the way to the store."

"Who, Glo?" Shondra asked with sleepiness still in her voice.

"'Memba that guy that was with Kendu a coupla weeks back when we came from shoppin'? Well I just kicked it to him and got his number. I'm 'posed to hook up with him tomorrow. Damn, that nigga fine," she said, twirling around like a high school girl in love.

"That's cool."

Shondra was deep in thought while Gloria was talking about KB. She was too wrapped up thinking about Junior to really pay attention to anyone else. She was so worried about him that she couldn't partake in her friend's good fortune in hooking up with a guy she really liked. Gloria continued talking, missing that Shondra was a million miles away. Finally, after Shondra stopped responding to anything Gloria was saying, Gloria realized Shondra wasn't listening to her story.

"Are you OK, girl?" Gloria asked.

"Huh? Oh, I'm so sorry, Glo. I'm just sitting here thinking about my baby."

"I understand. Come on and smoke some of this blunt with me and clear your thoughts."

"I think that's what I need to help me stop worrying 'bout him so much."

Gloria took a deep pull of the cigar filled with marijuana and fell back onto the couch next to Shondra.

"Damn, that's some good shit!" Glo said.

"Mmmmmmhmmmm," Shondra replied, blowing the cloud out of her mouth and nose.

"Yeah, this is what you need to get your mind right," Gloria said, filling her lungs with more of the ghetto herbal medicine.

"I know. I don't want to worry, but I can't help it. I just keep thinking something bad is going to happen to my baby. I don't want him to get hurt or get into any trouble, you know what I'm sayin', Glo? I just want things back to the way they used to be."

"I know, baby," Gloria said as she grabbed her and held her close to her bosom. "I know."

La was impatient and ready to start making money again now, so he and Junior were discussing how Junior wanted things to run. Junior wanted to make sure everything ran smoothly for both La's and his sakes. La was so thirsty for money that he didn't care about anything. He just wanted Junior to send him back with some work. His money was getting low and he was tired of staying at different people's cribs.

"Look, Junior, I'm just ready to get back ova there. I'm tired of stayin' up in that lady's crib like that. I mean, I appreciate your cousin letting me chill, but I need to get back to the hood and get this money."

"I hear you, La. I just wanna make sure this shit will run like clockwork 'fore I send you back out there. You know what I'm sayin'?"

"I hear you, man, but we been over this shit already. I need to get back on the block before niggas start makin' moves out there. Then there's gonna be more beef. Ya feel me?"

"Aight, let's just go over this shit one more time. I need to know you understand what it is I want you to do. You gotta stay low until I handle this shit with Stump and KB. Once I find out where the nigga rest his head at I'ma light his ass up."

"Shit, that nigga live in Bushwick, building 821," La informed Junior.

"You knew where that nigga live at? Damn, kid, you shoulda been told me that." Junior was wondering why La never said anything about knowing where Stump lived right after the shootout. They had been talking about it for over a month, and he

73

never once brought it up. Junior didn't have a good feeling about La not letting him know that bit of important information.

"I just remembered that shit when you was talkin' to your cousin the other day and he said something about a bitch he was fucking from Bushwick. I meant to tell you then, but I just forgot. Well now that you know, let's smoke him, and when niggas find out his ass got wet up, ain't nobody else gonna try no shit like that with us no more."

"You right about that, but I don't want you to be down with that. I'm gonna take care of it myself. He won't expect somebody to come solo, so I'm gonna catch his bitch ass sleepin'."

"I can dig it. That's smart. When I get ova there when you give me this work, I'm gonna find out what floor he lives on."

"Cool. Let's split this work up so we can get back to business."

Junior went into his pack and pulled out ten thousand dollars worth of work for La.

"See if you can get them two young cats that live in Lizzette's building to get on our team to work this shit off with you, and pay them 25 percent off every hundred. This way you can give them shifts so there'll be work out there twenty-four seven, and we'll probably make up for the time we lost since this shit happened. You down with that?" Junior asked.

Junior had been thinking about implementing this plan since the shootout. He figured he could have someone else working the block for him and have La pick up the money and give out the work.

"As long as I'm gettin' this paper, I'm all right with whateva."

Junior gave him the package and cab money to get back to the projects. After La left, Junior called Shondra's house.

"What's up, baby? I know I ain't been returning your beeps, but I'm trying to take care of this shit so I can come back home to you."

"I know, boo. It's been over a month and I've been worrying about you, especially when I beep you and you don't call me back."

"Don't worry about me, baby. I'm aight. Shit, I'm more worried about you. But, look, I need you to do me a favor."

"Anything you need, boo."

"La just told me what building Stump lives in, but I need to find out where the other nigga that was with him live at. I know he stay in Williamsburg, but I need to know what building, so keep your ears open for any info for me. I'm gonna get both them niggas, but I want to get the easiest one first, you know what I mean?" He wanted to make sure he got everyone involved in the setup.

"I understand. You know something, Gloria met the guy that was with Kendu. Remember that day I told you I passed him when we came from shopping? The guy that was with him that day?"

"Oh yeah, I remember. She kickin' it with that nigga now?"

"She told me that she got his number the other night and that she was supposed to be hangin' out with him that next day. I can ask her to find out for me."

"Yeah, but I don't want her to know he the nigga I got beef with if she don't already know. I don't need this nigga to figure out what's about to happen to his ass. This is real serious, Mooka. I'm gonna kill this nigga."

"Oh please, Junior." She started to sob. "Please, no, Junior. I don't want you to do nothing to get yourself hurt or locked up. Please, baby, can't somebody else do that?"

"Nah, I gotta do this one myself, 'cause dem niggas violated. Ain't nothin' gonna happen to me. He's the one that's gonna get it. That's why she can't know why you askin', feel me?"

Junior never imagined he would be planning to kill someone. He was a little naïve to the game and thought he would hustle without any problems because he felt he was smarter than the average hustler. His mind was changing now, and he felt as if he didn't have a choice in what he was about to do.

"OK, Junior, I'm gonna see if I can find out where he lives for you."

"Look, Mooka, I know that's your girl and everything, but you can't tell her shit. I can't trust nobody right now on this but you. Do you think she knows he was down wit' Kendu setting me up?"

"No. I don't think so. If he would have said anything about it she would have said something to me about it. I doubt he told her anything about that night."

"What about Kendu? You seen him around there lately?"

"I haven't seen him. They sayin' he went down South, but I don't know how true that is. You know how niggas be talkin'."

"Aight, that's cool, 'cause I just sent La back ova there with some work. I'ma get Du, too. I figured his ass was gonna get ghost so I'll just catch his ass after I take care of dem other two faggots. They the real threat. But trust me, once I take care of them, I don't care what part of down south he at, 'cause I'ma go down there and bury him too!"

"So when am I gonna see you, baby? I miss you so much. I'm used to sleeping with you next to me, and I'm lonely without you right now."

"Soon, ma, real soon. Let me take care of this business and we'll take a trip to VA or something. Just you and me, aight?"

"Look, Junior, I need some dick, straight up. I don't mean to sound like that, but I'm horny as hell for you."

"Damn, baby, I'm sorry. I been so caught up in this shit I'm slippin' on my duties to you as your man. Matter of fact, take a cab to Five Towns Motel in Far Rock in about a half hour and we can spend the weekend out there and catch up, aight?"

"Say no more, baby. I'm packing my overnight bag as we speak."

"I'm gonna leave right now. Just beep me when you're on your way so I can be outside waiting for you."

Junior grabbed some cash and went outside to find his cousin to see if he could give him a ride to Far Rockaway, Queens.

Kendu was getting worse. His habit was costing him over two hundred dollars a day, and he was broke. He'd been wearing the same clothes for over a month and was pawning his aunt's valuables to support his habit. He knew shit was getting out of hand when the younger drug dealers around his aunt's way started disrespecting him and treating him like a fiend. One day when he went to cop from one of them and was two dollars short, he told the youngster he would bring it back to him later.

"Yo, nigga, you act like I gotta license to sell this shit or somethin'," the dealer said. "You betta go suck a dick for the rest or take your bum ass somewhere else."

Kendu was hot as fire as he listened to the guy disrespect him like he was a crack head. At that moment he felt like grabbing him and beating him within an inch of his life, then taking his money and work to show him what he was really about, but he didn't have the heart at that moment.

Kendu didn't realize he was falling deep into depression. His life had changed so drastically in one fateful night. He made a bad decision in getting mixed up with Stump and KB, and now his best friend was his enemy. He was a ticking time bomb and was losing control. His thoughts were solely geared toward getting high in order to escape from the reality of his present situation. It wasn't evident to him that the disrespect he was experiencing was because he had the traits of someone strung out on crack. He was in denial. The reality was that he didn't have anything more to lose. He had gone too far and was spiraling out of control. His life had changed for the worse and he was at the point where he didn't give a fuck what happened anymore, which was a dangerous mindset for a man faced with his dilemma.

He had just used up all the fuel in his lighter, so he walked toward Key Food Supermarket to steal another one. On his way to the store he spotted one of the young drug dealers across the street standing on the corner talking to a girl.

"Ayyyy, yooo!" Kendu called out to him.

The guy looked around and noticed Kendu across the street.

"What, man?"

"I need to see you. What's up?"

The guy remembered Kendu. He had been copping from him all week. He told the girl he was talking with to hold on while he went to get that "fast money." As he crossed the street, Kendu quickly dug in his pocket for some money to flash on him, then pulled out an orange box cutter. When the guy got in front of him he had a serious look on his face.

"What you need, nigga?"

"I want to spend twenty dollars. You gonna give me a play, right?"

"Look, man, don't waste my fuckin' time, because I got shit to do. You get four jacks and that's it."

He picked out four capsules for Kendu. Kendu opened the box cutter and it made a loud clicking noise as the blade revealed itself from it's orange hiding place. Then he brought it down across the guy's face with one swift swing.

"OOOOhhhhhh shiiit!!!!" he screamed, dropping the bag and backing up.

His face opened up, exposing his pink flesh that soon turned red and started leaking like a kitchen faucet. Kendu scooped the bag off the ground and dug in the young dealer's pockets, then stepped back and brought the sharp blade down on the dealer's hands, which were covering his gash.

"Yeah, nigga, now look at you!" Kendu yelled. After watching the young boy screaming in pain, he made a mad dash back to his cousin's house. He left the guy on the corner bleeding like a pig as the girl across the street came running over screaming.

"Help! Help! Somebody please help him!"

The guy continued to scream, blood streaming all over his hands as he held his wound. The hysterical girl looked in the direction to where Kendu ran, then she ran to a payphone.

When he got into his cousin's house, Kendu started to think about the repercussions that were sure to come if anyone recognized him and found out he was the one who slashed the guy.

I bet them niggas know I ain't no joke now, though, he thought to himself as he opened the door to the room he was staying in.

"Damn, that lil nigga had a lot of dough on him," he said aloud while counting the bloody bills.

Kendu had close to one thousand dollars when he finished counting, and almost five hundred dollars in work. He had hit the jackpot. He knew this wouldn't be the last time he saw the guy, and he knew once his boss found out what happened there might be problems. As quick as that thought entered his mind, though, it left because he was planning on going to North Carolina to stay with his uncle. His attitude had really changed since the incident in the projects. He needed to get a grip on his life before something bad happened to him real soon.

Chapter 6
I'm ready to put y'all on.

La went on the other side of the projects to find the two little homeboys Junior planned on using to help get rid of the work he had. The guys were little terrors. They were young with a lot of heart, and weren't afraid of anything. They had always wanted to get down with him before, but he never thought about anyone selling for him since he worked for Junior. He did give them some work before and paid them fifty dollars, but he couldn't keep it up because it was eating up his profit. La was greedy for cash. Now that Junior wasn't going to be around for a while, he thought he would act like he was the man supplying everything. It would give him boss status in the projects, and he liked that idea. Once he told them he could give them double what he used to give them, he knew they would be ready to pledge their loyalty to him.

La was eager to get started again, although he knew he had deadly beef with Stump. He was aware of the danger, but he couldn't let his fear stop the flow of money. He would just be careful and make sure he kept a gun on him at all times. Stump was a dangerous dude, and La had to make sure he wasn't caught sleeping or that would be the end. La was hoping Junior would get Stump so he wouldn't have to worry about him anymore. But he thought best to put a plan of his own in action just in case Junior moved to slow on taking care of Stump.

"What up, Rock?" La asked, approaching the young guy wearing the Yankee baseball cap.

"What up, my nigga? What's poppin'? I heard you was bustin' your gun at some cats. You need me to body somebody for you?" he asked, motioning like he had a gun in his hand.

"Nah, that's aight, kid," La said, laughing lightly. "I got some good news for you and Dusty, if y'all still wit' it."

"What is it?"

"Where's Dusty? I want to tell y'all at the same time."

79

"He upstairs wit' a dirty. You know he like trickin' up his money on them bitches," Rock said, chuckling. "Matter of fact, let's go up there and throw a monkey wrench in his shit real fast."

"You crazy as hell, Rock. That nigga gon' kill you if you stop him from bustin' a nut and he payin' for it."

"That nigga ain't longwinded like that. He probably finished already and only been up there five minutes."

They rode the elevator up to the third floor. Dusty's grandmother had lived in the building since they were built over twenty years ago. His mother died when he was two-years-old and his grandmother had been raising him ever since. She was hardly ever home because she was a live-in home health aide for a wealthy family that lived on the upper east side of Manhattan, which gave Dusty free run of the house.

Rock stayed with Dusty because his mother was strung out on drugs. She was a bonified dope fiend and Rock never acknowledged her as his mother. He called Dusty's grandmother Mom. She took him in because she knew his mother didn't take care of him and she wanted to help out. She loved both boys like they were her own, and she cared for them financially and gave them guidance whenever they needed it.

Rock opened the door and went straight to the back while La sat down in the living room. The house was well kept, considering two young boys stayed there. Dusty came into the living room in his multi-colored boxers. He hugged La and slapped him five.

"What up, nigga? Damn, I thought you got hit in that shootout!"

"Nah, ain't shit happen to me," La said with bravado.

"You know how niggas be stretching shit. They was sayin' you got hit and was in the hospital. They said Kendu caught one in the back and died on the way to the hospital, and then they said Junior was shooting at the police and they cornered him and locked him up on attempted murder charges," Dusty told La.

"You know them niggas don't know shit. Wasn't nobody even out there when that shit went down. Kendu told me before the shit went down that most of them niggas on the other side was down with it because they didn't like Junior," La explained.

"Fuck dem crab ass niggas. They mad 'cause Junior getting dough in the hood and they don't know how to get with him, so they go against him. I heard niggas talkin' and shit, but I never fed into it because the nigga mad cool with me. He always look out for me when he see me and he hit me off wit' some ends when I ask him. Them niggas just hatin' 'cause they don't know how to get no paper out here. I did hear that Kendu flipped the script on you and shit. What went down with that?" Dusty asked.

"He came up to me and told me that Stump wanted to rob Junior and that he was gonna help him. He was working for Junior, too, so I couldn't figure out why he just flipped like that. He told me to stay away from Junior because he didn't want me to get caught up in that shit, but I thought about it and just told Junior what was going down. Junior went and got right, then gave me some iron to hold shit down. His cousin came through, and then I came out the building like Scarface and started bustin' at Stump." La was trying to make it seem like he kept it thorough as he told the whole story.

"You was bustin' at Stump?" Dusty asked, somewhat surprised.

"Hell, yeah! That nigga was trying to kill us. I was trying to make him go away for good!"

"I don't understand Kendu, kid. I mean, that was your man. Why would he just flip like that?" Dusty asked.

"Because he a closet smoker!" Rock said, coming back into the living room. "Joyce told me he was smokin' that shit, kid."

"Word?" Dusty asked, shocked.

"That's my word. She told me that shit a while ago. She should know. She smokes her damn self and I guess a crack head can recognize another crack head by how they act," Rock said.

"Do you think he really smokin'?" Dusty asked La.

"I don't know, man. I can't really say, but I do know he was actin' really funny about givin' that work and money up all of a sudden. You know something, none of that shit really matters because that nigga can't come back through here no more. Let me tell y'all what I came here for. That broad still back there?"

"Yeah, I just got some brain for free," Rock said, laughing.

"Yeah, right. That bitch ain't getting' nothin' else out of me with her raggedy ass pussy," Dusty said.

"Well look, boys, I'm ready to put y'all on if y'all ready to start working."

"Hell yeah!" they both said.

"How I want to do it is in shifts. I want my niggas to be out there twenty-four seven. I want the heads to know that we don't close. Whatever time y'all choose, you gotta stick with it. I want this shit to run like a real business. We can knock all the competition out the box if we stay open all day and night, plus my shit is bigger and better than Dre's shit in Bushwick, and better than Gino's shit in Williamsburg. So what y'all think?"

"I'm down. I'm gonna stick to whatever schedule you give me, bruh," Dusty said quickly.

"Ditto," Rock agreed.

"Aight, we gon start early tomorrow. I'm takin' the morning and y'all can split between the night," La said. "I'm gonna hit y'all both with your pack now and you take twenty dollars off every hundred you sell. Right now it'll probably be a lil slow, but you know once we out there it'll be clicking like I had it before." La was offering them less than what Junior had told him to pay them. La would just take the extra five dollars off every hundred and keep it for himself.

"Let me tell that bitch to get outta here," Dusty said. "You want some face or something before I send her ass outta here?"

"Nah, man, I want to take care of this shit and go home and bag up the rest of the work I got."

"Aight, man. She got a fat ass, though."

"I ain't gonna lie, La, for an older broad she real nice. You can't even tell she smoke that shit. I woulda hit it, but I didn't have no rubber," Rock chimed in, trying to convince La.

The Puerto Rican woman was on the bed putting on her bra when Dusty came into the room.

"I thought you were finished. I'm going back upstairs. Who else is out there?" she asked suspiciously.

"Rock and my man from the other side," he replied.

"I leave after they go."

"My man might want to get some head before he leave. You gonna serve him for me, baby?"

"I only do for you because we live in same building. I no want everyone to think of me like that, you understand, yes?"

"Yeah and no. If I pay for what I want and he pays too, then what difference do it make? I mean, he ain't gonna tell nobody if that's what you think. I'm gonna be working for him, and when you need credit or something, you can come to me and I'll look out for you just like you look out for me."

Her mind went into overdrive when he said he would be working for someone. Her habit was getting worse and it was becoming difficult to hide the effects of the drug because she was losing weight. Having Dusty right downstairs would be convenient for her, and then she wouldn't have to go out and cop the small, white rocks. Yeah, this would camouflage her addiction and no one would really know what she was doing. She couldn't let Dusty know what she was planning, though, so she decided to play it cool until he actually got the work.

"I understand what you say, but you no understand me. I no do this all the time. I just do when I need money. I no want everybody to think that I will do all the time, you understand?"

"Aight, fuck it. As long as I can still see you when I need to, I don't care. I was just trying to look out for my fam. We gotta take care of some business, so you gotta leave. I'll just tell him to go to my grandma's room while you leave. That OK wit' you?"

"OK, fine. Let me get dress," she said as she fixed her clothes. Dusty walked out the room to tell La to go in his grandmother's room so she could break out and they could finish their business. She walked out nervously, glancing at the door to see if anyone was looking at her as she departed.

"You know we didn't finish, and I already paid you so you know we gotta take care of this a lil lata', aight?" Dusty told her when she got to the door.

"No problema, papi," she said, flashing a smile and palming her round ass. "Just come up to my place. Ju have too many people in your house. And tell your friend he no need to lie to me either." She was letting him know that Rock came in and got served using game.

"I'll knock on your door around eleven tonight. That ain't too late, is it?"

"No, just come by. I'll still be up."

Lizzette was almost to the point of being strung out. She was performing sexual favors for money so she could support her habit. She chose Dusty because he was young and innocent. She knew he didn't have a girlfriend and was inexperienced so she used this to her benefit to get money out of him without having to go on the 'hoe stroll'. She was secretive about her drug habit and not too many people in the building knew. She did like Dusty because he was always willing to try something new, and when she gave him the combo—pussy and head—he was weak to all her demands. As she climbed the steps she thought about what he had just told her. Now it would be more convenient for her to get high. She wouldn't even have to leave her building.

When Dusty came into his grandmother's room after seeing Lizzette out, La had the work on the bed and was splitting it up for him and Rock.

"Come on, man, let's go in my room. If my grandmom catches us in her room doin' this shit, she'll fuck all of us up."

Dusty's room was well furnished. He had a black lacquer headboard, armoire, and two nightstands. It was unusual to find a young guy this clean and organized, and La knew Junior made the right choice by choosing them to be down. Rock and Dusty each got a one-thousand-dollar package and were told to only take out a two-hundred-dollar bomb at a time, just in case anything went wrong. That way they wouldn't be completely assed out. He told them they would each have to put twenty dollars of what they earned off every bomb toward a lawyer, so if they ever got caught they would have money for their own attorney. The problem with public defenders was that they didn't care about their clients because they didn't get paid that much. Their first solution to any drug case was to have the defendant plead to a lesser charge, whereas privately paid lawyers fought for their clients to stay out of jail. It was in their best interest to win all their cases in hopes of landing that one big profile case. Junior was the one who suggested having the workers put money away for a lawyer, but La made it seem to Rocky and Dusty as if he was the mastermind of the whole operation. After they went over everything, La and Rock left, and Dusty lay on his bed and thought of all the money he was going to make, finally.

Gloria and KB were getting tight. She really liked him and he seemed to like her just as much, but he was just a little weird. He didn't really talk about himself. He was more interested in her and what she wanted. He catered to her like a waiter in a fine restaurant. She had never been treated so nicely by any of the guys she ever dealt with before. This was a first for her, and she finally realized why Shondra loved Junior so much. KB and Gloria had seen each other every day since the night she met him going to the store.

They were coming from seeing a movie when KB asked her if she wanted to take the relationship to another level. The one thing Gloria really liked about KB was that he wasn't afraid to say what was on his mind. He didn't pull punches. He just laid shit right on the table and wasn't afraid of the repercussions. She told him she wanted to be his main girl, his only girl. She wanted to be exclusive with him and him alone.

KB hailed a cab from Forty-second Street and told the cab driver to take them to the Hilton on Fifty-third and Sixth Avenue. Gloria knew he really wanted to make it official now. He wanted to make love to her. The whole time they spoke on the telephone and went out, he never once made an attempt to have sex. That was another thing that made her like him so much. He took his time and didn't rush into getting the pussy like most niggas did.

The cab pulled up across the street from the hotel and they both got out and walked into the entrance of the building. Gloria had never been to an expensive hotel before. Most niggas took her to the four-hour spot or even fucked her in their homeboy's house. KB walked in and she stood in the lobby looking at the clean carpet and the people coming inside, their luggage being carried in by bellboys. She was so impressed that she planned on giving him the best fuck of his life. He wasn't ever going to leave her after she threw that good pussy on him. They got onto the elevator that looked as if it was made out of gold. When they got into the room, KB went to the bathroom and immediately jumped in the shower. She knew it was on. But before she lay on the bed, she pulled the top cover off to look at the sheets—no stains. They were white and smelled summery fresh. She picked up the remote and turned on the television. She flipped through all the channels and there weren't any pornos showing at all. This was no bullshit. This was the real deal.

Gloria was glad she had on her matching bra and panties, because if she didn't, there would be no way she would let him see her without her clothes. Shondra had always hipped her about that. Shondra told her that anytime she went out with someone she should always have clean, matching underwear, void of holes in case she wanted to have sex. It made the nigga know she was definitely a woman that took pride in her appearance and hygiene. KB came out of the bathroom with a towel wrapped around his waist. He had a hairy chest and a nice physique for a short guy, but she could tell he used to be chubby from the stretch marks around his midsection. The shower was still running as he came out of the bathroom, and he uttered one sentence.

"I left it on for you," he said as he walked past her and lay on the bed, dripping wet from his shower. She complied and went into the bathroom, grabbing a white washcloth from the sink counter and then taking off her tight-fitting dress and underwear. She looked around in the drawers and found a shower cap, and then jumped into the steaming, hot shower. It felt good, and she was getting horny thinking of how KB was just taking control of the whole night since he had made her his woman. Damn, she was happy. She finally got her a good man.

After her shower she stood in the mirror and admired herself. She knew she had a banging ass body. She had an hour-glass shape and her ass was perfectly round. Her breasts were full and her nipples were perky and always hard. She knew that when KB laid eyes on her nakedness he might cum prematurely. She wrapped the towel around her body, but it couldn't cover her completely, so she decided to just go without it. She toweled dry and left her skin a little moist with drops of water to make it glisten slightly. She walked out of the bathroom, went straight to the bed, and lay on it, pulling the sheets over her. KB had dozed off, but he awakened when she got into the bed.

"Damn, Gloria, you are bad as hell," he said, not really awake yet, but just getting a glimpse of her goddess-like shape.

"Well, damn, KB, you just don't care what you say, huh?"

KB got under the covers, took his towel off, and moved closer to her. She felt something hard against her thigh and moved slowly toward the bulge. He grabbed her shoulders and pulled her closer, kissing her on her mouth and neck while his hands ran down the small of her back and over her ass. He caressed and squeezed her ass cheeks as he humped her thigh. It felt good to her, so she moaned a little, grabbed his ass, and squeezed. He positioned himself so his shaft was over her shaved snatch. She felt him throbbing on her and pushed her cat against him hard, and he moved toward her, then grabbed her breast with one hand and placed his tongue on her hardened nipple. She gasped as she felt the warmth and wetness of his tongue on her nipple. He rotated his tongue around her areola, then sucked her nipple softly. She whined with delight and grabbed his thick pole, rubbing it on her wetness. He cringed and allowed her to take control.

"Give it to me," she whispered in his ear as she sucked his earlobe hard.

He inserted himself into her slowly and could feel the moisture of her hole engulf his manhood. He moved in and out slowly, savoring their defining moment and basking in its ecstasy. She let out low moans of delight as he quickened his movements, holding him closer to her so he wouldn't slip out of her sloppy wetness. She gyrated her vaginal area to enhance the feeling. As they became one they both began to move rapidly in unison.

"Oh my God!" she screamed. "I . . . I'm about to cum!"

"Hold on, baby. Wait for daddy. Don't cum yet!" he bellowed, the feeling coming to him almost immediately.

"K, baby, you are makin' me feel sooooooo goooood!" she wailed as her legs locked on her and her body began to shake.

"I feel you, baby. I can feel you cummin'!" he squealed in her ear.

The feeling lasted almost a full twenty seconds, and then they both lay on their backs when it was over.

"Damn, you good, Gloria," he said after catching his breath.

"You so damn big," she replied, squeezing his semi-hard pole.

KB turned to Gloria, positioned her head on his broad chest. While Gloria thought about how good his pipe game was, they both dozed off to sleep.

When Gloria woke the next morning KB was gone, but he had left a note on the nightstand saying he had gotten an important beep and had to leave in a hurry. It said he didn't want to wake her up because she looked so peaceful. He left a one-hundred-dollar bill for her to take a cab home. She felt bad that he had to leave, but she knew it must have had to be important for him to leave her alone in the room, especially after the night they had together.

Gloria sat up in bed and saw a breakfast cart sitting by the bed. There were waffles and Canadian-style bacon with fresh strawberries, fresh cantaloupe, and orange juice. She jumped in the shower, and when she was finished she sat down on the bed and ate her breakfast as she dialed Shondra's number. She was beaming when she called, and Shondra sounded happy for her. Gloria told Shondra how KB took her to the Hilton and how she fucked his brains out.

"Is he there right now with you?"

"Nope. He left sometime last night or early this morning," she said, her mouth full of waffles.

"Oh. Did he say where he was going, or he just left you there like that?" Shondra asked.

"He left a note saying he got an important beep and had to go," she replied as she drank some of her orange juice.

"So that's your man now, huh, girl?"

"Mmmmhmmm, yeah, girl. And he slayed me after he made it official. God knows that nigga is big as hell."

"He can't be bigger than that mule Junior got between his legs."

"Well, I can't say 'cause I ain't never seen what your man got, but I know MY MAN is big as a horse."

"I'm glad for you, Glo. I hope he makes you happy and keeps you happy. You really deserve that. So tell me something about your new man. I mean, I never met him and you know I got to check him out to make sure he doing my girl right."

"I know, girl, but he funny like that. He anti-social and shit. He say he don't like meeting people, but I told him he was going to have to meet you 'cause you my sista."

"What he say when you told him that?"

"He said he know he gotta meet you then. He said that he a little shy about meeting you because he want you to like us together as a couple. He promised that he would meet you real soon because he knows it's important to me."

"So where does he live?"

"He lives in Williamsburg with his mom," Gloria replied. "I think he stays there with her because she sick or something. I ain't really sure. Like I said, he don't really talk much."

"Well if he is staying with his moms 'cause she sick, that tells what kind of guy he is. You know what I mean?"

"Yeah, I guess. I really like him, girl. He's like the first guy that ever treated me like he gives a fuck about my feelings, not just getting into my draws."

"I feel you, girl, but you gotta be careful. Sometimes it's good in the beginning and then shit changes, so you gotta be careful how fast you let yourself go."

"I guess you right, but I'm hoping that things between us be something like you have with Junior. I want a man like that, a man that loves me unconditionally and treats me like that no matter who we are around, like Junior treats you."

"I hear you, girl, but you know he wasn't like that 'til we put time in together. We went through our shit, but we worked it out. There were times I thought we were gonna break up, but our love for each other kept us together. I had to swallow a lot of shit, and he did too. Going through all that is what made us closer. I want you to be happy, girl. I just don't want you to get hurt by no nigga again."

"Thanks, sis. I know you only looking out for me. I'm gonna take my time. I just hope he's for real."

"Well, for one thing you need to know a little bit more about him, you know. You should know as much about him as possible. That's how you'll know if he's real or not."

"That's true. We're gonna have to sit down and talk about a lot of things. I just hope I don't push him away."

"Well, shit, if that's the case, then you need to find out now so you'll know."

After talking for about an hour or so, Shondra made plans for her and Gloria to meet and get their nails and hair done.

"So when you get here just knock on my door. I'm gonna make the reservations as soon as I hang up," Shondra told Gloria.

"All right. I'm gonna finish eating this good ass breakfast and check out of this room at eleven. I'll come straight to your house because I already took a shower, so I should be there in about a half to forty-five minutes."

"OK, baby, I'll see you then," Shondra said and hung up the telephone.

Shondra went to her closet and pulled out some Jesus sandals and a white, linen, Ralph Lauren short set that Junior bought for her from Bloomingdale's. She had never worn it before. After she took her shower, she called her Dominican hairdresser located in Harlem and made appointments for her and Gloria. After she hung up the phone with the hairdresser, she beeped Junior and put on her outfit.

***

The day Kendu planned to sell more of his aunt's valuables to get money for a bus ticket to North Carolina, there was a knock on the door. He hesitated because no one ever came to his cousin's house. He was going to the back room to get his cousin's gun, just in case it was someone that found out about what he had done, but as he headed for the bedroom where the gun was stashed, he heard the front door crash open. A guy with a long scar across his face rushed into the apartment, pointing a gun straight at him.

"Don't move, motherfucker, or you're dead!"

89

Kendu put his hands up, scared to death. He was wondering if he could make it to the bedroom and get the gun, but the intruder had the drop on him.

"What's goin' on?" he finally asked, his voice quivering with fear.

"You 'bout to find out! Is anybody else up in here with you?" he shouted, looking around while keeping the big .45 auto trained on Kendu's head.

"N-n-n-noooo, nobody's here but me."

The gunman moved within arms' reach of Kendu and swung the gun at his head. Kendu felt an immediate pain on the left side of his head and dropped to the parquet floors, rolling onto his stomach and clutching the spot where he was hit. The gunman kicked him and Kendu could feel the barrel of the gun at the back of his head. Then the young guy Kendu had robbed came into the apartment. The gunman turned Kendu over on his back and asked the young drug dealer, "Is this him?"

"Yeah, that's that fuckin' crack head that sliced me," he said, hock spitting on Kendu and feeling the scar on his face pull.

"Please, man, please!" Kendu begged, rubbing the knot on his head.

"Shut the fuck up!" the gunman yelled. "Where's the shit you took? You better pray you still have it, 'cause if you don't, you gon' meet the devil!"

"It's in the room in the back under the mattress. Please, man, I'm sorry. I fucked up. I was high, man, on that shit, please, man. I can work it off for you. Please, man, don't kill me, please."

The gunman knew there was no possible way Kendu would still have any of the work or the money, but he wanted to see if there was anything else of value in the house to take for reparation.

The young drug dealer went into the back room to search for anything worth taking.

"Make sure you don't touch nothing with your bare hands in there," the gunman yelled.

"I'm not. I got my gloves."

The gunman made Kendu sit on the couch in the living room and kept the gun pointed to his face. Kendu could see nothing but the black hole and the long, black barrel. He had the worst feeling in his stomach. He couldn't stop shaking and his heart rate had sped up like a revving motorbike. The gunman held the gun on him and glanced toward the back to see if his accomplice had found anything. When his accomplice came back from the room, he was heated because he didn't find anything. Kendu was squirming on the couch, his body trembling uncontrollably. He had spent all the money and smoked all the product. He was trying to think of something he could give them that would compensate for the shit he took, but he had sold most everyting of value in his aunt's house.

"Look, man, I can get the money back for you. All you have to do is make a call. Please, man, don't kill me!" Kendu was reduced to real tears.

"I wish you shut the fuck up!" the young drug dealer said and punched Kendu in his face with a hard right.

Kendu knew the end was near. He knew they were going to kill him even if they did get all their shit back. He mustered up all the heart he had and tried to think of a way to get out of the deadly situation he was in. Since he had nothing to lose, he decided to try to grab the gunman and wrestle the pistol away from him. He figured that would come as a surprise to the gunman since he was the one begging for his life. He just had to wait for the right moment, and the way shit was looking to him, there wasn't any time to waste.

The gunman was standing over Kendu pointing the gun at his chest. He had a look of death in his eyes and a firm grip around the handle of the .45 caliber automatic pistol. His hand was steady, so Kendu knew he was not new to killing. The young thug was busy ruffling through Kendu's pockets looking for money, but then he did the unthinkable. He stepped across Kendu's legs, momentarily blocking the vision of the gunman, and that's when Kendu saw his chance.

In what seemed like slow motion, Kendu grabbed the barrel of the gun as the young thug made it across his legs. He caught the gunman by surprise and held on to the barrel of the gun as the gunman tried to unsuccessfully pull the trigger. Kendu held on with both hands and tried to yank it from his grip. The young thug started swinging wildly at his head as Kendu and the gunman tussled for possession. Kendu wouldn't let go. He held on because his life depended on it. The gunman was yelling for his accomplice to help him. The young thug ran to the kitchen and Kendu could hear the clanging of utensils. He knew he had to get possession of the gun or he would definitely die. He turned his body sideways and bit down hard on the gunman's hand. Within seconds he had the gun in his hand. He turned the weapon on the gunman and was about to pull the trigger when he felt a sharp pain in his back. The young thug was stabbing him repeatedly. He turned around and pulled the trigger, missing the thug. He squeezed off one more shot before falling down on his face. The young thug had dropped the knife when Kendu turned around, and he ducked behind a china cabinet when the first shot was fired. The gunman was on top of Kendu as he fell, and he grabbed the gun from his hand.

"I should shoot your ass for almost getting me blasted!" the gunman screamed at his cohort.

The gunman then put the gun barrel to the base of Kendu's head and made sure there would be no more mistakes. The boom was loud, and Kendu's brains were splattered across the nicely shellacked, parquet floors.

"Take the knife with you and leave," he told the young thug. "I gotta clean some of this shit up. Now go!" the gunman yelled as he looked down at the corpse.

He took a towel from the bathroom and wiped the doorknob he had touched. Then he went into the kitchen and wiped down the open drawer, taking out every utensil and putting them in a plastic bag. Then he went into the bedroom and wiped down the headboard and all the knobs in the room. He walked past Kendu, being careful to step over the blood. He didn't want his boot prints to play a part in the investigation. He grabbed the door with the towel and walked out of the apartment, closing the door behind him.

There were red- and blue-flashing lights in front of the three-story brownstone, and a crowd had gathered around the yellow police tape, eager to find out what had happened inside the building. Many of the people from the neighborhood were thinking the worst since this was not the first time they were witnessing a crime scene. A black van with the word CORONER painted in white letters on the sides pulled up among the police cruisers and unmarked detective vehicles. Three men got out of the van, pulled out a stretcher, and went up the steps of the brownstone, disappearing through the doors.

"What happened in there?" someone asked.

"I don't know, but I heard some gunshots. They must have come from in there," one lady commented.

"Whatever happened, I know that somebody in there is dead. You see that black van that pulled up? That means that there are dead bodies in there," someone else added.

"Who lives in that building?" another person asked.

"Ms. Brown owns the building, but I think she moved to North Carolina over a year ago. I think she left the building to one of her sons, but you don't see him much. I don't know who else lived in there, though," a next-door neighbor said.

There was silence as the stretcher came out with a body covered by a white sheet. No one in the crowd knew who the person was under the sheet. They whispered and asked questions, but no one had a definitive answer. Many of the people out there were making their own assumptions on what had happened, but no one actually knew who was murdered.

In the crowd there was a group of young men standing around not saying anything. One person in the group knew exactly what had happened. The person under the sheet was the guy that had robbed and cut him three weeks ago. The young guy with the newly acquired scar stood in the crowd with his friends and looked on, acting as bewildered as everyone else in the crowd. He was only there to see if anyone had any idea about what happened. He vowed he would get the guy back for robbing him and slashing his face in front of his girl. He couldn't let him live after that. When he came out of St. Mary's Hospital after getting his face stapled, he told his older brother, Drez, who was the supplier of coke in the area, what had happened. Drez promised him that he wouldn't have to worry about it anymore.

Kendu was dead at only nineteen-years-old. It seemed like he never had a chance. He was just another black brother that got caught in the fangs of a life void of love, discipline, and truth. He grew up not knowing the love of a mother because she died when he was eight after she gave birth to his little brother. He and his brother went to live with their grandmother who worked to support them, but unfortunately she was never home, so they basically raised themselves. Kendu had to learn the streets and made his own rules as he got older. He didn't adhere to anyone else's rules because there was no one to enforce discipline. His only truth was the sad reality of his doomed life. He was not taught he could be anything he wanted to be. There was no father figure to guide him, so he lived lies to compensate for all his losses. Kendu was a typical guy that grew up in the hood. He just never had many opportunities in life.

After Kendu robbed that young guy for his drugs, he knew there would be some kind of retaliation. He just didn't predict that it would come so swiftly. Kendu was a prime example of what could happen when young brothers didn't have a positive influence in their lives. He had planned to leave Brooklyn and go to North Carolina immediately after the robbery, but his drug habit persuaded him to stay longer. He spent all the money he had stolen, leaving him none to buy a Greyhound ticket and the day he decided to leave is when he heard that final knock on the door.

Chapter 7
That☐s what I do best.

Stump couldn't waste anymore time looking for Junior and Kendu over the shoot out they had. He still had to get money and doing capers was where he made his money. Robbing local dealers was just something he did just to past the time but he always had big jobs from his boy Drez.

Stump was standing in the middle of the living room explaining to the guys sitting on the couch the plan he had devised. All three men were sitting side by side listening to him intently, hanging on his every word. The men were all hardened criminals, guys Stump had an affiliation with from doing bids in Sing Sing and Attica.

Ray-Ray was a career criminal. He was muscular from being in and out of jails from the age of fifteen and he used his size to intimidate his victims. Roughhouse at 280 pounds was the guy that gave Stump his respect when he did his first bid. Stump had a run-in with him while going through processing in Elmira, and he and Roughhouse fought over some money. Roughhouse was known for his hand skills up north, but Stump changed all that when he broke his jaw with two wicked right hooks. Stump used to box Golden Gloves and was a prospect for the Junior Olympics until he got locked up. He caught another charge and was sent back to Rikers Island, and after they gave him an additional three years to his sentence, he ran into Roughhouse again in Sing Sing and they finished what they had started on the yard. In that encounter, Stump broke his will instead of his jaw. Rough lost his credibility and began to run with Stump's crew. The last guy, Murda Mike, lived up to his name. He was a cold-blooded murderer, but he had never been convicted for any of them because he left no witnesses. The only way the police could get him in jail was to plant drugs and a gun on him and give him a five-to-fifteen-year sentence for conspiracy to commit murder. Murda was a heartless muhfucka, and the worst muhfucka to run into late at night. They said when he was locked down in Sing Sing he got stabbed in his stomach and now had to wear a shit bag. He never let that cripple him, though. Instead it made him more dangerous. It was rumored that he killed more niggas than cancer itself.

All the men in the room respected Stump because he was all about business. He never let emotions get in the way of what he needed to do. They all knew from experience that Stump feared no one and nothing, and that included himself. When you dealt with a man that was not afraid to die and had literally cheated death numerous times, you were basically dealing with the devil, and none of them wanted to be an enemy to the devil, no matter how tough they thought they were.

Stump continued to lay out his plan to the men, and then there was a knock on the door. All the guys sitting on the couch got up, almost in unison, and pulled out their guns. Stump walked slowly to the door, but kept his back against the wall. He had a black, snub-nosed .44 Bulldog with a rubber pistol grip. As he got closer to the door, he yelled for the person on the other side to identify himself.

"It's KB."

"Oh, it's my man from 'round the way."

They relaxed after hearing that and put their guns back from where they were concealed. Stump turned the knob on the door and pulled it open. KB was startled because Stump was pointing the gun to his face.

"What the fuck is up?" he asked Stump, his hands raised to his face as if he could deflect a bullet if it was discharged.

"You tell me. Where you been? I beeped you over an hour ago."

"I was with my lady, man, damn. I just left her in the city. We were at Olive Garden eating dinner and shit when you beeped me. I had to leave her and take a cab straight here. You know how dem yellow cabs don't like bringing a nigga to the hood."

It seemed every time he was out with Gloria having a good time, Stump always beeped him and interrupted their time together. He knew Gloria was getting tired of him running and leaving her any time Stump beckoned.

"OK, I'll give you a pass this time, but in the future make sure you at least call me back and let me know something. You don't know whether it is an emergency. It's critical you call back and give me a time, because I set my clock to what you tell me, aight?" KB could tell that Stump was serious as he lowered the gun and let him enter the apartment. KB slapped everybody five, introduced himself, took a seat, and was briefed on what Stump was plotting.

Stump was planning to rob a coke spot Drez had told him about. He had been watching it for about two weeks and knew who he wanted in on it, and what their assigned jobs were going to be. The spot was camouflaged as a twenty-four-hour bodega. There were always two guys inside, and the drugs were located in the basement of the store. They didn't sell to people they didn't know, so it would be hard to get inside the store once they closed the gates at night. Stump knew the only way to get them would be in the afternoon when they least expected a hit, because they were busy most of the day into the late afternoon. What was attractive about this particular stick was that they could each walk away with over fifty thousand dollars if everything went smoothly. KB was going to be the wheelman as well as the lookout man. He would make the same amount, although Ray-Ray felt he shouldn't get the same cut as the rest because his job was the least dangerous. Stump spoke up for him and explained the importance of each person's job. The caper couldn't go smoothly if any one of them weren't present.

"Look, Ray, when we come out of the store wit' all that dough, where we goin'?" Stump asked.

"We gonna get in the car and peel out," he replied, lookin' at KB.

"Can you drive?" Stump asked.

"Hell yeah. I can drive like a bat outta hell!"

"OK, to keep the peace, you can be the wheelman and KB can be the shooter," Stump suggested.

"Nah, man, I need to hold the iron in my hand. That's what I do best. That's my thing. You know that, nigga!"

"Oh, OK, now you understand!" Stump turned to everyone and addressed them all. "I handpicked all of you specifically. I know what each of you are good at and capable of doing. I need the best men, and I believe I have the best. We all have things we're good at, and there are other things that we can do, but are not the best at. That's when you need help to balance the shit out. That's what I did when I chose this crew. So understand one thing, this shit will not fly unless everyone handles their job to the T. We all count on each other for this shit to go without a hitch. Does everyone understand me?"

There was no doubt in everyone's mind that this was a big lick. They knew they would have to be on their jobs and not slip, because one slip could be fatal for the whole crew.

Chapter 8
Let me get a ham and cheese.

KB circled the block in the stolen, white, commercial van and slowly drove past the store to see if there were any people inside. The rest of the guys were in the back of the van wearing masks and checking their guns to make sure the safeties were off. This was crunch time and there was no room for mistakes and no time to back out. Stump asked the guys if they were ready to "rock and roll," and everyone nodded in agreement. They were pumped and ready to take the money and leave without any casualties. Stump knew the guys they were about to rob were not going to go out without a fight. He anticipated it, but didn't tell any of this to his crew because he felt that they already knew how dangerous this caper was. There was way too much money involved for it to go off without at least one dead body.

"Y'all niggas ready?" Stump asked everyone, clicking his automatic and putting a live round in the chamber. "Park ova there by Lindsey parking lot and keep the van running. Don't turn that shit off for nothing. Got it, KB?" he asked.

"I got you, man. Don't worry. I got my end covered."

"I gotta make sure you can see us comin' out that muhfucka. Once you see us, mash the gas and pick us up!" Stump explained.

"I gotcha, man. I'm not gonna fold on you. Trust me, man."

KB pulled the van into the parking lot and parked between two other cars to look inconspicuous. The back doors opened and the crew of men all jumped out. Ray-Ray, Roughhouse and Murda Mike all walked toward the store. Roughhouse was to go inside and order a hero sandwich to keep whoever was behind the counter busy. Ray-Ray was to go to the back of the store by the cooler and act like he was buying beer. The back was where the door to the basement was. Murda Mike and Stump would come in last and announce the stickup once Rough and Ray had it secured.

"Let me get a ham and cheese hero with lettuce, tomatoes, extra mayo, salt, pepper, oil, and vinegar," Roughhouse told the man behind the counter.

"American cheese?" the Dominican man asked as he turned his back to put on the clear, plastic gloves.

"Yeah, American cheese. Can you heat it up for me?"

"Mmmhmm," he answered as he cut the Italian bread down the middle with a large butcher knife.

When Ray walked into the store he went straight to the back and began looking at the selection of malt liquor in the cooler. While he was back there he spotted the door on the floor that led to the basement. It had a padlock on it and was partially covered by empty boxes. Stump and Mike pulled their masks over their heads and pulled out their guns as they walked into the store. As the store door closed behind them, two Dominican men parked in a black Acura Legend with tinted windows observed the two men putting masks over their faces.

"Turn around and let me see your fuckin' hands 'fore I blow your face off!" Stump screamed to the man behind the counter.

Mike went around the side and kicked open the door to get entrance behind the counter. Stump slid the duct tape over the counter to Mike and he pulled off a piece and put it over the petrified man's mouth, duct taping his hands behind his back.

"The keys are under the sink, man, in a blue cup," Stump informed Mike.

"I got it," Mike reported as he headed toward the back.

Roughhouse and Ray-Ray were moving the boxes by the time Stump and Mike got to them.

"Roughhouse, you stay up here and keep whoever comes in this muhfucka inside. Don't let them leave," Stump directed.

"I gotcha."

Ray got the lock off the door and they all stood back and pointed their guns at the door.

"It should be two niggas down there. I'm goin' first. Y'all just hold me down," Stump told Ray and Mike.

Stump went down the stairs leading to the basement and clicked on a light that was hanging by a chain. As he got to the bottom he gestured for the other two to follow. He walked down a long corridor and could hear someone talking as he got closer to an opening where a light was shining. He turned around and put his index finger over his mouth, signaling them to be quiet. Ray and Mike followed behind him, moving silently like a cat preying on a mouse.

"They in there," Stump whispered, pointing to the opening at the end of the corridor. "I think they counting money."

As Stump got close enough to the doorway of the room, he could see the silhouettes of the men and heard them speaking in Spanish. He pulled out his second gun, the .44 Bulldog, and jumped into plain sight, pointing the guns at the three guys sitting around a table of money and powder cocaine. Instinctively, Mike was on his side with a .357 Smith & Wesson pointed at the men, and Ray was on Stump's other side with a nine-millimeter Beretta.

"Get down on the floor, NOW!" Stump screamed at the top of his lungs in his fiercest voice so there would be no questioning his seriousness. "If you move, you die, muhfuckas!"

Ray pulled out a black bag from his back pocket and went to the table.

"Anybody else in here wit' y'all?" Mike asked no one in particular.

"Hay nadie aquí pero satisfacemos no nos lastimamos," the short one replied.

"Oh, these muhfuckas want to play like they don't speak English, huh?" Mike asked Stump. "I think I better teach them English real fast!"

"Hurry up and get all that shit!" Stump told Ray.

"It's a lot of shit, man. I think we might need another bag," Ray said, filling up the bag.

"Just fill up the bag and worry about the rest later!" Stump replied.

Ray wanted everything—the drugs, money, and the jewelry the guys had on.

"Where's the tape?" Stump asked Mike. He wanted to tie up the guys.

"Man, I left that shit upstairs. Damn!"

"I need to tie these niggas up so they don't get frisky," Stump said.

"Fuck it. I'll help Ray and you hold them down," Mike replied.

Mike went over to help Ray put the money and bags of coke into the black garbage bag.

The guys in the car knew the spot was being robbed. When they saw Stump and Mike put their masks on they made a phone call to their boss. They were the lookouts for the spot and were there specifically for niggas like Stump's crew. They got out

101

of the car, pulled out two big knives, and headed for the entrance of the bodega. The taller man looked inside and could see Roughhouse standing by the counter eating a sandwich. He waited to see if any of the other guys were around, but didn't see any of them, so they rushed inside. When they got into the store, Roughhouse pointed the gun at them and told them to get behind the counter. He had no idea that they already knew what was going on.

"Get behind the counter, boys," he said, waving the gun toward the side of the counter.

"What's happening?" the slim one asked, hiding the knife behind his back.

"Don't worry about all that. Just get behind the fuckin' counter and you won't get hurt!" he said, his mouth full of the hero.

The taller one, noticing Roughhouse wasn't aware of what was really going on, lunged at him and plunged the knife into his chest. The short one brought his butcher knife down on the hand with the gun and it fell to the floor. Roughhouse backed up as both men continued to stick him with the knives in his midsection. He was fighting back and was able to grab the short one. He didn't know how many times he was hit, but he could feel himself getting weaker.

"Die, mudderfucka!" the taller one screamed as Roughhouse hit him with a hard right to his temple. The man fell to the ground out cold, and Roughhouse turned his attention to the short guy who showed no sign of fear. He looked at the Ruger on the floor and at the Dominican behind the counter who was frozen with fear. He watched the man on the floor that he had just knocked out to make sure he was really out cold. When he looked at the short guy, he could tell they were both were thinking the same thing. Roughhouse kicked the gun toward the entrance of the store. The Dominican hit Roughhouse again in his side. He winced from the sharp pain, but concentrated on making it to his gun.

Stump, Ray, and Mike were wrapping things up when one of the guys on the ground got up. Mike pulled the trigger of the .357 magnum and his body literally lifted off the ground and he was thrown into wall. He fell face first to the ground and you could see the gaping wound in his back.

"Ah, shit, we gotta off all of them!" Stump said, knowing Mike was thinking the same thing.

"I'm heading upstairs, fellas. I'm gonna see if Roughhouse is OK," Ray said, heading for the corridor.

"We're right behind you, kid," Stump replied.

"Usted los individuos va a pagar esto con su vida," the dark-skinned Spanish guy said.

"What, you fuckin' Goya bean eatin' muhfucka!" Stump yelled and placed his gun behind the man's head, pulling the trigger. Stump didn't understand what was said to him, but he knew he didn't like it. The other man on the ground began to weep uncontrollably, and Mike pumped two shots into his back, then stood over him and finalized his death with a bullet to his head. Ray was headed upstairs when he heard the shots. Although he cringed from the explosions, he knew they were home free. Mike looked at Stump and they both headed down the corridor to meet Ray and Roughhouse.

Ray dropped the bag when he saw Roughhouse on the ground tussling with a Spanish guy. He saw blood all over the floor and another Spanish man lying on the ground not moving. Ray immediately ran to Roughhouse. The guy struggling with Rough broke free just in time as he saw Ray coming to Roughhouse's aid. He jumped up and staggered out of the store. Ray emptied the gun at the fleeing man, but missed as the guy slipped out the door untouched. Roughhouse was coughing up blood and Ray tried to pull him to his feet, but he was too heavy. Ray struggled with him until he had him sitting in an upright position.

"We gotta go. We gotta get you to a hospital, man!" Ray screamed.

Stump and Mike came up and saw Ray trying to pick up Roughhouse.

"Get him outta here!" Stump ordered Mike while picking up the bag Ray had dropped. "What the fuck happened up here?"

"Some niggas stabbed him up. One of them on the floor," Ray replied.

Mike was helping Roughhouse out the door. Ray ran out to make sure no one had seen what was happening and to look for the van, but he didn't see it in the parking lot down the block. There was no sign of KB anywhere. Mike was helping Roughhouse along in the direction of the parking lot, but Rough was on wobbly legs and couldn't move fast. He was mumbling something to Mike, but Mike was concentrating on getting to the van as quickly as possible.

"Is the van out there?" Stump asked Ray as he came back into the store.

"I don't know, man. I don't see him. I thought he was supposed to be watching for the first nigga to come outta the store," Ray said nervously.

Stump told Ray to go to where the van was supposed to be. When Ray walked out the store he heard the boom of a gun going off and knew the guy on the ground was now dead if he wasn't before, then he heard another boom, which meant the guy behind the counter had met the same fate. The sirens were getting closer and everyone knew it would only be a matter of time before the police arrived on the scene. Stump made sure there would be no witnesses left. He tied up all the loose ends. Ray took off running to the parking lot, and Stump was right on his heels.

"Let me go, man. Go ahead. I can make it to the van," Roughhouse gurgled to Mike.

"I can't leave you like this, man. Just try to move a little faster."

"Just go!" Roughhouse knew he was slowing everyone else down, and he didn't want everyone to get caught on account of him.

Mike left Roughhouse leaning on a fence and ran toward the parking lot as the sounds of the sirens got closer. The van pulled up on the corner where Ray and Stump were running and slowed down so they could get in.

"Where the fuck was you, muhfucka?" Stump demanded to know of KB.

"The traffic police came into the parking lot and made me move because I didn't have a sticker. I just circled the block and I saw y'all two running."

"They stabbed up Rough, man. We gotta go get him!" Ray said to KB.

KB made a U-turn and headed back toward the bodega. Mike was running up the block, and when he saw the van he ran into the street to make sure they saw him. KB slowed down and Ray opened the back door for him to get in.

"Go get Rough!" Mike cried out to KB. He had a look of desperation on his face.

KB could see Roughhouse running and falling down. He couldn't keep his balance while he was trying to make it to the van. He could see the van and was trying to make it to where it was, but his legs wouldn't let him go any farther. He got to his feet again and tried to hop to the van. He was losing a lot of blood exerting all this energy. The van seemed so close, but his vision was getting blurry and he kept choking on his own blood. Roughhouse heard the sirens behind him and knew it was too late for him. He wanted them to wait, but at the same time he wanted them to go. There was no saving him, not now. It was too late. The sounds of the sirens were deafening and the blue and red lights could be seen flashing off the buildings. All the guys in the van were looking at him as he fought to make it to them.

"We can't get him!" KB broke the silence in the van. "We'll all go down if we do. There ain't no time!"

"Don't leave him, homey. He came with us and he's leaving with us. We not leaving nobody behind, cuz!" Mike said, his eyes filling with tears. It was weird to see Murda Mike getting emotional over death.

"We can't, man. We don't have no time and we'll get busted if we go get him," KB said almost in a whisper. "Look, the police are already in front of the fuckin' store." KB realized the seriousness of the situation. KB was the only one speaking up because the rest of them didn't want the responsibility of making the call on leaving Roughhouse. KB turned the van around and sped off toward Broadway. Ray, Stump, and Mike looked out the back window of the van and watched as Roughhouse fell down the final time, never to get back up again.

Chapter 9
Here love, don't lose it.

The unmarked police car rode past for the third time. The detectives in the car were hoping someone would run so they could go to the air-conditioned office and do paperwork and get off the hot streets, not to mention the streets were more dangerous this time of the year. There were more people on the street when it was hot than when the weather was cold. And more people meant more problems, and much more aggravation. Most detectives on the force just wanted to finish their tour and go home to their families, but there were a few that wanted promotions and tried to portray their favorite television cops like Baretta or *SuperCop*. Taylor and Burke were homicide detectives that used unauthorized tactics to pry information from suspects to help them solve cases. They would usually threaten people or plant evidence if they didn't get the results they were looking for. It had a lot to do with when they were both beat cops. They constantly fucked with young guys that didn't have a clue about the law and the rights that protected them under it. Once they had the suspects in custody they would sit them in the back of their unmarked car, and ride to deserted factories and tell them they had a choice to tell them what they wanted to know or wind up dead. They easily recruited informants this way, which made their job much easier when they were out on the prowl for an arrest.

"Why the fuck they keep passin' through?" La asked no one in particular.

"I know. It's not sweep week. That's next week," one of the workers said.

"Ain't none of y'all lil niggas dirty, right?"

"Nah, we clean. We don't hold no more since they got Rock with that bullshit ass possession charge," the lieutenant of the workers said.

Rock had gotten caught with half a blunt in his pocket and the detective that caught him found some vials of crack in a tennis ball in the grass next to where he was standing and tried to say it was his. Rock had a paid lawyer and his charge was dropped from felony possession to a misdemeanor, and he was given community service for having the half-smoked blunt.

107

"Yo, La, come here, man," Rock said as he opened the door of the Lincoln Mark V he was driving. He had got the car off a crack head that owed him three hundred dollars. When Rock threatened to kill the man, the guy gave Rock the car to clear up his bill.

"Whaddup, my nigga?" La asked.

"Kendu got murdered, kid."

"What?"

"Kendu is dead, man. They found him in Bed-Stuy in his aunt's house."

"Who did it?"

"I didn't get all the details, but I heard that it had something to do with him robbing some of the lil' drug dealers ova that way."

"Nobody don't know who did it?"

"I didn't get all that. I mess with this shorty ova there and she was telling me about some nigga that got killed in the building. When I asked her who it was, she said she only knew that is was Joe's cousin from Bushwick. I didn't think about it until she said that and then I knew it was Du. She said she didn't hear anything about who did it, but it was a rumor that it was the nigga that supplied that part of the Stuy with drugs."

"That's fucked up," La said, slumping down in the passenger seat of the car. "I knew that something like this was gonna happen because the nigga started fuckin' with that shit and wildin' out for no reason. Damn, Du!"

Rock went back to where he had picked up La and got out. La stayed in the passenger seat deep in thought. He couldn't believe his man was gone. He couldn't believe it had ended for him the way it did. La was flooded with emotions. He was thinking of how young Kendu was, how he must have felt, whether he knew he was going to die, if he was scared, and if it hurt. He also wondered if Kendu had suffered and if he felt alone in his last minutes. Then La promised himself he wouldn't go out the way Kendu had.

Rock was telling the workers to keep the customers from hanging around the building when they weren't copping because it brought heat to the spot. Just as he said that a blue sedan pulled up, and two detectives jumped out and walked over to where they were standing.

"How ya doin', Rodney?" the tubby one named Burke asked.

"What the fuck you dudes want? This ain't no donut shop!"

"Why all the profanity, Mr. Cooper? Are we addressing you in a vulgar manner?" the slim one named Taylor asked.

"'Cause y'all fuckin' wit' me, and I'm tired of y'all fuckin' wit' me when you see me somewhere," Rock said, frustrated. "Y'all want to check me and try to plant something on me like y'all did before, 'cause I got a lot of witnesses out here this time."

"Well we did have a reason to come see you, but since you insist on us checking you," Burke said as he walked up to Rock, "turn around so I can make sure you don't have anything on you that you shouldn't have, like crack, cocaine, or guns."

Rock assumed the position as he had so many other times since they busted him with weed. Taylor frisked him and pulled out a wad of bills.

"Now where did you get all this money from, Mr. Cooper?" Taylor asked, throwing the bundle of money to his partner.

"Why you worrying about where I get my money from?"

"Because that seems like a lot of money for such a young man like yourself to be carrying around in the middle of the day. Reggie and me work hard every day, and we still can't walk around with money like that in our pockets."

"It's $3,750 to be exact," Burke said after counting the money.

"Whoa! That's a lot of money. Now I'm gonna ask ya again, where did you get all this money from, Mr. Cooper?" Taylor asked Rock as he continued checking his pockets.

"It's my mother's money. I have to pay our furniture bill and some other stuff. Damn, man, y'all all in my fuckin' business. Why don't y'all just leave me the fuck alone!"

"Can your mother verify that?" Taylor asked.

"My momma ain't home. Yo, why don't y'all leave me the fuck alone!"

"There you go with that profanity again. All right, since your momma isn't home, I'm gonna let you keep the money. I wouldn't want your momma or you to have to sleep on the floor because you fucked around and got your furniture money taken from you."

Burke threw the money on the ground next to Rock's feet and the money flew everywhere.

"Oops, it slipped outta my hand. I'm sooo sorry."

109

Rock was clearly upset because they were embarrassing him in front of his workers. These officers were abusing their authority and their badges. The workers scrambled to pick up the scattering money.

"Be careful they don't pocket any of Momma's furniture money," Burke said, laughing. "You know you're not paying them that much," he finished and walked off to his car.

Taylor followed behind him, then turned around.

"Oh yeah, a guy from these projects was murdered." Taylor looked Rock directly in his eyes and continued. "Did you know him? I hope he wasn't a friend of yours because that's a terrible thing to happen to such a young guy. You better be careful out here, I wouldn't want to hear anything like that happened to you."

La was sitting in the car watching everything the crooked detectives were doing. He knew not to get out of the car when he saw them approach because he didn't need them to harass him like they did Rock. He was the backbone of the operation as far as they knew, and since Junior wasn't around, he had to keep a low profile so the police wouldn't know he was the man in charge. They would usually bust drug users for simple possession of drug paraphernalia and try to get them to reveal who the man behind the workers was, but most of the users didn't know, and the ones that had an idea thought better not to talk because of Rock. La didn't sell hand to hand anymore because he had workers. All he did was get the work from Junior and give it to Rock to distribute. He had come up quickly and the operation had grown to moving three thousand to seven thousand dollars a day. His clientele increased in three months so they had to make sure that after everyone copped, they left the area immediately. There was no hanging out around the building. He didn't even collect money from the workers anymore. Dusty brought all the money to him whenever the workers were finished. La made sure the workers treated every user with respect and he made examples of the ones that didn't. His operation was going better than planned, and he wasn't ready for it to end just yet. He had bigger plans ahead and didn't want anything to jeopardize his progress. The first thing he had to do was get rid of Stump then his other plan would go smoothly.

Rock was fuming after he picked up all the money.

"One day they gonna come around to fuck with me and I'm gonna kill both them muhfuckas!"

La walked over to Rock and pulled him by his collar into the lobby of the building.

"Look, Rock, you see they fuck wit' you every time they see you, right?"

"Yeah, man, and I don't even be doin' shit!"

"That's not the point. They know you now so they gonna keep fuckin' wit' you until they get something on you. That means that you gotta stay one step ahead of them. You havta make sure that you always clean when you on the block. You can't keep a lot of money on you, no weed, no liquor, nothing that gives them a reason to fuck wit' you. If you dirty and you see them before they see you, get ghost on they ass. But if they see you and you dirty, you gotta dash on them. Sooner or later they gonna get tired of chasin' and fuckin' wit' you because they won't never have shit on you. Outta sight, outta mind, my nigga."

"I hear you, but they be doin' foul shit. They even threatened me. They told me to be careful that what happened to 'Du don't happen to me!"

"They tryin' to push your buttons, kid, but you can't react 'cause them muhfuckas got a job to do just like you have a job to do. Your job is a lil' easier because you already know what they doin'. You make their job harder by making them try to find out what you doin'. They can think what they want, son, but without hard evidence they don't have shit. That's why I told you and Dusty to put money away for a lawyer. When you have a paid lawyer all them bullshit charges get thrown out and the judge gets pissed off because they keep wastin' his time with bullshit cases. You gotta buckle down, son. You gotta change up your format and throw them niggas off your scent."

La was finished his sermon for now. He wanted to see if Rock was gonna take his advice. If he didn't, La knew he would have to take his rank away or cut him loose. La felt he had come too far to fail because of one nigga's fuckup.

"I'm going on the other side and check on Dusty and his crew," La told Rock. "I want you to meet me at the crib at twelve tonight, OK?"

"I'll be there," Rock replied. He didn't like how La was acting all of a sudden, like it was his fault the block was hot.

***

The traffic was really heavy coming back from Virginia Beach. Shondra was in the passenger side of the rented Corvette asleep like a baby. She had really enjoyed herself with Junior. It

111

had been months since he took her out of town. They were supposed to rent a condo on Virginia Beach and spend the entire time on the beach and in the room, but Junior had decided to take her to Kings Dominion amusement park, too, which was a surprise for her. She enjoyed herself thoroughly.

The New Jersey Turnpike had been backed up since Exit 3, and Junior was just making it to Exit 6 after six hours of driving. The top was down on the red convertible and the wind was blowing gently on Shondra's brown skin. Junior looked over at her and thought about how much she was going through and how much he actually put her through. She rarely complained about anything he asked her to do for him, even betraying her best friend's trust by getting information for him on her new man, knowing he had fatal intentions. She felt Junior's life was more important than her and Gloria's friendship. Shit, she could find another friend, but if Junior died there would be no coming back.

Junior had a lot do when he got back to Brooklyn. He knew one day his street credibility would be tested, but he didn't know when. What he did know was that he played himself by becoming too comfortable when he first started hustling, and he made a promise never to slip like that again. It had been over three months since the shootout, and La was making him more money in Baptiste than Junior was making when he was out there himself. He had gotten kind of lazy and was just bringing the work to La and collecting the money to re-up. He knew he should be out there making sure everything was going right, but his excuse was that he wanted to take care of Stump first. He was waiting for the right time to get Stump because he didn't want the murder to lead back to him. Shondra didn't know everything he was plotting because he only told her what he needed her to know. Everything else he kept to himself, because if push came to shove, she wouldn't be able to give the police any info even if they pressured her.

Traffic let up and he finally made it to Exit 14C, the Holland Tunnel. He paid the tolls, took Canal Street to the Manhattan Bridge, and headed to Brooklyn. As he passed over the East River there was a sign that read, WELCOME TO BROOKLYN. A NICE PLACE TO VISIT, A GREAT PLACE TO LIVE.

What bullshit, he thought to himself as he rode down Flatbush Avenue.

"Damn, boo, we got back fast. We almost home," Shondra said, wiping slobber from the side of her mouth.

"Eeeewww!" Junior said playfully. "You want a Lifesaver or an ice cold bottle of Scope?"

"Oh, please, you know you love the way my breath smells."

"Yeah, after you eat a peppermint hamburger and drink a tall glass of Listerine. You been sleep since we left VA, girl. Why you so tired?"

"I don't know. I had so much fun at Kings Dominion and the beach. I'm still trying to make up for those all-nighters you pulled too."

"Well you know I got a battery in my back that never needs recharging."

He pulled over by a liquor store on Myrtle Avenue and jumped out, leaving the car running.

"You want something from outta there?"

"Yeah, get me a bottle of Bailey's," she said.

"Aight, I'll be right back."

He went into the liquor store and bought a small bottle of Hennessy VSOP and a small bottle of Bailey's for Shondra, then paid the Chinese man behind the counter. When he came out of the store he ran into an old girlfriend from high school—Charlene. He remembered that Muffin was her nickname. She was his first girlfriend in high school and she still looked good as hell. She had long hair flowing down her back with a caramel complexion, slanted eyes like a China doll, and a gold crown on the side tooth in her mouth. She was wearing some tight Guess shorts with a close fitting Tommy Hilfiger shirt that showed off her perky breasts. The shorts made her ass poke out like it was swollen, and her hips curved so deeply that they were busting the seams on the side of her shorts. When she stopped in front of him he remembered the thing that had attracted him to her the most—her legs. They snapped back because she was bowlegged and she looked like a stallion standing in front of him. At that moment he forgot Shondra was sitting in the car waiting for him.

"Hey, stranger. Long time, no see," she said in her high-pitched voice. She sounded like the singer Michele from Death Row.

"Wow, picture me seeing you after all this time. What's good, mama?"

"Damn, can a girl get a hug or sumthin'?"

"My bad," he said and grabbed her close to him, giving her a gentle but inviting hug.

"You look nice," she said, admiring him from head to toe.

He had on a Karl Kani jean suit with a pair of all white Air Nikes, an eighteen-inch cable with a house medallion, a gold nugget watch, and a bracelet with the letters JUNIOR spelled out in diamonds. She knew he was definitely getting money from somewhere with all the expensive jewelry he was wearing.

"Thanks. What you been up to, Muffin?"

"Nuthin' much. Jus' chillin'. Looks like you been up to a lot by all that shit you got on."

"Nah, ma, I'm jus' chillin', too. Where you on your way to?"

"To my girlfriend's house. She wants to hang out, maybe go out to the city and catch a flick and grab sumthin' to eat. Nothin' special. Why? You want to do something?"

"Yeah, why not?"

"You got a girl or you single, playa?"

"Um, yeah, she ova there in the car," he said, pointing to the red, drop top Corvette on the corner.

"Oh, I'm sorry, luv. I don't want you to get in trouble, so I'm gonna step off."

"Nah, it's not like that. I mean, you my friend. She ain't gonna bug out because I'm talking to you or if we go out or sumthin'."

"For right now, but what about lata?"

"Lata ain't here yet. Let's talk about that when we get there." He was putting his mack game down. "Why don't you give me your digits so I can get up with you lata?"

She pulled out a pen from her purse, ripped a piece of paper off the bag he was carrying, and told him to turn around so she could write her number using his back as support. That move was a dead giveaway. Whoever saw that would have known he was kicking it with her and that she was giving her number to him. There could be no mistake of a platonic relationship between them.

"Here, luv. Don't lose it or let anybody get it."

Junior took the number and balled it up in his hand. There would be no way he would let Shondra find that number. He didn't want to fuck up his chances of hitting Muffin's ass again.

"When you want me to call you?" Junior asked.

"Right now, but I know you can't because"—she looked at the car—"you look a lil busy. Call me when you get rid of your dead weight."

"Aight, I'm gonna give you a call tonight. We can go out lata," he said, smiling. "What time you have to be home so I'll know how long to plan our evening."

"My keys are my curfew, nigga!" she said and walked off, shaking her ass so hard it looked like she was walking in slow motion.

Junior was in a trance as she strode past the car and glanced at the passenger, rolling her eyes and shaking her ass even harder. When he woke up from the trance he realized what had just happened, and he knew he had to think of something to tell Shondra. She was definitely going to ask him who Muffin was. He walked slowly back to the car and opened the door, putting the bags in the backseat. He wasn't really sure if she saw anything, so he figured if she didn't say anything, then he wouldn't either. When he got into the driver's side of the car Shondra was looking outside the passenger's window, so he couldn't tell if she was mad. He pulled off and sped down Myrtle Avenue toward his cousin's house.

"I got to stop at my cousin's house for a minute, aight?" he asked, breaking the silence in the car.

"Mmmhmmm."

"What's wrong with you?"

That's when she turned to him and showed her true emotions. Tears were streaming down her eyes and her lips were quivering when she spoke.

"I don't know who that bitch was that you was talking to, but I know you, Junior. I know that you'll say it was business, but I know that's bullshit!"

"Yeah, I know her. I used to go to school with her and we were kinda cool. I ain't seen her in a minute and she was just talkin' to me about old times. That's all. Damn, I ain't know it was a fuckin' crime to have a female as a homey and shit!"

"I'm not stupid, Junior. She gave you her fuckin' number. I saw her writin' it down on your back and then the bitch got the fuckin' gall to sashay past me and roll her fuckin' eyes. I shoulda got out and snuffed that bitch!" She was furious now. "Then you gonna get in the car and don't say shit to me like nuthin' happened, like I ain't shit. That's so fuckin' disrespectful, Junior!"

"Aaah, come on, Mooka, I ain't thinking 'bout that girl. It's not even like that. I don't know why you all upset and shit. I'm with you, baby," he said, grabbing her head and putting it on his shoulders. She pulled back.

"Junior, I swear to God, if I find out that you fuckin' wit' that bitch, I swear I'ma kill you and her both!"

"Don't even worry about that shit, ma. I'm not looking for nobody. I got you. I don't need nobody else."

"I'm not bullshittin', Junior. I'm serious!"

"Aight, ma. I ain't bullshittin' either."

Junior knew she was serious, and he did love her, but he was just a man. He was thinking with his dick instead of with his heart. Shondra was quiet the rest of the way to his cousin's house, hoping that Junior wouldn't violate her trust, but she knew she didn't stand a chance against the pretty, light-skinned girl with the fat ass.

Junior pulled into the parking lot and got out of the car. His cousin Craig was shooting dice so he stood on the side and waited for him to finish rolling.

"What up, cuz? You just gettin' back?" Craig asked.

"Yeah, man, I need to get in the crib to get something," Junior said as he started walking toward the building.

"Aight. These niggas trying to break me," he said as he turned to the group of guys who stood in a circle waiting for him to roll again.

"Head Crack!" Junior screamed as he went into the building.

As he waited for the elevator he thought about how his cousin had his projects on lock. Anything that was sold in there, Craig ultimately supplied. He had workers and sold weight to some of the dealers. He treated the dudes in his projects well, making sure anyone who wanted to make some money had the opportunity. He had a strong crew of workers and gorillas who were not from the projects but came to regulate whenever Craig had major beef or had to go to war. His street credibility was never questioned by anyone in the projects, but there were always the nonbelievers. That's when he made examples of the ones that tested his abilities. One guy was found on the roof of a building with both his hands cut off at the wrists. The police found the hands in his pockets balled up with ten, crisp, one-hundred-dollar bills in each of them. There was a note that read, "Don't get caught wit' your hands in my pockets!" That one wicked act was how he kept potential thieves disinterested in his operation and kept his workers loyal to a fault. Craig was also likened to the Godfather because many of the tenants in the projects came to him whenever they needed a favor. He would help them with any situation—from financial assistance to personal safety—and they would be indebted to him until they paid off the favor.

Crime was kept to a low in Craig's projects because his operation was organized. He didn't venture out to the neighboring areas because he wanted to keep the peace. He made it a point to spread the love every chance he got. He would sponsor basketball games for the youth, support after-school programs for the community, and he even enforced a twenty-four-hour-a-day tenant watch program. The regular blue and whites couldn't get any convictions because his operation was impenetrable, but he was being investigated by the feds. Craig was addicted to the notoriety more than the money, and his high came from eluding law enforcement. Junior had taken notice of how his cousin ran his operation and tried to emulate some of his characteristics and procedures.

The elevator stopped on the twelfth floor and Junior stepped out into the dimly lit hallway. He went to the exit door and walked up the rest of the three flights to the fifteenth floor. Craig had told him never to ride the elevator exactly to his floor just in case of an ambush, and that's how Junior conducted business when he was at his own spot. Craig was always thinking like that. That's why his operation in the projects ran so damn tight.

Junior pulled out the keys, entered the apartment, and immediately went to the alarm system on the wall to deactivate it. He then continued past Midnight, Craig's all black Pit bull. Craig had Midnight professionally trained, and his attack commands were in Chinese. He was a vicious dog and only three other people besides Junior could come into the apartment without Craig. If you didn't know it was the projects, you would have thought you were in a posh apartment in Trump Towers. Craig had Italian leather furniture in the living room with plush carpeting and a big screen television with cable. The kitchen had a dishwasher installed and all three bedrooms had king-sized bedroom sets with thirty-six-inch Sony televisions.

When Junior walked into Craig's room, Midnight came behind him and snarled a little. It was instinctive because no one was allowed into Craig's room if he wasn't present. It took some time, but Craig had trained Midnight to let Junior go in without him being there, and it seemed that now Midnight was just letting Junior know it was OK, but not to make any funny moves. Midnight was just protecting his master's property. Junior understood because Craig's room was where all the money and drugs were kept when he re-upped for the projects. But Craig never kept all the money or drugs in there for more than eight hours.

Junior took out four thousand dollars. He was going to give Shondra fifteen hundred, and then he had to pay off some of the lookouts he had in the projects who La didn't know were out there. He walked into the kitchen and got his gun from the freezer. Craig had at least two guns in every room of the apartment, even in the hallway. Junior was taking his gun because he was going to Baptiste. Although there were guns already out there, he didn't want to get caught driving up without one on him. He had spoken with La and La said that nothing had jumped off since he'd been back out there, and that the operation was going strong. Junior believed him but wanted to be prepared if something did jump off.

Once downstairs Junior saw that Craig was raking the players in the dice game. Most of them had somber looks on their faces. Junior walked up to Craig and told him he took some money and his gun and was on his way to drop off Shondra at home.

"Yo, Tiko, take the bank for me while I talk to my cuz real quick," he told one of his young workers. He put his arm around Junior's shoulder and walked with him toward Junior's rented car.

"You sure you aight going back ova there?"

"I'm good. I been through there droppin' off work. Plus, since La's been over there he ain't had no problems."

Craig stopped midway to the car out of earshot from everyone in the parking lot.

"The one that was stayin' ova here with you after that shit jumped off?"

"Yeah, you know he got it jumpin' over there again."

"Oh word? So shit still movin' out there?"

"Yeah, he doin' like seven thousands dollars a week. I need to be over there so I can watch that money and the workers, you know what I'm sayin'?"

"I hear you, cuz. Just be careful. You know you gotta keep your eyes open at all times. Now you have to watch out for the Ds and that nigga, and if you hear something you gotta handle your business. Make the barrel bend. You understand me?"

"I got you, cuz. I see how shit really goes down now."

"You got your burner, right?"

Junior pulled up his shirt, revealing the black pistol in his waist, and Craig flashed him an approving smile.

"You gonna start chillin' back ova there, huh?" he asked. He wanted to make sure his cousin was ready and not frontin' for him.

"Not like that. I'm just gonna pick up the paper and make sure everything is everything and then I'll be back over there full time, eventually. I want to take care of that nigga first before I get back in my groove ova there so that'll be one less thing for me to worry about while I'm out there. I need to take my guns back over there before I get too relaxed. I'll talk to you about that a lil later on. OK, I'm out."

Shondra had fallen asleep again and Junior pulled off and headed for Baptiste projects to drop her off and finally check on La.

L. J. Miller

Chapter 10
Nobody is ready for change.

"What's wrong, baby?" Gloria asked KB as she got up from the bed. KB had not been responding to her sexual advances for weeks, and she was worried that he might be seeing someone else. This was the first time he wasn't reacting to her sexually, and she knew something was wrong. She just didn't know what. "You all right, honey?" she asked again with worry in her voice.

"Yeah, I'm OK," he said with no real emotion at all.

Since the robbery KB had been uneasy because Roughhouse had died and he felt a sense of responsibility. It had been on the front page of the *Daily News* the next day, and the article said the police had promising leads on the assailants. No police or detectives had been to his mother's house inquiring, and none of the guys said anything about detectives or police paying them a visit. Stump was acting as if nothing tragic had happened that day, and when KB spoke to him on the phone, he was already planning another job for them.

The last time KB saw all the guys was when they went to Stump's house to split up the money. There was over two hundred fifty thousand dollars, and they split it equally five ways with Roughhouse's cut going to his mother and sister. They didn't know where the money came from because Stump had someone send it to them anonymously to help with the funeral. Stump told the guys that they couldn't attend the funeral because it would probably be swarming with undercover cops looking for anyone that could give them information on the robbery, and he didn't want anyone to take the chance.

Roughhouse died a terrible death and KB couldn't get the image of him trying to make it to the van out of his mind. Nor could he get over how he was the one to make the fatal decision to leave Roughhouse behind. This was really tearing him down mentally, but he couldn't tell Gloria because he didn't want to chance it leaking out and getting him locked up. He didn't want any mistakes or sorries. If he was implicated in the robbery, he would be going down for murder, and that carried a sentence of twenty-five years to life.

"You look like you're deep in thought. I know something's wrong, baby, because you've been so restless at night and jumping in your sleep. Tell me. Maybe I can help you, honey. I'm here for you, K. I want to be here for you."

"I told you it was nothing!"

"Now I know it's really something since you flippin' on me for being concerned about you. Whatever it is, baby, I'm not the cause, and if I am let me know and I'll change. If I did something, K, please tell me. I'll make it right, I promise. I love you, baby. It bothers me to see you like this, especially since I know you're not really like this. Please, baby, I just want to help you. Don't you understand?"

KB didn't want her to think it had anything to do with her. He didn't want her to blame herself, so against his better judgment he decided to tell her what had happened. He was hoping that telling her would ease his mind because he hadn't told anyone about the robbery since it happened, and it was eating away at him inside.

"Come ova here," KB told her.

Gloria had a look of horror on her face as he told her the complete story from the beginning to the tragic end. After he finished telling her she sat on the bed with her mouth wide open. She had heard about the robbery on the news, but never dreamed KB was involved. She didn't believe he was capable of doing shit like that. KB looked at her and tried to reassure her that he wasn't in danger of getting locked up because the police didn't have any evidence on who committed the crime. She looked at KB, not knowing who he really was at that moment. Gloria knew KB was sort of thuggish, but she didn't know he was into what he had just told her. Four people died because of what he did. She was wondering if he was capable of harming her if she were ever to do anything to him he believed warranted that kind of behavior. KB was looking at her with a blank look on his face. She wasn't afraid of him. She was more in shock about what he had told her.

"K, baby, I don't know what to tell you," she finally said. "I mean, I don't know what to say to that. One thing I do know is that I will stand by you no matter what. I love you, K, and I'm going to do whatever I can to help you whenever you need me."

KB looked Gloria square in her eyes and couldn't believe he had just told her what happened that day, but what really had him bugging was that she said she was with him no matter what. He had never met anyone that felt that way about him, and he could tell she was sincere by the tone of her voice and the expression on her face.

"Yo, ma, you don't know how much that means to me. This has been worrying me because I don't want to get caught behind this bullshit, and I feel fucked up because I feel like I'm the reason the nigga is dead."

"Look, K, I knew something was bothering you because you been actin' real funny and shit. I thought you was seeing another bitch or something because I couldn't get you to perform in bed like you normally do."

"You know I would never step out on you, Glo. You the best thing that I ever did. You're all I need. I love you, too, girl, for life."

They both lay on the bed and she began to stroke him gently. He responded by moving with her hand in an up and down motion. She pulled down the zipper on his Iceberg jeans and pulled out his manhood. She slid her wet mouth over his hardness and began to suck him slowly, looking up at him as she continued to slurp him. He was enjoying it. His eyes were closed and he was moaning every time she sucked his tip. She was glad to be pleasing him, and she sucked him harder until she felt his spasms. He was about to explode and she could feel his shaft pulsating in her mouth before his eruption. The lower part of KB's body began to move left to right quickly. She applied pressure to his hips and moved her mouth up and down, sucking hard as she came down. He exploded into her mouth and she could feel the warm and creamy liquid shoot straight down her throat. It was salty and it was the first time she had ever swallowed a baby, but her intentions were to solidify her relationship with KB. This would definitely seal the deal. She finished sucking him dry as a desert and he became limp and unable to move. She had drained all his energy. Gloria got up off him and admired his limp body lying there, not able to move. She was just that good. She was good enough to satisfy her man and have him love her for real.

KB and Gloria hopped into a cab after checking out of the hotel. Gloria had her head on his shoulder as the cab sped across the Williamsburg Bridge. KB was taking her home. They were planning to go away for the weekend, so he wanted to see Stump before he left to let him know he was gonna be gone for about three or four days. He wanted to spend some of the money he had made on Gloria. Stump told him there was another hit that was supposed to be taking place real soon once he got the details. Although the last robbery didn't go right, and Roughhouse got murdered, KB did like the payoff. He made more money on that one robbery than most people in the hood made in a year. He knew the risks were high, but all he did was drive the getaway car. He really wasn't involved in the more dangerous part of the stickup, and he still got an even split. What better way to make money?

Gloria woke up when the cab pulled up in front of her building, and they both got out and went into her building.

"Hold up," she said as KB pushed the button for the elevator. "Let me go knock on my sista's door and see if she's home."

"Aight. I'll see you upstairs."

"No, I want you to meet her. She's been dying to meet you. I told her so much about us and how you got me strung out, and she wants to see the nigga that got her sister's nose open."

"All right, I'll meet her."

Gloria knocked on the door and waited for someone to answer. KB stayed down by the elevators, not really wanting to meet Shondra. He knew she was Junior's girl, and he didn't know if she knew he was down with Stump or that he was there the night of the shootout. KB was careful not to tell Gloria he was there that night because he wasn't sure if she would tell Shondra, and he couldn't risk that. He wasn't sure if Junior knew he was there that night, but he knew how the hood talked. Just in case, he fixed the gun in his belt and leaned against the door of the elevator. Gloria was about to leave when she heard the locks on the door start clicking.

"Who is it?"

"It's me."

The door opened and Shondra's little brother Tim was standing in the doorway wearing plaid boxers.

"Shondra's not here, Gloria."

"You know where she at?"

"I don't know."

"All right, Tim. Whenever she gets in, tell her to come upstairs. I don't care what time it is."

"I'll tell her."

Just about at the same time Gloria was talking to Tim, Junior and Shondra pulled up in front of her building and sat in the car talking. While they were conversing, Junior was looking around to see who was out. He hadn't told La he was coming by because he wanted to see if the operation ran exactly the way he said it did. There was a young guy standing on the corner of the building across the street, obviously the lookout. Another guy was standing in front of the building. He had to be the one serving the heads. Junior watched as a customer came up to the guy in front of the building and how he sent him inside to cop. He observed the lookout on the corner who nodded his head, letting the seller know that everything was clear. After about thirty seconds he went inside the building and the lookout seemed to be talking into a headset.

Junior was surprised. It looked like La had made some changes to how they served the customers, and it looked like a good system. Junior explained to Shondra what was going on, and they both watched as the two guys rotated positions so if detectives or narcs were riding by they wouldn't see the same person standing on the corner. Junior watched them for about an hour and realized the traffic was steady and the guys were handling their business correctly. Junior was looking at it as if he were a narc. They wouldn't be able to get them on a possession because everything was done out of sight. The operation La had in place looked like it was tight.

When they got into the apartment, Shondra went straight in her room and took off her clothes to take a shower. Junior went into the room, sat on the bed, and turned on the television. It felt funny being in the room and not seeing all the things he usually had there that made it home for him. He lay back on the bed, looked up at the ceiling, and breathed in deeply. He lit a cigarette and closed his eyes. After he finished his cigarette he dozed off until Shondra came out of the shower. When she came into the room she dropped the towel to the floor as she closed the door behind her. The noise of the closing door woke him up. He looked at her as she got the Johnson & Johnson baby oil and sat on the bed. She poured some in the palm of her hand and massaged both hands together, then lifted one of her legs and spread the oil evenly up and down her thick thighs.

Junior got up off the bed and helped her oil her body, caressing her supple breasts and kissing her neck at the same time. She was getting aroused, and he slid his hand down to her split, feeling her wetness mixed with the oil on his hand. She winced a little, and he continued to massage her clit as she lay back on the bed and opened her legs to him invitingly. He placed his tongue on her nipple and felt it harden as he sucked it gently, all the while fingering her sweet, wet insides. She began to move in a circular motion and he switched nipples. Her body felt like silk and he was getting stiff as a log. The bulge in his pants was uncomfortable, but he continued to please her. She began to move to the motions of his fingers, and he switched positions. His hands were on both nipples, squeezing them lightly, and his tongue was licking the hardened clit that was poking out of its hiding place. She whined and squirmed with delight as he continued licking and sucking gently while squeezing her nipples. She let out a loud moan and he knew she was ready to orgasm.

He jumped up off her, stood back, and looked at her body trembling. She looked up at him and gave him a look like a wounded puppy, begging him to finish what he had started. He spread her legs wider and put his face back to where he was before, sucking and licking her rapidly. She exploded immediately and her body shook frantically. He kept his hands locked on her hips like a C-clamp, not allowing her to get away. She was fighting so he would release her, but he kept his grip on her and continued to lick her quickly. She fought so much until another snowy feeling came over her. She was having her second orgasm and she screamed and shook even more violently than the first time, and then she relaxed after some seconds had passed. She closed her eyes, breathing hard, and her body became limp. Her clit felt raw as he slowed down to a light licking. She was finished.

After washing off his face, Junior went back into the room where Shondra was putting on a Nike jumpsuit.

"I'm about to go check on my work," he said to her as he pinched her on her ass.

"OK, baby. I'm gonna go upstairs and see Glo. Tim just told me she was down here looking for me."

Junior fixed his gun in his waistband as he turned and walked out the door.

KB was about to leave Gloria's apartment when Shondra knocked on the door.

"Who is it?" Glo asked as KB stepped away from the door.

"It's me, girl."

Gloria unlocked the door quickly and opened it for her girlfriend. KB sat up on the couch and brushed his pants leg off. Shondra walked into the apartment and hugged Gloria's neck.

"What's up, girl? I missed you."

"I know. I ain't seen you since you been back. Did y'all have a good time?"

"You know I did. Hmmm, you must be KB."

"Yeah, I'm KB," he said, outstretching his hand to hers.

"Oh no, hun," she said, grabbing him and hugging him. "You family. You got my girl all sprung and shit. So how are you? I heard a lot about you."

She purposely hugged him to see if he was strapped. The hard, metal gun that pressed up against her as she hugged him confirmed her suspicions.

"I told you she was cool," Gloria said, smiling.

"Yeah," he said, blushing slightly. Shondra did seem cool to him. She gave him a nice reception and he had expected her to give off some negative vibes.

Shondra thought KB was a handsome dude. She liked his build and he dressed nice. He had a boyish look to him and he seemed a little on the shy side.

"So, Mr. KB, you from Williamsburg, I hear?"

"Yeah."

"My girl tells me that you the man in her life now. You better treat her right or you're gonna have to deal with me."

"I'm goin' to go get that blunt from the room. Don't scare my baby off now, girl." Gloria said leaving Shondra and KB alone in the living room.

"So what you do, mystery man? Seems like you don't talk much."

"I just be chillin', you know."

"How long you lived in the 'Burg?"

"All my life."

"What side you live on?"

"Meserole."

"Oh, so you must know Gino and them niggas?"

"Yeah, I know Gino. We went to the same school."

"You seem cool, KB. I hope I'm not being too nosey asking you twenty-one questions and shit, but that's my girl and she really likes you. I just want to make sure that you and her vibin' on the same shit, you know what I mean?"

"I hear you. She told me how she used to be and how you changed her. I respect that about her because she didn't have to tell me shit, but on the same token, I can't say where we'll end up, but I'm feelin' her. That's why I made her my girl."

127

"Roll this shit up," Gloria said to Shondra as she came back into the room, passing her a blunt. "We should all go out sometime," Gloria suggested. "Me, you, KB, and Junior."

That statement took both Shondra's and KB's breath away. Now both their identities were confirmed for each other. KB looked at Shondra to see what she was gonna say to the suggestion.

"That'll be cool. We should hook up and go out," she replied, licking the blunt, then lighting it. She kept her cool because she had anticipated Junior's name coming up.

"We goin' to Atlantic City this weekend," Gloria said as she passed the blunt to KB.

"That's cool. What hotel y'all stayin' in?" she asked KB directly. "Caesar's Palace's rooms are nice, especially the suite."

"I'm thinking about the Trump Plaza," he replied as he checked his pager. "I gotta use the phone, Glo. 'Scuse me, Shondra," he said as he got up and walked out the room to use the phone.

"Damn, he don't talk much, do he?"

"Not really. I told him about that. He all anti-social and shit."

"Well do he at least talk to you? I mean, does he tell you anything about himself, like personal shit?"

"Yeah, we talk, but he's not really big on talking."

"You need to know your man, girl, like who his homeboys are, and where he at when he not with you."

"You don't even know where your man is twenty-four seven, girl. You know how niggas is," Gloria said almost defensively.

"Bullshit. I know where he tells me he is. He don't necessarily have to be there but he do tell me and I do know who his homeboys are," Shondra replied, letting Gloria know that her relationship was a far cry from what Gloria was dealing with.

"I know, girl. I just don't want to seem like I'm sweating his every move. I don't want to push the nigga away by being too much in his business. You understand what I mean?" Gloria was being sincere. She had always wanted a good man, and KB seemed like he was the one. He treated her nice and she didn't want to do anything to mess up what she had with him, although she always listened to Shondra when it came to men.

"I hear you, girl, but you need to know more about him. I'm not sayin' he hidin' shit from you. I'm just sayin' you need to know who you fuckin'."

"I know."

"Look, Glo, you know I want you to be happy. I just don't want you to slip up and make any more mistakes with no-good-ass niggas. I'm not saying that KB is a no-good nigga. I'm just making sure that you know more than just his name for your own benefit."

KB walked back into the room and Shondra got quiet. Gloria stared at the floor.

"I got to make a run real quick, hun. I'll be back lata on tonight," KB said as he headed to the door.

"OK, baby."

Shondra looked at him and wondered where he was going. She watched as he kissed Gloria passionately. She saw how Gloria melted right there in front of him, not hiding her emotions. She had thoughts of how Junior was so much like that, even after they'd been together over four years. Gloria went out into the hallway with KB and asked him where he was going. She was unconsciously doing exactly what Shondra wanted her to do.

"I'm goin' to handle some business."

"I'm just askin' because I hope you're not goin' to fuck wit' that nigga, Stump."

"That's my man, baby. No matter what happens, that's my man. You gotta understand that."

"I just don't want you to get into any more trouble. That's all, baby," she said, rubbing his back.

"I'm good. Don't worry," he replied as he pressed the button for the elevator.

Gloria walked back inside the apartment and held her arms out for a hug.

"What's that for, girl?" Shondra asked.

"Because I know you love me and only want the best for me."

"You know that, girl."

Gloria was holding Shondra tight and Shondra sensed something was wrong.

"What's wrong, Glo?"

"It's KB. I do know something about him, and it's bothering me."

"What is it?"

"You remember that shit that happened by Lindsey Houses, the coke spot that got robbed?"

"Yeah, I think so. Didn't like three or four people get killed?"

"Well KB and his crew was the ones that hit that store. They robbed and killed the two Dominican guys and one of his homeboys died fighting off one of the other Dominican niggas. They had to leave him because he couldn't make it to the getaway car," she told Shondra, almost sobbing.

Shondra was shocked to hear that KB was involved in that robbery, but then her mind shifted and remembered he was capable of doing something like that because he tried to rob her man. She began to wonder whether the outcome would have been similar if KB and Stump had succeeded in robbing Junior.

"Damn, that's fucked up. He don't look like that kind of dude."

"Looks can be deceiving. That's why I said you were right, because I wouldn't have found that out about him if I didn't push the issue."

"Well tell me something, who was the guys he did it with?"

"Some nigga named Stump. He 'posed to be the ringleader, and then there were some other dudes. I can't remember their names."

"You ever meet the one named Stump? Where he live at?"

"Nope, I never met him, but I do know he live in Bushwick projects because that's where KB said they met to go over the details before they did the robbery, and that's where they split up the money."

"That's right. The news said they got away with something like two hundred thousand. KB must got some money now."

"Yeah, that's how we goin' away for the weekend. He said he wanted to spend some of the money on me."

"Well I'm gonna go back downstairs 'cause I'm tired as hell. Come down in the morning so we can finish talking, and let me know when y'all leaving, all right, girl?"

"All right. I'll be down there in the morning. See ya later."

***

When Junior got to Rock's building there were a bunch of young guys standing in the front. They were staring at him hard and he didn't recognize any of the faces. One of the guys blocked the entrance, making Junior go around him to get into the building. Junior braced himself to swing at the guy, but the young boy was ready and swung on Junior first. The right hook to Junior's jaw made him fall back onto the black fence. As he stumbled backward he pulled out the silver nine millimeter and took off the safety. He pointed the gun toward the guy that hit him and then fanned it around to the crowd of guys that looked like they were ready to run.

"Back the fuck up!"

"Be easy, duke," the one that hit him said.

Junior walked up to him and put the gun to his face, patting him down to make sure he didn't have a burner on him. Then Junior turned to the other guys and told all of them to lift up their shirts and turn around to make sure they were unarmed as well.

"What the fuck? Y'all lil niggas don't know who I am?" he asked with a look of death in his eyes. Junior didn't know if the guys were part of Stump's goons, so he prepared himself to kill all of them in an instant if they were.

"Nah, man, we don't know you. Who you?"

Junior looked at him and swung the gun at his head. At the same time he squeezed the trigger, making it discharge. The guy dropped to the ground holding his head with both hands. The other guys thought Junior had shot their friend in the head because it happened so fast. All their expressions changed to fear.

"I'm the nigga that did this to you!" He turned to the other guys. "If y'all don't know me, you better get to know me, or fuck around and wind up wit' a hole in your forehead."

All the guys looked at Junior and figured they had fucked with the wrong nigga. They all stood there wondering if he was going to do something to them next. The young guy he hit was on the ground in a fetal position holding his head, moaning as Junior stepped over him and grabbed him by his shirt.

"Who you down wit, nigga? And if you lie to me, get ready to close your eyes for good!"

"I ain't wit nobody. This my crew."

"I should kill you!" Junior whispered in his ear. His voice was laced with cyanide as he said it.

"Yo, man, I swear I ain't down wit nobody." He cried. "Please, man, don't do this to me."

Junior stepped over him, went into the building, and ran up the stairs to see if Rock was home. He wasn't worried about the young boys because after what he had just done to their man, they knew they were fucking with a soldier. They would remember Junior and make sure they wouldn't make the same mistake again.

La and Rock were in the hallway when Junior came out of the exit. They had heard a gunshot and was going to investigate.

"Whaddup, Junior?" La asked as he walked over to give him five.

"Ain't nothin'. I just pistol-whipped some lil niggas in front of the building."

"Word, what happened?" Rock asked, pulling out his gun.

"The nigga stole off on me and I pulled out my gat and split his wig."

"Come on, let's go back down there and see who them young cats was," La said, already running down the stairs. La really didn't like the fact that Junior had popped up on them like that, and he wanted to show Rock he was in charge by acting like he could put everything back in order.

"I handled that shit already," Junior said. "They don't want it. Trust me."

"Well we gon' make sure them lil' niggas don't violate like that again," Rock said. "This my fuckin' building, and I don't remember hiring no security guards."

They ran down the stairs, but by the time they got outside the young crew that was out there was gone. There was blood on the ground, though—evidence that Junior handled the situation effectively.

"I see you put in a lot of work," La said as he headed toward the back of the building. "Them lil niggas couldn't have gotten far."

They spotted the crew of guys walking toward Bushwick projects.

"That's probably them right there!" Rock said, running towards the group of guys walking..

"Aaaay, yoooo!" he yelled. The kids turned around and saw Junior, Rock, and La, and they took off running up the Ave.

"Y'all better stop before I send some slugs at y'all lil asses!" Rock yelled, running with the gun in plain sight.

Two of them stopped and the rest kept running. Rock caught up with the two and told them to tell their homeboys to stop and come back. They complied, and the other three came back, reluctantly copping a plea all the way back.

"Look man, we don't want no beef," one kid said. "Duke already bust Danny in the head."

"Shut the fuck up. I want to know who the fuck y'all lil muhfuckas is!" Rock said.

"I'm Danny," the one that got his head busted said.

"I'm Fizz," the youngest looking one with braids said.

"I'm Darrell," the third one said, looking nervous.

"Leroy," the brown-skinned, skinny one said.

"Jeff," the shortest of the crew said.

La and Junior stood there and just looked at them. They were all no older than fifteen, but they looked like they were down for whatever. La looked at Junior.

"You let them little niggas front on you?" La asked.

"I told you the lil muhfucka stole off on me. Look, La, don't make me body shorty."

"Nah, man, I'm just sayin', shorty must got some heart to front on you like that. I'm not trying to play you. I'm just surprised that these lil niggas was tryin' to muscle you, that's all."

La knew Junior was not a pussy by any sense of the word. He'd seen him fight, bust his gun, and now pistol-whip some niggas.

"Why was y'all niggas posted up in front of my building?" Rock asked.

They looked at each other, then Danny spoke.

"We was tryin' to find a vic."

"In front of my fuckin' building, nigga?" Rock asked with fury in his voice. "Where the fuck y'all from?"

"Bushwick projects."

A light bulb went off in Junior's head. He wondered if he had made a mistake by letting them go. Stump was from Bushwick. Suppose he really did send some amateurs at him. They had definitely caught him slipping.

"Look, youngin's," La started, "I understand y'all tryin' to get money and shit, but y'all can't get it over here like that." Then he looked at Junior. "If you want to make some money, then we can put y'all lil asses to work."

"We're down," Danny said, still holding his head.

"Aight, y'all need to take your boy to Woodhull Hospital to get his head looked at," Rock told them. "And tell them that you fell off the monkey bars or something if they ask how your melon got cracked."

"I'm going to get that nigga back for bustin' my shit like this!" Danny boasted as the boys were walking away and out of earshot from Junior, La, and Rock.

As Rock, La, and Junior headed back to the building, La began telling Junior about the recent news on the streets.

"Yo, Junior, you heard what happened to Kendu?" he asked, not knowing if Junior knew or not.

"Nah, what happened to him?"

"Somebody murdered him in his aunt's crib," La told him. "The police don't know who did it, but I heard one of them niggas over in the Stuy did him. The hood is sayin' that he got killed because he started robbing those young dealers over there, but I don't know how true that is."

"You said he was smoking, right? It might be true then. He might have thought that them little niggas over there didn't put in work if they got robbed. Who knows," Junior said, then continued. "La, I know that was your man and shit, but you know I had beef with that nigga, so I'm not feeling sorry for him like that, because if we would have bumped heads, the same thing would have happened."

"I know. I'm the one that told you what the nigga was up to, remember? Don't sweat that, my nigga. Du knew what he was doing when he started fuckin' with that shit. He saw how that shit fucks niggas up. I talked to the nigga 'bout it, but he denied it. I knew, though, 'specially when he started talking reckless and shit. That was my man and the whole nine, but we make decisions out here in the field and we gotta live with that. I guess I just gotta charge it to the game." La was tried to sound unemotional while he spoke..

"Well it's a done deal now. You gonna hit his fam off with something?"

"It's just his lil brother and his grandma. I hit them off already," La replied.

"That's peace. I'm 'bout to take care of that nigga, Stump. I can't let that shit go like that. That nigga tried to murk me," Junior said.

"I ain't seen that nigga since I been back 'round here. I think he know what time it is," La said.

"If that nigga come 'round here bullshittin', I'm a put two slugs in his dome piece." Rock said.

"Yo, Rock, I gotta talk some business with La, so let us go up to your crib so we can talk privately," Junior said.

"Cool. I'm gonna go on the other side and check up on these niggas and Dusty."

"Ay, Rock, you know you gotta put up your toast before you go over there," La reminded him.

"I know. I stash it near that abandoned building before I get on the block."

"All right, see you in a few," La replied.

Junior and La took the elevator up to the crib and once inside Junior asked La how things were going.

"It's sweet. Shit is really going good. It's been hot out here recently, so I changed the way the workers handle the custies. I make sure that nobody is holding and that there is a lookout for every shift. The one that serves stays out of sight in the building, and the one steering makes sure that the head leaves out the back of the building as soon as they cop. We have headsets that look like a Walkman, and the lookout tells us when he sees Ds coming through. After thirty minutes to an hour everyone rotates their positions. The money that is made is put in a mailbox until Rock or Dusty comes to pick it up. They usually come through every hour, or they chill over there to make sure that shit is running straight. We keep four guns out here, one stashed in the back of the building, one in the building, one across the street in the bushes, and one in a locked mailbox."

"Damn, La, you really impress me. I was watching how this shit was running while I was sitting in front of Shondra's building, and it looks like you got everything under control."

"We pullin' in about ten to fifteen Gs."

"How many workers you got out there?" Junior asked, calculating in his head how many workers were on the payroll.

"I got eight niggas workin', but only three work the overnight shift."

"That's cool. And about them lil niggas from Bushwick, I don't want them on the payroll. I need to take care of that nigga in Bushwick before I try to put work out there, you know what I mean?"

"I don't think that's gonna be a problem. I can have Rock and Dusty watch over them until you take care of that business. Nobody out there gotta know that it's our shit."

"No, La, I don't want them niggas on the payroll. After I take care of that business, then you can recruit them, but not before. You hear what I'm telling you?"

"I hear you."

"Once I take care of that nigga, then we can concentrate on expanding the operation to the other projects around us. I found out that Gloria fuck with the nigga KB. He live in the 'Burg. I still didn't find out what floor Stump lives on yet."

"Shit, we can body that nigga first then," La said, referring to KB.

"Yeah, but I want to get the head of the snake first, you know what I mean?"

"I feel you. Once the head is gone, the rest of the body can't function." La replied.

"In the meantime, we gonna get this money, but we can't sleep on this nigga for shit. I see you holdin' shit down lovely out here right now, but I'm gonna be on the scene again. I'm gonna let you run shit, and I'm gonna play the back so you can shine, my nigga. You good with that?"

"This your shit, son. I'm a lieutenant and you're the general. You just keep shit comin', and I'm gonna keep getting shit off for you."

Junior looked at La, trying to figure out if he was being sincere. Junior had learned from experience that the power of money could make the best of friends turn to enemies. He was hoping La was loyal. He hoped he wasn't making a mistake by leaving La in charge of the operation.

"Oh yeah, the Ds is hot on Rock over here, so he just pick up money. He got picked up with some weed, and since then the Ds been on him every time they see him on the block. He don't hold anymore, so if they roll up they don't get him with nothing but money. When he got picked up I used the money you told me to save in case any of us got locked up. I only spent twenty-five hundred on a lawyer."

"That's cool. Now you know why I said to save that money. See how it comes in handy?"

"You right. I'm glad, too, because I sure wasn't comin' outta my pocket for no lawyer."

"Yeah, but you gotta understand, either way it goes, you have to because if you don't look out for one of your own, they can turn state on you and fuck up your whole operation. So you have to make sure that you take care of them. Once they come home then you can handle them whichever way you see fit."

"I got you, Junior. You right."

"What's up with Dusty?"

"He be watching the workers and paying them at the end of the week. Most of the time he be with that Puerto Rican crack head bitch."

"Who, Lizzette?"

"Yeah, I think she got that nigga sprung on the pussy. He always got the bitch in the crib with him late nights and shit."

"Damn, I didn't know she had him like that."

The last time Junior linked up with Lizzette she was far gone on her drug habit. She beeped him and he told her to meet him at a hotel on Broadway. She still had a nice body, but it wasn't as tight as it was before. When they got into the room she wanted to get high first, and he noticed she wasn't putting it in blunts anymore. She was smoking from the pipe. It was a turnoff for him, but he still let her give him brain. After he busted a load, she wanted another hit, but he wasn't about to give her anymore without any money. She begged and pleaded and offered more sexual favors, but he declined her offer. Then she asked him how long he had the room for so she could get some more money. She left the room and came back about twenty minutes later with about seventy-five dollars. Junior didn't ask her where she got it from. He just gave her the product and let her blast off. While she was getting high she passed him the pipe like she was passing him a blunt. Out of reflex he slapped the shit out of her hand and kicked her out the room. He knew that was a dope fiend move, trying to get him hooked on the drug so she could get high as long as he had product.

"Shiiiit, the bitch don't even give me head no more 'cause he be actin' like that his main shorty," La said.

"Well I hope he don't let that bitch know what he be doin'. When they on that shit ain't no tellin' what they'll do if you don't give them what they want." Junior knew what the outcome of fucking with a fine crack head could be if a nigga wasn't focused.

Junior was really impressed with how La was handling everything, and despite his apparent cockiness, La was in total control of the operation. He did like the fact that he was aware of what was going on, and at the same time made changes when necessary. La had really learned a lot from Junior, and he deserved to be in the position he was in. La was fast becoming Junior's right-hand man, and he hoped things between them wouldn't change. They walked over to the block where La was going to show Junior firsthand how things were running. Junior's pager went off and it was Shondra's code.

"That was Shondra. I'm gonna go see what she wants. I'll meet you in the back of the building in a few."

"Aight. I'll be right here twistin' up this blunt."

Shondra was sitting in the living room when Junior walked through the door.

"Whaddup? Something wrong, baby?"

"Well no, not exactly."

"So what's up?"

"I saw KB. He was upstairs in Gloria's house."

"What!" Junior exclaimed. "He still up there?"

"No, baby, he left a little after I got up there."

"He know that you my girl?"

"Yeah, it came up in conversation. Glo was saying that we all needed to hang out together."

"What did he say when she said that?"

"He didn't say nothin', but that's not what I want to tell you. When he left, Gloria told me that him and Stump are the ones that robbed that coke spot by Lindsey."

"Word? Them niggas the ones that did that shit? One of the dudes got killed doing that shit."

"I know, baby. That's why I want you to be careful when it comes to KB."

"He told her that shit?"

"She said he told her everything in detail."

"He a stupid muhfucka. He don't even know her like that. Suppose she gets heated wit' him, his ass is finished. And they'll charge him for those bodies too. He good for twenty-five to life for that shit."

"I thought about that too, but she ain't gonna drop dime on that nigga. She in love with him already. I can see it in her eyes and hear it in her voice when she speaks the nigga's name."

"Did she say where he was going when he left?"

"No. I left right after him to let you know what I found out."

"I need to hurry up and get at them niggas."

"Junior, I got faith in everything you do. I just want you to be careful. I don't trust him and Stump."

"I wonder if he told her if they planning on trying to get at me again?"

"I don't know. She didn't mention anything like that to me. As far as I know, she don't know that KB had anything to do with that shootout with you."

"I know that's your girl and everything, but I doubt she would tell you if he did tell her anything about getting me, especially if he got her fucked up on him the way you say he do. There ain't no way she gonna give up info like that. Trust me."

"You right, baby. So what you gonna do?"

"What I need to do is find out how this money is flowing out here. That's what I need to do."

"Be careful, Junior," she said, hugging his neck. "I love you."

"You heard that Kendu got murdered, right?"

"No, I didn't hear nothin' 'bout that."

"La told me that some niggas in the Stuy bodied him because he was running around robbing dealers out there."

"So how La takin' it?"

"I know that was La's man and all, but you know I was gonna set it on him for tryin' to set me up. I think La dealin' with it, but at the same time I ain't grieving for that nigga. La said that he was smoking that shit, so he gotta charge it to the game. I think that shit clouded the nigga's judgment and he just started making fucked up moves."

"Well you know you can't trust everybody and everything, Junior," she said. "That was his homeboy from back in the day. They grew up together, so you know he gotta be feelin' bad." She felt as if Junior had something to do with Kendu's death, but he just wasn't telling her.

"Yeah, but you know niggas get older, and with age comes wisdom. I think La is starting to see that this game is real and you have to stay true to it or become a victim. Du *was* a good nigga, but he let the game control his actions instead of letting his actions control the game. La knew what the outcome was gonna be when he told me what the nigga was planning. I guess he stayed on the winning side, for now."

"You need to be careful, Junior. Everything is starting to change. Are you ready for the change?"

"Nobody is ready for change. You just have to be aware and make adjustments. I see that everything is different since that night. That's why I'm taking these calculated steps. I'm making sure that there's no mistake when I go after those dudes. Don't worry, Mooka, change is inevitable, and knowing that change is coming puts me one step ahead of everyone else. Being ready is a state of mind. I'm processing what happened and making the necessary moves to make sure that I don't come out in a body bag. I was born ready. I got the best of both worlds, ma," he said as he closed the door behind him.

KB was sitting down in Stump's living room listening intently to the details of the new robbery he was planning. He was looking at Stump thinking he was really crazy. Stump wanted to stick up a club. The same crew from the last robbery was there minus Roughhouse. It felt awkward to be sitting in the same spot again going over the finer points of the robbery, knowing what had happened the last time. Stump had set it up near perfectly. The one thing he didn't incorporate into the plan was someone coming into the spot and resisting the robbery, and that's how Roughhouse got killed. There was a new face in the crew that KB didn't recognize, and Stump didn't formally introduce him. He looked younger than KB and had a long scar down the side of his face, which made him look especially grimy and treacherous. He didn't really seem interested in what Stump was saying. He seemed more focused on Stump himself and KB was wondering if Stump or the other guys peeped it. It was funny they weren't introduced, especially since he knew everybody there but him. KB made a mental note to watch the new guy's every move when the day came to do the stickup. He didn't trust homeboy for a second.

"My man is a bouncer at Love Castle, the club on Flushing Ave.," Stump was explaining. "Him and his crew will be at the front door so it's gonna be easy for us to get our guns in. He said the owner is a big heroin dealer and keeps most of the dough from his transactions in a safe in his office upstairs and that picks up the money on Saturday nights while the club is in full swing. On that night some dude is throwin' a party for his man that just came home from up north, so that can be more money because he said duke is a big time coke dealer from Manhattan. We're gonna rob everybody in the club, plus the owner. We can pull it off because there won't be no guns in there but ours, except for the owner, but I'm gonna have the drop on him."

KB was looking around the room as Stump was talking. All the guys had their eyes fixed on him as if he was a preacher giving a sermon, and none seemed apprehensive about the details of the crime, but KB wasn't feeling him when he said he wanted to rob everybody in the club. He felt if the party was for a big-time dealer then most of the patrons would be dealers and would make the robbery much more difficult because they wouldn't be willing victims. KB had a bad feeling about this one. He didn't want to be down, but he didn't know how to back out of it.

Stump finished explaining the details of the job and told everyone it would be about three weeks before everything would go down, but he wanted everyone to meet at his house the night before the robbery so he could go over everyone's jobs. He also wanted everyone to stay at his place that night so they could go to the club the next morning together to check out the layout and go over how everything was supposed to go down. Once everyone agreed to the plan, all the guys got up and left. When KB was on his way out the door, Stump called him back.

"What's up, nigga?" Stump asked.

"Nuthin'."

"I still ain't forgot about that lil nigga from Baptiste that was bustin' at me. You been 'round there lately?"

"Nah, man, I been chillin', spending that dough," KB lied.

"When I catch that lil muhfucka, I'm gonna body him. He probably thinking shit is sweet because I ain't been back out there at his punk ass, but I had to take care of that coke spot first, you know what I mean? You know what happened to the other kid, right?"

"Who, Kendu? Man, somebody killed that nigga."

"I know. My man Drez, the one with the long scar, he the one that bodied him. Just so happens that the faggot ass nigga robbed one of his workers. He lucky I ain't catch his ass first. One down and one to go. You gotta find out if Junior still be over there getting money. If he is, let me know. I'm not gonna wait like I did the first time. Soon as you find out, make sure you let me know. You ready to do this next stick I got set up, nigga?" he asked KB as if he knew he had cold feet.

"I'm ready. How much dough you think is gonna be up in there that night?"

"I'm thinking like 350 Gs altogether. It could be more. Everybody in the club that night is gonna be a bonus, feel me?"

"That's a lot of dough, and I ain't even spent all that other dough yet." KB said.

"Shit, all that dough, that wasn't shit. I probably got fifteen Gs left from that shit. I don't hold onto money like that because it got blood on it. I try to spend it as soon as I get it." Stump informed KB.

"After this stick I'ma go away for a minute, ya know what I'm sayin'?"

"Where you goin', nigga? After this stick I got another one set up and I need you to drive for me."

"How long after? I mean, I just wanna go away for a little vacation."

KB needed to get away for a while because he wasn't really into the robbing and murder he had experienced since hanging with Stump.

"I want to hit this jewelry spot after the club. My man's sister works there and she told him that her boss be having jewelry that's imported from Italy. He be dropping off half a mil or better to the spot."

"So when you gonna have it all set up?"

"Probably like a week or so after this one, but we gotta do it on a Thursday because the nigga only comes there once a month. When he comes he drops off enough shit 'cause he a wholesaler for all the expensive jewelry shops."

"I'm down," KB said, trying to act like he was really with it.

"All right, just make sure when I beep you, you call me right back. I need everybody to be at my crib at the same time, so don't be late." Stump closed the door as KB walked out.

La and Rock were in the back of the building smoking weed when Junior walked up on them. They were sitting on some benches next to the back door with their backs to him.

"Pass Junior the blunt," La said to Rock without turning around.

"Yo, how you know it was me?"

"I told you I got this shit on lock. They let me know anytime somebody comes through the front or back of the building while I'm out here," he said, revealing the small walkie-talkie he had next to him.

"I'm feeling this. I like the way you got this shit clicking," Junior said, passing the blunt back to Rock.

"I like it too. It makes the po-po's job harder. They won't ever catch anybody dirty out here. I'm ready to start doing hand-to-hand and make some extra money," Rock said, mimicking like he was serving a crack head.

"You ready to start . . . shiiit, I'm ready to start with the way things going over here. The only thing you gotta worry about is running out of product," La said.

"And that's not gonna happen because I got that shit covered," Junior said.

Junior sat back there and watched as the heads came through the front and exited through the back of the building. Rock was the enforcer on his shift. He was there in case any stickup kids came or a head tried to get fast with the money. He kept a steel pipe and wooden plank with nails in the grass by the door.

Rock once used the plank on a crack head that thought because he was older than one of the workers he could get over on him threatening him with bodily injury if he didn't give up the drugs. The worker gave the crack head the drugs, and when the head left out the front of the building with the product he radioed to Rock and told him what had happened. Rock caught the head as he rounded the corner and hit him in his knees with the wooden plank. The crack head screamed as he hit the ground, holding his knee. Rock swung at his head, missing intentionally to scare him. The crack head had his hands up in the air pleading with Rock, but Rock wasn't interested in what he had to say. All he wanted the crack head to know was he didn't tolerate any robbing of the workers. He made him empty his pockets and took back the product that the crack head stole. Rock did let him keep what he copped fairly, and then he helped the crack head to his feet and hit him one more time in the gut to let him know he meant business. Rock never said a word when he beat the crack head because he wanted him to wonder how he knew he had robbed his worker. He wouldn't try it again, and probably would warn any other unsuspecting crack heads thinking of robbing any of the workers that it wasn't worth the ass whooping.

Junior saw about four Gs move in the three hours he was out there with them. He was very impressed with La, and the only thing that would make everything complete would be when he got

Stump and KB. Then he would feel a little more safer about being out there. If he got Stump, then the word would be out that he was not to be fucked with, although most niggas had already figured that out since the shootout he had with Stump. The hood always knew more than the police. It knew Junior would bust his gun if needed, and it didn't matter who it was. Junior took solace in knowing that even though he was never confronted with any problems like that before, he had handled the situation well. When he had the shootout with Stump, he was scared at first, but when he heard the sound of the gunfire he had got extremely confident about what he was doing. That feeling could be contributed to him just going into survival mode when confronted by a dangerous situation, but in any case, he felt in complete control of the situation.

After the shootout Junior's attitude changed drastically. He always knew that as a hustler he would encounter dangerous situations, but until it actually happened to him, it isn't real. Stump opened up the reality of what Junior was doing, and if Junior planned to stay in the game, he had to adapt and have a killer instinct to ensure his continued existence. He had to take off the kid gloves because although he didn't think he was a major player to the niggas in that hood, he was. In the neighboring projects like Williamsburg and Bushwick, there were hustlers getting their grind on, but Junior was the first, real dealer in Baptiste Plaza. Junior always believed the niggas that lived in Baptiste never thought about selling drugs because they didn't have a capitalist spirit like him.

***

Junior remembered how he began hustling. After living with Shondra for a while, he noticed her oldest sister Dee Dee always had shady looking characters coming in and out of the house late at night. But it wasn't until one night when someone came to the door looking for her that he realized she was smoking. Dee Dee didn't have the look—you know, the missing teeth, dirty clothes—nor did she have the characteristics, like the constant game to get money or the habit of stealing. However, the person on the other side of door had the seasoned look of a smoked out crack head. Apparently Dee Dee gave the crack head money to cop what she wanted and they would get high together in her room.

After a while, Junior heard Dee Dee arguing with the person in the room because she obviously wasn't getting her money's worth. The crack head apparently was tapping the bottle before he gave her the drugs. Because of the recurring incident of getting beat out of her money, Dee Dee started to cop for herself, and that's when the effects of the drug started to show. Dee Dee began stealing from her mother and started making up excuses of why she always needed money. She would take her food stamps and sell them for cash to obtain the hard, white rocks that came in little plastic vials. Junior would watch as Shondra and her mother unsuccessfully tried to get her off the drug by taking her money away from her and trying to keep her in the house, but it was all in vain. She was already hooked to the point where she could lie with a straight face and cry on cue.

Junior never felt any real sympathy for Dee Dee. He just didn't like to see what she was doing to his girl and her mother. Dee Dee would be out on a mission all night, then come in early the next morning and sleep all day.

One night Junior stood outside and watched how many times she went to Williamsburg. He counted about twenty times, and if she was copping at five dollars a hit, that was at least one hundred dollars, and in just one night. Then he wondered how much he could make if he had all the heads in the projects coming to him. The next day he decided to call his man Shon from Farragut projects. Shon was one of the biggest dealers in his projects. Junior had kept in touch with him through the years, so when he was ready to be introduced to the game, Junior went to see him.

"Yo, Shon, I want to get started in the game," he said.

"Word, kid? I thought you said you wasn't gonna fuck with this shit. What happened? You seeing green skies now?" he asked, wiping down his all-white BMW 525.

"Where my girl live at, ain't nobody slingin'. I want to open up shop ova there."

"What projects you talkin' 'bout?"

"Never mind all that. Just let me know if you can put the God on or not."

"I can do that. I sell jumbos. I got the biggest nicks this side of the projects and in the Fort. That's why them niggas over there hot with me. They clientele come way uptown to cop my shit."

"I got two hundred dollars. Let me get forty jumbos. I'mma break them down to regular nicks and see if I can get it poppin' ova there."

"All right, but you could come off better if you let me hit you off with a pack and we split sixty forty. That way you don't have to worry about baggin' shit up."

"Nah, that's all right. I don't wanna work for nobody, plus if something goes wrong, that'll kill our friendship, and I like you just the way you are."

"I hear you. You don't want to play Indian. You want to be chief. I can respect that."

Junior took the work Shon gave him and stopped off to the smoke shop on Broadway and Myrtle to get some vials to start his new career in drug selling. Once in Shondra's room he emptied all the vials out onto a mirror and transferred the contents into the smaller vials, doubling the amount he started with. He went out in the front of the building to find a crack head to test his work. He was hoping it would be better than whatever they were copping from Williamsburg and Bushwick, so he could stop the traffic and have them come to where he was selling. When the head came back, his eyes were wide and his mouth was twisted. He was nodding his head, letting Junior know the product was good. Junior told him for every five new customers the crack head brought to him, Junior would give him one free. The head agreed, and by the next morning Junior had sold out.

"Damn", he thought to himself. I just doubled my money in one night. This is where it's at.

Junior went to see Shon again and spent all of what he had made that night and continued to do this for months until one day his cousin asked him who he was copping from. Junior told him he was getting the jumbos from Shon and breaking them down. When his cousin heard that he laughed out loud and told him he was getting beat every time he spent a gee with Shon. He informed Junior that he could buy the crack in weight from Manhattan. Junior was happy with the money he was making, but hearing he could make more, he decided to see what his cousin was talking about.

Junior remembered hearing his cousin talk about going uptown on 141st and Amsterdam, so he immediately took a trip uptown to find out how he could get his own product. Blind to the fact of where he was going, he was determined to cut his spending with Shon and possibly triple his profits.

That's how Shon's able to sell jumbos. Slick mulhfucka, and he wasn't gonna tell me shit. He was gonna keep lettin' me cop from him at regular price, Junior thought.

A Dominican guy walked up to Junior and asked him if he was looking to cop. Junior was taken off guard at the shady character that was speaking to him in broken English.

"What you got?"

"We got hard and soft. What ju lookin' for?"

Junior didn't know what he meant by hard or soft, so he said hard because he thought that must mean crack.

"OK, come weet me," the Dominican said as Junior followed him around a corner. As he followed him other Dominican guys were yelling for him to cop with them.

"How much you spendin', papi?" Junior's Dominican asked once they reached their destination.

"I got a gee."

The Dominican pulled out a calculator and started pressing buttons.

"I give you fifty-nine grams, papi."

"All right," Junior said, not knowing how much that really was.

"Give me the money," the Dominican man said while holding out his hand.

"Nah, papi, I gotta see the shit first," Junior said, wondering if he was about to be robbed.

"OK, papi, my name is Raul. I go get it for you. Stand in the hallway, OK?"

If Junior had given him the money first, the guy never would have come back. It would have been a rookie mistake Junior would have just had to take as a loss.

"All right, Raul, I'm Junior," he replied, shaking his hand. "If this shit is good, then you'll see me again real soon."

"I got fish scale, papi, the best perico out here. Ju be back, trust me," he said as he ran up the stairs.

When he came back they made the transaction and he gave Junior a Ziploc bag filled with three slabs of beige, crystallized rocks that looked as if they were cut from a pie pan. Junior put the bag in the front of his pants and got ready to walk out of the building.

"Wait, papi, let me go first to make sure it clear."

Junior stayed by the door, peeking out through the plate glass window. He watched as the Dominican man motioned for him to come out. As Junior exited, he left in the opposite direction from which he originally came, and headed to the A train on 145th Street.

Junior didn't know how much fifty-nine grams normally costs, but when he got back to Shondra's house and made the calculations, he figured that he was paying seventeen dollars a gram. He bagged up the whole thing and came out with approximately thirty-four hundred dollars worth of merchandise, which gave him a nice profit. He almost let out a loud yelp as he thought about how he had shortchanged himself the whole time he was copping from Shon where he was just doubling his money. Now it was on.

Junior had plans of blowing up, and he was going to use those projects as his stepping-stone to success. He was the youngest dealer in the area at the tender age of seventeen, and he was his own boss. He was making more money than he had ever seen, and he was enjoying it. He was learning the game fast, and he soon became a threat to the other dealers in the neighboring hoods. He realized how Shon was able to sell jumbos and incorporated those same tactics, beginning to take over the drug business in Shondra's area.

At that time, things were good, but Junior was soon to find out that nothing stayed the same forever.

Chapter 11
You got it goin□on.

Junior dialed the number and waited for someone to answer. A sexy voice on the other line greeted him.

"Hello," the female said.

"Um, hello. This is Junior. Can I speak to Muffin, I mean, Charlene?"

"This is her. Who's this?"

She didn't recognize his voice because it was the first time he had called her since getting her number three weeks ago.

"This is Junior, ma. What da deal?"

"Nuthin'. I'm just chillin', just gettin' in the crib."

"Well if you just chillin', I got sumthin' that you can do."

"And what might that be, sweetie?"

"I can make tonight your night, or I can make it our night."

"That is so corny," she said, laughing, "but I'm with it."

"It's been a long time, Muffin. You still lookin' scrumptious and shit. I'd love to see if you feel the same."

"Whateva, nigga. Just because I used to sex you back in da day don't mean you can still hit when you feel like it."

"I ain't sayin' that. I'm just sayin', we got a lot of catching up to do, that's all."

"Well if tonight's my night, I'm hungry tonight, so let's go get something to eat."

"That's cool. When you want me to pick you up?"

"Give me about an hour. I gottta shower and get pretty."

"Shit, ma, how do you improve on all that beauty?"

"You still gamin', huh, nigga?"

"It's game if you have an opponent. It's the truth when you dealing with a star." Junior's game was flawless.

"All right, baby, you got it. Let me give you the address."

"I'll see you in an hour," he said after she gave him the information.

Junior went to Shondra's house to tell her he wouldn't be coming back that night because he had to take care of some important business. Afterward, he went to Craig's house to take a shower and change his clothes. He was still driving the rental he had used to go to Virginia. He had paid for an extra month because he didn't want to take it back yet. As he pulled up in the parking lot of the Tompkins Houses he looked at Craig's clean, 190E Benz and thought, *Now that would impress the shit out of Muffin.*

"Yo, cuz," Junior called out.

"What up, my nigga?" Craig asked, walking over to greet him.

"I need to borrow your whip tonight. I got this chick that I want to pick up, and I need your wheels to seal the deal on the pussy."

"As long as she ain't no chicken head, because you know they can't even ride in the backseat," he said, throwing the keys to Junior and laughing.

"You probably remember her. It's Muffin, the chick I used to fuck with in high school."

"You talkin' 'bout the redbone with the fat ass? Hell, yeah, I remember her, and I remember you wouldn't let me hit it either."

"That was my girl back then, nigga, and I probably won't let you hit it now either, 'cause the ass is much fatter."

"Make sure you strap up. You know how you like raw doggin' them hoes."

"Don't worry 'bout what I do with my piece, nigga," Junior responded, playfully punching at Craig's midsection.

"Ay, yo, I want you to hang out with me in a coupla weeks. I'm throwin' my man a coming home party. He just did six joints."

"You know I don't do the club scene, son," he told Craig.

"I know, but you gonna be with family. Ain't nuthin' gonna jump off in there, and if shit do get outta hand, there's gonna be mad artillery in there. Let me find out you nervous about hanging out wit your big cuz and enjoying yourself."

"All right, let me think about it."

"So tell me, what happened when you went back over to your spot?"

"Yo, my nigga got that shit on lock. It almost reminds me of how you got shit over here clicking. He got shit running real smooth. The only thing I gotta do is collect my dough and keep work on the block. That shit is sweet, son. He got like four niggas on payroll and three soldiers on the team, and all dem lil niggas is thorough."

"I hear you, but hear me real quick before you go. That shit sounds sweet, but if you not on the scene, then you won't know what's really goin' on because you not out there. So just because you got extra time on your hands, don't take it for granted that everything is going smooth. Once you not on the scene, niggas start changing the rules and your original setup, and if you don't agree, then you got beef. You understand me? Remember, out of sight, out of mind."

"Yeah, I got you, cuz."

"All right, now go ahead and bust a nut for me, too."

Junior rushed upstairs and took a shower, then put on an all black, velour Sergio Tacchini sweat suit, a black and white Nike T-shirt, and a pair of white Nike Air Max with a black swoosh. He had to pull the strings on the pants tight because he was taking his black pistol grip .38 revolver with him. He looked at himself in the mirror and liked how the eighteen-inch, gold cable with the house piece looked against the black and white T-shirt, and how the jacket brought out the gold nugget watch on his wrist. If nothing had changed about Muffin, he knew she was a gold digger, and this outfit would make her give the pussy up because it was screaming out, "this nigga got money!"

Junior wasn't planning on paying for shit except dinner and a hotel room. The only thing she was gonna get out of him was a meal and hard dick, and he expected head along with dinner and the potential hotel visit. Junior was dressed to kill, literally, and he knew when she saw him and saw what he was driving, her pussy would be doing somersaults. He was planning to slay that ass, so he made sure he drank two Guinness stouts before picking her up.

The two-story house with the green canopy looked dilapidated and abandoned. Junior checked the address again to make sure it was the right crib, then he beeped the horn. The house looked creepy to him, and he started hoping it was the wrong address, because as good as she looked, she couldn't possibly be living in those conditions. He beeped the horn again, pulled out his toast, and placed it in his lap for precautionary measures. Although shit wasn't looking right, the thought of beating that pussy up was all he was looking forward to. He finally got out of the car, still gripping his gun, and turned off the headlights, leaving the yellow parking lights on. He walked up to the broken, black gate and pushed it open. It scraped the concrete as he pushed it open because it was off the hinge. Then he looked up at the front door and started climbing the steps. When he reached the top of the last landing, arriving at the battered, double wooden doors, he tried to peek inside to see if the building was abandoned. As he peered through the glass pane in the doors, he couldn't see anything because the curtains shielded the glass, so he looked for a doorbell, but the fixture on the side only revealed what used to be a doorbell. He turned around to descend the steps of the abandoned building when he heard the door fly open. He quickly turned back around, poised to pull his pistol from his side and fire.

"I'm sorry. Are you looking for someone here?" a young lady in a pink housecoat asked him.

He put the gun behind his back, hoping she hadn't noticed it.

"Aah, yes, ma'am. I'm here to pick up Charlene," Junior said.

"Oh, you must be Junior. She's getting ready. She told me to check if you were out here because no one would be able to hear you knocking. I'm sorry. Would you like to come in?"

"Um, no, thank you. I'll just wait for her in the car."

"You have to excuse the condition of the building. I just recently purchased it, and as you can see, there is a lot of work that needs to be done."

"Oh, that's no problem."

"Where are my manners? I'm Ms. Turner, Charlene's mother," she said, extending her hand to Junior.

When Junior used to go with Muffin, he never had the chance to meet her mother because she was always working. It was evident where Charlene got her fine looks and tight body from, because her mom was definitely a superstar, even in that housecoat.

Junior was holding the banister of the stairs with his left hand and the gun in the other hand behind his back. He was faced with a dilemma because she extended her right hand out to him, and he couldn't use his right hand to shake because that was the hand that held the gun.

"Hey, Ma, why didn't you tell me he was out here?" Charlene asked, suddenly appearing behind her mother.

Junior saw his chance and switched the gun to the other hand, shaking Ms. Turner's hand as she turned around to look at her daughter.

"I'm sorry. I was inviting him in. I didn't want to just leave him standing here on the stoop."

"Oh, OK, so you met my moms, huh?" Muffin asked, switching her attention to Junior.

"Yes. She was keeping me company while you were getting ready."

"Thanks, Ma. Don't wait up for me. I'll be in late."

"Well don't come in too late."

"Don't worry, Ms. Turner, I won't keep her too late. We're just gonna catch a movie and go out to eat," Junior said to show that he was a respectful young man. But his true intentions were to dick down her daughter with no grease.

Charlene and Junior made their way down the stairs, and as they walked to the car Junior got a good look at what she was wearing. She had on a jean skirt that stopped just short of her thick thighs and showed off the form of her hips. Her legs were bare and looked silky smooth. She had on a tight, white shirt that exposed her belly button. He couldn't figure out if the shirt was supposed to look like that, or if it was just too small for her. Her footwear consisted of white Reebok classics with some white pom pom socks. She smelled of White Diamonds. Muffin looked good and smelled even better. He put his arm around her waist before they reached the car and palmed her ass gently to test her. Even through the denim he could feel her softness. He couldn't wait to get between her legs.

"You driving this?" she asked when she saw the car.

"Yeah, I drive this when I'm with someone special," he said, applying more pressure to the grip he had on her ass.

"So how many special people ride in here?"

"A couple, like my moms, sister, aunt, you know, special people."

"OK, wise guy," she said as she sat in the passenger seat.

He purposely walked past the front of the car so she could get a better view of what he was wearing, then got into the car and pulled off. He was taking her to the Promenade to set the mood. Once they got there they walked around and looked over at Manhattan. The skyline illuminated the cool night.

"The city that never sleeps," Muffin said.

"I bet their light bill is high as hell."

They walked to the far end and looked at the ferry to Staten Island as it passed by, and then gazed at the Statue of Liberty. He turned her around to him and placed his hand on the small of her back where the curve of her ass began. She nuzzled her head into his chest, gazing into his eyes, and he kissed her passionately. She pushed her front onto him and grinded against him, placing one of her legs between his so he could feel the warmth of her middle. He put his hand under her skirt and ran it up and down her thick thighs, squeezing her ass gently. She moved closer, enjoying the tingly feeling his touch sent to her kitty.

"Come on, baby," she whispered in his ear. "Let's go get something to eat so we can finish this on a full stomach."

"I can get full off of you right here," he said as he stooped down and lifted her skirt up. She had on a pair of fire red bikini panties and he pulled them to the side and inserted his index finger into her awaiting snatch. She cocked her leg up on the rail, giving him room to operate and forgetting she was outdoors in a public place. He kneeled down and licked her clit with the tip of his tongue while moving his fingers in and out of her pulsating tunnel with precise movements as she squirmed and moaned with delight. When her legs got weak and trembled, he removed his tongue and took his finger out of her passageway, looking up at her. Her eyes were closed and when she finally realized he had stopped midway to her orgasm, she looked down at him licking the finger that was covered with her passion juices. This made her pussy vibrate even more. That was the most erotic and freakiest shit any man had ever done to her, and she wanted him to finish her off. He rose to his feet and looked at her blinking softly, and kissed her again so she could taste her own sweet fluid. Her cat was pulsating and she could feel herself getting sticky as he rubbed his huge pole onto her through his thin sweat pants.

"DAMN!" was all she could say as he grabbed her hand and led her like a zombie to the car.

Muffin walked back to the car thinking of nothing but sexing Junior as they drove over the Brooklyn Bridge to the South Street Seaport. Junior parked in a twenty-four-hour parking lot and they both walked to Uno's restaurant for dinner. Once inside, Junior went straight to the bar and ordered a double shot of Remy XO for him, and a Blue Hawaiian for Muffin as they waited to be seated. Midway through their drinks the waitress seated them and handed them menus. Muffin ordered the shrimp platter with butter sauce and lobster tails, and Junior had the steak dinner with a baked potato. It was always like a gold digging broad to order the most expensive shit on the menu.

As they ate, Muffin couldn't take her eyes off Junior. He had changed so much over the years since high school. She never thought he would turn out to be so good-looking and well groomed. His hair was cut in a low Caesar with waves spinning, making you seasick. His attire was flawless and everything fit him well, actually fit him perfectly as if it were an Armani suit tailored to his exact build. His big, bulky jewelry accented with diamond chips, and the big, bulging wad of money that was evident in his pocket were the bonuses to the physical attraction she already felt for him. He was definitely not the Junior of high school days.

The Junior of high school days was book smart. He was in all the gifted classes and excelled at every subject. He wasn't a nerd or anything. He just didn't seem the type to turn out the way he did. He seemed more like the dude that would go to college and get that job working for a big corporation. The young man sitting in front of her undeniably impressed her, not only with his looks and style, but especially with his sexual antics that floored her and had her wanting to get with him again. When they were together back in high school they had sex on two occasions and he wasn't experienced. He would just get in and bust a nut in five minutes, if that long. The only thing he had going for himself back then was his pole. His shit was big, thick, and shaped like a hook. She looked at him now as a totally different person, a young man on the rise, and she wanted to be with him when he reached the top. All she saw was dollar signs and an easy life, and she wasn't going to let nothing or no one stand in her way of getting just that.

Junior sat back and ate his meal, thinking of nothing but finishing off what he h ad started with Muffin. She was one fine ass bitch and soft as hell to boot. He was beaming with confidence and knew he had her in his clutches with the little stunt he had pulled at the Promenade. He knew she probably never encountered anything like that before, and she would literally be begging him for some dick now, instead of him sweating her for the pussy. Most niggas either denied licking twat or honestly didn't do it, but Junior found out early that eating pussy could get any girl sprung like a broken coil. He perfected his style of lovemaking, learning different things from prostitutes, porno movies, and trying out new moves with Shondra. He found out if you stopped right before a woman orgasmed, their body still went through the motions, but the explosive feeling subsided and they yearned for that climax. Once he found that out, he used it to his advantage. The bonus to that was he was blessed with a lot of beef and his pipe game was just as good. He planned on making Muffin sweat him more by taking her to a suite at the Marriott on Forty-second Street in midtown Manhattan. He figured she had never been there before and that would be the icing on the cake. Yeah, he would spend a lot of money, but his plan was to show her the dough without giving her any. He wanted to make sure he had her mind fucked up, giving him full control of what transpired between them, because he didn't want her controlling the outcome of the night.

As he finished up his steak and potatoes he looked up at her with his bedroom eyes and flashed a devilish grin. She understood his eye language and what he was insinuating, so she finished up her platter and he asked for the check. The Uno waitress was flirting with Junior openly during their meal. She would purposely put her back to Muffin and ask Junior if everything was to his liking. She came back six to eight times during the course of the meal, each time rubbing up against him with her ass, bending over and revealing her breasts, and even making a comment on how tight her uniform was so he could see her camel toe through the thin black pants she was wearing. Junior didn't think Muffin peeped what was happening, so he didn't mention it. When she brought the check he left his number on the back of the bill and a one-hundred-dollar tip that would ensure a phone call from her sometime during the week. As they got up to leave, Junior pulled Muffin's chair from under her and let her lead the way out.

"Ooops, I forgot my purse. I'll meet you outside."

"Aight, I'll go get the car and pick you up in the front."

As she went back to the table to get her purse, Muffin scooped up the check and took the tip.

That bitch think she slick but she won't get this fuckin' tip, she thought as she picked up the one-hundred-dollar bill and looked on the back of the check. She took a pen out of her purse and scribbled out the number Junior had left on it. She took a dollar out of her Louis Vutton purse and wrote the words: YOU'RE LUCKY I'M IN A RUSH, BITCH, OR I WOULD FUCK YOU UP! Then she walked up to the register and paid for the meal with the money Junior had left.

Muffin was street smart and had peeped everything the waitress was doing all night. She was used to that type of reaction from both bitches and niggas. It was part of the game. Shit, that's how she got Junior the day on the corner by the liquor store. She walked past the waitress, passed her the note, and shot her a look that could freeze fire. As she strutted out the door she shook her ass extra hard, knowing the waitress was watching. The waitress rolled her eyes as she read the words on the back of the dollar. She would have to be more subtle the next time she wanted to get somebody's man.

Once Muffin made it to the car, Junior took the FDR to the Forty-second Street exit and drove up to Eighth Avenue past the peep shows and nude bars. He pulled into the Marriott valet parking, got out, and went to the front desk. He got the executive suite on the fortieth floor and he and Muffin rode the elevator up to the room. The elevator amazed Muffin. It was all glass and you could see outside onto the street while you rode up. Junior opened the door of the suite and Muffin stood in awe as she looked at the biggest and most luxurious hotel room she had ever seen. Junior walked over to the mini bar, took out two rock glasses, and filled them both with ice and poured them both a drink. She didn't know how to act and didn't want him to see that fact, but the truth was she was completely taken aback by the room. He passed her the drink and went through the double doors to the bedroom where she watched as he took off his jacket, revealing his sidearm. Yeah, he was a true hustler. The gun on his hip solidified that for her. Muffin was in seventh heaven as she took a sip of her drink and joined him in the bedroom. He was sitting on the edge of the bed rolling up a blunt.

"Turn the cable on."

She walked past him, tripped over his feet, and fell hard in the space between the bed and the dresser.

"Hee hee." He chuckled. "You aight, ma? You ain't even had none of this sess yet and you trippin' all over yourself."

"It's them big ass duck feet," she said, getting up off the floor. "You meant to trip me up."

"You right, baby. What better way to make you fall for me?"

"Look, baby, you don't have to trip me to make me fall for you. You're doin' a good job already."

"You make it easy, Muff. All your beauty is magnetic and you pulling me in," he said.

"I hope so, babes. You got it goin' on in more ways than one."

They smoked and talked about old times. The herb was making Muffin horny and she was getting wet for Junior. She took off her top and lay back on the bed, blowing Os as she rubbed her thighs. Sensing things were getting heated, Junior grabbed her hand and led her to the Jacuzzi in the adjoining bathroom. She disrobed immediately as he filled the tub and the water began to bubble. She stepped in as sexy as she could and waited for Junior to enter behind her. He left and returned with two champagne glasses and a bottle of Dom Perignon in his hands.

This nigga is not playin' no games. This shit is straight outta the movies, Muffin thought.

"Damn, baby, what you tryin' to do, make me fall in love wit' you?"

"If that's what it takes to make you a part of me, then hey."

"I'm not gonna front, Junior, you really doin' it to me. You doin' and sayin' all the right things, and right now I'm on a merry-go-round and I don't want it to stop."

His manners were working a part of her emotions she didn't want revealed, and he was doing it without sexing her first.

Got her ass! he thought to himself.

"Like I said, Muff, you make it easy. You so different from the other chicks. They look for what they can get outta a nigga first before looking at what they got in a nigga. Most girls think that money is everything, how much they can get outta a nigga and shit. I'm different, ma. I got a lil bit of change, but it means nuthin' if I don't get to spend it on someone that I feel is worthy. Chicks that are interested in my pockets more than the nigga that's wearing the pants turn me off. I don't like females that expect clothes and jewelry as soon as a nigga busts a nut, because that means they sellin' pussy, and if I wanted a prostitute I would go on Eleventh Ave. At least I know what I'm gettin' for my money, you feel me, ma?"

Muffin moved closer to him in the Jacuzzi. He was being real and she respected his honesty. She felt like he was trying to tell her what position she could play in his life if she was going to be real with him.

Junior was playing on her emotions hard. He was hoping if he came at her with an unorthodox approach he would have her mind, giving him total control of her actions. He wanted to find another person other than Shondra that he could trust, and who would do anything for him. He felt a female was the only candidate for that kind of trust, and he was banking on Muffin. He felt that females were more loyal than guys in this game only because they dealt with emotion differently. He felt that if he could get a female to fall deep in love with him that she would remain loyal to him as long as her love for him stayed strong and during that time he would be able to trust her to do almost anything for him.

Muffin was zoning. She never had a guy kick it to her like that before. Junior was changing her mind about him, and she was really feeling what he was saying to her. After tonight she was going to stick to him like glue if he let her. Although she knew he had a girl, there was something different about him. He wasn't afraid of expressing himself to her. He was open and revealed a lot to her, and that meant a lot. He was the first man to make her feel the way she was feeling, and it felt good. She grabbed his hand and got out of the fizzy water, leading him to the bed. He followed her like a puppy, and when they reached the bed she sat down and grabbed his other hand.

"I want to please you, daddy. I want to make you feel better than any girl has ever made you feel in your life."

Junior stood there looking down at her beautiful face. He had sealed the deal. She was sprung. Her emotions were overflowing and she wasn't trying to hide it.

"Daddy, I know that you got a girl," she said, stroking his pole gently. "I'm willing to play second only if you guarantee me that it'll be just me and her. I can tell that you are different from all the rest of the niggas I ever wasted my time with, and I want to show and prove to you that I can be your right hand from now on. Whatever you ask of me, daddy, I will do it without question. Just promise me that we will be together."

She put him in her wet mouth and started making slurping sounds as she looked up at him to make sure he was enjoying it. The sounds he made told her he was into it. She sucked the head of his snake and went around the rim with her tongue. As she positioned her head upright she grabbed his hips with both hands and tried to insert all of him into her open mouth. She inched it in slowly, deep throating his huge mass. He got excited and started pumping in her mouth like it was her pussy, and she let him. She squeezed her jaw muscles when he pulled out and opened wide when he went in. He started moving in and out rapidly, and she knew he was close to climaxing. She felt the hot jism release into her mouth, going straight down her throat. This was the first time she had swallowed. She held onto him and continued slurping until he was completely drained. His body relaxed and she continued to suck on him until he started moaning loudly. She looked up at him and his eyes were closed, showing complete satisfaction. She was pleased to know she had made him feel good.

She took her mouth off him slowly and licked up and down his shaft, then she rose to kiss him. They both fell onto the bed and then he took control. He spread her legs and began licking the inside of her thighs. She was already wet as he rubbed his finger across her clit. She winced a little and started swiveling her hips. As he put his tongue on her clit she felt tingly all over again like at the Promenade. He was a master at what he was doing. After licking her to her climax, he inserted his staff into her slowly, taking his time. She was beside herself with pure pleasure. He sucked her nipples gently and then he did something that she had never experienced. He put his hands under her ass and began fingering her asshole. It felt weird at first, but he was being methodical in his motions. She felt his finger enter her asshole little by little until he was working both his finger and cock simultaneously in each hole. She began to shiver as the pain and pleasure consumed her entire body. She was about to detonate like a dirty bomb and began making noises she had never heard come out of her mouth before, and then in an instant she was screaming at the top of her lungs.

"OHHHHH MYYYY GGGGOOODDDDD!!!!!"

She had cum so hard her legs were shaking like someone was electrocuting her. He continued to thrust his pole in and out, quicker and quicker. She wasn't in control of her breathing. It was like she was having an asthma attack, and then she came again and screamed a second time in delight.

"GGGGGOOOOOODDAAMMMMNNNIITTT!!!!"

Her legs muscles tightened and she was finished. Junior continued until he came, then rolled over beside her. She was sweaty and utterly confused. This was the first time someone had actually made love to her, and the first time she had a double orgasm. This wasn't fucking. This was how someone made love to you. Then she began to cry and couldn't stop.

"I'm sorry, baby, did I hurt you?" he asked in a concerned voice, propping himself up on his elbows.

She threw her arms around his neck and squeezed tightly, burying her head on his shoulders.

"Junior, I love you."

L. J. Miller

Chapter 12
To the love of money

Things were going so good in the hood that La decided to take some of the workers to Ryders, a neighborhood strip club. One of his friends from school told him they were having a lock in and he decided he'd take some of the workers to show them a good time. La's intention was to try to build a structure of trust and loyalty among the chosen workers. He wanted to be sure when the time came for them to bust their guns for him that they would do it without hesitation.

"Y'all niggas ready to go?"

"Yeah!"

La knew they were going to enjoy themselves thoroughly, because he was paying for everything. They were going to be in there the whole night and he expected to get them sucked and laid without them worrying about coming out of their pockets. La chose these particular guys because they were the ones that made the most money on the block and were something like his inside informants. They would tell him everything that was going on in the hood from the workers who weren't happy, to the heads that were going to other spots to cop. La liked playing the boss and liked being in total control of what happened on the block. He called the shots and was the boss as far as he was concerned.

La and the workers arrived at the strip club in the new Acura Legend he had purchased three weeks ago. When they pulled up there were a lot of people waiting on the line to get inside the strip club. La walked up to the door with his crew of four men and walked straight in, bypassing the people waiting on line. He was a regular, so he got VIP service. He didn't have to pay at the door, and he had his own table. The workers had never been to this club before, so they were impressed with the star treatment extended to him.

La walked to his table, which had two bottles of Moet sitting in ice buckets waiting for him. They all sat down and La popped the cork and poured everyone a drink.

"To the love of money and power!"

Everyone clinked their glasses together and drank the bubbly liquid down. The club was full of beautiful women in exotic lingerie, thongs, and bikini sets. Three strippers came over to La's table and sat down between the boys and La. They were gorgeous—big breasts, round asses, and thick thighs. The boys were drooling as they watched one of them give La a lap dance right at the table. La was acting as if he wasn't interested. He did this because he wanted them to know the treatment was nothing special to him. He was used to a beautiful woman grinding herself against him, at least that's what he wanted them to think. The strippers would do whatever he wanted because he was a hustler and hustlers doled out big money. They would work their way around to all the big spenders and linger with the ones that spent the most. The boys continued to drink and were enjoying themselves. La told them to go to the stage and gave each of them one hundred dollars to tip the girls. They practically ran over to the stage to see all the fine strippers and see which one they would be able to get with in the VIP room.

On stage were three strippers who knew La very well. He usually had two of them meet him at a hotel for a threesome. He would pay them five hundred dollars each for their services. They loved when La came around or beeped them. They would drop whatever they were doing because they didn't have anyone that tipped as much as he did.

One of the girls, Bubbles, was talking with a guy with a long scar down the side of his face. The guy was trying to get her and her friends to go with him to a hotel and have a ménage a trois. He was flashing a knot of money, but she wasn't interested because he looked treacherous. She had experiences before with shady characters that used money to persuade her to go with them and then refused to pay for her services. This guy looked like one of those characters. She kept trying to reject him in a nice way, but he was being very persistent. La walked by the stage to see how his boys were getting along with the strippers, and that's when Bubbles got his attention. When she saw him, she whistled and he looked up at her and went to greet her. As he walked over to her he felt her soft, velvety ass and slid a twenty-dollar bill in her thong. She stooped down and whispered something in his ear, and he nodded, then laughed and walked off to where his boys were sitting.

"Yo, my man, you know that ho, Bubbles?" the guy with the scar asked La.

"Yeah, what's up?" La answered.

"Nah, I'm tryin' to get the ho to do a threesome with her girl, but she frontin' on me."

"Aight, so what you want me to do?"

"I'm saying, if you know her like that, just tell her I'm good peoples and that she safe with me," he said, pulling a brick of money out of his pocket to prove he had bank.

"I hear you, bruh, but I ain't that ho's pimp, and I can't co-sign for you 'cause I don't know you like that."

"My bad. My name is Drez. I got shit locked down in the Stuy," he said, putting his hand out for a shake.

"I'm La. I hustle out of Baptiste and I got that shit on lock ova there," La replied, shaking his hand and letting him know he was getting money too.

"What up, La? Look, kid, I'm trying to get these hoes to go to my hotel after this shit, and she flakin' on me. You ever got down with dem hoes like that?"

"Yeah, I got them a couple of times, but like I said, I can't really vouch for you like that."

"How about you come to the room wit' me so they know e'erything is e'erything?"

"I don't know. I got my boys with me right now."

"I got my boys, too, but it could be just you, me, and them hoes. Shit, we can bring six and make it a real party if you come."

"Aight, let me go talk to her and see what's up."

"That's cool, fam. Come over to my table when you set it up. I'm sitting over by the VIP," Drez said, pointing to a table in the corner that was roped off.

The table he was sitting at was reserved for the heavy rollers, niggas that had real paper. The people in that section usually spent no less than five thousand dollars, and Drez was in that section. This peaked La's interest in him and he decided he would help him out as much as he could just so he could make himself more popular to his workers. Once they saw him over in the roped off VIP section he would gain more respect. He walked over to Bubbles and asked her if she would be willing to take five of her friends to a hotel with him and Drez after the lock in. Bubbles trusted La, but she had heard a lot about Drez. He was a cold-blooded murderer who got his respect from killing rival dealers. When La asked her, she wasn't too eager to say yes because she didn't feel safe going anywhere with Drez, even if La said he would be there to make sure everything went all right.

"I don't know, La, baby. I heard a lot about that nigga, and it ain't all good."

"I know, baby, but I'm gonna be right there wit' you. I'm gonna make sure you safe, baby. Don't you trust me?"

"La, baby, do you really know this guy like that? I mean, I heard he killed some nigga from 'round your way a while back in the Stuy for robbing one of his workers. He killed him, La."

"Nah, I ain't heard about that, but I'm saying, baby, you gonna be with me, so you safe. You don't have to worry about nuthin' happening while I'm there with you." La was so caught up in trying to get her to go with Drez that what she said about him didn't register, he didn't put two and two together. Knowing Drez was a real baller made him gravitate to him more. No one would dare fuck with him if he was affiliated with a known murderer. And when he thought no one, he meant NO ONE.

"OK, baby, I'm only gonna do this because you givin' me your word that everything is gonna be all right."

"That's my baby."

He was sure getting her to go with them would put him in good with Drez, since Drez was unable to get her to commit to going with him alone.

La walked over to the roped-off area and Drez waved him in. He poured him a glass of Dom and looked into La's eyes to see if he was successful in getting him what he wanted.

"It's a go?" Drez asked, blowing smoke out his mouth from the blunt he had between his teeth.

"Yeah, I took care of everything."

"That's good. So when's it going down?"

"Right after the lock-in. I didn't tell her where 'cause I don't know where we goin'."

"That's cool. I'm at the Radisson in midtown," Drez said. "I'm gonna let my boys take my Jag and we gonna ride in the limo I rented."

"OK. When you ready just come get me at my table ova there."

La wasn't intimidated by Drez. He didn't have time to be because he was too impressed by his status and power. La had a brainstorm, when they freaked off with Bubbles and her friends, he was going to see if Drez would be interested in making a move with him to take over Baptiste from Junior's clutches.

***

Something about the way KB was acting lately was making Gloria nervous. He wasn't himself for the past two nights, and tonight he was getting ready to leave her again. He told her he wasn't going to be back until late Sunday night, and when she asked him where he was going, he wouldn't tell her anything. Gloria wasn't big on being nosey, but ever since she had the talk with Shondra, she really wanted to know more about her man.

He was in the bedroom making a phone call because his beeper had gone off, and she was about to do something she never did before. She was about to invade his privacy and eavesdrop on his telephone call while he was in the bedroom. She went into the kitchen, hit the mute button on the telephone, and picked up the receiver.

"I'm getting ready to leave in a minute," she heard KB saying to the person on the other end of the line.

"Yo, don't be late, nigga."

"I won't. I'm on my way out as soon as I hang up," KB said.

"I'ma need you to pick up those other guns from my man before you come to the crib. I can't go because I'm waiting on the bouncer to come and give me the exact time to go there."

"Where at?"

"Go to the auto shop on Pierce Street. I already called and told him that I'm sending somebody to pick them up for me."

"Aight, I'll go pick them up and meet you at your crib once I get them."

"Make sure you take a cab from the shop. It's a lot of big shit he givin' you and you don't need to get stopped on the street wit' all that artillery. It's enough to go to war with the marines."

"I hear you. I'm out. See you in a minute."

Gloria hung up after she heard KB put down the receiver on his end, and rushed back to the living room. Now she knew why KB was acting so suspiciously. He was about to do another stickup.

KB was sitting on the bed thinking how stupid he was for calling Stump back when he beeped him. He should have just went straight to his crib and said he never got the beep. Now he had to go pick up an arsenal of guns. Obviously they were the guns they would use when they robbed the club Saturday night. He knew he was going to be taking a chance going to get the guns, but there was no way around it for him. He would either do it or get done by Stump, which was not an option.

KB got up off the bed and put on his jacket. Now he had to go face Gloria and tell her he wouldn't be coming back until Sunday, hopefully. He couldn't tell her where he was going, because he promised her he wouldn't do anymore stickups. He wished he hadn't told her about the last robbery he went on with Stump. Then he would be able to tell her anything and she would believe it. After he told her what happened, she was always hounding him about getting into trouble with Stump, and she was always trying to find out where he was when he wasn't with her. Damn, how he hated lying to her, but he had no choice this time.

"Where you going?" Gloria asked.

"I gotta go take care of something."

"When you comin' back?"

"I'll be back lata on."

"Why you lyin' to me, K? Why won't you tell me where you goin'?"

"Come on, Glo, let me go and take care of my business. Don't put me through this shit."

"You know you about to go do something real stupid, K. Why you lyin'?"

"Look, Glo, I gotta go take care of some business. Just let me go."

"What business, K? Is it wit' that killer, Stump? I know you going to see him. I know you 'bout to do some more stupid shit. I don't believe you, K. You say you love me, but all you do is lie and keep shit from me. If you love me, K, you won't leave right now. If you really, truly love me, you'll stay here."

KB didn't want her to cry, and he didn't understand why she was so emotional. He had something to do and that was it. It wasn't anything for her to cry over. If he didn't go she would really be crying—at his funeral.

"Get out of my way, Glo," he said, pushing her to the side and opening the door. "I said I'll be back and that's it. Just relax."

"You gonna just leave me like that? You don't love me, K. You don't know what love is!" she screamed as he opened the exit door and went down the stairs. "Fuck you!" she said to herself, and she meant it.

Shondra was watching a movie on the VCR when her phone rang. She saw on the ID that is was Glo calling.

"What up, girl?" she asked as she picked up the ringing phone.

"You was right. I don't know shit 'bout that nigga."

"What you talkin' 'bout?"

"KB. He goin' out to do some more dumb shit with that nigga, Stump. I was listening on the phone when he was talking to him. The nigga treat KB like he his son. He told him to go pick up some guns and he ran outta here like his father sent him on an errand. I asked him where he was going and don't you know that black muhfucka lied to me in my face? I started to tell him that I knew what he was about to do, but I was scared he might fuck me up for listening in on his phone call. I'm scared for him, Shondra. I don't want nuthin' to happen to him. That nigga Stump is bad news."

"Did he say what they were gonna do? I mean, do you know exactly what they gonna do?"

"No, but I know that he going to pick up a whole bunch of guns from some auto shop on Pierce Street. Whatever it is, I think it's major because the nigga was telling him that there was enough guns for them to go to war with the United States."

"Damn, that's really serious."

"I'm coming downstairs, Shondra. Leave the door open for me."

Good, Shondra thought. *That'll give me time to beep Junior.*

Shondra beeped Junior and put in her code to let him know to call right back, then she continued watching *The Usual Suspects.*

Junior was on his way uptown with Muffin. They had spent every day together since the night of their first date. She was in love, so in love she was willing to do any and everything he asked of her. He asked her to go with him to cop, and like a good soldier, she agreed. They were on the A train going to 145th Street. He had almost forty Gs on him and was a little nervous, but Muffin had his .45 auto in her purse. He showed her how to take if off safety and just aim and pull the trigger if necessary. She was down with whatever he said as long as he was with her. He would be frontin' if he said he wasn't catching a lil bit of feelings for her, but he knew he couldn't go there with her because of Shondra. He loved Shondra with all his heart, and she was his for real road dog. She was the one that was there for him when he needed someone most. Nah, he couldn't violate the bond they had just for Muffin.

"This is the A train to 205th Street, 145th Street next stop. Please watch the closing doors," the conductor said over the train's PA system.

"Come on, ma, that's the stop where we gettin' off."

"Mmmmm, daddy, I love being in your arms. You know you spoiling me, right?"

"Yeah, I know, but you gotta be on point right now. We 'bout to take care of some serious shit."

"I got your front and your back, daddy."

The train doors opened and they exited the train and walked up the stairs. The sun was beaming down. It was a cool day and there were a lot of people out on the streets. They walked up the hill toward Broadway, then turned on Amsterdam Avenue. Junior took this route a thousand times and every time he made this trip he had butterflies until he made it back to Brooklyn. They walked hand in hand like a couple and went into a corner bodega to buy some cigarettes.

"This is the first time that I'm bringing somebody with me, so just relax and do what I tell you. What up, Ponchito?" Junior said to a dark-skinned Dominican. "You ready for me?"

"Jes, papi, but who is this chiquita with you?"

"This my girl. It's been hot, so I'ma have her carry my shit for me. Is that a problem?"

"No problema, but joo know she can't come upstairs, papi."

"Bullshit. I been coppin' from Venezuelo for years. If I can't bring my girl, then I'ma find another connect."

"Let me see if it's OK first, papi. Sigame."

They followed closely behind and when he got to the door he tapped on it three times and waited for a response.

"¿Quién está allí? (Who's there?)" the Dominican woman's voice asked from behind the door.

"It's Ponchito. Diga a Venezuela que su amigo esté aquí." He told the woman that he wanted to see Venezuelo, and that he had someone with him. "Y eso él tiene una muchacha con él." Then Ponchito explained that Junior had a woman with him.

"Un momento."

The door opened and a big-bellied Dominican man beckoned Junior and Muffin inside, hugging Junior on sight and shaking Muffin's hand.

"Come in, come in," Venezuelo said, showing them to the couch. "Did Ponchito give you a hard time, amigo?"

"Nah, not really. This is my girl, Charlene," Junior said to Venezuelo. "I brought her with me so she can carry the shit for me, because it's hot over here."

"No problem, my friend. Just last week the policia run up in my other apartment across the street. They no get nothing but they make big mess in there. You hungry? Mia, you hungry?"

"No, thank you," Muffin replied.

"I'm good," Junior said.

"OK, so let's go into the other room. Excuse us, mia," he said, picking up the remote control and handing it to her.

Muffin took the remote and started channel surfing. She sat back and looked around the modest apartment. Pictures of Saint Mary, little statues of religious prophets, and rosary beads hanging on the frames of pictures were littered throughout the small apartment. She was looking for a family portrait, and when she didn't see one she figured this was just one of Venezuelo's girl's houses. *Niggas is the same no matter where they're from!* she thought.

"I want two kees," Junior said to Venezuela as they sat down in the bedroom that was transformed into Venezuela's office.

"No problem. You moving up, I see. Business must be good."

Venezuela was Junior's connect and had the rawest coke that side of Manhattan. His coke looked like it had diamond crystals in it and was pure as a virgin in a monastery. Venezuela liked Junior because he never came short and always conducted business in a professional manner. Venezuela didn't allow many hustlers in his home, but he had grown to trust Junior over the years, and wanted to make him feel more comfortable when they did their transactions.

"How much you lettin' me get it for?" Junior asked.

"Thirty-four thousand. I give you extra half ounce because I have new product from Peru, better than the other shit from Colombia," he said, smiling at Junior. "I no have it long, so you get as much as you can before I run out. This perico will make your business do even better."

171

"Let me go get the money from my girl."

Venezuela got up with him and went to call a runner to bring the two kees over to him.

"You hungry, ma?" Junior asked Muffin again as he counted out the money. "Because this is gonna take a little time."

"No, I'm all right. You about to give him all that money?"

"Don't start asking no questions now, Muff. Just sit back and chill till we done."

"Oh, I'm sorry, daddy."

After Venezuela put the cash in the money machine and verified the amount, they went into a kitchen where he cooked up the two kilos of coke, then weighed it out on a triple beam when it dried. Venezuela put the finished goods into a bag and Junior took the Ziploc bag filled with the product in the shape of pies, and put it in Muffin's pocketbook. Venezuela gave Junior and Muffin a hug before going into the back room.

"I'll see you in two weeks."

Ponchito was downstairs waiting for customers when they got to the lobby.

"Joo straight, papi?"

"Yeah," Junior replied, the butterflies fluttering around in his stomach.

He passed Ponchito a one-hundred-dollar bill and waited for him to give him the all-clear signal. Then he and Muffin walked out hand in hand and crossed the street, heading for the train station.

"Don't look back," he told her as a blue and white patrol car drove by slowly. Just then his beeper started to vibrate and he quickly turned it off without looking, not wanting to draw any unnecessary attention to himself. He would check it when he got back to Brooklyn. Muffin was nervous because she knew if the police were to stop them and found out she was holding drugs and a gun in her pocketbook, there would be no way around getting locked up.

"Don't be nervous, ma," Junior coached. "They not the one that jump out on people. They probably on them Dominicans' payroll."

"I'm all right, baby."

When they got to the train station all the tension was eased.

"How much shit is this?" she whispered to Junior.

"Two kees," he replied, looking down the tunnel, impatiently waiting for the A train to arrive.

"That's a lot, right?"

"Ummmhmmm," he replied, not trying to engage in a deep conversation.

"I did good, right, baby?"

"You did fine, luv. You my Bonnie," he said, reassuring her that she was more than his mule. "You wanna learn how to bag up when we get to Brooklyn?"

"Anything for you, baby, anything for you," she said as a train finally pulled into the station.

Dusty and Rock were watching the workers when they heard on the walkie-talkie that noccos (detectives) were circling the block. Rock informed the lookout to get off the corner and go across the street and sit on the side of the building, then he told the workers in the back to get clean just in case the Ds jumped out on them. They all complied and stood in a group like cattle in a herd, watching for predators. La came up and asked what was happening. They explained the police were hot and they were slowing down for a minute.

"Yo, Rock," he said, "go on the other side till shit quiet down on this end. You know if they see you they gonna fuck wit' you. Take the money on the other side and go through the back when you leave."

"You right. I hate the fuckin' po po. Ay, Dusty, give me that dough you got on you," Rock said.

"What up, Dusty?" La asked as he turned his attention to Dusty. "I ain't seen you in a minute. You aight?"

"I'm good. Just spending time with my lady."

"Yeah, that bitch got you sprung, nigga," Rock said.

"Chill with the bitch, shit. That's my girl now, duke."

"Oh, now that's your girl? Nigga, she ain't nuthin' but a pretty Puerto Rican closet smoker," Rock said.

"Chill, Rock. Don't you see he serious?" La asked.

"Don't tell him shit. When I snuff him, he'll know I'm serious."

"Ahh, man, you gonna beat me up ova a ho? You my man and the whole nine. You mean to tell me you'll let a crack head come between us?"

"I already told you, that's my lady, nigga. Why you just can't respect that and stop dissin' her in front of me?"

173

"'Cause she a crack head, that's why. Why don't you find you a regular chick to make your girl? Why you gotta go get a crack head?"

"Aight, y'all both chill out before this shit gets serious," La said.

"Shit, he act like she somebody. Everybody 'round the way done hit that. Even Junior done test drove that shit."

Dusty started walking up on Rock and La grabbed him to avoid the confrontation.

"Don't hold him. Let him go. He want to scrap over that ho, then I'll fuck him up and bring him to his senses."

"Ain't near one of y'all fighting. Just chill out. Go 'head, Rock, and take that money to the other side and put it up."

Rock started to walk away as La and Dusty talked.

"That's why his ass don't be out here no more. He be chasin' down that bitch. You better check to make sure he ain't in the closet with that bitch," Rock yelled as he walked toward the other side of the projects.

"See what I'm talkin' 'bout?" Dusty asked as he broke free from La and ran down the street behind Rock.

Rock didn't see Dusty until it was too late. All he felt was pain in the back of his head. He stumbled forward and his hands broke his fall.

"What up, nigga?"

Rock scurried to his feet and threw lefts and rights in a furious barrage, knocking Dusty backward onto the wall of the building.

"Look, B, don't make me hurt you ova no ho," Rock said to Dusty as he grabbed both his arms. "I'm just keepin' it real with you, my nigga."

"Fuck you!" Dusty screamed as he wrestled free and swung at Rock's head. He missed, but he connected with a left to Rock's jaw. Rock winced from the blow, then continued his onslaught of punches to Dusty's midsection and face. By the time La and the workers reached them, the fight was over. Dusty was threatening Rock, who was sitting on top of him like a chicken waiting for an egg to hatch.

"Get the fuck off me!" Dusty was screaming.

"Get off him, Rock!" La said.

"I am. I just want him to understand why he got this beat down. That bitch ain't worth it."

Rock got up off of Dusty and backed up immediately, waiting for round two, but Dusty just got up and kept with his threats.

"Look, it's already hot out here. We don't need no more heat," La said. "Y'all niggas squash this shit and let's get back to business. Y'all hear me?"

"Yeah," they both said reluctantly.

"I'm gonna talk to you in minute, Rock, I gotta go over on the other side. Me and you," La said to Dusty, "we gotta talk right now. Let's walk."

As Dusty started to follow La, La continued speaking.

"Look, kid, you know Rock your man, and you know that he wouldn't say shit to hurt you. He just trying to look out for you. You gotta see the positive in what he's sayin'. Ask yourself a question, have you been out here on your shift lately?"

"Not really, but that's only because—" Dusty started.

"That's what I mean," La interrupted. "You can't give no excuses, son. This is some serious shit we dealing with out here. When you not here on your shift, Rock is the one that takes your slot and you still get paid. He see that you slippin' and he just tryin' to get you to get your mind back right before it's too late. Ain't nothing wrong with fucking with them bitches, but you can't fall in love with them. You gotta remember that they want what you got access to, so you don't even know if she wit' you for you, or for that shit you can give her. You feel me, kid?" La found himself preaching as Junior would have done with him.

Dusty's pride was hurt. He felt like everyone was coming down on him. He didn't see Lizzette as a crack head. He saw her as a woman that cared about him.

The truth was that Lizzette had Dusty's mind all fucked up. She used his immaturity to get what she wanted from him. He was giving her money and product almost every night they were together. She stopped him from going to her house, using a bullshit excuse so she could spend all her time at his house around his stash. Lizzette was cunning. She used her beauty and sexual experience to get Dusty to do things he normally wouldn't agree to.

One night Lizzette used her womanly wiles to get him to do the unthinkable. He got high with her. They were having sex and she told him if he took a toke of her blunt it would make him last longer. He was skeptical at first, but she put a lot of pressure on him and he folded. Dusty took the blunt from her and pulled on it. The weed and crack combined together gave

175

him an unusual high. He was speeding from the cocaine, but also feeling the depressant of the cannabis. His heart rate increased, and then he was overcome with a panicky feeling. Lizzette studied his reaction, then put his dick in her mouth and sucked him to his climax. She figured if he reached his peak he wouldn't be able to distinguish what it was that made him feel so good. As the night continued they smoked more and more, getting higher and higher. Then she took him to his graduation. She introduced him to the pipe. Dusty was so high and his mind was so jumbled that he didn't realize what he was doing to himself, and by the time he did, it was too late. She coached him and taught him how to get the full effect of the blast by holding the smoke in his lungs for a long period of time, and before the night was out Dusty was a product of his own destructive ways. During the following days, Dusty found himself married not only to the drug, but also to the perpetrator of his habit. He tried to refrain from indulging, but the more he fought the urge, the more Lizzette cajoled him. It was a losing battle in the end. He was in love with both of them—the woman and the drug.

La continued to talk to Dusty, but he didn't seem interested in what La was telling him. He was wondering if his main man Rock really knew what was going on with him. He was hoping his ways and actions didn't show he was strung out on the same product he was supposed to be selling. Dusty tried to focus on what La was saying but his mind was flooded with too many thoughts. He was too far gone and didn't know how to ask for help.

"I hear you, La. I know I been slippin', and I should be on top of my game, but to keep it real wit' you, she got me fucked up in the head real bad."

"That's what Rock was saying. He musta peeped it and told you, but you so caught up you not hearing him." La had the feeling there was something more to what was going on with Dusty, but he didn't want to speculate.

"Look, La, I'm gonna get back on my job. You don't have to worry about this shit no more."

"Aight, I hear you, but this the last time, Dusty. Rock been carrying you for a minute now, and I know he tired."

"I know and I respect that. You got my word, La. I'm back to work."

Dusty slapped La five and walked off. It was the weekend and he needed to make some money because he had to meet Lizzette later on that night.

KB got out of the cab on Flushing Avenue and walked up the walkway to Stump's building. Some young guys were out there gambling as he passed by with the big duffel bag full of guns. When he got inside he saw someone serving a crack head by the stairs, which was unusual in Stump's building because he didn't allow any drug selling in front of or inside his building. When he got upstairs everyone was sitting around drinking and smoking weed.

"What up, K?" Stump asked, passing the blunt.

"Nuthin'. I didn't know you were slingin'."

"What you talkin' 'bout?"

"I seen some young nigga serving a head in the lobby. I remember you sayin' that you told all dem young cats that they couldn't hustle in front of your building, so I figured it must be your shit that they selling."

"WHAT!" Stump boomed. He didn't like drug dealers. It didn't take any heart to sell drugs to an addict, and it didn't take any skill to make the money, but there was another reason he hated drug dealers. He had lost his mother to an overdose when he was seven-years-old.

The dealer that sold her the lethal dosage was his father, and he had left her to die. Stump stood in the doorway of her bedroom as he watched his father pack his belongings as his mother lay shaking and foaming at the mouth on the cold, wooden floor. The dealer never noticed his son, motionless, tears streaming down his cheeks, standing there watching, but unable to utter a single word. His father grabbed her "tools" and any other evidence that could prove he had been a witness to her death, and rushed out of the bedroom, literally knocking young Stump to the ground. The door slammed close and Stump made it to his feet, slowly walking into the bedroom to help his dying mother. He cried out her name in hopes of getting a response, but her eyes stayed rolled up in her head, showing only the white portion, and her violent spasms continued. Stump heard the door slam again and the noise made him jump. When he turned around, his father grabbed him by both arms and lifted him up in the air, shaking him violently.

"You betta not tell nobody I was here, you lil bastard, or you'll wind up like your dope fiend mama!" his father yelled. Young Stump was speechless and scared shitless. The dealer put him down and pushed his face down to the colorless corpse on the floor. "Look at her! If you say anything to anybody, this is what's gonna happen to you!" Stump was horrified when he released him and he ran to the corner and slid down the wall, staring blankly into space. His father looked at him, satisfied he would be in the clear, then left for the final time. When the police and paramedics arrived five hours later,

they found the overdosed woman sprawled on the floor and young Stump in the same spot, sitting in his own feces and urine. He was in shock. And that may have been the reason they didn't ask him any questions about what had happened to his mother. And ever since then Stump couldn't stand anything about drug dealers or slingin'.

Stump opened the duffel bag, pulled out a sawed-off shotgun, and headed for the door. The rest of the guys got up on cue and followed him out. KB thought he was going to stay behind, but Stump beckoned him too, because he wanted him to ID the kid he saw selling in his building.

When they reached the lobby no one was there, so Stump opened the door and went outside. There was a group of young boys in front of the building, but when they saw Stump and the shotgun, they took off running.

"Don't run, you little muhfuckas, 'fore I make y'all a fuckin' memory!" he yelled, pointing the shotgun in their direction. "Which one of them sold in my building?" Stump asked KB.

"That one over there," KB said, pointing the guy out as the young crew looked at him like the snitch he was.

"Danny?" Stump asked, pointing the shotgun at the young boy's head. "This my lil man." He looked at Danny, flames in his pupils. "Why the fuck would you do that? You know I don't tolerate that shit in my building. Get the fuck in the building, all of y'all!"

They all filed into the building and were shocked when they saw all the guns aimed at them. Visions of dying were on all their minds.

"Empty your fuckin' pockets," Stump screamed. Everyone complied and Danny was the only one with drugs on him. Stump scooped up the vials of crack and money and handed them over to KB, along with the shotgun, and then in a flash he slapped the spit out of Danny.

"Whose shit is this?"

"Rock and La."

"Who the fuck is Rock and La?"

"Them niggas from Baptiste," KB interjected.

"Get the fuck outta here. You workin' for them muhfuckas?"

"We robbed one of their workers a couple weeks back, and to stop us from sticking them up they gave me work so I wouldn't hit them again."

"So you took they shit and then you gonna come here and violate, is that what you're telling me?"

"It's not like that, Stump, man. Ain't nowhere to sell out here, and I know nobody sells outta this building. All I was trying to do was get some clientele and then tell them I was gonna be over by the fence."

"I tell you what, lil' nigga"—he grabbed him by his throat and threw him against the wall—"tell them niggas from Baptiste that I got they shit, and if I catch you or any one of your homeboys around my building again, I'm gonna dead y'all. Now get the fuck outta here!" he yelled as he kicked Danny in the ass.

"You believe that shit?" Stump asked KB as they went back into his building. "Them the same niggas I was gonna rob, ain't it? I see them muhfuckas really don't believe that it can happen to them. Now they all up in my projects tryin' to get money. They must really think that this shit is over. I'm gonna kill them niggas one by one. That's my word on my mama's grave. Before it's all over, I'ma make them projects a ghost town. I'ma light that shit up like the Fourth of July."

"I didn't know them niggas was back out there hustlin' after that shit went down," KB replied.

"It don't matter. They not gonna be out there for long. This time I'ma do it right, just me and you, K. You hear me, man?"

"You know I'm wit' you, man."

"Well let's deal with that after we do this stick."

"Did your man ever come by and tell you the time?"

"Yeah, he said we need to be there by one. The owner comes between one and three and doesn't stay long. He drives a black Beema. We can do it two ways. We can either get him when he comes out, or we can go up in there and get him and everybody else in that muhfucka. I prefer to go up in there and get everybody else with him, because that's how I plan to pay my man, 'cause he ain't gettin' none of that money in the safe. What y'all think?" He was asking everyone's opinion, but he already had his mind made up.

"I'm wit' gettin' everybody up in there," Murder Mike said.

"Fuck it. Let's go all out," Ray-Ray said.

"Let's get 'em all," Drez said.

"What about you, K?" Stump asked.

"Shit, I'm just the driver. It makes me no difference."

"Nah, kid, not if we go up in there. We need another head up in there with us. You know how many muhfuckas gonna be up in that piece?" Stump asked.

KB's heart dropped when Stump said that. He didn't want to go up in there with them fools. He wanted to stay out in the van where he felt he had a better chance of not getting hurt or caught. He knew from the beginning he wasn't cut out to run with Stump, but his desire for recognition along with greed had gotten the best of him. He never realized he would have to get involved so deeply, but now his back was against the wall and there was no way around it.

"I know, but who gonna drive the van?"

"You still gonna drive. You gonna be the first one to leave. I already got this shit mapped out, kid. E'erything gonna be aight."

There was a knock on the door and Stump got up and answered it in his usual style—guns drawn and standing close to the wall.

"Who is it?" Stump asked.

"Stone."

Stump looked through the peephole, then opened the door slowly and greeted his friend, the bouncer. They walked to the bedroom in the back of the apartment and closed the door behind them, then emerged from behind the door about twenty minutes later, and the bouncer left as fast as he came.

When Stump locked the door he went into the living room and yelled, "IT'S ON!"

Chapter 13
Love hurts, baby.

It was late when Junior called Shondra back. He showed Muffin how to bag up and he was relaxing in the stash house drinking cognac and smoking herb. He was gonna use Muffin and make her a part of his team. No one had a female thoroughbred on their team, and Junior was gonna make her the most dangerous part of his clique.

"What up, Mooka?" he asked into the mouthpiece of the receiver.

"What took you so long to call me back, Junior?"

"Come on, you know I had to go take care of my business. I told you I was gonna make a major move. Now we gonna live like real kings and queens."

"I hope that's all you doin'."

"Go 'head with that shit. Now tell me what happened."

"Gloria came down here a while after you left and was telling me some shit about KB. She said the nigga was plotting to do something else with that dude Stump."

"What did he tell her?"

"She listened in on his phone conversation and said he was talking to Stump and that Stump told him to go get some guns or something like that and to meet him at his house afterward."

"Did he mention my name or anything?"

"She didn't say he did. I mean, I really don't know. I don't think so."

"What the fuck you mean? Either she said it or she didn't."

"Why you flippin' on me? I'm just telling you what she came down and told me. Damn!"

"I'm sorry, ma. It's just that I want to get them niggas 'fore they get the drop on me. I'm trying to make some power moves, and I ain't gonna be comfortable until I know them dudes is taken care of."

"I'm scared, Junior. You know they killed those Dominicans over in Lindsey."

"Fuck that shit. Fuck them niggas. I'ma put them niggas to rest when I catch them."

"I just want you to be careful, baby. I'm just worried, that's all."

Muffin came into the room and Junior looked at her and put his index finger over his mouth to let her know not to say anything while he was on the phone. Muffin, being the intellectual woman she was, figured he was talking to Shondra. She walked over to him, pulled down his zipper, and commenced to giving him head while he was on the phone. She knew he wouldn't be able to continue his conversation as long as she was sucking his insides right out of him. Junior began to breathe heavy as his conversation continued with Shondra, and he tried to contain himself, but Muffin was sucking on him like a vacuum.

"What's wrong, Junior?"

"N-n-n-nothing, ma. I caught a pain in my side . . . mmmmm," he managed to get out. "I'ma call you lata', aight?"

"You not comin' here tonight?"

"Mmmmhmmm, I'll be there lata. I gotta go."

Shondra wasn't crazy or stupid. She heard slurping noises in the background as he hung up the phone. She knew he was there with a girl, and she had warned him about fucking around on her. She dialed his beeper number again and again. She was going to do that all night until he came or called her back.

***

"You made up your mind?" Craig asked Junior as he and Muffin walked to the car.

"About what?"

"You hangin' with me or what?"

"I don't know, man. You know I got to get to work with this shit I just got."

"Come on, man, it ain't like you go out all the time. You could bring your pretty lady with you, too. Don't you want to go clubbin' Saturday, ma?"

"Sure, why not?"

"See, your girl wants to hang, so you might as well just bring her with you so both of y'all can enjoy yourselves."

Muffin was looking at Junior, hoping he would take her out to the club, which would give her a chance to let all the bitches know she was next in line, after his girl. She loved the spotlight and knew a lot of girls wanted to be with Junior, especially since she had hooked up with him. It was always like that when a nigga became a hot commodity.

"Come on, daddy, let's go out together. I like to dance, too, you know."

"Aight, but I'm not stayin' long." He walked over to Craig and whispered to him. "That's some foul shit you just did, but payback's a muhfucka."

"You'll get over it, kid, once you hear that loud music and see all them hoes in there on your dick, then you'll be thanking me," Craig whispered back.

"How so? You just told me to bring sand to the beach."

"Don't worry about that. Them hoes gonna let me know, and I'll put you on. Don't worry..Just come and have a good time."

"I'll be back later. I need to talk to you about some things. I just made a power move and I want to make sure everything's gonna run right in the hood when I put it out there."

"Shit, nigga, it took you long enough. I was waiting on you to make your move so you could come play with the big boys."

"Whateva. I'm 'bout to blow up so fast that it's gonna make niggas in the hood hate me more than they do now. I'm a major player now, baby."

"On the real, we gotta talk about putting this shit together so that none of us have to be in this shit too much longer. I love the game, but you gotta know when to hold 'em and when to fold 'em. Shit is getting kind of thick out here and you know election year is coming up. You fed status now, baby. No more blue clothes coming atcha—all suits—so you gotta be weary of how you move." Craig knew his little cousin's status was about to change, and he wanted him to be aware of how serious things were going to get for him.

Junior looked at Craig and was amazed at how he had changed his demeanor like a chameleon. One minute he was talking shit about partying, and the next minute he was talking like a scholar of the game. Junior listened intently to everything Craig said because Craig was a vet in the game, and his shit had been running smooth ever since his first bid. When he came home, his jail reputation followed him. He was known at every compound from Rikers Island to Sing Sing. Tompkins was a dangerous place to live with robberies and shootings every day, but Craig had used that to his advantage. He recruited all the hard heads and offered them the opportunity to put their guns down and make some steady money. Some were reluctant, but most of them got on board and crime in the projects diminished without the help from the president, mayor, borough president, or any other politician looking to get elected for another term. Craig eventually took control of all illegal activity in the projects and gained respect from the very young to the very old. He was known to end beefs permanently with bodies gone missing or being found dead in other boroughs. Craig was a kingpin in the projects. He was known and respected in all boroughs, and he was the boss of Brooklyn in his own right.

"I'm telling you, man, I think that nigga smokin'," Rock was telling La.

"How you know for sure?"

"He be actin' different and shit. He always with that bitch. I mean, always. If a nigga spend that much time with a broad and she smokin', he gotta be smokin' with her. That shit just don't fly with me, La."

"I hear you talkin', B, but you gotta be sure, you know what I'm sayin'?"

"How sure you gotta be? I mean, if a nigga start actin' different and changing his ways, that's a sign that something ain't right. Look at Kendu. Was he actin' funny to you?"

That question took La back. He thought about his childhood friend and how he was actin' funny and even talking different near the end. He stopped hustling like he used to, and Joyce told La that Kendu never had work when she wanted to cop from him, and when she did cop, it looked like the bottles were tapped. He remembered when he and Kendu were talking about crack heads and how they would never try it because they saw what the effects did to the users. They promised each other they would never try it, no matter what, but now his friend was dead because of it. If Dusty was on crack, La wanted to save him, especially because he was unable to save his own best friend.

"I can't lie, son, there were signs that something wasn't right, but because that was my man, I didn't want to believe that shit was for real. I don't want Dusty to go out like that, so I'ma make sure that he is smokin' before I try to help him. I can't go to him and dis him like that and be wrong. Feel me, son?"

"That's my dawg and I got eyes. I see that he ain't right in the head, and it ain't because he fuckin' with that bitch and she got him sprung. It's something else and I'm not trying to lose my peeps over no bitch that's tryin' to get him strung out so he can feed her fucked-up habit. I already dealt with that shit once with my moms, so I ain't tryin' to lose the only family I got left to that shit."

"Any money been short lately?"

"Nah, but you wouldn't be able to tell because he got grip and he keep a stash in the crib. I seen him give that ho like fifty dollars worth of work like she was on the books with us. When I asked him about it, he told me that she bought it. The bitch smart. She keeps him away from me because she know that I be pullin' her card right in front of him. That fight we had wasn't the first time we got into it ova that bitch. One day I came in the crib and the whole back room was smoky. When I went to the back he started flippin' and told me to get out. He told me if I violated his space again that I wouldn't be able to live there no more. The bitch came out the room and she was zoned out. I could tell she was beaming up because her eyes was wide as hell and when she started talking her mouth was twisted. I know he was buggin' because he would beef crazy when I want to blow weed in the room but he lets that bitch turn his room into a crack house. Believe me, son, right then I knew that they was doin' that shit together. I broke fool on her and the nigga came to her rescue like Super Save-A-Ho. I was wondering why he would flip on me ova a crack head smoking in the crib."

"Let's go up there now."

"He changed the locks after that. That's why I don't be ova there like that no more. I told you that the bitch practically stay every night with him."

"Well, let's go to her crib and I'ma ask her straight up."

"What? You think she gonna tell you he smokin'?"

"Not just like that. You gotta know how to make people tell you what you want to know. Come on, let's go find her and Dusty."

After going to Lizzette's apartment and not finding her there, they went to Dusty's house and knocked on the door. No one answered, so they went downstairs to wait out front for him. Lizzette was coming into the building when they reached the lobby. La turned to Rock.

"Follow my lead," La told Rock. "Ay, yo, can I talk to you for a minute?" La asked Lizzette, blocking her path.

"Hi, no, papi. I'm in a rush right now. I'll talk to you when I come back out."

"Look, miss, I need to talk to you right now. It can't wait."

"OK, papi, calm down. Tell me what it is that you want to talk about."

La grabbed her by the arm and pulled her with him into the exit. She started to resist when he started pulling her toward the exit because she was afraid. She wanted to scream, but she was fearful that would make matters worse.

"Where the fuck is my shit?"

"What ju talkin' 'bout?"

"Don't act like you don't know, bitch," Rock said menacingly.

Lizzette's hands started to shake. She was consumed with fear and her mouth and throat were getting dry.

"I swear I don't know what ju talkin' 'bout. Please tell me."

La pulled out his gun, backed away from Lizzette, and pointed it to her face.

"I'm gonna give you ten seconds to get my work or my money. If you don't, I'm gonna splatter your brains all ova the wall."

"I no have no work or no money for ju. I don't have nuthin' of yours. Pleeeeez, you makin' a mistake."

"No, bitch, you made the mistake because I went to see Dusty to get my money for the shit he sold and he told me he gave you the work on credit and you smoked all my shit up, so now I want my money or my work or you're gonna have a hole in your head."

"What?" She sobbed. "He lyin'. He didn't give me shit on credit. We smoked that shit together that he had."

"Stop lyin', bitch. My man don't smoke that shit!"

"I no lyin', baby. Ask your friend. He know."

"Don't look at me. I don't know shit, bitch!" Rock said.

"Yes, baby, ju know. Ju came in one night and we were smoking then."

Lizzette was afraid Dusty smoked up La's entire product and was now trying to pass the buck to her to take the blame off himself. She had to find a way to prove she didn't do it all by herself.

"Look, papi, he upstairs right now waiting for me to come back with some more stuff. He gave me this money." She pulled out some money from her pocket. "I'm supposed to get it from Louie because he said he the one that looks out. That's who he told me to go to."

La knew she wasn't lying. Louie was the only worker that gave out deals.

"Give me that!"

"What else you got?" Rock asked.

"I no have nuthin' else. I swear to Mary."

"I'm only gonna tell you this once." La was standing in front of her, his face and hers so close together that they were nearly kissing. "If I catch you around my boy again, I'm gonna ram that glass dick you be sucking down your fuckin' throat. Do you understand me?"

"Y-y-y-yes."

"Now get the fuck outta here, you fuckin' ho!"

Lizzette fell over herself trying to get out of the building. She was glad she didn't get hurt, but she was furious with Dusty for setting her up like that. La didn't have to worry about her seeing Dusty anymore, because after that shit Dusty lied on her about, she wasn't going to give him the time of day anyway. As far as she was concerned, Dusty was dead to her.

"I told you he was smokin' that shit. That bitch just confirmed it," Rock said.

"Yeah, that's fucked up. I don't know how niggas can get strung out on that shit, 'specially when they see what it does to them crack heads," La said.

"Now tell me how we supposed to get the nigga to admit he's smoking'?" Rock asked.

"I don't know. I'm just gonna tell him that I know and that if he wants help, I'll help him."

"That shit ain't gonna work. I told you how he flipped on me, and I'm his man."

"That's all I can do. But check it, if he don't want no help, son, I gotta cut him loose. I can't have him on my team if he fuckin' wit' that shit."

"I know, man," Rock said sadly. "I don't understand that nigga. I mean, he knows what I went through wit' my moms. He know I can't deal with that shit again."

La knocked on Dusty's door and put his ear to it. He heard someone ruffling around and backed up when he heard the footsteps getting closer.

Dusty looked out the peephole and saw La and Rock again. He didn't open the door the first time they came because he was waiting for Lizzette to bring back their "get high."

"Open the door, Dus. We know you in there," La yelled through the door.

Damn! Dusty thought to himself.

"Aight, hold up." He went to his room and opened the windows, lit an incense, and hid the glass pipe and other tools he and Lizzette used to get high.

"Come on, Dus," La said impatiently. Dusty went back to the door.

"I don't want that nigga comin' in my house," Dusty yelled to La. He was referring to Rock.

"Come on, man, we need to talk to you," La said.

"Fuck it, La. If the nigga don't want me around, then I'm ghost. Just let me know what happened."

"Aight, I'll see you in a few," La said to Rock. "Open the door. Rock just left."

The locks clicked and the door opened slowly. Dusty turned around, went into the living room, and sat on the couch. La closed the door behind him, followed Dusty into the living room, and sat on the loveseat across from Dusty.

"What the fuck that nigga Rock wanted? He know he ain't allowed in my crib no more."

"He worried about you, kid. I'm worried about you."

"What y'all worried about me for?"

"Look, Dus, you know you my lil nigga, right?" La started. "I'm just gonna tell you what I know."

Suddenly Dusty had this funny feeling in his stomach. His worst fears were coming true. La had found out he was smokin' crack with Lizzette. How was he going to deny it? How could he look at him with a straight face and lie? He and Lizzette already smoked up the rest of the package he had left, and if La came for the money or the work, he knew he was gonna come up short. He was in a precarious situation and felt like he was shrinking as he looked at La and waited for him to drop the bomb.

"I just saw that bitch you fuck with and she told me some disturbing shit. First she told me that y'all both smoked up my pack. Now I'm gonna ask you man to man if you fuckin' wit' that shit, but before you answer, I want to tell you something first. If you tell me you not fuckin' with that shit and I find out you lying to me, I'm gonna hurt you, straight up. Now if you come clean and tell me you need help, I'm gonna help you, and when you kick the habit, you'll still have your position here. Now, tell me what's up?"

Dusty put his head down.

"I need help, kid," he mumbled.

La went over an sat on the couch next to Dusty, hugging him without saying a word. Dusty had said enough.

When Shondra rolled over and didn't feel Junior next to her, she jumped up out of the bed.

I know that nigga ain't leave without telling me shit, she thought to herself. She walked through the house to see if he was there, and when she realized he left without at least saying goodbye, she became irate. The previous night when he came in she had confronted him about being with someone else, and he lied and told her she was bugging. She didn't have any proof, although she knew she wasn't bugging as he asserted. She knew she heard some slurping noises before he hung up the phone that one time, and she knew those sounds came from someone sucking his dick. He left in a huff, but when he came in later that night he made love to her and the show of love and affection had calmed her down temporarily.

Now that she was up and he was gone, she was pumped up again and couldn't help but think about who he was with. Shondra loved Junior and would do anything in the world for him, but she would not tolerate him cheating on her because she was so loyal to him. She couldn't understand why he would do that to her, especially when she had proved her love for him endlessly. She didn't understand what was happening to them.

"Who is it?" Shondra yelled from her room to the person knocking on her front door.

"It's me, girl," Gloria responded.

Shondra went to open the door and when Gloria entered, she was in an upbeat mood.

"What the hell is wrong with you?" Shondra asked.

"I think that instead of me crying ova some nigga, I should just take it for what it's worth and move on with my life," Gloria said.

"Ohhh Kaaay . . ."

"I see it like this, sis. If a nigga don't love you enough to keep shit real, then why push him? I'm only giving as good as I'm gettin'. I'm all cried out. I'm not puttin' my heart into somebody that ain't returning the same love," Gloria said, expressing her new attitude.

"What? Did KB call you and upset you with some more bullshit?"

"That's the point. He didn't call. He knew that I was upset before he left. If he was so concerned, he would have at least called a sista to make her feel better, but he didn't. Whatever it is he's up to, it's more important than my feelings, so I'm sayin' fuck it. I'm not gonna let this shit keep upsetting me. I'm gonna keep going forward. Fuck this fake love shit."

"All right, honey. When did you get this revelation?"

"Last night. I was crying my eyes and heart out for someone who probably wasn't even thinking about me. I told myself that I was wasting my tears on someone who didn't appreciate the kind of love I had showed him, so I figured that I better learn to love myself first because I know I won't hurt me. I believe that he cares for me, but he just doesn't love me as much as I love him, so I just can't give more than I'm getting anymore."

She would have told Gloria to leave that, but she was finding it hard to take her own advice.

"What you gonna do when he comes back?" Shondra asked.

"I ain't gonna do shit. I'm gonna act the same as far as he's concerned, but I'm gonna look out for my own feelings. I'm not gonna let his actions dictate my emotions anymore. He's a man. I'm gonna give him his space, but in the meantime I'm gonna enjoy myself. I can't lie and say I don't love that nigga, but I'm not gonna let my love for him make me crazy. Fuck that, it's about me," she said, snapping her fingers and turning around.

"You right. We should never love a nigga more than we love ourselves, 'specially when they don't show us the same kind of love in return. It's fucked up that we gotta get our feelings all hurt up and shit before we realize how foolish we really be actin' when it comes to these niggas."

"Well, girl, I'm ready to go out and celebrate. You wanna hit the club tonight?" Gloria asked, shaking her hips. "I'm ready to get down and dance my pretty black ass off, and who knows, somebody might notice me."

Shondra wasn't in the partying mood, but she couldn't let her girl go out by herself, so she agreed to go with Gloria to a club.

***

"I'm trying to straighten that shit out right now," La was telling someone on the telephone. "Just have your man meet me to drop off the guns." La hung up the telephone and looked at Rock. "You think you'll be ready to do what we was talking about?"

"I'm ready right now," Rock said.

"I think we should wait a couple more days. I'll have them heaters by then. My man is supposed to be bringin' them ova later on."

"I knew this was gonna have to be taken care of sooner rather than later. Even though shit is kinda smooth out here, you have to make sure you cover all the bases," Rock said.

"I know, and once this shit is done, we gonna be on our way, baby," La said, slapping Rock five.

"I'm with you, nigga, all the way. You tell Junior about Dusty yet?"

"I been beepin' that nigga today and I was hittin' him last night, but he ain't called me back yet and he was ova here last night at his girl's house. We need to get another package because we running low and that shit Dusty fucked up set us back. I hope that nigga don't think I'm gonna eat that loss because I'm not. He should have been out here too. Shit, if you didn't put me on, I would have never known that nigga was smoking that shit with that bitch."

"Where you sendin' him?"

"They got this inpatient spot up in Manhattan on 126th and Edgecombe. He'll be in there for six months, then they'll transfer him to an outpatient spot closer to home until he's fully rehabilitated."

"That's cool. I'm just glad we caught him before he was really out there and strung out."

La's beeper went off and it was Junior, so he and Rock went to the payphone on the corner to call Junior back.

"What up?" La asked as he heard Junior's voice on the other end.

"I got your beep. I was busy. That's why I didn't call you back. You finished?"

"We gettin' low. It's time to re-up."

"I'll be over there in a minute."

"Aight, I'll be on the block."

Junior pulled up in his cousin's Benz, got out a block away from the spot, and walked through the back of the projects. When La spotted him coming up he got off the benches and met him halfway.

"Let's go to your crib," Junior said.

La followed him to the car and they took the short drive to his building. La got out, and Junior grabbed a blue gym bag from the backseat before getting out. Once inside La's apartment, Junior took out the contents inside the bag. La stood and looked at all the bagged up crack and was in awe. He had never seen that much at one time. He was wondering what Junior was up to.

"I just copped a couple days ago. This is some new product. I need you to give out some samples to the custies and see how they like it. This shit is supposed to be better than what we have now."

"Damn, the bottles are bigger. What happened?"

"We on the come up, babe bruh," Junior said, smiling. "We 'bout to take this shit to the next level. I want to have this shit pumping through all the surrounding hoods," Junior said, pulling on a cigarette he had just lit. "Oh, yeah, there's something else, La. I got this chick that I want to put on. I want her to pick up and drop off for you. I need Rock to be with me over in Tompkins. You'll still have Dusty and you can let him take over for Rock."

"That's cool, but Dusty's fucked up."

"What you mean?"

"Dusty's smoked out on that shit. That bitch Lizzette turned him out," La explained. "Rock pulled my coat to it and I handled it. Tomorrow he going to a rehab so he can get cleaned up."

"What the fuck! What's wrong wit' these niggas? Don't they see what that shit do to a muhfucka? Shit!"

"I know, man. I was thinkin' 'bout how that shit killed 'Du. When I found out about Dusty I wanted to make sure that I did something to help him out before it was too late."

"That's good. I'm glad you handled this before it got outta hand. Well now I gotta think on how I'm gonna do this."

"Don't worry. I got things on this end, so you can concentrate on what you gotta do over in Tompkins."

"Boy, seems like you got e'erythin' covered, huh? I knew you were the right pick for this."

"Man, I got you. You ain't got to worry 'bout shit as long as I'm out here."

"Let me think about it and I'll get back to you, aight?"

"That's peace."

"You want to go hang out wit' me tonight?"

"Where at?"

"Some club on Broadway. My cousin is throwing a party for his man that just came home. You down?"

"Nah, I got this chick I'm gonna check out tonight. We'll hang out another time."

"Aight then, I'll give you a hit tomorrow on what I'm gonna do. I'm out."

**

The warm water felt good against her skin as Muffin sat in her bathtub. She was taking a bubble bath before getting ready for the party. The white foam in the tub covered her naked body, revealing only her knees that popped up every now and then when she shifted her position. She lathered herself with the bubbly water and her skin felt like silk as she moved her hands up and down her thighs. She closed her eyes and began to think about Junior and how good his lovemaking was. Unconsciously she started to play with herself, massaging her clit and rubbing her breasts. Her nipples hardened as she pinched them gently, and her cat pulsated from the gentle touches to her middle. Muffin was fantasizing about how Junior initiated foreplay before making love to her. She was stuck in her dream world about their intimacy, and before she knew it she was moving and moaning to every good feeling going through her body. As the time passed the water gently rippled with every movement of her gorgeous body, and soon she climaxed, awakening her from her sexual dream.

Muffin dried herself off and went into her bedroom to lie down. She flopped down on the bed with her arms sprawled out, naked as a newborn baby. She was deep in thought about how lucky she was to have Junior come into her life again, and how she didn't have any plans of letting him go. She turned her head to the closet where the Nina Ricci silk dress Junior bought her was hanging on the door. Once she put it on, she knew she would be the hottest thing in the club. It was a French designer dress and she was shocked when she looked at the price tag when he purchased it. He had spent eight hundred dollars and didn't even flinch. She couldn't wait for him to see her in it because there was no denying her shape. When she tried it on it conformed to every curve of her body. She knew she was shaped like a thick stripper with an hour glass figure, and her lovely looks were the bonus. She loved the way Junior lusted for her and how he never acted jealous because he was confident, something else that attracted her to him. She knew Junior liked her, but she wasn't sure how much. She wanted to do everything in her power to please him. She was his bottom bitch in his stable of whores.

"Girl, what the hell you doin' lyin' on your bed naked like that?" her mother asked as she entered Muffin's room.

"Why didn't you knock?" Muffin asked back, getting up and putting on her pink robe. "Damn, ma, you don't give me no privacy and respect."

"Look who's talkin'. This my house, lil girl. I was comin' in here to tell you that Junior called and said he was coming over here in about an hour."

"OK, thanks, ma."

"Baby, you really like that boy, don't you?"

"Yeah, ma, he's real nice. He treats me good."

Her mother sat on the bed. She was about to have a talk with her daughter that she wished she had with her before she encountered all the bad men she met.

Muffin's mother was from the streets of Brooklyn, born and bred. She had her share of good men, and she most definitely had her time with the gutter niggas. She had Muffin at a young age. She was only sixteen-years-old when she met a smooth talking hustler named Juicee. He wined and dined her and showed her the fast life, flashing big wads of money, which enticed her. She didn't know the streets until she met him, and he showed her the hustler's life at an early age. Muffin's mother got pregnant and lost the shape that once had Juicee begging to hit it, so he strayed to her best friend. And when Muffin was born, Juicee denied her existence.

Muffin's mother tried to raise her daughter to the best of her ability, but because she was a youngster herself, she had failed miserably, and had neglected Muffin through the years. She never had the chance to teach Muffin to love herself first and not to look to a man for that affection. She worked hard, long hours, and when she came in late nights from work, she was always too exhausted to spend quality time with Muffin. This ultimately ruined their relationship because Muffin was neglected emotionally, and lacked the maternal love to mold her into a woman. Her mother always wanted a mother-daughter relationship with Muffin, but time had passed her too fast, and Muffin grew up on her own and relied on the streets to teach her what her mother couldn't.

"Listen, Muffin," she began, "I see you have that sparkle in your eye over that boy. I just want to tell you somethin'. I'm not preachin' to you, baby. I just want to give you some advice, OK?"

Muffin never talked to her mother much about her relationships with boys, so what was happening right now seemed weird to her, but she invited the conversation.

"I'm listenin'," she replied.

"Sweetheart, there are two kinds of guys out there—the ones that respect women, and the ones that women respect. I've noticed that the fella you're seein' is very respectable, but you have to be careful of his intentions. A lot of guys see women as revolving doors or notches on their belts. The way you can make sure that they maintain respect for you is to keep your self-respect. Don't ever sell yourself short, and never settle for less than you're worth. A real man will respect that about you."

"What if he has a girl already?"

"You shouldn't play second to anyone, because that is a sign of weakness. It means that you are settling. However, if you do play second, then you should get double what the first one gets, be it emotionally or financially. Always remember your position if you agree to play second. You are limited in what you can do in that relationship, because if you don't know what part you play, when you slip up, he will let you know. The mistress might receive expensive gifts for substitutions of missed dates, broken promises, or absence of quality time. Remember, if he has someone else, you will not get the special times like his birthday, Thanksgiving, Christmas, and New Year's. These are lonely holidays if you're the mistress. You also have to remember that you can't have another man because *he* will never be open to playing second. Baby, if you're this man's mistress, you may become dependent on him if he's taking care of you financially. You have to be careful to monitor your emotions and not let them take over, because if you do, he may see you as a liability to his relationship with his main girl and get rid of you before you can cause any problems between them."

"I really like him, ma, and I know he has a girl, but that doesn't bother me because he treats me good and I spend more time with him right now than she does. Tonight we goin' to his cousin's party. Wouldn't he take his girl if it was like that?"

"Listen, sweetheart, you have to be able to understand your position as well as play it. You have to know where you stand and be sure that you don't overstep your boundaries. You can't become a slave to your heart. We tend to make bad decisions when we think with our hearts instead of our heads. Our judgment is clouded by emotions and feelings that could lead us to definite heartbreak. You must make him know that you do care for him, but would leave him in a heartbeat if he was to violate you in any way. And, baby, that's something you will have to stick to because if you say it and don't act on it, that is another sign of weakness, and that will be your greatest disadvantage in your relationship. It's OK to love him. It's even OK to lust after him, but you can't become obsessed because that will destroy your virtue as a woman and you may find yourself doing things that you wouldn't normally do. And depending on how he really feels for you, he may cut you loose and save himself the headache of dealing with you."

"I don't want to play myself with him, ma, but I really do like him and I believe that he will be all mine in the end. I mean, I know about his girl and all, but that's not gonna to stop me from doing what I have to do to be his girl."

Muffin's mother could see her daughter was emotionally caught up with Junior. She knew from experience that most men thrived on having a woman who understood they had a girl at home, because they didn't have to hide anything from them, and at times that could lead to disrespect. She knew it was too late to tell her daughter she was in an unhealthy relationship because she was already obsessing over the guy. From her own experience, she knew it was rare that a nigga would leave his main girl if his side girl already knew about his situation. Why would he?

"The only thing I can tell you is to follow your heart, baby, but use your mind as your guide. Then everything should work out in your favor. Love hurts, baby, and it's unlike any physical pain in the world," her mother said, giving her the longest and tightest hug she had ever given her daughter in her life.

196

Chapter 14
Wow, y□all rollin□deep.

"Get down!" Junior was yelling at Midnight. Craig's pit was jumping on him as he came out of the bathroom from taking a shower. Midnight was excited because Junior had been playing with him a lot since spending so much time at Craig's crib. Craig had told him not to play with the dog because he was strictly there for protection and nothing more. Junior went into the room to get dressed for the club. His cousin was already downstairs with his crew. They were all standing in the parking lot. Everyone was going to leave from there to go to the club. Craig told Junior earlier he wanted to show up in the club with about thirty people deep to show strength.

Junior looked out the window and could see all the guys and girls hovered around Craig. He was the center of attention and Junior kind of envied the love his hood showed him. He wanted his crew to love him similarly, but it wasn't like that with him. La's attitude was changing, and he had a strong feeling that it wasn't for the better. Junior didn't grow up in La's area, but he hung out there a lot when he was young, so he felt like he was a native.

As he thought about La and his role in his organization, Junior remembered the jewel his cousin Craig dropped on him when he first started hustling in Baptiste.

"In order to get respect from the niggas around there, you have to remember that you gotta gain their love and respect without them disliking you," Craig had said. "That's hard to accomplish because you are not born and bred there. They will always see you as an outsider. You will have to do things that they have to respect as men and fear as gangsters. You have to make them believe that their hood is your hood. You have to make them believe that you are a native to that hood. In other words, lil cuz, you have to love thy neighbor's hood. If you fail to make them respect and fear you, you will not last long out there getting money, and they will run you out or kill you, so be careful. Niggas get jealous where money is involved, so you have to make sure that anyone that wants to eat can be fed, or at least offer them something to keep them happy. Never put all your trust in anyone, and never let them know everything. Always switch up. Never keep the same routine. Be *hard to figure out, because who you think is your friend will fool you. This game has no loyalty,"* Craig said, finishing his sermon.

As Junior got dressed this night he couldn't get hustling out of his mind. He was feeling like he had given La too much control, which was causing Junior to lose his place in the operation. Most of the workers were really under La's order.

He put on a blue, double-breasted suit with a black, silk shirt and a pair of black Stacy Adams. He complimented the shirt with a gold rope chain with a medallion, and his gold nugget watch. Craig walked into the room with an impatient look on his face.

"Y'all niggas ready to break out?" Junior asked, picking up his gun.

"Yeah, nigga. We was waiting on you."

"Before we go, I gotta go pick up Muffin from her crib."

"That's aight. We'll follow you."

They took the elevator down and walked into the parking lot to the awaiting throng of people. Everyone was in their Sunday best, and almost everyone had a forty ounce in their hands. Junior greeted everyone in the parking lot. There were faces he didn't recognize, but the love was so thick it didn't matter. They all stood around talking and joking for a while, then everyone started going to their cars. Craig announced that they were going to follow Junior to pick up his lady first, and from there they would head to the club. When Junior pulled up in front of Muffin's house, she was impatiently waiting on her stoop, but was amazed at the fleet of cars that pulled up behind Junior. She felt like a celebrity when she got into the car.

"Wow, who are all dem people in those cars behind us?"

"Those my cousin's peoples."

"Wow, y'all rollin' deep."

"Yeah, that's how we roll to make sure we don't have no problems. When niggas see you deep like we are, it discourages them from starting any beef."

He was trying to convince himself of that, because he was really hoping nothing jumped off at the club.
***

The black van was parked across the street from the club. KB was in the driver's seat and the rest of the crew was in the back loading up the guns. Everyone had on black pants with black matching hoodies. There was a big turnout at the club, and people were already standing on line waiting to get inside. There were so many females on line that you would have thought Eric B. and Rakim were performing that night.

Whoever throwing that party must have a lot of love, KB thought to himself.

"You see the bouncer out there?" Stump asked KB.

"Not yet. It's packed out there."

"The nigga said he'd come out about the time the owner normally pulls up," Stump said.

"Well he didn't come out yet. Oh, wait, that's him right there, I think," KB said.

"Flash the headlights one time real fast. I want him to know this is us."

KB flashed the headlights quickly and the bouncer acknowledged their presence by nodding his head in their direction.

"Now we gotta wait till we see this nigga pull up," Stump said.

"It's a lot of muhfuckas out there, and you can imagine how many are inside. How we gonna get all of them to cooperate?" KB asked.

Stump detected fear in what KB was asking, so he pulled out his gun and pointed it at KB's head.

"With this, my nigga! You nervous or somethin'? I can't let you go up in there if you scared, because a nigga might smell it on you and you'd be the cause of this shit not going according to plan. I'm gonna ask you one time, dawg. You down to do this shit or what?"

KB's heart was racing. He knew he didn't really have a choice.

"You know I'm down, man. I was just sayin', it's a lot of niggas out there and I'm sure that your man is probably lettin' some of them in with they toast."

"He ain't lettin' nobody in there wit' no heaters. I already told him, and he said he ain't lettin' nobody in wit' no guns!"

The line was moving slowly because the bouncers were searching everyone before letting them enter the club. The bouncer was checking every male thoroughly, turning away a few that had guns on them. The girls had their pocketbooks checked by a bouncer on the inside with a flashlight, and a female was there to pat them down as well. A cab pulled up to the front of the club and two females dressed in black, DKNY cat suits and hooker boots got out. Every nigga on the line stopped what they were doing momentarily to gawk and lust after the statuesque females. They strutted to the entrance like racehorses and disappeared inside.

Craig's crew all parked around the corner from the club and entered through the back. Craig had paid the bartender to let them in because they were exclusive guests of the host. The crew of twenty males and ten females emerged into the club like superstars. All eyes were on them as they filed through the backdoor. Most of the guys had guns, as well as some of the females. Craig made sure they would be able to get their guns in through the back. He had tried to talk to the bouncer and offered him some money, but he was uncooperative, so Craig found someone else who was willing to let him in with the firearms.

As everyone moved to make room for the others to come in and get stamped, Junior was fixing the burner in his waist. After adjusting it and feeling self-conscious that some of the people in the club had noticed what he was doing, he decided to give the gun to Muffin. He removed the large, .45 automatic from its hiding place, put the safety on, and passed it to Muffin, who put it in the large Gucci bag she was carrying.

The inside of the club was illuminated in crimson red light. The music was deafening as the crew made their way past the bar. There were people on the dance floor dancing to Shabba Ranks's latest song. The smell of marijuana in the cloudy air made it evident that the crowd was doing more than dancing and drinking. As Muffin shuffled through the crowd, she began gyrating her hips and moving to the beat of the music blasting out of the speakers. Although it was a little dark, the crowd noticed Craig's crew walking toward the VIP section. There were two bouncers standing on either side of the ropes separating the VIP section from the regular crowd. The crew approached the entrance to the section and the bouncers stood there, blocking the entrance until they got confirmation of everyone who was in the crew. Craig went to the front and showed the special tickets that were given to him to allow him entry to the section. Everyone placed their hands under a UV lamp that showed the ink that was stamped on their hands, then walked up the steps to the VIP section. Some of the females in the club were watching to see who was being allowed in so they could put their bid in once the VIP guys came back down to the dance floor.

The VIP section was usually a second dance floor in the club, and was very large. Once up there you could look over the rail and down on the crowd. There were people already sitting at the tables containing complimentary bottles of Moet. Craig saw his friend, Jock, the one the party was for, and they embraced. Jock was muscular and wore a red tank top and white, baggy, linen pants with red gator shoes. He had beautiful women with him at his table. Craig introduced Junior to him and they too embraced. Junior pulled up a chair to Jock's table and sat.

The section was even more packed since Craig's crew arrived, but there was standing room for the rest that couldn't get seated at the tables. Meanwhile, down below in the crowd there were two females in black cat suits that were focusing their attention on Junior.

About that time a red car with alloy rims pulled up in front of the club. A slender man dressed in blue dungarees and a white shirt got out, walked to the passenger side, and opened the door. KB and the rest of Stump's crew were stooped down on the side of the van, all with their guns out and their hoods on. The owner had arrived. Stump was already waiting on the side of the club for the slim man to get out of his car and enter the club. He wanted to get to him before he got inside, because there were still people on line waiting to enter the club. KB watched as Stump coolly walked up to the man as he closed the passenger's side door. Stump whispered something in the man's ear. The man looked shocked, but kept his cool. They both walked around the building and out of sight. When the bouncer saw that, he began to quickly let everyone into the club. As the last patron entered through the black, steel doors, he motioned to KB.

"Come on. Let's move!" Ray-Ray said, walking toward the entrance of the club. He turned around to see if they were following. "Come on, Drez, Mike, K, we gotta get in there so we can have the drop on them niggas."

In his mind KB knew he was going into a death trap. There was no way they would be able to get all the people in the club to cooperate, but he didn't see another option for himself.

As they stood by the door, Ray-Ray told everyone to holster their guns and take their positions once they got inside the club. The door opened and the bouncer let them in, following behind them without saying a word. KB made his way over to the DJ booth and Ray-Ray went toward the backdoor. KB never saw where Drez went. They stood in their positions waiting for the sign from Stump. KB's legs felt like spaghetti, but he had to go through with it now. It was too late to back out.

Junior was on the dance floor with Muffin when he felt a tap on his shoulder.

"So, muhfucka, this is what you been doin'?" Shondra yelled in his ear over the music. Junior turned around and was shocked to see her standing there. He was caught totally off guard.

"What the fuck, nigga? You can't say shit?"

Junior grabbed her by her hand and pulled her through the crowd toward the bar. He noticed then that she wasn't alone. Gloria was standing right next to her in a black cat suit, too, but she didn't notice he had been with Muffin because she was eyeing some other niggas in the club. He left Muffin on the dance floor without telling her anything. Shondra was resisting, but he kept a tight grip on her until they reached the bar.

"What the fuck you doin' up in here?" Junior screamed.

"No, muhfucka, that ain't the question. What the fuck you doin' in here wit' that bitch?"

Stump and the owner walked up the stairs to his office, unnoticed by the horde that was in the club partying. As they approached the steel door, the owner was praying he made it out alive. He didn't want to make any sudden moves. He wanted to cooperate fully in hopes that Stump would just take the money and leave. The owner opened the door to his office, and as soon as he did so Stump pulled his gun from the inside of his hoodie and stuck it to the back of the man's head. Stump made the owner open the safe, and then he tied the owner's hands with an extension cord and duct taped his mouth. Stump emptied the contents of the safe into the bag. There was a lot of money in it like the bouncer had told him, and there were two big handguns in there too.

The owner lay face down on the ground beside a desk in the office, looking like a captured slave. Stump went over to the two-way mirror that overlooked the club. Stump could see out, but no one in the club could see inside. He looked out into the crowd to see if his people were positioned where they were supposed to be. He saw KB standing by the DJ booth. Ray-Ray was by the bar, Murder Mike was at entrance, and Drez was by the VIP section. The bouncer had his boys scattered all around the club. As Stump stood there looking over the crowd, he knew this was going to be the hardest part of the robbery, but it was not going to deter him from the plan. He was ready, willing, and determined to go forward.

"I can't believe you dissed me like this!" Shondra was saying to Junior, tears welling up in her eyes. "I never fucked around on you. Why would you do this to me?"

"It's not what you think, baby. My cousin asked me to come at the last minute. I really didn't want to come, and you know clubbin' ain't my thing."

"That's not it, Junior. That's the same bitch that gave you her number when we got back from VA."

"Let's just get the fuck outta here so we can go home and talk. I can't hear shit in here."

"Hold up. I gotta let Glo know I'm leaving."

Shondra saw Gloria dancing with two guys. They had her in a sandwich and were grinding and groping all over her to the hip-hop music blaring in the air. Shondra was making her way to Gloria when all of a sudden the music stopped and there was a loud bang. Her heart skipped a beat when she heard the boom because she didn't know what was happening. Some people started screaming and started heading for the closest exits, only to be stopped by gunmen in hoodies backing them away.

"Everybody get the fuck on the ground!" a voice yelled over the PA system.

No one moved, and then there was another loud boom. This time everyone got low. Junior immediately scoured the crowd, looking for Shondra. He wanted to make sure she was all right. His mind was racing, and then he remembered Muffin and began looking for her because she had his heat in her purse.

He noticed all the gunmen had on black hoodies with their guns out. There were two guys near him at the bar and they were hustling people to the center of the club. Junior moved with the crowd in hopes of making it to his cousin's crew or Muffin.

"We want your money and your jewelry. If any of you niggas want to play super hero and turn this robbery into a homicide, just be sure that you look around. The nigga next to you might be with us, so just cooperate so everyone can go home."

Craig and Jock were already thinking of a way out of the situation. Most everyone in their crew was strapped, but they didn't want to make any quick moves because they didn't know who was down with the robbery.

"Yo, how many do you see out there with guns?" Craig whispered to Jock, who was stooping down with the rest of the crowd.

203

"I counted five niggas in hoods, but I see about three more with guns."

"It's about forty of us. I think if we can get close to the niggas with the guns, we can have the drop on them. Once them niggas see that we outnumber them, they might break for the door," Craig said.

"We hafta blast 'bout three or four of them off top to let them know we not bullshittin'," Jock said. "Shit done really changed out here, huh? I mean niggas got enough balls to rob a club?"

"Man, niggas will try anything to get paid, ya know," Craig replied. "I'm not going out like this."

"Ain't that a bouncer that was at the door?" Jock asked as he looked over to the crowd gathering in the middle of the dance floor.

"I don't know. I came through the backdoor."

"Yeah, it is that muhfucka! He set up this shit. That's why he was being so thorough at the door tonight. Black bastard!" Jock was pissed. "Since he the one that set this shit up, he's gonna be the first nigga to catch the heat from my biscuit."

"Let's make our way to the middle so we can get a good position," Craig said as he started to move to the middle of the floor with the rest of the crowd.

The crowd was complying with the gunmen, and money and jewelry were being passed to the four men with black bags. There were two guys standing around them with their guns drawn, pointing them randomly at everyone. No one in the crowd tried to make a move out of fear of being the first victim. The women were crying and shaking hysterically while some of the guys had looks of revenge in their eyes. Gloria and Shondra were together and they were both crying uncontrollably.

"What the fuck is goin' on?" Gloria sobbed.

"I don't know, girl. I just hope they take what they want and just leave," Shondra replied, sobbing.

The guys collecting the money and jewelry made their way over to where Shondra and Glo were stooping down, and Gloria looked up and noticed KB standing over her. Her eyes got as big as saucers and she was about to scream out his name, but thought quickly against it. She put her jewelry and what little cash she had in the bag, and stared in his face with the evilest glare she could give him. He didn't say a word. He just kept moving through the crowd as if he didn't see her. Shondra noticed him, too, and her heart dropped. She knew if he was there, then Stump was there too, and if they saw Junior she knew they would kill him.

"Oh shit!" she whispered to Gloria. "That was your man and he didn't even say shit to you. That's fucked up!"

"That muhfucka!" Gloria wailed. "How could he do this shit? I knew he was up to something, but I woulda neva thought he would do some foul shit like this."

"I gotta find Junior. If KB in here with Stump, they might kill him when they see him."

"Why would they do that?" Gloria asked, puzzled.

"Because they tried to rob him when they had that shootout," she blurted out.

"What?"

"They the ones Kendu was trying to set Junior up for."

"Why you never told me that? That means that you knew about KB before I met him?"

"Look, Glo, I gotta find my man before these niggas find him first, because I don't want nuthin' to happen to him."

Muffin and Junior were stuck in the middle of the crowd. She had passed him his burner and he tucked it into his waist.

"It's not a lot of them," Muffin whispered to Junior.

"I see about seven niggas with guns and the dude up in the DJ's booth," Junior said.

"Those guys we were with, don't they have guns?" she asked.

"Yeah, I need to find out where they at. I know they gonna do something."

"They need to do something because these niggas don't look that deep in here. I hate niggas that do foul shit like this."

"I know, but that's what they do. You can't knock anybody's hustle, only when it causes you grief. Oh, shit!"

"What?" She looked at Junior and could see him pulling his gun slowly from his waist.

KB was walking toward him, but didn't see him. Junior tried to shield himself from KB, not wanting him to see him and recognize who he was. Junior put his head down and peeked up at the guy that was in front of KB.

"Put everything in the bag!" the gunman was saying to the men and women that were stooped down on the ground. KB was standing behind him, waving the gun around the heads of everyone. Junior's heart was beating rapidly and his hand was sweaty from gripping the gun so tightly. As KB got closer to Junior, Muffin noticed who Junior was staring at. She grabbed his gun and squeezed off three shots in KB's direction.

BLAM! BLAM! BLAM! There was loud screaming and everyone got up and rushed the exits, trying to get to safety. There were more shots immediately after the first three and people were falling over each other, trying to get out of the club. KB had gotten hit twice and had fallen to the ground. He was bleeding profusely from his wounds and his gun fell out of his hand when he hit the floor. Someone had picked it up and started blasting away at the other gunmen, and all hell broke loose.

Craig had shot two of the gunmen in the head and they died instantly. His crew was positioned around the club and had most of the gunmen at bay. Jock and his crew were shooting anyone that had a gun as they made their way to the exit. The exits were crowded from the club-goers trying to escape the mayhem going on inside. Craig kept his back to the wall as he moved close to the exit so he could see who was coming in his direction. The screaming was deafening, but he kept his eyes moving around the entire club to make sure no one snuck up on him. He was looking around for Junior and someone else from his crew, but it was mass pandemonium and the people running were blocking a clear view.

Craig made it to the exit and he caught a glimpse of the bouncer Jock was talking about. He stayed close behind him. The bouncer was looking nervous as he made his way through the crowd. He was looking back and pushing people as he headed for the bar. Craig stayed behind him with his gun down by his waist. As he got to the back exit he pulled up his gun.

"Ay, muhfucka!" he shouted.

The bouncer turned around and was met by the barrel of Craig's gun. The bouncer dropped his hand and backed up to the door that led to his potential freedom if he could make it out. Craig pulled the trigger and a loud boom was heard as the bouncer was lifted off his feet, hit the exit door, and fell out into the darkness of the night. Craig turned around briefly to see if anyone was looking, then he walked over to his still-breathing victim and put the gun to his head as he lay there shaking. He pulled the trigger one more time, putting the bouncer into eternal darkness.

Gloria was kneeling down screaming for help for her wounded boyfriend. KB was losing a lot of blood. She was afraid to leave him there and go get help because she feared he might expire on her. Shondra walked over and offered her help.

"Get the fuck outta here, bitch!" Gloria screamed. "You wanted this shit to happen. That's why you was asking me so many questions about him. I hate you, you fake bitch!"

Shondra couldn't do anything but look at Gloria. Her heart dropped. She couldn't deny what Glo was saying. The reality of what Shondra had been trying to do really came through as she looked at KB on the ground and how hurt her friend was.

"Who the fuck did this to him!" Gloria asked, cradling his head in her lap.

"I . . . I . . . I don't know."

"OOOOOHHHHH, God, please don't let him die, please, God. I'm sooooo sorry."

Shondra got up and went to find someone to help him.

"Where the fuck you goin'?" Muffin asked Shondra as she tried to leave through the entrance of the club.

"None of your fuckin' business, bitch!" Shondra said as she pushed her way past her.

Muffin grabbed her by her arm and turned her around, pointing Junior's gun in her face. "It is my business, bitch. You need to leave Junior alone!"

"What, bitch?"

Shondra knocked the gun from Muffin's hand in a sweeping motion and hit her with a barrage of punches to her face, then grabbed her hair and swung her against the wall of the club. Muffin was dazed and slumped to the ground. Shondra stomped her in her face numerous times to seal the win. Muffin was curled up trying to block the onslaught of kicks to her mid section and face as Shondra kept stomping her and screaming.

"You fuckin' bitch!" she yelled over and over. As Shondra continued her assault on Muffin, someone walked up behind her and hit her in the back of the head. She felt a sharp pain, and then everything went blank. The person that had hit Shondra in the head helped Muffin to her feet and out of the club. Junior saw the guy that hit Shondra, but he was too slow in getting to him, so Muffin and the man both disappeared into the crowd and made it outside the club.

The sound of sirens could be heard as people ran to their cars trying to get away from the chaos that was happening inside the club. There were bodies lying around, some dead and others with serious injuries. After going outside and trying to find

Muffin, Junior noticed paramedics and police vehicles pulling up, so he went back inside to help Shondra. She was lying on the ground unconscious. He knelt down next to her and put her head in his lap. When he saw two paramedics come into the club with stretchers, he waved them over to him and they took over. Junior looked at her one final time, then made his way to the back exit. He pushed open the door and the cool wind alerted him of a wound he had suffered inside the club. His shirt was sticking to his upper body from the blood. It was empty in the back, except for the body of the bouncer. Junior stepped over him and quickly made his way back to Tompkins projects.

The van pulled up in front of Stump's building and everyone got out. Stump was carrying two bags, and Mike and Ray each had a bag of their own. Drez also had a bag and there was a girl with him. They went into Stump's apartment and threw the bags on the floor.

"Now tell me who this bitch is again?" Stump looked at Drez.

"This my little cousin. Some bitch in the club was stomping her out, so I knocked the bitch out and brought her with me."

"What about KB? Nobody know what happened to him?"

"I don't know. I heard a gunshot and I grabbed the bag I had and got to the door. There was niggas in there with guns and they was blasting, so I shot my way out the club. I didn't see KB," Ray-Ray said.

"I saw him with some nigga that must have been down with the bouncer's crew, but when I heard the first gunshot I ran out the booth. I hit two or three niggas that was shooting, then I seen a bag on the ground so I grabbed it and headed for the exit. I didn't see KB after that," Mike said.

"So nobody know if the nigga dead or not?" Stump asked.

"I'm not gonna lie, I saw mad niggas on the ground. I can't say if K was one of them, but there was mad bodies around and a lot of them wasn't moving. I thought we was the only ones that was supposed to be holding," Drez added.

"Yeah, I don't know what happened with that, but other than that everything worked out good. Aight, we gonna split this shit up now."

He dumped the contents of the bags onto the floor. There was jewelry, money, and wallets in the bags that Drez, Mike, and Ray had. The bag Stump had contained stacks of money.

"What about her?" Mike asked, pointing to Muffin.

"After we split the take, I'ma take her home," Drez said.

"Nah, she gotta get gone now," Stump said.

"Aight, I'm gonna put her in a cab. I'll be right back."

Stump grabbed Drez's arm as he rose and whispered in his ear.

"You betta make sure she don't say shit, cuz!" And with that Muffin followed Drez outside.

"I didn't know you was down with that shit. I thought you was getting crack money in the Stuy. You got too much money to be doin' that dumb shit," Muffin said.

"You can never have enough money. This is how I got down in the beginning. The opportunity came, so I took it. Ya know what I'm sayin'? Who was that bitch that was duffin' you out?"

"I was in there with my man, and that bitch was his girl."

"Huh? Who your man?"

"Junior. He hustle out of Baptiste."

"He got a man named Lakim?"

"Yeah, you know him? He getting major paper. I just bagged up some shit for him this week."

"How deep is you and that nigga?"

"I love that nigga. He got me open. That's why I was gonna off his fucking girl."

"Look, Muff, you need to stay away from that nigga. I don't want you gettin' caught up in any shit that's about to go down with him. You hear me?"

Drez was her cousin and he used to live with her when they were younger. He was a live wire and was always into grimy shit for as long as she could remember.

"Why, Drez? What you up to now?"

"Look, cuz, just stay the fuck away from dude, ya hear me?"

"But why, Drez? He's so cool."

"Let me put it to you like this. The nigga La don't want him in the picture no more, and he told me that I could put my work ova there if we get rid of him, and over there is a gold mine, so that's what I'm gonna do. And, Muff, don't go running your mouth to the nigga."

A cab pulled up and she got in. As he closed the car door she heard him say, "Blood is thicker than water." As the cab pulled away she could see Drez walk over to the payphone on the corner.

La looked down at his pager as it vibrated.

"This should be him right here," he told Rock as they both walked to a payphone. La dialed the number in his beeper and waited for the person on the other line to pick up.

"What up? Everything a go?" La asked.

"Yeah, I just came back from handling some shit. I almost didn't make it out," Drez replied.

"You ready?" La asked.

"Nah, I'll tell you when," Drez said.

"OK," La said, looking at Rock and nodding his head in agreement.

"I'm out. I'll beep you and give you all the details," Drez said.

"Gotcha, peace." La hung up the phone. "It's on, baby. He gonna beep me back with all the info."

"That's peace. Once we get this nigga out the way, the rest is easy," Rock said, patting the gun in his waist.

"Yeah, but the nigga ain't no slow leak, so you gotta be on point."

"I got this. Trust me."

"I hear you, Rock, but you gotta be careful."

"I'll meet you upstairs in a minute," Rock said as he turned to leave. "I gotta go check on that money real quick."

"Aight, I'll be up there waitin'."

Rock went to make an important phone call.

When Junior made it to the projects there were people standing around in the parking lot. He could see that some of the females were crying. He immediately thought something had happened to his cousin Craig.

"Damn, nigga, I thought you got hit up in there," Craig said when he saw Junior.

"Nah, I'm all right."

"Damn, man, I can't believe that shit happened," Craig said.

"You know I know who did that shit, right?" Junior asked.

"Word, who set it up?"

"Remember them niggas we was bustin' at a while back in Baptiste?"

"Yeah."

"It was them. I saw one of them in there and my bitch peeped it, and when the nigga got close she grabbed my ratchet and aired him out. That's when shit went berserk in there. I think she flattened the nigga. I just saw him drop and that was it."

"You look like you need to go to the hospital, nigga," Craig said, looking at Junior's blood-soaked shirt. "You got hit too?"

"Nah. I thought I did, but it was just a graze or something, 'cause I don't have no hole in me. Duke was fucked, though. He was spitting blood and the whole nine."

"Fuck that, nigga. I hope he die. They killed one of my men in there. My man Jock told me the bouncer was down with it, too. I caught his faggot ass and layed him out by the backdoor."

"Is everybody else all right?"

"Yeah, but I thought you got caught up in that shit. That's why everybody out here was buggin' out. They thought them niggas bodied you. I'm glad you all right, and I'm sorry I made you go out with us."

"It ain't nuthin', but check it. I need to find out if my girl is OK. I saw this kid hit her in the head with a burner. Drive me to the hospital so I can check on her," Junior said while checking his vibrating pager. It was Rock's code.

"Give me a sec. I want to change out of these clothes," Craig said.

"I might as well go upstairs and clean up a lil bit myself and make a phone call," Junior said.

Shondra was being put on a stretcher as police and the coroner swarmed the club, collecting bodies and evidence. Her head was pounding and she was still a little dizzy from getting knocked out. The air was cool outside and there were bystanders wondering what happened in the club. Police were questioning some of club-goers that were wounded in the melee and the flashing lights from the squad cars and ambulances made it seem as if the party had been moved outside. The EMT workers were asking her questions, but she was too dazed to answer. Too many things were running through her mind. She was thinking about the bitch that pulled the gun on her, if Junior was OK, how her best friend Gloria was doing, and if KB was dead. The EMT worker lifted the stretcher up and was about to put her in the ambulance when she heard Gloria's voice nearby screaming.

"NO, NO, NO!" Gloria yelled. Shondra lifted herself up from the stretcher and saw Gloria grabbing an EMT worker and trying to get into the back of an ambulance. He seemed to be telling her she couldn't ride with KB, and she was upset. Shondra was paralyzed with grief as the cries of wounded people echoed in her ears while the ambulance she was in pulled off, but there was one distinct sound that drowned out all other sounds. It was Gloria's wailing.

The money was being split when Drez got back to Stump's crib. He immediately noticed Stump putting money aside for KB.

"Anybody hear from KB?" Drez asked.

Nobody answered.

"Everybody pick out a piece of jewelry you want. We'll take the rest to the hock in mid-town tomorrow," Stump said.

Ray-Ray picked out a gold rope chain with a round medallion. Mike picked out a nugget bracelet, Drez took a Figaro chain with a crucifix, and Stump took an Italian link chain with a diamond encrusted pendant and a herringbone chain with a crucifix for KB.

"The rest of this is going to the hock and we'll split the rest of the dough tomorrow. Take y'all shares and get out," Stump said.

Everyone picked up their stacks and headed for the door. Drez started to count his money stack and Stump walked over to him and knocked it out of his hands and onto the floor.

"You think I can't count, or you think I'm trying to beat you out of some money, nigga!"

"Nah, man, I was just seeing how much it was. That's all."

"Count that shit when you leave. Now get the fuck outta my crib, nigga."

The inside of the hospital was cold. Junior hated hospitals because they had a funny smell. He walked past the security guard in the emergency room and went to the clerk and asked if they had a patient that came in a short time ago by the name of Shondra.

"I don't know, there has been a lot of people who came in tonight." The clerk saw the concern in Junio'r eyes. "You can go back there and see if you want," the clerk said, pointing to the double doors behind her.

Junior pushed the doors open and entered into the emergency area. He spotted Shondra on a bed sitting up, and when she saw him her eyes lit up. He made his way over to her and he hugged her as she cried hard on his shoulders.

"The police in here, baby, and they asking a lot of questions," she said.

"You OK?" he asked, feeling the bump on the back of her head.

The question brought back the reason she was in the emergency room.

"Yeah, but that bitch you fuckin' wit' pulled out a gun on me, Junior. She was going to shoot me."

"What?"

"Yeah, and I knocked it outta her hand and I was beating the shit outta her and then somebody hit me in the back of my head."

"I'ma kill that bitch!"

"I don't even know why you shittin' on me. I'm a good girl."

"Look, I'ma talk to you when you get outta here. Right now I'm gonna go handle that shit."

"OK, baby, be careful." She blew him a kiss and he vanished through the doors.

Junior parked in front of the rundown house and got out. He saw Muffin looking out of the window as he exited the car, so he slammed the door to let her know he wasn't there for a pleasant house call. He figured she was coming down when he didn't see her face in the window anymore, so he leaned on the hood of the car and waited. One of the double wooden doors opened and Muffin emerged from the dilapidated structure of the house, offsetting its ugliness by her radiant beauty. With the grace of a swan she continued down the stairs, then she saw the look of disgust in his eyes and stopped abruptly at the bottom of the stairs as he advanced toward her menacingly.

"What's the matter, baby?" she asked him, backing up as he moved closer to her.

"What the fuck happened at the club?"

"Please, baby, let me explain first—"

"Why the fuck would you do that shit, Muffin?" he screamed as his open hand found her cheek and twisted her head to the left.

"Uuugh! Please stop, Junior! Please!"

"Why should I, bitch! You pulled a gun out on my girl!"

"Please, baby, I'm sorry. I was jealous."

He backed up, realizing what he was doing, then he turned to leave.

"Junior! Wait! Baby, please! Junior!"

"You fucked up, Muff. Stay the fuck away from me!"

"Junior, wait! There's something I need to tell you."

The way she said it made him stop abruptly. All of a sudden there seemed to be a sense of urgency for him to listen to what she had to say.

"Baby, I found out your man is trying to set you up." She began telling everything she had learned from her cousin. "I didn't know if I should go against the grain, but I knew in my heart I had to tell you. All I ask is that you don't do anything to my cousin. That's all," she said when she finished the tale.

Junior was heated. His cousin Craig told him not to trust that nigga from the time they had the shootout with Stump, but Junior went to bat for La and told Craig he was good peoples. Now he was faced with the same bullshit all over again. Muffin was sitting on the stoop looking at Junior, not knowing his intentions. She knew she made a grave mistake by telling him, but if anything happened to him she wouldn't be able to live with herself.

Junior was already in think mode. He looked at Muffin and couldn't help but thank her in his mind for saving him from another setup. There was no denying her love for him. He was feeling indebted to her for what she had told him. He walked over to her and stroked her hair gently, then whispered in her ear.

"I appreciate what you just told me, but you on probation until I take care of this shit. You understand?"

Like a humble servant she bowed her head down and invited his touch, apologizing again for what she did at the club.

"I'm not gonna promise you anything about your cuz 'cause I gotta look out for me. You feel me?"

He wasn't sure about how close she was to her cousin, and didn't want her to tip him off, but at the same time he didn't care because he was already warned. He preferred the element of surprise, but if that couldn't be avoided it would have to be an all-out war.

"I told you because I don't want anything to happen to you, daddy, and I don't want nothing to happen to my cousin either, but if it's a choice, I choose you. And if something happens, I'll charge it to the game."

Just what I wanted to hear, Junior thought. *I knew this bitch was thorough.*

"I'm out, but I'm gonna call you later on," Junior said.

"OK, but please call me, and I'm sorry, baby. I hope you forgive me."

She watched the car pull off down the street and stood on her stoop wondering if she had just signed her cousin's death warrant.

L. J. Miller

Chapter 15
No more bitchin☐

Stump was enjoying his early morning shower. As he let the hot, steamy water beat down on his body he wondered what had happened to KB. It had been a week since the robbery and he hadn't heard anything from him. He sent one of his boys to his house and anonymously gave his cut from the robbery to his mother. He grabbed a towel from the rack, got out of the shower, and got dressed in his room. He put on his bulletproof vest, a precaution he took every day after the unfortunate time he was shot up. He grabbed his twin nine-millimeter Glock automatics and tucked them inside his waistband, then he snatched up some money and headed for the front door. He looked out the peephole, which was part of his normal routine, then turned the knob slowly and pulled open the door. He hesitated in the hallway, thinking he had left something behind, but couldn't remember what, so he put the key in the door and locked it.

When Stump's door slammed, a figure in the exit staircase pulled out a gun and stood close to the exit door. As Stump's footsteps grew louder, the man in the staircase knew his victim was getting closer and he readied himself by the door. Stump walked down the long corridor and headed for the back staircase, unaware that a gunman was waiting for him. He didn't like waiting for the elevator, so he rarely took it. He went to grab the knob on the exit door and it flung open. He was face to face with the gunman who had a big, black gun pointing right at him. Before Stump could react, the hooded gunman let off two shots to Stump's midsection, sending him tumbling backward into the corridor. The noise from the gun echoed throughout the building as the gunman fired off three more shots. As one of the bullets pierced through Stump's thigh, he managed to pull out both guns and return fire while slumped against the wall. The gunman jumped back into the exit and slammed the door shut as the bullets from Stump's gun hit the metal door and created huge, round cylinders on impact. Stump was trying to get to his feet, but his thigh wound prevented him from getting up quickly, although the vest had stopped the penetration of the bullets that were targeted at his chest. The gunman in the exit attempted to open

217

the door, and as he did so Stump squeezed off more shots to stop him from coming into the hallway. The deafening echoes from the gun blasts could be heard throughout the building. The gunman opened the door and fired off a shot so he could peek into the hallway to see how badly Stump was wounded.

Stump was leaning on the wall and kept his guns pointed toward the stairway door that the gunman was hiding behind. There was silence for what seemed like an eternity, and then there was another loud boom, but it came from the other end of the hallway. It got Stump's attention and he looked down the hallway. Someone else was standing at the other end of the hallway, and the face seemed familiar to him. Stump now knew he had been set up because he was being ambushed. He never thought anyone had enough heart to try to hit him inside his own building. He mustered up all the strength he had left in his body and fired two shots off in the direction of the other gunman, then ran to the second exit while writhing in pain. He was feeling death coming on his heels as he tumbled down the concrete stairs, hoping to get to the lobby. He heard footsteps behind him, so he stopped on one of the floors, opened then slammed the exit door as if he had gone out on that floor, but really he just continued down the stairs.

The first gunman came rumbling down the stairs, determined to finish Stump off, but he was thrown off by the slamming of the exit door. He stopped briefly on that floor, but heard faint sounds coming from the stairwell below, so he continued down this time, treading softly so he wouldn't be detected. Stump stopped on the second floor because of the pain in his legs and chest. He reloaded his clip, put his back against the wall, and tried to regain some strength. He was almost to the lobby of his building.

As the gunman crept down the stairs he could hear heavy breathing. As he approached the bottom of the stairwell landing, he rounded the corner of the stairs and pointed his gun at Stump, who was unaware of his presence at the top of the stairs. He was surprised Stump was still standing after being hit by his powerful magnum. He aimed for his head to make sure the job would be complete, and one more loud boom rattled the stairwell. Stump stopped moving. The gunman quickly ran down the stairs and put an exclamation point on his work, then ruffled through the pockets of the corpse and took everything, removing the guns from Stump's possession.

Once the killer finished, he ran to the roof of the building and crossed over to an adjoining building. There he took off his black hoodie and sweats, and put them in a bag, and threw them down the incinerator on his descent to the lobby of that building. He walked out of the building into the sunlight and watched as a crowd gathered in front of Stump's building. As he walked down the lane in the direction of Baptiste Plaza, the gunman wondered if his accomplice had made it out safely as well.

La was sitting in his living room waiting on Rock when he heard a knock on his door. He walked to the door, gun in hand, and looked out the peephole.

"Who is it?"

"Drez."

La opened the door and Drez walked in.

"So what up with this nigga Junior? When we gonna get at him?" Drez asked.

"I want to take care of it this week, but I don't want to do it over here," La said. "I don't want his people to think that I had anything to do with it, you know what I mean?"

"I hear what you sayin'. So where you plan on doin' it at?"

"I don't know. That's what I'm thinking about now. The only place I know he hang out is in Tompkins, and it's hard to catch him on that side of town."

"I just found out my lil cousin fuckin' him. They was together at that club I stuck up. I told her to stay away from that nigga, though."

"You told your cousin?"

"Look, nigga, that's my lil cuz. I don't want her getting caught up in this shit, you understand?"

"I hear you, but suppose she tell the nigga? Then what?"

"She ain't gonna say shit!"

"You sure about that?"

"Yeah, nigga, that's my fuckin' cousin. She ain't gonna go against the grain for that nigga. I'm family. You scared. Maybe you ain't ready to play boss, nigga."

"That shit don't work on me, son. My heart don't pump Kool-Aid, bruh."

"Aight then, stop worrying about that bitch ass nigga and let's set up this shit."

219

"I'm waiting on Rock now so we can do this shit right."

"I say get the nigga wherever we can get him. I don't have time to play secret agent wit' you. All it'll do is waste time."

"I'm just sayin', I don't want to make it a war. That'll slow down the money flow."

"Is that right?" Drez asked.

"I'm just letting you know how I want it be done."

"On da real, bruh, you can't tell me shit. You ain't calling no shots if I'm laying down the murder game, so you can't tell me NUTHIN'!"

The knock on the door startled La. He went to the peephole and saw it was Rock and let him in.

Drez was still talking when Rock came into the living room and sat down. He listened to the conversation that was already in progress and it seemed like they weren't agreeing on something.

" . . . and that's why we gotta do it now and not wait," Drez was saying.

"I hear you, but I don't want to take no chances on anybody linking it to me."

"I'm not feeling what you saying right now. Sounds like you having a change of heart, bruh."

"Man, look, if we gonna do this, it gotta be done right, bottom line," La said, sounding like a broken record.

"Well let's get it done then. No more bitchin'."

"You ready, kid?" La asked Rock.

"I'm waitin' on you."

La looked at Drez and then spoke to Rock again.

"Let me iron out the rest of the details with Drez, but it's goin' down soon, aight?"

"Aight, just let me know," Rock said.

"We gonna let you know, lil man. There's gonna be some major changes taking place very soon," Drez added.

"I hear you," Rock replied.

"You'll bust your gun if you have to, right?" Drez asked Rock.

"I always bust my gun if I have to," Rock replied matter-of-factly.

"See, that's what the fuck I'm talkin' 'bout!" Drez shouted, looking at La.

"Yo, beep me when y'all map this shit out. I'm goin' on the block and check this money," Rock said.

Then Rock slapped both men five and walked out of the apartment.

L. J. Miller

Chapter 16
Let me tell you what karma is, nigga.

There was a heavy police presence around the building as the two detectives walked over to the taped-off building. For Taylor and Burke this was not an unfamiliar sight. They were immune to dead bodies in the hood. It was commonplace for black males to escalate a small incident into something more serious with murder becoming the end result. As a stretcher passed by them in the lobby of the building, Burke stopped the attendant pushing the stretcher and pulled the sheet back to see if there was a recognizable face under it. Taylor stopped him and asked him to make a wager. If it was a convicted felon they both knew, then he would buy lunch. But if it was someone they didn't know, then Burke would take Taylor to lunch. Burke agreed and pulled the sheet off, just enough to reveal the face. They weren't surprised to see that it was Stump, aka Henry Billings. He was a terror in those projects.

"Somebody must have finally got tired of his shit," Burke said, pulling the sheet back over the body.

"It was just a matter of time before somebody got to him. I guess he wasn't that lucky this time."

"Let's go check out the crime scene," Burke said.

They looked at the white outline of where the body rested last and observed a bulletproof vest that was obviously worn by the deceased victim.

"This is where it ended for him," Burke said, kneeling down on the ground.

"I wonder if he knew it was his day or not," Taylor said, climbing the stairs to look for more evidence.

They went to the floor where the assault took place and where the police were already gathering evidence. Taylor and Burke looked at the holes in the exit door and the shell casings on the ground in the exit and the hallway.

"Wow, I'm surprised it didn't end here. It looks like he didn't go without a fight," Taylor said.

There were no weapons, but there were plenty of shells. Taylor walked to the other end of the hallway where he discovered something unusual. There were two shells lying near the exit. He called his partner over.

"Seems like he was ambushed," Burke said upon seeing the shells.

"Yeah, seems like there were two gunmen. I guess they wanted to make sure he didn't get away."

"His reputation exceeded him. There was no way they wanted him to get out of this alive. This was a hit."

"Seems like he got hit, but was able to return fire. The shells at the other end of the hallway tell that story," Taylor said.

"I guess they didn't expect him to have on a vest. The holes in the exit door prove he was trying to sustain the gunfight. The guy on this end must have fired some shots to help the guy in the other exit." Burke was trying to figure out the last minutes of Stump's life.

"I know one thing, they were using some high-powered guns to get him," Taylor observed.

Taylor and Burke did the routine of knocking on doors and asking the tenants if they heard or saw anything, knowing the answer would be the same at every door. No one wanted to be a witness to a homicide, because they feared retaliation. Taylor and Burke knew most of the hardened criminals in the area, and they made it their business to keep their ears to the streets to find out who was who in the hood. They were hoping they would get a lead through one of their informants, because they seriously doubted anyone was going to come forward voluntarily with any pertinent information. Although there were many that were probably glad Stump was dead, they were not going to give up any information on the assailant, even if they knew anything. If anyone told the police something, and someone in the hood found out, the person would be marked for death. The code of the streets was never to snitch. Burke and Taylor knew this code, but it was mind-boggling to them that people young and old lived by these ridiculous codes.

The crowd that gathered in front of the building wanted to see if the rumors were true about Stump being dead. There were young and old in attendance. Some were crying and others were joking around as if his death was not serious. A lot of old people cried because there was another senseless death by the hands of one of their own. They couldn't help but feel depression and sadness from the genocide. Many of them had raised some of the kids in the neighborhood that turned out to be criminals.

The room was silent except for the periodic beeping of the life support machine that KB was hooked up to. Gloria was sitting in a chair beside his bed keeping vigil. There were so many tubes running from him that he resembled a string puppet. He wasn't conscious and was breathing with the help of a respirator because his lung had collapsed. Gloria spoke to him and read him passages out of the Bible. She wasn't giving up, although the doctors were only giving him a 50 percent chance for a full recovery because of his injuries.

Gloria was getting prepared for KB's second surgery when Shondra came to visit. Gloria hadn't seen her since KB was shot and didn't want to see her because of how she put a nigga in front of their friendship. Shondra entered the room, not waiting for an invitation, and placed the balloons and card she had bought on his nightstand. Gloria gave her a wicked look and Shondra walked over to her and sat down in the chair across from the bed.

"Glo," she started, tears welling up in her eyes, "I know you don't want to see me or talk to me. I really want you to know that I'm so sorry for betraying your trust and our friendship."

"I don't want to hear shit from you, bitch. Please get the fuck outta here!"

"Please, Glo, just give me a chance to—"

"Give you a chance? Give you a chance? Why the fuck should I give you a chance? Look at him, Shondra." Gloria looked at KB lying in the bed. "Did you give him a chance, did you give me a chance, huh? Did you give us a fucking chance? You was only thinking about yourself!"

"I know, Glo, and I'm sorry."

"You're sorry? I'm sorry too, bitch. I'm sorry I ever trusted you. I'm sorry I ever met you, and I'm sorry you ain't value our friendship. Now get the fuck out!"

That statement tore into Shondra like the bullet that tore into KB's chest. She knew now that their friendship was completely over.

"What up, Junior?" La asked, speaking into the phone.

"Ain't nuthin'. What's up on your end?"

"We dry out here. We starting to lose our customers because we don't have enough work for all the shifts. I got the workers on a tight schedule, so a lot of them getting mad. Some of them going ova to the competition 'cause ain't enough work."

225

"I know shit fucked up right now, but there's a drought because of that big bust in Miami, so my connect don't have nothing right now."

"You don't have nothing stashed that you can give me to hold me down until he comes through?" La asked desperately.

"Nah, kid, I ain't got shit. I gave you all I had from the last time I copped."

"Aight then, man, just make sure you beep me and let me know when you get right."

"Yeah, I got you," Junior said and hung up the phone.

This was the second time La had beeped Junior about getting some more work. Junior was waiting until there was no work over there so he could put his plan into effect. La had tried to lure Junior to the projects to talk about Dusty a week ago, but Junior knew if he went there he wouldn't return. That's when he knew he had to put an end to the bullshit. He had collected all the proceeds from the last package from Rock. He was going to cripple La by breaking him down piece by piece. When La called again and told him most of the workers defected to the competition because they weren't making any money, Junior knew it was time. La's power was gone and he was going to show him who the real boss was.

There weren't any workers in front of the building when two men in suits, one carrying a duffel bag, entered the building across the street. It wasn't an unusual scene lately for the streets to be empty, because there hadn't been work in the projects for weeks. The two men went into the building and walked up the six flights to the roof. Once they reached the door to the roof they opened it slowly and stepped out into the cool night, walking around to make sure no one was up there with them. The gravel beneath their feet made a small crunching noise as they patrolled the roof. From the roof they had a bird's eye view of the street, and a good look of anything coming into or leaving the building. The guys went into the duffel bag and took out two black work jumpsuits and put them on, then took out two high-powered rifles with scopes on them and placed them on the wall of the roof. After they got into their uniforms, they placed padlocks on the roof doors, then took their position by the edge of the roof and waited.

Junior pulled out a vest from Craig's closet. It was an official police vest Craig had gotten from one of his girls on the police force. He put it on over his white T-shirt and strapped it to him using the Velcro straps, and then he donned an oversized hoodie. His frame looked a little bulky, but he would hide that with a leather jacket. He grabbed two .45 automatics and a .357 snub-nosed Magnum revolver. He tucked the two .45s in his waist and placed the revolver in a holster and stuffed it in the middle of his back. He looked at himself in the mirror and was satisfied with the way he looked, so he grabbed his keys and left.

Junior pulled up to a phone booth, beeped La, and sat in the car and waited for him to call back. He had circled the projects already and no one was on the block. When he felt the vibration from his beeper he looked down and saw that there was an unfamiliar number on the screen.

"Hello?" the voice on the other end of the phone asked when Junior called the number.

"Somebody just beep me from this number?" Junior asked.

"Who's this?" the mysterious voice asked.

"Somebody beeped me from this number. If there's somebody else there, ask them if they just beeped somebody," Junior answered.

"Hold on."

"Hello," La said, picking up the phone.

"Yeah, what up, nigga?" Junior asked.

"Nuthin'. You straight?"

"Yeah, I got it. Where you at?"

"I'm at a broad's house in Lindsey. You already in the hood?"

"Nah, I'm not over there yet. I'm on my way, though. Matter of fact, why don't you meet me on the block?"

"Why don't you just come to the crib instead?"

"I got some loose so I want to go out there and let the heads check it out and let them know that shit clicking again. You can take the rest of the shit back to the crib when I get there."

"I can send one of the workers out there so you don't have to go out there yourself. Ain't no need for you getting hot for nuthin'."

"It shouldn't be that hot out there now 'cause ain't no work been out there about three weeks, right?"

227

"Yeah, that's true. Aight, I'll meet you around there in fifteen minutes."

"Aight, son," Junior hung up the phone and quickly dialed another number to let his people know he was on his way.

"Damn!" La exclaimed as he sat down on the couch and rubbed his head.

"What's wrong? Was that him?" Drez asked.

"Yeah."

"Then why you draggin' around like that? You ready to move or what?"

"He want to meet in front of the building on the block."

"OK. I'm going over there."

"Wait, I gotta beep Rock."

"You do that. I'll be in the back of the building waiting."

La called Rock and told him to meet him on the block.

Drez walked into the building and went out the front to see if Junior had arrived. There wasn't anyone standing in the front of the building when he peeked out, but the two gunmen on the roof saw Drez and had their sights on him, following his every move until he disappeared into the building.

Junior pulled up on the side of the building and got out. He walked around to the front to make sure his cousin's boys were in position on the roof. He looked up and when he saw them, he put up two fingers and they replied by putting up one finger and waving it. He had planned everything up to now, but this was the part he couldn't plan. He had to play this one by ear, and that's what made it so dangerous. As he stood there he wondered if La was coming himself or if he would send someone else. Junior was nervous and was taking a chance standing out there in the open.

When La got to the building he saw Drez sitting on the benches in the back. He couldn't believe the dumb muhfucka was sitting on the benches in plain sight. What the hell was he doing? La walked into the building and went to the front to meet Junior. Junior heard the door opening and moved off the wall, wanting to see who was coming out of the building.

"What up, nigga?" La asked, walking up to Junior and slapping him five.

"Same ol', same ol', playa. What's poppin'?"

"Waitin' on you, boss. Shit been dry. You ready to put that new shit out here?"

"Yeah, go get a head so they can test it out real fast."

"Aight, let me go see Pee Wee."

"Here."

La took the product and went into the building. Junior waited for him to get on the elevator before entering the building. Junior walked to the backdoor and peeked out of the small, triangular window and noticed someone sitting on the benches. He couldn't make out a face, but he knew he wasn't one of the workers. Junior hurried back out to the front and waited for La to return. He was glad La didn't embrace him because he didn't want him to feel the vest he was wearing under his jacket. The roof gunmen's palms were sweaty as they gripped the long barrels on their high-powered rifles.

La returned with a smile on his face.

"Damn, Pee Wee said that shit made his dick hard," Law said.

"Good, that's all I needed to hear," Junior said.

"Where the rest of the shit at? I'm ready to put that shit out here now."

"I got it in the car. It's already bagged up."

"Good, that means I don't have to worry about doing it."

Junior looked at the greed in La's eyes and it disgusted him.

"How many workers you got left?" Junior asked.

"I'm down to three right now."

"Damn, them niggas ain't show no loyalty. You shouldn't let them eat. You can't trust niggas that'll bite the hand that feeds them, you know what I mean?"

La looked back at him and hung onto the words like a trapeze artist. His palms began to get sweaty and his legs became weak. Junior grabbed him by his collar, pulled out the .45, and pulled him to the far side of the building away from the door.

"I'm gonna ask you one time, kid. That nigga in the back, is he waiting for me?" His gun was pressed up hard in La's ribcage.

"I don't know that kid."

"Wrong answer. Look on the roof, my nigga. You and that dude in the back is dead!" Junior said with ice in his voice.

"Hold on, Junior. I don't know what the fuck is going on. I just came out here to meet you for the work, so I can get this shit clicking again. I don't know what you talkin' 'bout. That's my word."

229

"We'll see. What's the signal? Is he 'posed to come out when you go back in the building?"

"Man, I don't what the fuck you talkin' 'bout, Junior. You buggin'."

"You know how I know you lyin', La? 'Cause if you didn't know him, you woulda asked if he was wit' me when you came through the back of the building. I don't got no time for your bullshit. If you don't tell me what duke doing back there, I'm gonna leave your brains on the wall!"

La hesitated and Junior hit him in his head with the butt of the pistol. La let out a loud scream.

Seconds later, the front door of the building flung open and Drez emerged, gun in hand. Junior kept La in front of him and pointed the gun in Drez's direction.

"What, muhfucka!" he screamed.

"NOOOO!" La screamed.

Junior squeezed off a shot and the bullet hit the door. Drez opened fire, hitting La as Junior used him as a shield. La's screams were heard all through the hood as Junior let off more shots in Drez's direction. The bullets hit the divider in front of the building, chipping away at the cement as Drez stayed behind it for cover. La dropped to the cold concrete as Junior continued to fire his pistol. The two guys on the roof couldn't get a clear shot of Drez. Their view was obstructed by the partition he was hiding behind in the front of the building. Junior made a mad dash to the corner of the building, letting off shots as he ran, hopeing that would keep Drez from returning fire. Drez peeked around the partition and saw Junior fleeing. He ran to the back of the building with plans of ambushing him.

Junior stopped short when he got to the side of the building and peeked back around to the front. His heart was racing as he looked up on the roof of the building across the street. The guys were waving their hands, motioning for him to go back to the front of the building. He ran back to the front and peeked around the corner. There was no sign of Drez or La. Then the guys on the roof pointed to the far corner of the building.

Drez was peeking through the door to the back of the building, waiting to see Junior. He could hear La moaning in the hallway but couldn't help. He didn't mean to shoot La, but he didn't have a choice. La was propped up against the wall in the lobby and there was a streak of blood from the front door to where he was resting by the elevator. Drez slowly pushed open

230

the backdoor, hoping to catch Junior. Then he heard a loud bang that came from behind him, and the force of the hit instantly threw him out the door. He fell to the ground and turned to look behind him, but the door closed too quickly. How did he let Junior sneak up behind him like that? He never thought to check whether Junior had doubled back on him.

Drez's gun slid to the benches when he fell and he tried to get up, but the wound to his back wouldn't allow him to move. He was face down and could feel the pain in his back. He continued to try to pull himself to the benches to get his gun, because that was the only chance he had to survive. Then he saw some black, Chukka Tims stop in front of him. He looked up and was shocked to see Junior standing over him, pointing a gun to his head. He was stupefied. If Junior was standing in front of him, then who had shot him in his back? Did La double-cross him? Junior walked to the benches and picked up Drez's gun, then stood over him again.

"So, you Muffin's cousin, huh?" Junior asked, turning him over on his back and pointing the gun to his forehead.

"Fuck you, nigga!" Drez groaned. He knew this was it for him.

"I guess blood ain't thicker than water, huh?" Junior replied and then he realized who Drez was. "You the nigga that pistol-whipped my girl in the club. Let me tell you what karma is, nigga. It's fate, and yours is sealed! Yo, fam, La didn't tell you that I ain't that predictable? You made a fuckin' mistake when you got with La, dickhead. Y'all thought y'all was gonna take ova my shit jus' like that, huh, muhfucka?" Junior kneeled down to the wounded man as he spoke into his ear. "You didn't think shit was gonna play out like this, did you?"

That was the last thing Drez heard before everything went dark.

Junior took everything out Drez's pockets, including his ID, then he threw some drug capsules into the grass next to Drez.

La was still slumped over by the elevator where Drez had dragged him after Junior ran. He didn't know how bad he was hit, but he was having trouble breathing and was losing blood. He could see Drez standing by the backdoor peeking out, then he heard footsteps coming from the staircase. As the sounds grew closer he tried to rise to his feet, hoping it was help. Rock appeared from the staircase with gun in hand and when he saw Drez he squeezed the trigger, and Drez was thrown outside. La looked up at Rock, who walked calmly over to the backdoor and slammed it shut.

"You a dirty muhfucka, La."

"What the fuck you talking about?"

"How can you be so fucking foul? The nigga treated you good. He gave you total control of shit out here, and your ass was frontin' like it was all you the whole time. I knew, La. I been knew you was a dirty muhfucka. You the same nigga that said what your man Kendu, God bless the dead, did to Junior was foul, and then you turn around and do the same dirty shit! You's a grimy ass nigga, son. And, yo, let me tell you, that nigga Drez, well he the one that bodied your man. Did you know that, La?"

"How you know that, Rock? How you know that nigga murdered my man?"

"Doesn't matter now, nigga. He dead!"

"OK, Rock, you got this. You played it right and you played me. What now?"

"That's just it, La. I'ma leave you here to die. If you make it, then your maggot ass may deserve to live, but trust and believe me, you won't be able to live ova here no fuckin' more, and if I see you 'round here, La, I'ma put ya lights out for good—eternal darkness, nigga!"

Rock walked out of the building, leaving La slumped against the wall bleeding. Junior was standing in the back of the building when Rock came out.

"Where that foul ass nigga at?" Junior asked.

"He dead."

"You sure?"

"Not really, but if he wasn't, he will be," Rock said as he counted the money Junior handed him.

"Well, one thing's for sure, he ain't running shit out here no more. Now it's time for us to blow up!" Junior said, giving Rock a package.

Chapter 17
You believe her.

The restaurant was crowded so they had to wait to be seated.

"Table for two?" the short waiter asked as he handed them menus.

"Yeah."

"Smoking or non-smoking?" the waiter asked as he led them toward the back of the restaurant to the smoking section.

"How this nigga gon ask me smoking or non-smoking and automatically walk to the smoking section? I'm going to fuck his head up. Watch this," Junior said.

The waiter walked over to a table in the smoking section, stood by it, and waited for the couple to sit down.

"Here you go," he said.

"Is this the non-smoking section?" Junior asked.

"Uh, no, this is the smoking section."

"Why the fuck we ova here then?"

"Uh, I thought you . . ."

"Smoked? How the fuck would you know? Did you wait for the answer? Now take us to the non-smoking section, asshole!"

"I apologize, sir. I made a mistake."

"See what you gotta go through just to get a nice table out this muhfucka. I swear I get tired of this kind of treatment when I'm spending a lot of dough."

They took their seat and looked over the menu.

"Order anything you want, baby girl," Junior told Muffin.

Muffin was looking over the menu, but she didn't have an appetite. Junior was spending a lot of time with her lately and she was enjoying every moment with him, but she knew the real reason for all the attention. She found out Drez was murdered and Junior told her he was there, but wasn't the one that killed him. She wanted to believe him, but she was having mixed feelings because she was the one that told him about what Drez and La were planning. When she told Junior, she did ask him not to hurt her cousin, but he never promised, so she didn't know if she should believe what he was telling her. It happened almost a month ago, and since then Junior was spending every waking moment with her. She enjoyed the lovemaking and the gifts, but she couldn't get her cousin's murder out of her head. She was overwhelmed with guilt because if she never told him what she knew, Drez might still be alive. Now she was in a very awkward place and didn't know if she should leave Junior alone and tell the police, or go with her heart and forgive him. It was a hard decision for her to make, but she needed to do something because it was affecting the way she acted when she was with him.

"You ready to order?" Junior asked her, interrupting her deep thoughts.

"Yeah, gimme the garden salad."

"That's all you want, honey? You ain't been eatin' much lately. You on a diet or sumthin'?"

"Nah, baby, I'm just not hungry."

Junior knew what was bothering Muffin. She had been acting funny ever since he told her he was there when Drez was killed. He didn't have a choice in telling her because she was the one that told him about the setup, and if he denied any involvement, he would have to worry about her going to the cops. He began to spend more time with her to keep her happy and to keep an eye on her. He figured if she was happy, she wouldn't snitch on him, and if he was always around, she wouldn't have the chance to snitch. She seemed happy most of the time, but there were times she looked like she was deep in thought and that's when she zoned out. This worried him because he wanted to trust her, but he had already experienced betrayal from niggas that were supposed to be true to him, and the way she was acting made him wonder how trustworthy she really was. He was glad that through it all there was still one person he could trust his life with, and that was Shondra.

While Junior sat in the restaurant wining and dining his mistress, Shondra was sitting in the living room on the couch crying her eyes out. Gloria still wasn't speaking to her, and Junior was spending less time with her. She was feeling like she had lost the two people she loved the most, and then she heard a knock on her door. She walked over to the door without thinking and opened it.

"Good afternoon. Ms. Brown?" the detective asked.

Shondra straightened up when she saw the two detectives at her door. She was thinking the worst, so she tried to brace herself for bad news.

"Yes, I'm Ms. Brown. Is there a problem?"

It was Taylor and Burke.

"Actually, yes. Can we come in for a second?" Taylor asked.

Shondra moved from in front of the door and let them in, motioning for them to sit on the couch.

"Would you two like something to drink?" she asked.

"Sure, thanks. Ms. Brown, I want to ask you some questions if you don't mind." Taylor was doing all the talking.

Shondra went into the kitchen, poured two glasses of Pepsi, and handed them to the men on the couch.

"Do you know someone named Junior?" Taylor asked, taking a sip of his drink.

"Yes, I do. Why?"

"Well, Ms. Brown, we need to ask him some questions. Do you know where we can find him, or is there a number where we can reach him at home?"

"No."

"Ms. Brown, this is a very serious matter. Any information you can provide us with will give us an opportunity to try to help him, you know, give him a chance to clear up any accusations against him."

"What accusations?"

"It's not actually accusations. It's more like finger pointing. Someone has mentioned his name in the connection to a murder about three weeks ago. The person that's pointing the finger isn't really credible, but we have to follow up on any leads, even if we believe them to be false. That's why we would like to talk with him so we can exclude him from the investigation."

"Well, if I see him, I'll let him know what you guys told me."

They both rose and headed for the door.

"OK, thanks for your help. Whenever you hear from him you can have him call us and we'll question him and clear his name as quickly as possible." Taylor handed his and Burke's business cards to her, then walked out the door.

"You believe her?" Taylor asked Burke in the hallway.

"Hell no. The bitch is protecting him. We'll have to catch him on the streets," Burke replied.

"Well, one thing's for sure. I don't think she is going to be the one that hands him over to us," Taylor said as he opened the door to the unmarked police car.

The waiter brought a garden salad for Muffin and Junior had the Galleto al Balsamico Antico, which was a fancy Italian name for grilled chicken, fried vegetables, and roasted potatoes. They both ate their meals quietly as a live band played soft music in the background. Junior decided to address Muffin's long silence.

"What's wrong, baby girl? It's like you have a lot on your mind but you don't want to share anything with me. I thought we was better than that. You know if something bothers you, it bothers me. You my lung, mama." As he spoke he placed both her hands in his.

"Oh, baby, I love you so much," she said as she squeezed his hand. "I don't know what's wrong with me, baby. I don't want to make you feel that I'm hiding anything from you, because I will never do that, baby. I don't really know what's wrong, Junior. So much has happened and I guess I'm depressed. I don't know."

"It's just that I'm worried about you, baby. It's like you're not happy anymore like you used to be. I be trying to do things to make you happy, and it doesn't seem to be working."

"No, baby, I appreciate everything you've done for me. I mean, you are the best. It's me, baby, not you."

"No, don't blame yourself. I know that you've been through a lot. I want to understand you. I want to be there for you, and I want you to trust me, my words, and my actions, because it's all true to what we have built together. I want you to know that my love for you is real. I need you to feel my love, baby."

"I do, Junior. I don't doubt how you feel for me. In the beginning I wasn't sure, but I always wanted you to love me the way you do right now. I feel your love, baby, and I don't want that to change. You are my heart, Junior. You make me smile, you make me feel safe, and I love that feeling and don't ever want to lose it."

"I know that you're still mourning over your cousin, and it's kind of foul for you to be with the nigga that was there when he died, and that's why I want you to know that I understand you having mixed feelings about being with me, but I need you to know that I am not the one that killed him. I would never lie to you about something like that, Muff. If it wasn't for you, baby, shit would have went different that day, so I gotta keep it real wit' you. Do you understand what I'm sayin'?"

"Junior, I can't lie, baby. I've been feeling responsible for my cousin's death. I told you what he told me because I didn't want anything to happen to you because I love you, but I didn't want anything to happen to him either because he my family. Now I feel guilty like I'm the one that killed him. It's because of what I told you that he's dead, and I feel like shit."

"Come on, let's get outta here so we can talk. I don't want you breakin' down in here." He rose, threw some money on the table, and grabbed her hand and led her out of the restaurant. He remained silent until they got in the car, and then he continued where they left off.

"Look, Muff, I'm really sorry that your cousin got killed, but you know something, I'm glad it wasn't me. That might sound fucked up to you, but you have to understand the game that I'm in. Niggas be wantin' me dead jus' because—no reason, jus' because. Think about it, ma. My man was trying to get me bodied. This game don't have no loyalty. Finding out that your cousin got killed had to make you feel fucked up because you knew that it had something to do with me. You might even have wished when you first heard about it that it was me instead of him because of your guilt. I gotta respect that because that was your family, and blood is supposed to be thicker than water. I remember you sayin' that if something happened to him you would charge it to the game. Well, I did the same for La. His betrayal was something that I didn't expect. I trusted him with my whole operation, and he was dishonorable. That's his charge. Imagine how I feel now, though. I'm not the one that bodied Drez, but I was the nigga he was looking to kill. Now I'm seeing his cousin, who put me on to what he was planning to do. I feel fucked up, too, Muff. Sometimes I wish that I didn't meet you so that you didn't have to make that decision. I feel like that because I feel your pain when I look at you. I don't want you to second-guess your decision, but at the same time I don't want you to be glad that you didn't. One thing I can tell you, Muff, is that I know you love me. I know how you feel for me is true, and I trust you, baby. And believe me, it's hard for me to trust anybody after all this shit, but I trust you. I trust you because I know you love me for real."

Muffin was beside herself emotionally. Junior's statement reduced her to tears. She had grown to love Junior, and after hearing all this she felt he was really in love with her. The tears streamed down like a waterfall and she became weak. This was the feeling of true love. She didn't say anything else to him. She just leaned over and buried her head in his chest.

Rock was making a mitt in the projects now that Junior had made him second in command. Things were looking up for Rock and he was enjoying the money he was making. The only thing that troubled him was that he was still hot as a firecracker in the hood. Taylor and Burke still fucked with him every time they saw him on the block. Now they were asking him about a murder.

"Yeah, well you betta watch your back. Word on the street is that his friends are looking for the guy or guys that did it," Taylor said.

"OK, and you're telling me this to say what?" Rock asked.

"I'm just telling you what I heard, and it came from a reliable source. You resemble the description they gave us on the perps," Taylor responded.

"Don't we all look alike to y'all anyway?" Rock asked with his head cocked to one side.

"Smart ass! You know something, Rock, I have a strong feeling you had something to do with it, and if you didn't, you know who did. If you tell me what part you played in it now, I can promise you won't go to jail for coming forward." Taylor was lying.

Rock knew Taylor was bullshitting him. There was no way he would walk if he told him he was involved.

"Well you don't have to worry about that, 'cause I don't know nothing."

"You little bastards make me sick. You think you so smart and slick. I really don't care what happened. It's just our job to find out, and I promise you, Rock, when I get the evidence I need to put you behind bars, I'm going to make sure that they throw your ass under the cell."

"Damn, man, I told you I don't know shit. Why you so mad at me? You act like it was somebody you knew personally."

"You little fuck!" Burke grabbed Rock by his collar. "You really think I won't make your mother childless?" Burke whispered in his ear. "If I catch you late at night by yourself and no one is around, I will kill you!"

"Look, Burke, I don't know why you screaming and threatenin' me like that. I don't know what happened, and trust me, if I did, I would tell you because the shit happened in my hood. So please stop threatenin' me." Rock said it loud enough for everyone in earshot to hear, just in case Burke was serious and Rock wound up mysteriously dead.

"Fuckin' smart ass nigger!" Burke said and released his hold on Rock, which sent him flying into the side of the building. "You on my shit list, you black bastard!"

After that incident the detectives continued to come around every day, time implying they were getting closer to solving the case. They kept trying to offer Rock a way out if he gave them information that would help them close the case. Rock was beginning to get nervous because he knew if they ever found out he was involved they would make sure he was prosecuted to the fullest extent of the law. Things were going too good for Rock now, and he wasn't looking for it to end due to him getting locked up, so he was seriously contemplating telling the detectives something that would ensure his freedom.

Shit, Junior the one that killed Drez. I only shot him, he reasoned.

This was the typical reaction of anyone who found himself in a precarious situation, especially when faced with extensive jail time. Rock was enjoying being "under-boss" of the operation. He liked how all the females flocked to him, and he was definitely enjoying the money he was stacking. All that would be in jeopardy unless he did something to secure it.

Rock was doing better than when La was in charge. He was moving whatever Junior gave him like a truck driver on the Interstate. Junior had dropped off a kee for him and he was already down to four Os, and it was only a week later. Unlike how La did it, Rock didn't wait until the workers were completely out. He would pay them on the ends. Junior liked it that way because he got paid first, and the workers liked it because they always had money and were able to save. Rock had gained a lot of respect in the hood, and since Stump's death, there wasn't any threat of a worker getting robbed or killed over drug money.

People in the hood were treating Rock and Junior differently. They had become ghetto celebrities. After what happened to La and Drez, it seemed as if everyone knew it was them, but no one was willing to snitch because they feared death would be the retaliation. Rock knew how thorough Junior was from Stump's murder. He was the one that devised the ambush on Stump. When Rock told Junior that La wanted him to do the hit on Stump, Junior told Rock to go ahead with it, but he wanted to be there to make sure everything went OK. La never knew Junior was the actual mastermind of the hit. Junior scrapped La's idea once Rock told him what he had planned, because he said if he did it La's way, he would never have made it out of the building without getting caught, so Junior planned the murder, down to the last detail.

The phone was ringing, but no one would pick up. This worried Shondra more and more. Her friend wasn't returning any of her calls. She had been calling Gloria's house since she heard that KB had come home from the hospital. She wanted to see if she could repair their friendship, but she never could get in contact with Gloria.

Shondra's frustration was amplified by the absence of her man, whom she hadn't seen in months. Junior hadn't spent any time with her since the incident with La and Drez, and when she beeped him he rarely answered her pages. She was spiraling into a depression and was beginning to question their relationship. This was a time when she needed him the most, and he was unavailable. The fact that she lost her friendship because of her decision to betray Gloria for his benefit weighed heavy on her heart. He didn't seem to care about what she was going through now that it was all over. She knew he had things on his mind, too, but she was his girl, his Bonnie, and he wasn't showing her any love or understanding. The only thing she could think about was him cheating on her with that girl from the club the night KB was shot. Thinking that he was still with that same girl was inevitable. Why else wouldn't he return her calls or come see her? What other explanation could there be? The more she thought about it, the more upset she became, and when a woman started to think about infidelity in her relationship, she was likely to do anything. Shondra went to the phone and dialed Junior's pager number, putting in 911. If he didn't call her back, she was going to go find him.

KB was still in pain but he was healing quickly. He was already walking without the cane they gave him in physical therapy. Gloria had stood by him the entire time he was in the hospital. From the time he arrived at the hospital to the day he left, Gloria's face was always the first thing he saw when he opened his eyes. She would wash him, read to him, and feed him. His mother wasn't even there as much as Gloria. Glo was there so much that the nurse brought a recliner into his room so she would be comfortable when she slept in there at night. KB was grateful she was by his side. There was no doubt in his mind that she loved him. She kept her ear to the street and kept him abreast of what was happening in the hood. She told him how many people died the night he was shot. She told him Stump got murdered in his building and that the police had no witnesses, and most recently she told him about the incident that happened with La and Drez in her projects. The image of the girl pointing the gun at KB was ever fresh in his mind, and he knew he was lucky to be alive.

With Stump, there was a certain honor he had when it came to his crew. There was seventy-five thousand dollars cash and a gold chain in a bag on his bed when he came home from the hospital. He knew it was from Stump. That's why it bothered him to hear of his brutal murder, but for some reason he felt free, as if he was released from some invisible bondage. KB felt his life was spared for a reason, and he mentally made a pact with himself to live a safer existence. Sometimes people didn't get second chances, but he was given one.

KB looked over to Gloria who lay across the bed in a deep sleep. He was supposed to be going to therapy in a little while, but he didn't want to wake her. She looked so peaceful. She had literally been taking care of him with no complaints, and he wanted her to rest. He walked to the mirror and pulled up his T-shirt, looking at the bandages that went all around his mid-section and over his chest and shoulder. He stared at himself in the mirror and internalized the drastic change his body had been through. His health had changed in the course of one night. He lost a lot of weight while in the hospital, and he wasn't able to get around as easily as he used to. KB was afraid. He didn't know if he would ever recover 100 percent, but he was grateful to be alive. A single tear formed, then rolled down his cheek. Since being shot he found himself more emotional and somewhat religious. Gloria's weekly Bible readings may have contributed to this new behavior. He wiped his cheek and grabbed the cane from off the bed.

"Hey, honey, whatcha' doin'?" Gloria asked, waking from her sleep.

"Nothin', ma. Get your rest. I'ma go to therapy."

"OK, wait. Let me get dressed." She rose from the bed and headed for the bathroom.

"Look, ma, I appreciate all you've been doin' for me. Just let me go to therapy myself. I'll take a cab there and back. You stay here and rest, OK?" KB wanted to do something on his own without help. He was starting to feel handicap.

"It's OK, baby. I don't mind," she yelled from the bathroom with toothpaste in her mouth.

"Nah, ma, let me do this on my own. It's been a while since I did shit for myself, you know. I wanna know that I can, baby, feel me?" he asked her as she gently put her arms around his waist.

"I'm sorry, baby. I've been so caught up in trying to get you back to how you were that I ain't realize the improvements you've already made. You right. You should go to therapy by yourself. Shit, it'll give me a chance to clean up this damn room." Gloria kissed him gently on his back, got his sneakers from the closet, and placed them by his feet.

KB loved the fact his girl was so understanding to his needs. She really understood how he felt without him really getting into it with her. He put on his sneakers, wincing when he bent over to tie them.

"Aaaah, that's why I gotta keep goin' to therapy. I gotta get used to bending ova without feeling so much pain."

"Well, baby, you've had plenty of bed rest. You've been eating right, and you've even exercised while you were here, so you are definitely improving faster than they expected."

"You right. Call me a cab now so by the time I get downstairs, it'll already be there."

"All right. I'll just clean up your room for you while you're gone and run down to my house and get some more clothes. You don't mind that I've been stayin' here with you this long, do you, baby?"

"Come on now, is that a trick question?"

"Just had to make sure, baby."

Gloria was surprised to see Shondra standing in front of the building when her cab pulled up. She hadn't spoken to Shondra since the day she dismissed her when she came to KB's room and acted like she was so concerned about him. She vowed she would never forgive her for her blatant betrayal of their once solid friendship.

Shondra noticed Gloria as she emerged from the cab that pulled up in front of their building. She watched as her friend stepped out of the cab wearing a tight-fitting sweat suit that showed off the perfect form of her body. As Gloria approached the building, Shondra could see that she wasn't looking at her. She knew Gloria might still be mad, but Shondra felt Gloria could at least acknowledge her existence. Shondra stepped in front of her, partially blocking the entrance so Glo had to face her. Gloria walked past her and shoved her aside. Shondra lost her footing and stumbled over to the wall. She didn't get upset, but she felt she deserved a spoken word if she was going to do all that.

"Damn, Glo, if you gonna push me, you can at least speak to me!"

Gloria walked to the elevator and pushed the triangular button to summon its arrival. She refused to recognize Shondra's presence.

Shondra followed her into the building and stood behind her.

"Come on, Glo, I know you're still mad, but please give me a chance. I'm so sorry! I really am!"

The elevator opened door opened for Glo to get on. Shondra grabbed her arm, preventing her from getting on, and Gloria turned around and slapped Shondra hard in her face.

"Don't touch me, bitch. Don't ever put your raggedy ass hands on me again!"

Shondra's face shifted violently from the force of the slap, and in that instance she forgot the purpose of her standing there with Gloria and became defensive, an instinct she had inherited from the many fights and scuffles she had in the past. She swung her fist, connecting to Gloria's face, and continued to assault her until Gloria found the power to push her off momentarily. Shondra backed up, but was back on Glo like a cheetah on a gazelle. She punched her in her face and pulled her hair, trying to get her off balance. She swung her into the mailboxes, then stomped her as Gloria covered up. Shondra was screaming as someone came into the lobby and pulled her off of Gloria.

"Bitch, you crazy. You musta' bumped your fuckin' head thinkin' you could slap me and not catch a beat down! You really musta forgot who the fuck I be, bitch!"

Some guys that came in the building to see what was happening were helping Gloria to her feet as she tried to regain her composure. She looked over to Shondra, who was still going off in a tirade about how bad a bitch she was when it came to fighting. Gloria was furious. She knew she didn't have any wins with Shondra on a physical level, so she decided to beat her with her words.

"You stinkin' bitch. You 'posed to have been my best friend. How the fuck could you do me the way you did me? You is a lyin' bitch." Shondra suddenly stopped with her ranting and raving and calmed down, remembering her purpose for stopping Gloria in the first place. She listened to Glo go on about their friendship. "You acted like your relationship with Junior was so fuckin' good, and the whole time you was frontin', bitch. That's why you was willing to fuck up what I had with my man, because your shit was already fucked up. You was getting info out of me about my man and running back and telling that nigga, thinking that would make shit better between y'all. You stupid, bitch. That nigga still was fuckin' on you, and when you seen me happy with my man, it made you mad. Why, bitch? Why didn't you want to see your *best friend* happy? You played it off like he was such a good nigga to you, and the whole time he was fuckin' on you. I didn't know you was jealous of what me and my man had. I didn't know that you hated to see me happy. Now I know the truth about your miserable ass. You can't live a lie, you stupid bitch, 'cause it's bound to come out."

Shondra was standing there with her mouth wide open. She was shocked Gloria was putting all her business in the street like that. There were a lot of people from around the way that didn't know too much about her, much less her relationship with Junior. She was embarrassed and wanted to just go in the house and forget everything, but she couldn't let Gloria get the last word.

"You don't know what the fuck you talkin' about, bitch. I always looked out for you, you stupid ho! You was always jealous of me, bitch. You always wanted my life, you always wanted to be me, but you couldn't. Well, fuck you, bitch, and that nigga you fuckin'. I wish he did die!" Shondra knew that last part would pierce Gloria's heart.

Gloria rushed Shondra, although she knew there wasn't anyway she could win a physical fight. Shondra sidestepped and uppercut her, and then kicked her in the ass as she fell to the ground.

"You can't win, bitch, so you betta stop while you ahead."

"Shondra, you wish my man died? Well I hope they get your bitch ass man for all the shit he did. Everybody knows he had something to do with that shit that happened in the back of La's building. When my man get better, bitch, I'ma tell him to slap the shit out of you for tryin' to set him up, you dirty, stinkin' bitch!"

"You threatenin' me, bitch! You wait till my man get ova here. I'm gonna get him to kill that bitch ass nigga, and after that I'ma stomp your ugly ass out!"

"Shondra, the telephone!" Shondra's brother had opened the door and yelled out into the hallway to his sister, unaware of the commotion going on in the hallway.

"Oh yeah, bitch, that's my man right there. I'ma tell him what's goin' on, so you betta be gone by the time he gets here!"

"Whateva, bitch. That nigga probably won't even come anyway, his faggot ass!" Gloria screamed loud enough for her to hear before she closed the door.

Shondra was on fire when she grabbed the phone that was dangling in the hallway.

"Hello?" she screamed into the receiver.

"Yo, what the fuck is wrong?" Junior asked.

"Why the fuck it took you so long to call me back? I been beeping you all week and you ain't return none of my calls. Why!" Shondra was upset. She was furious because of Gloria had said to her was all true. She knew Junior was seeing that girl, and she didn't know what to do.

"I told you why, ma. I'm busy takin' care of shit out here. I gotta make sure that shit is going right out here or I'll fuck around and lose e'erythin'. What's wrong? You put 911."

"I just got into it with Gloria. She threatened me, tellin' me that she gonna tell KB that I was the one that tried to set him up and get him to kill me. She said that she gonna tell him to get you too!"

"Word? Where they at now?"

"She just went upstairs. That nigga wasn't with her, though. She mighta been comin' from his house 'cause she was gettin' outta a cab when I saw her."

"Well I'm on my way ova there. I'ma pistol whip that bitch and make that nigga come see me. Nigga know what it is wit' me. He got blasted and he still poppin' shit. That's my word I'ma bury his ass too! He gonna wish the devil took him when he had him the first time. Look, just stay inside till I get there, and leave the door open. I'm on my way right now."

"OK, but when you get here we need to talk, 'cause I'm tired of your bullshit!"

"Whateva. I'm on my way! Make sure you leave the door open!"

Muffin was standing at the door while Junior was using the phone. She knew he was going to sneak and call Shondra sooner or later, but she didn't think he would be disrespectful and call from her bedroom. She heard the whole conversation and was pissed off when he came into the living room where she was sitting. She prepared herself for the lie he was about to tell her about why he had to leave so abruptly.

"Ay, Muff, I gotta go check on somethin' 'round the way. My boy got some problems," Junior said, putting on his black, leather jacket.

"Your boy, huh?"

"Come on now, ma, don't give me that. Soon as I take care of this business, I'll be back here with you and we can finish what we was doin'."

"I ain't worried, baby. Take your time and be careful out there."

Junior kissed her gently and walked out the door. She walked to the window and waited until he got in his car, then went into her bedroom and pressed redial on the telephone.

"Hello?" Muffin said when Shondra picked up the phone.

"Hello, who is this?"

"It's me, you ugly bitch!"

"Who the fuck is this?"

"You know who this is, bitch! Why the fuck do you beep him so much? Don't you get the message when he don't call back. HE DON'T WANT YOU NO MORE, BITCH. GET OVER IT ALREADY!"

"You fuckin' ho! Why don't you tell me where you at so I can finish fuckin' you up? You was lucky last time, bitch!"

"No, bitch, you was lucky. Look, when my man get ova there please tell him when he finished helping your measly, broke down ass to hurry home and don't forget to bring me a shrimp roll back."

"Ooooh, bitch, why don't you come here and tell him yourself, or you scared?"

"The only thing I'm scared of, bitch, is looking at yo' ugly ass. Give it up, Brusilla. He mine now and you can't do nothing 'bout it. Junior like pretty things, sweetie, and ain't nothin' pretty 'bout you."

"I'll find out where you live, bitch, when he comes here. And when I do, watch your back and your front. If you think you're so cute, I'll change all that when I slam your face on the concrete!" Shondra slammed down the phone.

Muffin laughed, but she was furious with Junior when she sat down on the couch and thought about how deceitful he was to her.

Shondra was going to stand outside and wait for Junior. Her anger wouldn't allow her to stay in the house and wait. She went into her room and snatched her jacket off the hanger and a card fell on the floor. It was one of the cards the detectives had given her when they came to her house asking about Junior. She bent down slowly and picked it up, then went in the hallway and paused by the telephone.

Junior didn't have a gun on him at Muffin's house, so he had to call Rock so he could get strapped before he went to Shondra's.

"Yo, you got iron in the crib, right?" Junior asked Rock over the phone.

"Hmmhmm. What's up, man? You got some beef?"

"Nah, not really. I gotta take care of that bitch, Gloria. She fuckin' with my girl."

"Oh OK. That's why you need the toast?"

"Yeah, nigga. By the way, how shit goin' out there?"

"It's goin'. I'ma need to see you in a minute."

"Cool. I'll take care of you after I take care of this bullshit."

"Aight, I'll be in the crib waitin' on you." Rock hung up the phone.

Junior pulled up in front of Rock's crib and went upstairs to get the gun. He knocked on the door and Rock opened it and let him in.

"Where the iron at?" Junior asked as he followed him to the back.

"Right here." Rock passed him a nine millimeter.

"Let me pick what I want, nigga."

"This the only one I got up here," Rock said with a suspicious look on his face.

247

"Aight, fuck it. I'ma dirty this shit up, so don't expect it back."

"It's yours."

"I'm out. I'll get wit' you lata, boy," Junior said, slapping him five.

Rock had given Junior the gun he had used to kill Stump.

Junior decided to enter through the back of Shondra's building in case KB and Gloria were in the lobby waiting. He pulled out the gun and opened the door to the hallway slowly, peeking his head in to see who was in the vestibule. He holstered his heat, proceeded up the three stairs to Shondra's door, and turned the knob. He was upset the door wasn't unlocked, especially since he told her to leave it open for him. He knocked with his special knock and kept turning around to make sure KB wasn't lurking in the stairwell while he waited for someone to open the door for him.

Shit, she knew to keep the door open for me. She knew I was coming, he thought as he stood there waiting for her to open the door.

"Freeze. Police! Don't move, motherfucker, and don't turn around!"

Fuck! Junior thought. *How the fuck . . . who the . . . Damn! Somebody done set me up.*

Printed in the United States
106601LV00003B/34-39/P